TO HAVE OR TO HAVE NOT . . .

It had taken strangers coming into their lives and introducing them to new interests to make Maggie realize how dull her married life had become. Before, when she and Doug were completely happy together, change was something she feared; now they both welcomed it.

It hurt a little to see Doug leave, knowing that he would not be back until the next day. His deliciously masculine body would not be lying naked and warm beside her, welcoming her touch, her kisses. She'd been without his sex for weeks and the strain was beginning to bother her, yet hard as she tried she could not bring herself to go to bed with anyone except Doug, simple as it would be to have Mike Ballantine. With Mike, she'd found a part of her that had never been allowed expression before; something wild and frivolous and daring.

Now she found herself asking if it wasn't time for her and Doug to discuss their future before they were pulled farther apart. But an arguing voice asked if she really wanted to go back to her old ways. She knew she wasn't ready for that, but neither was she ready to be totally free of Doug. The word divorce still frightened her. Was that because she'd no longer have an excuse to refrain from having sex with other men?

Maggie knew that if she couldn't have Doug, then it would be Mike . . . and she was adult enough to admit that the idea was very exciting.

But afterward? Ah, that was what she was most afraid of. Afterward.

ATTENTION: SCHOOLS AND CORPORATIONS
PINNACLE Books are available at quantity discounts with bulk purchases for educational, business or special promotional use. For further details, please write to: SPECIAL SALES MANAGER, Pinnacle Books, Inc., 1430 Broadway, New York, NY 10018.

WRITE FOR OUR FREE CATALOG
If there is a Pinnacle Book you want—and you cannot find it locally—it is available from us simply by sending the title and price plus 75¢ to cover mailing and handling costs to:

> Pinnacle Books, Inc.
> Reader Service Department
> 1430 Broadway
> New York, NY 10018

Please allow 6 weeks for delivery.

____Check here if you want to receive our catalog regularly.

PINNACLE BOOKS　　　　　　　　　NEW YORK

This is a work of fiction. All characters and events portrayed in this book are fictional, and any resemblance to real people or incidents is purely coincidental.

LIVE FOR TODAY

Copyright © 1982 by Ben All, Inc.

All rights reserved, including the right to reproduce this book or portions thereof in any form.

An original Pinnacle Books edition, published for the first time anywhere.

First printing, January 1982

ISBN: 0-523-41172-3

Printed in the United States of America

PINNACLE BOOKS, INC.
1430 Broadway
New York, New York 10018

Take therefore no thought for the morrow; for the morrow shall take thought for the things of itself. Sufficient unto the day is the evil thereof.
(Matthew 6:34)

LIVE FOR TODAY

Chapter 1

The day was as dark as her mood. It was a rainy Thursday and as usual the house was quiet.

Maggie leaned against the bay windows in the den feeling the glass cold against her forehead and the crackling fireplace warm at her back. As she watched the rain-water puddle on the lawn, she wondered if it had been the right thing to ask Alice over. She needed a woman's advice, but she wasn't certain Alice Maitland was the right woman to give it, especially since none of her three marriages had been successful. Alice would be the last person to advise sensibly an "up-till-now" happily married woman on her marriage problems. But there wasn't anyone else Maggie could talk to. Alice and she had been best friends since kindergarten. Although they had grown apart when Alice discovered boys at age fourteen, it never occurred to Maggie to develop a new best friend. Over the years, however, Alice always seemed to be there whenever Maggie needed her, and vice versa.

Maggie touched the pane with her fingertips and looked out through the rivulets of water sliding down the glass. She knew what Alice would recommend before hearing it. *Get out*, she'd say. *Chuck the whole thing. You've proven you could bring up two nice kids, so why stick around and let them watch you grow old and miserable. Start living for yourself, kiddo.*

Alice had always seemed anxious to toss away anything that became a problem, including husbands, pregnancies . . . anything. It wasn't that Alice Maitland was a heartless, destructive person; it was just that she was free-spirited and enjoyed her own definition of happiness. She lived for herself and saw nothing wrong with that. Her philosophy was simple enough: "As long as I don't seriously hurt anyone, I do whatever pleases me." And obviously no one was seriously hurt by her several divorces; Alice had come out of each one all the wealthier, all the more independent and seemingly happier, and still on friendly terms with all her ex's.

Maggie sighed. She was bored and restless and, at thirty-six, felt very old. Each day she found she spent less and less time sitting in front of her mirror. It had taken her a mere three minutes to put on her makeup. She didn't want to see the wrinkles, the tiny age lines that were tugging at the corners of her eyes. Doug said she was imagining things, that there were no age lines, no sags, no wrinkles, that she was more beautiful than ever . . . which Maggie interpreted to mean, "You are getting old."

That's why she needed to talk to Alice. She needed a woman's opinion about her present discontent with her life and herself. How could a man—particularly a husband—be objective enough to understand and sympathize? The inside of a woman was only duplicated in another woman. She wanted Alice to reassure her that her life wasn't finished. She wanted to hear Alice say, "Don't listen to a man's advice, particularly a husband's. What do husbands know about a woman's wants and needs? Sex, that's all men think about. And they think getting it up is all they're responsible for."

Doug wasn't like that. True, he had a stronger sex drive than she, but most men did, especially husbands who were pushing forty and intent on performing as actively as they did at twenty. Besides, Doug had admitted his foolish mistake when he took up with that Phyllis Bracken a few years back. No, unlike Doug, it wasn't a new lover Maggie wanted, it was a new life. Still, that wasn't completely true either. She didn't want a new life, just a new *way* of life, of which Doug would most assuredly disapprove, as would the kids. The life that had started for her and Doug twenty years ago was falling apart.

She thought about all the years that had led to the solid security and comfort now surrounding her. Now that she had it she felt it weighing her down, smothering her with its insured dependability, and she felt terribly guilty about it. She was married to the only man she had ever wanted to marry; they had two lovely, almost grown, children, a boy and a girl; their home was in the smarter section of the suburbs, where she had always wanted to live. Everything was perfect. They weren't exactly rolling in money but they were very comfortable and wanted for nothing. There wasn't a single flaw in all of her married life.

Maggie continued to stare out at the pelting rain. Not a flaw, she thought as she pushed herself away from the glass. That was the problem. Her life had no flaws, no pitfalls, no excitement; it had no color, no flair, and there didn't seem to be any hope of adding any if she continued the way she was. She had gained her perfect end. Everything she'd ever dreamed of wanting she had. There were no more anxious moments about unexpected expenses, sudden emergencies with which she and Doug had to struggle. All her golden days were in the past, packed away with memories of a perfect love affair and their romantic notions of living happily forever after. So here she was in her quiet paradise of muted clouds, free from harsh lights and jagged edges. Hers was a life of smooth lines and equable patterns—and she was sick to death of it!

She looked around the room at Doug's re-upholstered chair beside the fire; everything so steady, so comfortable, so protective. This was her future, the rest of her life, and already she was weary of its monotony.

The pang of guilt hit her again. It didn't seem right to be bored with everything so right. If only she had something to fuss about she'd be more content. She almost welcomed those nights a few years back when she had sat up angrily waiting for Doug, knowing he was with that other woman. At least that had been a reason to get up and fight for the happiness and security that was now boring her. Perhaps that's what she needed, a challenge; something to get up and fight for.

She had come to realize her futile future only last month on her thirty-sixth birthday. For the first time she saw her life as it was and as she was living it. She recognized the fact that it was finished and gradually slipping into a colorless tomorrow. She came to the decision then that what she needed was a different tomorrow. She wanted a whole different future, but still one of which her husband and children would approve.

Now came the rub. There wasn't a single thing she could do to become the free woman she wanted to be without depriving or inconveniencing her family. That's why she wanted to talk to Alice. She needed Alice to bolster her resolve, her courage to break away from the usual ties of wife and mother. Alice would teach her how to deafen herself to Doug's and the children's complaints.

Her thoughts were interrupted by the ringing of the doorbell. She hesitated. The bright, clear ring shattered something intimate and delicate that had permeated the room seconds before. The ringing was suddenly an unwanted intrusion that seemed to chip away a little of her resolve; and as she stood there undecided, she felt her determination begin to slip.

The bell sounded again, this time impatiently. Maggie clenched her hands until the nails dug into her palms. She started toward the foyer, but again she hesitated. After a moment, with long deliberate steps she went to the door and put her hand on the latch. After taking a deep breath she pulled opened the door.

"Hell, I thought for a moment you changed your mind and went out," Alice said. Maggie thought her voice sounded a little louder than usual, as though she were talking to someone across the room. And her face looked a little flushed. Alice collapsed her umbrella and stepped inside. She glanced at Maggie, then did a double take. "My God, you look terrible! Is it that time of the month or are you pregnant again?"

"Heaven forbid," Maggie laughed, rolling her eyes. It felt strange to laugh.

"You wouldn't be the first," Alice cautioned.

"I'm too smart for that."

"Let's hope so."

The mere sight of Alice's bright expression seemed to bring promise into Maggie's life.

Alice dropped her coat and hat across the umbrella stand and walked past Maggie into the den. Maggie watched her enviously for a moment. Alice was so determined, so self-assured. She was indeed a handsome woman, tall and stately, well shaped, well coiffed; every move she made was made with a definite purpose in mind. Yet there was something lopsided about her today. She moved a little unsteadily, as if she'd been drinking.

Alice said, "I could sure use a drink, kiddo. Mind if I help myself?" She went to the liquor cabinet without waiting for Maggie's answer. "Bitch of a day." She poured a healthy jigger of Scotch over some ice cubes. "Normally you and I play tennis on Thursdays, right? Well, what with the rain and all, I, contrary to tradition, went to my office." She tasted the drink. "Imagine, five million job openings and not a single applicant." She dropped into Doug's easy chair and put her feet up under her. "We're supposed to be in a recession, according to the government. Do you know we shot the whole advertising budget running ads in all the papers and trades and turned up only thirty lousy applicants in one week? Christ, I don't think people want to work anymore. It's too damned easy to eat something you're allergic to, blow up like a puffer fish and go on welfare . . . let Uncle Sam pay the bills." She patted the tight little bun at the back of her head and smoothed down her already smooth hair. The new severe hair style suited her. Maggie merely stood quietly waiting for Alice to settle in. That was Alice's way. She always had to let her private inner spring unravel to a comfortable tautness before getting down to the real business at hand. And today, Maggie decided, she was unusually taut, so that explained the drinking. The one she'd just fixed was obviously not her first this afternoon.

After lighting a cigarette and taking another sip of her Scotch Alice eyed Maggie carefully and said, "So what's up?" Without thinking she added, "Is Doug fooling around again?" The minute she said it she wanted to bite her tongue. She'd heard Doug was seeing that Phyllis Bracken again but by the look on Maggie's face Alice couldn't tell if Maggie was aware that her husband was up to his old tricks. Maybe the slip wasn't completely out of place, Alice decided. Once before she'd alerted Maggie to her husband's indiscretion. After all what were best friends for? But no, now wasn't the time because what Alice had heard was pure gossip and it had come from a rather unreliable source. She'd do some checking on her own before saying anything to Maggie, if anything needed saying. After studying Maggie's expression, Alice came to the decided conclusion that Doug's fooling around wasn't what was troubling her friend.

Maggie shook her head. "No, that isn't it." Odd how the old pain of Doug's infidelity had lost all its hurt. It hadn't been all that long ago that she'd suffered the embarrassment of being the last to find out her husband was sleeping with another woman, a woman who had once professed to be a friend. It was something she'd never thought Doug capable of and perhaps if it hadn't been for Alice, she might never have found out about it.

Maggie found herself staring at Alice's drink. It looked tempting, especially the way the amber glistened against the ice. She started toward the liquor cabinet, then checked herself and went to stand beside the fire. "It's really nothing, Alice."

"Nothing, my foot. You aren't the type of girl who calls her best friend out on a day like this, knowing that particular best friend melts like sugar in the rain." She rattled the ice cubes and almost emptied the glass. "Something's wrong," Alice said. "You always look like a drooping sparrow when you're upset about something. Let's have it." She took a drag on her cigarette and blew the smoke up at the ceiling. "Besides, you always spend rainy days gluing pictures in your family album or stitching up something in that sewing room of yours."

"Am I so predictable?"

"Like sunshine in summer."

Maggie bit down on her lower lip. She felt angry without knowing exactly why.

Alice leaned forward. "Hey, what's bugging you? Do I see a glimmer of discontent in those big, flashing eyes?" She half smiled. "I was wondering how long you were going to continue playing the happy little homemaker." She sipped her drink. "Even as a kid you always tired of things quickly. Is that what this S.O.S. is all about?"

Maggie looked at her with surprise.

"Don't look so astonished. I've known for quite a while that you've been batting your head against these walls, trying to get loose. I just didn't think it was my place to insinuate mutiny into your perfect little life."

Maggie let out a deep sigh and leaned back against the

mantlepiece. She ran her hands through her hair. "Predictable and obvious, is that what I am?"

"Obvious when your husband's away on a convention and you start flirting with the guys at the club."

"I never," Maggie gasped, looking wounded.

"Oh, come off it, kiddo. Every time Doug goes away on those dumb business things you start making googoo eyes at the tennis pro or whoever is available, not to mention that Saturday when you held court at the bar for the benefit of the cute new barman."

Maggie felt embarrassed knowing that Alice was right. But the flirtations were harmless; it was just that she wanted some attention.

Alice said, "I know you're climbing the walls with boredom. Remember, kiddo, I know you as well as you know yourself, maybe better. You never were much good at hiding your feelings, good or bad."

It was as if a wall collapsed and all her frustrations spilled out into the street. "Oh, God, Alice, I'm so bored I could scream!"

"So go ahead and scream. Then do something about it."

"Like what?"

"It all depends on why you're bored. If it's sex, find a lover. If it's your home life, change it."

"As simple as that?"

Alice threw her cigarette into the fire and got up to fix herself another drink. "As simple as that," she said. "Why does everything have to be complicated?"

"How?"

Alice half turned as she poured more Scotch over the ice. "How what? How do you change your home life or how do you find a new lover?"

"Home life."

Alice smiled and made a helpless gesture. "For a moment there I thought it was your turn to try out new bed sheets."

"Sorry to disappoint you." She hadn't meant for it to sound caustic, but it came out that way.

"Well, if you want to change your home life I'd suggest you go out and find yourself a job." Alice started back toward her chair. She felt wobbly. "Whew, it's either getting very hot in here, or I don't need this drink."

Maggie waited for her to settle in the chair. "What kind of a job could I get?"

"I just got done telling you, kiddo, that employers are yelling their heads off for help."

"Experienced help," Maggie corrected.

"Yes and no."

Maggie thought for a moment. "No, Doug would never agree to my going to work."

"Then join a church group. Donate your time to some charity or help out on some political campaign. Those political types are always up to their stiff society necks with tea parties and fund-raising things." She made a vague gesture.

Maggie shook her head. "They'd throw me out of church, I'm nervous around sick people and I hate politics with a passion."

"Then get a job whether good old Doug likes it or not. Hell, girl, it's your life, not your husband's."

"We don't need the money." Maggie knew she was snatching at straws but she also knew she wasn't qualified to be paid to do anything.

"So donate your salary to a worthwhile cause. Give it to me. I'm not proud." Alice was feeling very relaxed.

Maggie laughed. She decided to fix herself a drink anyway. "Oh, I don't know, Alice. I feel that if I don't get out of this house I'll go bananas, and yet. . . ." She finished fixing a highball and began pacing back and forth before the fire. The logs crackled like the frustrations that started to build up inside her again. The walls were back up and the boxed-in feeling had returned. "I have wracked my brain trying to find some solution to the way I feel."

In a low, quiet voice Alice said, "Why don't you stop pacing and sit down and try to spell it out for me."

Maggie stopped. "You just got done telling me that you know me better than I know myself; you tell me the answers."

"Okay, I will," she answered, falling back in the chair. "First off, bear in mind that a person's self-interests are the most important thing in the world to them. Second, think of the *now*; the future can always be adapted and the past can always be exaggerated, but it's the present you gotta concern yourself with. If you find it boring, then for Christ's sake change it."

Maggie raised her glass in salute and grinned. "I didn't realize that your three marriages turned you into a philosopher."

Alice laughed. "Not my three marriages, kiddo, these three Scotch-on-the-rocks. I stopped off and had one before I got here." She returned the salute. "It's the usual thing for divorcees to do on rainy days—and it beats gluing pictures or sewing dresses." She took another swallow, and blinked her eyes. "You know I'm really starting to feel a glow."

"Really, Alice," Maggie said impatiently when Alice started to get up to fix herself another drink. "Don't you think you've had enough? I didn't ask you here to watch you get plastered."

Alice pushed aside her glass. She turned to Maggie, looking rather contrite. "You're right, kiddo. I am getting a snootful, aren't I?" Suddenly she felt a stinging behind her eyes and before she knew what was happening the tears brimmed her lids and ran down her cheeks. "Oh, hell," she said as she brushed them away. Maggie noticed the tears and frowned. Alice said, "Rainy days also make me cry. Didn't you know that, kiddo?" She fumbled for a handkerchief.

"Alice," Maggie said, going to her. She wanted to put her arm around her but as long as they'd known each other they had never acquired that physical intimacy that some women had with one another. "What is it?"

"Shit, I don't know. Don't mind me, Mag." She took a deep breath and blew her nose. Staring straight ahead of her, seeing nothing, she sighed again and said, "It was just a year ago today that Eddie walked out on me. Good old Eddie. The life of every party. The best stud in town. I really loved that bastard."

Maggie felt helpless. In all the years she'd known Alice, she'd never once seen her cry; she always thought her incapable of tears. Alice represented strength and hardness; nothing penetrated her tough facade. She'd always been like that. And from what she'd seen of Eddie Baxter he was a perfect complement to Alice: Fun-loving, cold, and unfeeling. They were an ideal match.

It was odd for Maggie to stand there and suddenly see how wrong she'd been about Alice all of these years. Alice Maitland was as capable of being hurt as anyone. It was so much a surprise to Maggie that she felt she'd just been slapped in the face by a total stranger.

"Alice," Maggie stammered. Her heart went out to her friend, yet that old reserve that they both were so careful to build between them over the years was as strong and impenetrable as ever. Much as she wanted to comfort her, Maggie found herself incapable. "I didn't know," she managed to say.

Alice, unconscious of Maggie's astonishment, said, "No one knew, kiddo. Not even Eddie. You know me, all mouth and no guts when it comes to letting my feelings show. Always the big sport. Good old Alice." She blew her nose again. "Oh, hell, kiddo, Eddie and I were a great team. Two of a kind. Both of us always too busy trying to get a laugh to sit down and honestly tell each other how we really felt. I know he loved me as much as I did him, but we were too damned busy trying to prove to each other that we believed in independence and equal rights and nobody needed anybody but themselves." She let her eyes slide toward Maggie. "Try fucking yourself alone in bed. It ain't easy, kiddo, let me tell you. And they'll never invent a vibrator that feels and smells like a man."

She tapped out another cigarette. "Jesus, look at me," she said, holding out her hands to show how badly they were shaking. "Every time I think of that guy I get unstrung." She lit her cigarette and leaned back. After a moment she pushed herself forward and slapped her hands on the arms of the chair. "Hell, I think we got the scripts mixed up, Maggie. It's you who are supposed to cry on my shoulder. Isn't that why I came over here?"

"No, Alice, really. I never. . . ." She let the sentence dangle and hurriedly replaced it with, "I shouldn't be burdening you with my stupid problems. It's just that I never. . . ."

"That you never thought I had a serious bone in my body, right?"

"No, nothing like that," she said self-consciously. "It's just that you were always so independent about everything."

"Callous is the word, kiddo." Alice crushed out her cigarette. "Let's not talk about me. I do enough of that to the walls of my apartment. How about some coffee in the kitchen? Housewives are supposed to work wonders over cups of coffee sitting at a kitchen table."

Maggie smiled. "Coffee coming up," she said as they started out of the room.

To be honest, initially she'd asked Alice over to act more or less as a sounding board. She'd expected Alice to listen and advise her to chuck her marriage, her husband, her kids, and go off on a tear with some idyllic lover in a flashy sportscar, to some exotic paradise—all of which advice Maggie would ignore. It was the actual sound of her own complaining that Maggie wanted to hear. She wanted to hear her discontent spoken out loud, put into words, words that vibrated against walls and ceilings and fell on human ears other than her own. She thought that by actually hearing the sound of her complaints—in the presence of another human being—it would help her understand them better.

Now, perceiving a sympathetic side to Alice Maitland, Maggie felt more inclined to linger over coffee and open up her fears, knowing they wouldn't be trampled on like so much confetti, fun to play with but hardly of any importance afterward. She cradled her cup, letting the heat sting her hands. "The housewife in her kitchen—is that all there is to me? That's where I need advice, Alice. Am I really too realistic about everything?"

"Like what for instance?"

"Everything. I have the feeling all of a sudden that everything I always dreamed of having isn't really worth it now that I have it. It's all material stuff that wouldn't bring a quarter of its worth if I had to get rid of it."

"I wouldn't exactly consider Doug and the kids material stuff. You don't know how fortunate you are to have them. Listen to one old gal who knows what she's talking about." Yet far back in Alice's mind was the nagging gossip that Doug was being unfaithful again and Maggie's marriage could well wind up on the rocks—but she forced it out of her mind for the time being. She'd check it all out later.

Maggie said quickly, "I didn't mean Doug and the children. I know how lucky I've been in that regard, even if. . . ." She looked uncertain and put down her coffee cup.

"Even if Romeo strays every now and then," Alice said. She reached out and patted Maggie's hand. To Maggie the touch felt warm and comfortable and she wondered idly why they'd never touched before this.

"Even that," Maggie said. "I know Doug would never walk out on me, especially for some other woman. We truly love one another, Alice. I know that for a fact, just as I know you and I are sitting here drinking this coffee."

"And still you're fed up?"

"Not fed up with Doug or David or Julie. Fed up with myself, I suppose. I feel I haven't done anything with my life. Oh sure, I have a great house and a marvelous family, but suddenly that isn't enough, Alice." She looked thoughtful, her mind going back over the days. "The day after my last birthday I was standing at the living room windows looking out at the sky and realizing all the things that were going on outside my confined little world right at that exact moment. Millions upon millions of people live in this world and if I'm lucky I'll come into personal contact with maybe a hundred in a year, if that many. Good Lord, Alice, do you realize that I actually look forward to my hairdresser's gossip every Wednesday, much as I disapprove of Richard's graphic descriptions of his trips to the steambaths? At least it gets me out of my mundane little life for an hour or so."

Alice merely frowned at Maggie's mousey hairdo and got up to refill her cup. "You really ought to let me make an appointment for you with Jean-Claude. He'd do wonders for that dull mop, and especially rinse out those gray strands. I can't for the life of me understand why your stylist hasn't done something about that."

Maggie slammed the cup down on the saucer so hard she almost shattered it. "Christ, Alice, you haven't heard a single word I said."

Alice casually refilled the cup and put in another two teaspoons of sugar. "Sure I have, kiddo. I just wanted you to get it all out. You always were one to ramble around the edges and never get to the heart of things. Now tell me, honest injun; what started all this sudden discontent?" She sipped her coffee, watching Maggie over the rim of the cup. "Haven't you been getting screwed enough?"

Maggie impatiently waved the remark aside.

"Don't try to cover up, Margaret. Every marital problem starts in the sack."

"Why must you always bring everything back to sex?"

Alice saw her discomfort. So there was something wrong in the sex department; she could see it in Maggie's eyes. It might not be a major problem but by Maggie's expression there was a suspicion of something being amiss. Alice said, "Look, whenever a wife suddenly gets antsy to go into the big bright world it's because she's not getting any kick out of what she once got a kick out of. If you want my advice, buy yourself a book on how to improve your sexual techniques and I'll lay you odds you will be too busy dreaming up new ways of doing it to have time for anything else."

"Seriously Alice," Maggie said, "I'm bored out of my skull." Her sex life with Doug was her business and she certainly wasn't going to gossip about it with Alice. "Doug has his world outside this house, just as David and Julie have theirs. Why can't I have mine?"

"You can. But from the way you're talking, you're bored with this house, while Doug and the kids aren't. They come home to it for security whenever they feel threatened. In your case, you're feeling threatened and the first thing you want to do is run away from your security."

"But can't you understand that it's my security that's threatening me?"

"I don't buy that. You're looking for excitement and you don't have the slightest idea of what to do with it when you find it. You've never been able to cope with what goes on outside your world, Maggie; Doug and the kids are doing it every day. Mark my words, within a month of unshackling yourself from all this . . ." she made a sweeping gesture ". . . you'll find it crashing down around your ears. You're what keeps it all from falling apart, don't you realize that?"

Maggie gave her a disgusted look. "Well I'm sick and tired of being the old supporting pillar."

"Everybody needs the old pillars, kiddo. Hell, without old pillars how would anyone know there once were great people and civilizations?"

Maggie put her hands over her ears. "Oh, spare me any more of your cheap platitudes, Alice. I'm sick and tired of the way I'm living. I want to come home at night just the way Doug does. I want to know what's going on out there; I want to be a part of it."

"Yeah, sure. Everybody wants to be *with it* today. Just remember, that all those people who are trying so hard to be *with it* today are completely destroying their tomorrows."

"Damn it, Alice, are you still drunk? Stop with the aphorisms. What did you eat for lunch, Bertrand Russell?"

Alice winked. She really did still feel a bit giddy. "No, the guy I ate was much younger and, oh my God, was he hung!"

"You're impossible." She swept up her cup and saucer to pour herself a refill.

"Look, Maggie. All kidding aside, if you really think you want to go out and fight tigers, then go out. I personally think it's a terrible mistake because you've never been on a safari before and you're going out without a guide. But, if that's what you want, then by all means go to it. But don't say I didn't warn you. And above all else, kiddo, before you walk out the door make sure you know the real reason you're walking. Don't put it down to being taken for granted by your family, or the feeling that you're getting old and life is passing you by. They are just excuses. If you really dig down deep inside yourself you'll come up with the real reason you want out. Maybe you want more sex, or a younger lover, or adventure, or danger, or excitement. Whatever the truth, it is going to be a threat to what you have right now and once you leave your *present* behind, you've lost it and you'll never be able to come back and find it the way it was originally. When it's gone, it's gone for always. So all I can say, kiddo, is make damned sure you have a good reason to chuck all this for something you don't know anything about."

Maggie listened; yet she wasn't listening completely. True, she knew nothing of the world outside, but it certainly couldn't destroy what she already had. She wouldn't let it. After all, how could she possibly know if she was satisfied with her life if she had nothing to compare it to? She'd married Doug Hampton when she was eighteen and David was born less than a year later. Julie was born a year and a half after that. Before Doug she'd lived another protected life, watched over by fearful, anxious parents, a custodial father who believed no woman was born with a brain, only beauty and charms to please a man. She'd never wanted for a single thing in the whole of her life. Her mother protected her from the evils of liberty, her father from the evils of living. In school she took academic courses, learned Latin and the romantic languages, certainly nothing so commercial or crass as the useful study of shorthand or typing or bookkeeping. According to her father, anything to do with money or business was most unladylike. At home her mother saw to it that she learned to sew and embroider extremely well.

She'd met Doug in 1960, the year John Kennedy defeated Nixon in the presidential election. Doug didn't get involved in the Vietnam war because by then he was a family man with a wife and son to support. And the years following were good ones, although a mirror image of the years that had gone before. Her parents' advice and guidance had proved right. She cooked and sewed and kept a tidy, orderly house for a devoted husband and healthy children. But all that was behind her. The whole world had changed, and yet she was still exactly what she had always been. She was stagnating and regardless of Alice's dire forewarnings, she felt that it was only right that she change—and damn the consequences!

She said as much. "I guess I more or less made up my mind before you got here, Alice. If I don't leave the nest now I'll start hating it, which will really destroy it for everyone."

Alice gave a helpless sigh. "Well, if that's what you feel you must do, then do as I said earlier, get yourself a job."

"And as I asked earlier, what kind of a job? I can't do anything."

Deep down, Alice didn't want Maggie to change from what she'd always been. Maggie represented a kind of goal that Alice knew she herself could never achieve, but having it all personified in Maggie was almost like having it herself. It was selfish of her, she knew, but Alice couldn't help the way she felt; she'd always been selfish and always would be.

Begrudingly Alice answered, "You'll learn. There's always some tightwad willing to take on an inexperienced soul so that he or she can work them to death for starvation wages. You're a natural."

"I've thought maybe I could work in a department store, or perhaps a dress shop."

Alice shook her head. "You'd wind up on your feet all day and it'd kill you in a week. Find something where you can rest your buns on a chair all day. It's easier on the varicose veins."

"How about office work, filing or reception maybe?"

Alice shrugged. An idea suddenly struck her. "Tell you what—come to the agency tomorrow and I'll fix you up with one of my counselors. There's a form I ask applicants to fill out and by your answers my people can usually steer you toward the kind of job you're most suited for." She glanced at her watch. "Oh, hell, it's later than I thought and me with a heavy date. Christ, I'll never look twenty-two by seven-thirty." She stood up and winked. "Just between you and me I'd never look twenty-two after a six-months tour of duty at Main Chance. Which reminds me; I'm going to that spa in Arizona next week. You know the one, The Golden Cactus. Want to go?"

Maggie shook her head and grinned. "I don't need a health spa, I need a reclamation center. As for you, you can still pass for a child bride without the help of those spas you're hooked on."

"God, don't start putting ideas of marriage in my head. I'm suddenly feeling very vulnerable after that brief crying jag." She sighed as she looked around the kitchen. "I guess all this homesy-folksy atmosphere got to me. Tell you what, next time we have one of these soul-baring conversations, let's do it over lunch at some very smart, expensive restaurant in the city where we both get dressed in our best Halston frocks."

"I don't own one," Maggie said, giving her a gentle shove toward the door.

Alice cocked an eye. "I've noticed," she said sarcastically. "Which further reminds me, kiddo: If you're intent upon going out to shoot the tigers, you'd better buy yourself a gun." She fingered the material of Maggie's dress then pinched the roll around Maggie's middle and added, "And think twice about going to that spa with me next week."

Chapter 2

The rain had stopped, the late afternoon shadows were beginning to make patterns on the lawn. As Maggie sat in the window-seat of her sitting room she mulled over what Alice had said and came to the conclusion that Alice didn't want her to change her life. She wanted Maggie precisely where she was, here where Alice could call and find her at home whenever Alice wanted to gossip or needed to take a break from her work. She wanted Maggie available for tennis on Thursdays and for shopping on Friday afternoons. Doug and the children were no better; they'd all object and for the same reason: they'd be inconvenienced.

Maggie idly felt the roll of fat around her middle. She really was getting a bit out of shape, but it wasn't all that bad yet. She hated the thought of dieting. It was so much easier to close one's eyes to faults rather than go through all the trouble and discomfort to correct them.

Maggie bit down on her lower lip. She had to go out into that outside world at whatever the cost. Her decision was followed immediately by the question Alice raised. What was causing this sudden discontent? The real reason. Was it just because she was tired of being alone all day, or was there something deeper in this desperate need to be outside her home, her life? She was happy with Doug, or at least she thought herself happy, except for the tedium of the day when he and the children were away.

She concentrated on her life with Doug. Sexually she had to admit there wasn't the so-called passion that was there in the beginning, but that was normal for two people after being married as long as they were. She had to face the fact that not too many years ago Doug had almost left her for Phyllis Bracken. If their marriage was as perfect as Maggie supposed, why had Doug been tempted into Phyllis' arms? After he'd stopped seeing Phyllis he admitted that it had only been a need on his part to feed his male ego. Well, if that is the case then perhaps, Maggie thought, her female ego needed to be fed by someone other than her husband.

Was that what Alice was insinuating—that Maggie wanted to get out of the house and have other men admire her, proposition her?

Maggie stood up and walked toward the mirror over the dresser. She could just see the upper part of her reflection but that was enough to convince her that no man in his right mind was going to fawn over or make sexual overtures to this middle-aged, rather dumpy housewife from New Jersey. Maggie touched her hair and smoothed the hip line of her matronly dress. She could use a new hair style and a rinse; in fact, everything about her was dated, including her hemline, her makeup, even the tiny print in her dress. She pinched her waist again and grimaced, noticing that the sausage roll wasn't diminished when she was standing up, only camouflaged under her beltless shift. She cupped her breasts; at least they could still pass as firm and youthful. The rest of her was a disaster, she decided with a sinking heart, and—thinking of Alice's parting remark—there was no way she was going to be young and beautiful by tomorrow.

She pulled open the doors of her closet and began sifting through her wardrobe, holding up this dress and that. None of them was right for the picture she had of herself penetrating the jungle (as Alice referred to it). They were, of course, most suitable for the image that was expected of her at the club—that of the proper, middle-aged wife of a successful building contractor living in the proper section of Saddlebrook Estates, just across the Jersey palisades from Manhattan.

Up until recently that image had suited her, but it didn't satisfy her now. She wanted chic gowns, expensive hair styles, twice-weekly manicures, a fascinating career complete with an attaché case filled with important papers from the office and fast dinners in the microwave.

She frowned at her reflection and her fantasy was drenched by the rain that began pouring down again outside. What office? What career? she asked as reality swept back into the room. She didn't know the first thing about working in an office; besides, she hated fast foods cooked in the microwave.

Ah, but it would be so exciting, she told herself as she threw the best of her dresses across the bed and went again to sit in the window-seat and stare out at the new sheets of rain. She thought for a long time, carefully counting off the things she was qualified to do and those she was not.

One by one the ideas that came to her had to be discarded for obvious reasons, the most obvious of which was the fact that she had no proof of any special kind of education other than a high-school diploma. She'd been too busy taking care of David and Julie while Doug broke his back pouring concrete and tracking home endless tons of dirt and mud from the construction sites he worked on from six until dark. For Doug the endless drudgery had paid off in the end, but Maggie felt no further ahead than the day she returned from their honeymoon. Her lifestyle had improved, of course, but the household monotony was still there, just the same. She still saw Doug off after fixing him a hearty breakfast. She still rode herd over David and Julie, much as they resented it. They were all grown up, they told her; they weren't kids anymore; they didn't need a doting mother clucking over them.

Maggie smiled. Well, they'd soon find out what it is like to get along without the doting mother, the ready meals, the dependability of having a full-time housekeeper.

She glanced at the dresses she'd thrown across the bed. None of them were suitable for job hunting . . . a bridge party with the girls, perhaps, but certainly not looking for a job in New York. She'd just have to have new ones. Her watch told her it would be hours before Doug and the kids were due home. Rain or no rain the dress shops in town were still open.

As she was trying on a rather plain blue silk she felt again the nagging doubt about what she was doing. Did she want to dress for the attention of others, particularly other men? She shook her head at her image in the glass. No, she wanted to look smart and sophisticated, modern—*with-it*, as they say. But her conscience asked again, "But isn't that why you want to look that way, so men will look at you? Come on, Maggie, face the truth; you want to find out if you can still catch a man's eye."

Wrong!

She frowned. Of course she wanted to be attractive to men . . . but also to women. It wasn't sex she was setting out to find, it was merely a job, something to occupy her time, improve her mind as well as her disposition. It was the Alice Maitlands in this world who put all the emphasis upon sex. I am not Alice Maitland, Maggie told herself as she decided on the blue silk, because it was the one that best hid the sausage roll around her middle. She just wanted to meet new people.

Later that night she was doubly convinced of that as Doug took her into his arms and began caressing her breasts. He'd gotten home later than usual and said he was tired, but the minute they'd gotten into bed his erection made a liar out of him.

Despite her eagerness to respond to him, there was something different about Doug tonight. It was as if he were somewhere else, but intent upon proving that he could still arouse her as he always did. The pattern of their sex had changed tonight. The preamble was never this direct; foreplay was something they'd grown out of, heading right into the main event, an outgrowth of their familiarity.

She wanted to question him about the unusual scent that clung to him. A new soap, more than likely, but it had a sweetness that clashed with his personality. And he was doing different things to her, things she wasn't certain she enjoyed; but then he was inside her and all her questions, her doubts scattered.

It was when he was deep inside her, the pressure of his body pounding heavily against her own excitement that she reminded her conscience that she wasn't looking for any outside sex. Doug was more than enough. There couldn't possibly be a better husband or lover than Doug.

She pushed herself up to meet his onslaught, wanting him deeper and deeper inside her. She heard her voice, low and gutteral, moaning in pleasure. The heat of his body was overpowering, devastating. The strength of him made her head light, her mind senseless. She was reaching climax after climax and would surely faint from the sheer ecstasy if he didn't release her from the delicious torment he was subjecting her to.

"Doug, oh my God, I can't take it anymore," she moaned.

He pounded more mercilessly, more viciously as he felt his approaching orgasm. "God. . . ." he breathed as bolt after bolt of his searing lust spurted from his very core and gushed into the welcoming warmth of the woman he loved.

A stillness floated down from the blue plaster ceiling, a stillness so dark and thick that it suffocated their quick, heavy breathing. Doug rolled onto his back, putting his hands behind his head. A tiny, guilty sob caught in his throat; he released it with a sigh.

Maggie turned her head and smiled at his seemingly contented profile. She inched closer and draped an arm and a leg across his naked, sweating body. "Good?" she asked. There was a smugness in her voice as she studied his face.

"Umhuh."

Maggie let her hand slip down over his flat, muscled stomach. He was still as young and handsome as when she married him. His face had gotten a little more weathered, but it only added to his good looks, accentuating his square jaw and his piercing steel-blue eyes. His hair had always vacillated between blond and brown, depending upon the season of the year; and if it had grey streaks like her own, she hadn't noticed.

"Doug?"

"Huh?" His voice was getting heavy with sleep.

"Would you mind terribly if I got something to do to occupy my time during the day? You and the kids don't really need me full time anymore and I have so much free time on my hands."

"Whatever you want, hon." His voice was far, far away.

"You know I've been bothered a lot recently with the idea that I'm not involved in anything. I'm closed up in this house all day and I haven't a clue as to what's going on outside except for what I see and hear on the TV."

Doug let out a deep sigh and reluctantly turned toward her. "Maggie, if you want to get yourself something to occupy your time, I just got done saying you have my blessing." He pecked her mouth. "Now can I get some sleep?"

"Thank you, darling," she said, hugging him tightly. "Alice said she would get one of her counselors to screen me tomorrow morning. Are you sure you don't mind?"

He wasn't listening. "Go to sleep. Do whatever you want."

Doug's breathing became slower, more even. A moment later he was sound asleep. Maggie rolled over on her side and hugged her pillow. She felt happier than she had in a long while. Tomorrow would be different, different from all her yesterdays. She smiled contentedly and let her eyes fall shut.

She was still wearing the same smile and humming a gay little tune as she fixed Doug's bacon and eggs.

"You sound happy this morning," Doug said as he kissed her cheek and sat at the table.

"I'm going to Alice's agency this morning to see about a job."

"Job?"

Her smile faltered a little. "Remember? We talked last night. You said you didn't mind if I got a job."

"You didn't say anything about getting a job; you said you wanted to occupy some of your free time."

"Well, it's the same thing, isn't it?"

"No, it isn't the same thing. I. . . ." He didn't finish. Julie and David came into the kitchen, involved as usual in one of their seemingly unending arguments . . . although they called them "discussions."

They were bright, good-looking young people, Julie too grown up at sixteen to suit Maggie, and David far too mature. It was hard to accept the fact that he'd be graduating from high school next month. They were, Maggie found, at that age when nothing was important except themselves and their own world of rock music, parties, cars, and dates. Very little else mattered; not even parents, who represented discipline and restrictions, which had no place whatsoever in what they considered modern living.

Neither of the youngsters greeted their parents, but then who ever said "Good morning" to the household fixtures?

Maggie put a bowl of cereal, toast, and milk in front of David, who attacked it immediately.

"Just juice for me," Julie said. "I'm on a diet."

Maggie didn't argue, knowing how useless it would be. Anyway, as soon as Julie met her girlfriends they'd have their milk shakes and pastries just to establish their mutual resistance to parental authority.

Maggie wanted to talk to Doug but by the way he was concentrating on his food it was obvious he didn't want to pursue their conversation. She put her plate on the table and took the chair next to his. Doug immediately checked his watch and said, "Damn, I'm late." He got up and pecked Maggie's cheek. "I'm going out on that Palisades construction site today so I might be late getting home tonight, honey."

"Again? You're working late every night these days."

"Speaking of working," he said, "We'll talk about that business of your getting a job when I get home." He gave her another quick kiss and was out the back door pretending he didn't hear her calling his name.

She didn't feel like asking her children's opinion, so when Julie said, "What job?" Maggie merely said, "Nothing important; just something I've been thinking about."

She wasn't going to let Doug dissuade her. She was going into New York to see Alice and her counselor regardless of what Doug said.

David said to his sister, "I've got that graduating committee meeting in half an hour so if you want a lift to school let's go."

Julie gulped down her juice and grabbed her books. "Don't forget, David, you promised to speak to Vince Lockwood about taking my friend Pam to the senior prom."

One minute there had been a trembling of talk and activity and a second later it was as if silence had taken on material form and had crowded down around her, over her, under her like thick mats of quilted dust. It was only when she found herself alone with the deafening stillness of the house that she found herself becoming more and more eager to start out for her appointment with the employment counselor.

She didn't like herself as much in the blue silk as she had yesterday. It made her look fat and lumpy, but then she was fat and lumpy, she told herself as she glanced at herself in the mirror and wondered why she hadn't noticed in the shop that the pleats in the skirt made her hips broader. Oh well, she thought with a sigh, it was too late to do anything about it now.

A warming breeze replaced the wet grey of the day before. Any signs of the previous rain huddled out of sight, kept there by the promise of a perfect day. Maggie saw the sparkle of the day as an omen of good fortune. Unfortunately, drifting across a corner of the sky was a dark cloud from yesterday. And to add to the omens she felt a little hesitant setting out after Doug's parting remark.

Oh, what the hell, she decided as she got into the car and started the motor. Going for an interview with an employment counselor wasn't exactly getting a job. Doug had said they'd talk about her going to work when he got home. Okay, so they'd talk. If she had a prospective job in her pocket, their talk would be more specific, it would have a more definite point of reference.

She sped along with the traffic heading for the Park-and-Ride lot where she'd change to the bus for Manhattan. The turn-off for the lot was directly ahead. She pulled up behind the last car in line and inched her way forward. As she began looking for a vacant parking slot she found herself thinking of their sex last night. Doug had seemed somehow remote. She shrugged. He was tired, that's all, she told herself.

She began concentrating on her overall sexual relation with Doug, deciding that he had to be the best husband a woman could want, but then he was the only husband she'd ever had so insofar as sex or anything else was concerned, she didn't have anyone to compare Doug to.

She found a space, got out of the car and locked it, then hurried toward the bus that was getting ready to pull out for New York. Within thirty minutes the bus lumbered through the Lincoln tunnel and started up the curling ramp to one of the upper levels of the Port Authority terminal.

As she took the escalator to the main level she couldn't help feeling the sudden excitement of the city itself. Everywhere she looked people moved. There was no mistaking the fact that she was no longer in suburban New Jersey; she was in a world of total motion and noise, a life where people moved or rode toward definite goals and destinations. The thriving activity made her forget completely about purse-snatchers and muggers and all the undesirable things said and written about this fabled city with its jostling people and yellow taxi cabs.

Her heels clicked across the marble floor toward the Eighth Avenue exit and she felt herself getting lighter, walking faster. She stopped just outside the door and allowed the increased intensity of the place to overpower her as people bumped and shoved her on both sides. Here was her magical escape from the monotony of her life. That is what the city meant to her, had always meant, although she'd never been ready for the escape until today.

Alice's office was over near Fifth Avenue on 44th Street. Maggie turned to her left and, unlike everybody else, waited at the intersection until the "walk" sign flashed on before crossing Eighth Avenue. She'd always marveled at the complete disregard New York pedestrians had for traffic and the traffic had for pedestrians. It was like people fighting against machines, each trying to prove to the other that they are the more important, the more indestructible.

She hadn't gone a hundred paces toward Fifth Avenue up 42nd Street before she found herself feeling that she belonged here, despite the tawdry arcades, the porno theatres, the pimps and derelicts lounging against the buildings. It was as if an alien force had taken possession of her and had changed her dramatically from the protected New Jersey suburbanite to a sophisticated, decisive New York career woman. She tried not to glance at herself in the store windows for fear her confidence would vanish at the sight of reality. She refused to think that the blue silk pleats made her hips broader or that her hair was a little too matronly for the new Maggie Booth Hampton, the "cosmopolite." She was being possessed by the city. New York was gathering her up with its influence. Everyone around her had a strange obsessed expression about them, and as she walked deeper and deeper into the city she felt the same obsession coming over herself, reminding her that only the obsessed get what they want out of this life.

Alice's building was in the middle of the block, closer on 44th Street to Sixth Avenue (she could never refer to it as the Avenue of the Americas) than to Fifth, so she found herself retracing her steps. She didn't mind, however; the sunless streets, the dingy buildings were strangely intoxicating. It was like walking in a paradox. The more unkept everything was, the more beguiling it all became.

She found the building and took the elevator to the fourth floor. The minute she walked off the elevator she was assailed by noise and bustle that sounded exactly like Alice.

Chapter 3

"Mrs. Maitland is tied up with a couple of people from the American Civil Liberties Union. Something about percentages in placing blacks and gays," the receptionist told her.

Maggie's eyebrows went up. She figured the receptionist to be no more than a year or so older than Julie, but she had already had acquired something hard and earthy in the way she talked. Was that one of the side effects that came with city sophistication? Strangely enough the girl's voice triggered a weird sense of excitement, yes, even of decadence and danger.

"Are you Maggie Hampton?" the man asked as he came up to her. He was somewhere in his late twenties, maybe early thirties, very good-looking in a short, slight sort of way, with thin yellow hair and a bright clear face. He had that squeaky-clean air about him, yet there was a tiredness about the eyes that didn't go with his smile. He was a night person, Maggie decided, noticing the sallow tinge to his skin.

He picked a piece of lint from Maggie's shoulder, grinned his boyish grin and said, "I'm Andy Carver."

Maggie's hand went instinctively to the spot where the lint had been, expecting him to apologize for his forwardness. He didn't. By the way he smiled it was obvious that he felt he'd done her the ultimate favor.

He said, "You're much too lovely to be blemished by a piece of lint." He made a motion toward what Maggie surmised was Alice's private office and said, "The boss lady is going to be tied up for awhile. She told me you might be coming in. Come on. I'll get you started with the paper work."

Walking alongside him she found Andy Carver was just about the same height as herself. He'd looked taller when he first came up to her, but then he was a man and in her mind all men were supposed to be taller. He couldn't be more than five feet six or seven, she decided, but he walked with the air of a giant and the grace of a dancer.

He ushered her past dozens of cubicles into a large square room with partitions separating the desks lined against the walls. The place had a starchiness about it, everything being so square, so crisp, so made-of-maple. There was not the aura of aluminum and chrome and glass that Maggie had expected. This was a comfortable, at-home place, and she wondered why frivolous Alice had gone to so much trouble and effort to make strangers feel so cozy. A spider's web came to her mind, but she dismissed it.

"You're from New Jersey, right?" Andy said as he handed her an application blank. It was obvious that Alice had filled him in a little bit.

"Yes. Saddlebrook," she answered.

"The Estates? My, how utterly posh," he said, raising his eyebrows almost to the hairline. He nodded toward the application blank Maggie started to fill in. "Surely you aren't here looking for a job?" He sounded like Julie.

"Yes," Maggie said, feeling guilty. "Is there anything wrong with that?"

"No. I just . . ." he made an awkward gesture and fell silent.

As Maggie filled in the blanks she tried to decide whether she liked this Andy Carver or not. He seemed a bit snobbish, but very congenial, very friendly. Overly friendly in fact. That bit about the lint-picking had smarted; intimate gestures such as that she reserved for very close friends. But then he was young and obviously his definition of friendliness included intimacy. Unfortunately people who were too friendly made Maggie suspicious.

As she worked, Andy talked. He mouthed his words too precisely, too perfectly to suit Maggie. There was an unreal quality about his voice that made him sound out of place, as though he should be on a stage or in front of a microphone, not behind a desk in an employment agency. He oozed theatrics in the way he waved his hands, the way his mouth turned down when he said something unpleasant. He wasn't genuine somehow.

Andy pushed back his chair and stood up. He motioned toward the dark-haired, dark-eyed woman who was settling herself behind a desk directly opposite. "Rita's here. The boss-lady left instructions that Rita was supposed to talk to you. I had no idea it was about a job. I hope Alice knows what she's doing. I thought you two were friends." Before Maggie could affirm that Andy hurried on, "Now look, don't let Rita get to you. She's our token Chicano just like Ned's our token black." He nodded to a nearby empty desk, then leaned conspiratorily toward her and half whispered, "And I'm the token gay, in case you haven't guessed." He pursed his lips and said, "We're very integrated."

Maggie felt a jolt in her stomach but forced a smile. "I see," she managed to say.

"I hope you don't mind my frankness," he said. The barrier was suddenly down and he was very swishy both in tone and manner. "That's just the way I am. Personally I'm claustrophobic; I simply abhor closets." He chuckled, then sobered immediately. "Alice says I'm too open, that I have a sadistic need to shock people." He shrugged. "Maybe, but I think of myself as being a totally honest, open person. I am what I am and I don't kid either myself or anyone else."

"That's admirable," Maggie said and was glad they were standing in front of Rita Gant's desk so there would be an end to this discomfiting conversation.

Andy made the introductions. "Now don't let Rita bug you, Mrs. Hampton. She's a total you-know-what, but she's terribly good at her job." He winked at the frowning Rita Gant and said, "*Hasta la proxima vez, señora.*"

Rita curled her lips and snarled, "Get lost, *Puta*." She spoke with a thick Spanish accent.

Maggie felt the current of intense dislike pass between Andy and Rita Gant. It was so spiked with hatred that she actually shivered. She fumbled with the application form she carried and offered it to Rita. To try and calm a little of the tension left in Andy's wake she said, "Are you from Mexico, Señora Gant?"

"Havana." She took the form and started to look it over. "And it's *Mrs*. Gant."

Maggie twisted the straps of her purse. "I see," she said. "I studied Spanish in high school. I try to use it whenever possible. It's such a beautiful language; I'd hate to lose my knowledge of it."

Rita seemed not to have heard a word. She was reading the application and from the way her expression darkened she obviously did not like what she read. She shook her head. "You didn't even fill in your home address. What is it, please?"

Still trying to establish a little more relaxed atmosphere Maggie said, *"Mi dirección es . . ."*

"Oh, for Christ's sake, Mrs. Hampton, speak English. Your Spanish is terrible."

Maggie was so taken aback by the woman's outburst that she felt tears gathering at the back of her eyes. "I'm sorry," she muttered, searching for a handkerchief. She blew her nose and tried to keep herself as calm as possible. "615 Corning Terrace, Saddlebrook Estates, New Jersey," she said after a moment.

Rita shook her head again as she wrote in the address. "Another rich, bored housewife."

Maggie felt her back stiffen. She didn't have to tolerate this woman's rudeness. "If you are intent upon being uncivil, Mrs. Gant, perhaps another counselor is available." She got out of her chair.

"I'm the only one right now," she said in a bored tone. Ignoring the fact that Maggie was standing over her, Rita said, "You don't have any experience, I suppose?"

Maggie hesitated. "No."

Rita reached for a card file.

Maggie continued to hesitate but decided finally that she felt a little foolish standing glowering at the woman. She reseated herself.

Rita said, "What do you think you'd like to do?"

She tried to calm herself, tried to ignore the dislike she felt for the woman. "Oh, I don't know. Anything."

"Anything includes a large variety of some very unpleasant occupations. Ditch digging, for example. Would you like to dig ditches?"

"Really, Mrs. Gant." She pushed herself forward in the chair. "Are you always so unpleasant?"

"Look, honey. I'm doing Alice a favor by cutting short my lunch hour to try and help you out. I would like to get this over with as quickly as possible so that I can get back to spending time with my Spanish-speaking applications, girls who *need* a job." She snapped the application form as though it were a whip. "You aren't qualified for much, I see. Do you type?"

"No." The coldness in Maggie's voice could have frozen water. "Perhaps I could wait on table, or something like that."

Rita breathed a sigh. "Being a waitress isn't something an inexperienced person gets paid to do. First of all you need to know how to handle people, food, and money. You're on your feet all day long and you obviously are thin-skinned so a lot of customers would have you hopping mad in five minutes, customers like me, for instance. No, you'd make a lousy waitress. You have to be damned good to get a decent job waiting tables." Rita scanned her cards. "You don't run any kind of office machines, I suppose?"

"I do not." She twisted the strap of her purse so tightly it hurt her hand.

"I didn't think so." She flipped to another card. "Saleswoman." She glanced at Maggie. "No, I don't think they'd even consider you."

"Why not?"

Rita made a face. "It's Bonwit Teller, honey. Very high class dressers work there. They wouldn't let you in the employees entrance."

Maggie gasped, feeling her blue silk dress turn to polyester. She sat feeling utterly humiliated and about two inches tall as Rita finished leafing through the card index. When she replaced them in the drawer and pushed it shut she said, "Nothing. You aren't qualified for anything."

Maggie couldn't hold her temper in check. "That, Mrs. Gant, is only your opinion. Surely I could be a receptionist or a bank teller or something along those lines."

Making it obvious that she was gathering up all her patience, Rita said in her heavy Spanish accent, "First of all, *Señora*, bank tellers have to be trained and you are too old to be considered for any training program I know of. And as for being a receptionist, they would not look at you; receptionists are always very young, very well groomed, very attractive ladies, not bored housewives from the suburbs looking for a thrill to pass their time until their man gets home."

Maggie jumped from her chair so fast and with such anger that she kicked it backward, sending it crashing to the floor. She knew from the noise that everyone in the office must be staring at her back. She didn't give a damn. "You are the most insufferable, tactless woman I have ever met, Mrs. Gant. Thank God I have no experience for any type of work lest with my luck I would wind up in an office working alongside the likes of you. *Adios, Señora Gant*," she snarled.

Rita Gant was grinning at her and Maggie saw in that grin the utter contempt Rita Gant had for Anglo-Saxons. It was without mistake a racial grin and Maggie had a terrific urge to reach out and slap it from her face.

Rita said, "Go home and speak Spanish to your cleaning woman, Mrs. Hampton. That is where you belong, whether you appreciate it or not."

Maggie heard about racial prejudice, of course, but she'd always equated it with whites hating blacks and blacks hating whites. In Saddlebrook Estates there was the color barrier, even where it wasn't supposed to exist, but no one spoke of it and everyone outwardly treated everyone else as an equal, even if deep down inside prejudice was still generated.

She heard Andy Carver call her name and out of the corner of her eye she saw him start toward her, but she wanted nothing to do with him and his openness, nor for that matter did she want anyone to speak to her. She was completely shaken and wanted to go home where she belonged.

As Maggie hurried past the reception desk, dabbing at the corners of her eyes to protect her mascara, Alice hurried after her. "Maggie. Wait!" Maggie ignored her.

"Maggie!" Alice called again, this time closer, close enough to grab hold of her arm.

Maggie shook herself free. "Leave me alone, Alice. This is humiliating. I've never been so furious in my life."

To her surprise she heard Alice chuckle. Maggie turned and glared at her through her angry tears. Alice saw the contempt in Maggie's eyes and said, "Hold on, kiddo, don't throw those daggers at me. This is the big, real world you wanted so badly to get involved in." She linked her arm in Maggie's and steered her toward the elevators in the hall. "There's a nice little restaurant in the cellar of the next building. Go have yourself a cocktail or coffee or something; I'll be finished up with these right-wingers in about ten minutes and I'll join you."

Maggie didn't want to be consoled. "No, really, Alice, I would rather go home."

"Quitting on your first day out. I'm surprised at you, Maggie. You weren't so easily beaten down when we were kids."

Maggie looked at her with wide, angry eyes. "You don't know what that dreadful woman said to me, Alice."

"I have a perfectly good notion of what she said to you. That is why I think you should have a nice quiet cocktail and wait for me to join you. Besides, I had cleared my lunch time for you anyway, so don't make me have to waste it by work. Come on, kiddo. The place is called Mario's and it's awfully good. I want to talk to you, Maggie. Wait for me." Alice's eyes went dark. "I think we should talk."

True to the promise she'd made herself, Alice had checked out the gossip about Doug and didn't like the facts she'd found. It looked like Doug and Phyllis were up to their old tricks and she felt she owed Maggie, her best friend, the truth about what was going on.

Maggie no more wanted to linger in New York than she wanted to find a dead cat in her bed. To her the entire city was suddenly filled with Rita Gants, all insulting and hateful, all out to reap revenge on the "Gringo" or "Whitey" or whatever pet prejudicial phrase they reserved for white people. She had never felt bigoted before, but she knew it was germinating inside her and she kept telling herself that she should not give a woman such as Rita

Gant the satisfaction of letting that seed grow. She was sensible enough to know that if she ran back to the security of her uncluttered, uncomplicated life right now the hurt and resentment would always be with her, sharp and clear. Alice was right. She should try and compose herself and leave New York with at least the memory of a pleasant, jovial lunch with an old friend.

"Fuck the bitch," Alice whispered and winked.

The very crudity of the remark made Maggie smile. It seemed to be at least a modicum of revenge against Rita. "Okay, Alice. I'll wait for you downstairs. Don't hurry. I'll be okay, believe me."

"I know you will, kiddo. I depended on that. Be with you as soon as I can. Order me a dry Manhattan, make it a double. That will give me a reason to cut these jokers short."

There weren't many people in the little restaurant, but the few that were there appeared to be of the discriminatory type. Discriminatory, she thought as she sat at a table for two near the window that looked out on the steps leading to the street. She felt awful. She would never in her life speak to anyone the way that perfect stranger spoke to her.

People were terribly cruel, she decided as she ordered an Old Fashioned and Alice's dry Manhattan. There had been no conceivable reason for Rita Gant to have been so cutting, so malicious. She was just a vindictive woman who harbored a deep-seated hatred for reasons only she herself could know. Or did all non-white people feel the same, only hid it better? Was there a deep resentment in everyone who wasn't white? She'd never understood why one race hated another, why one religion insisted on trying to destroy another religion, why one form of government wanted everyone to believe in its way. She had been taught to be kind to all people, to live honestly, fairly, treating everyone as she would treat herself. For the first time ever she realized that she had truly led a sheltered life and the rude awakening that had just come at the hands of Rita Gant had shaken her badly. She would never forget the experience, or the resentment in that woman's eyes.

"Stop brooding," Alice said as she slipped into the chair

in a flurry of clanging bracelets and enticing perfume. "Where's my drink?"

Maggie rallied. "He's bringing it. You didn't take long."

"I had a little chat with your favorite employment counselor. My, she sure took an instant dislike to you. I had no idea she'd react that strongly. Of course it didn't help to have Andy introduce you. She hates his guts more than anyone's, including mine. She wouldn't tell me exactly what she'd said to you but obviously by the way you looked and the way she spoke she must have gone for the throat."

The cocktails were set in front of them. When they were alone again, Maggie said, "Why on earth did you insist that Mrs. Gant counsel me if you knew how prejudiced she was?"

In a cool sensible voice Alice said, "Because I think you need to be reminded of what you have to put up with when you leave that cozy little retreat of yours in Saddlebrook Estates." Alice rested her elbows on the table and leaned forward. "Look, kiddo, I'm sorry Rita got so rough but she does have a lot of personal problems which all of us in the office take into consideration when we see how she treats people. Oh, she treats her own kind just as cruelly as she treated you. She's hooked on some kind of self-righteous fanaticism." She leaned back and sampled her drink. She smacked her lips and took another sip.

"Really, Alice," Maggie said with exasperation. "You tolerate the untolerable. You always have. I can't find a single reason for your sticking up for Rita Gant. A hard life and personal problems are no excuses for rude, vicious behavior."

"I'm not sticking up for her. I'm stuck with her whether I like it or not. She was assigned to me by some Latino Committee representing the Cuban Embassy. They rent floor space in my place. I'd love to kick her brown ass right out in the street but my hands are tied."

Maggie waved her hand. "Let's forget Rita Gant. It was a mistake to come here in the first place. Let's just have a nice lunch and I'll go back where I belong—which will please Mrs. Gant very much, I'm sure."

Alice gazed at her drink with a devilish smile tickling her lip. "What exactly did she say?" she said.

Maggie felt her brow crease into a frown. She toyed with her drink. Maybe she should get it all out and then forget it. She shrugged and said, "She just told me I was totally incapable of doing any sort of work."

"Which you knew before you came here," Alice reminded her coolly. "Certainly that didn't upset you."

"No," Maggie hedged. "It wasn't that; she said other things."

Alice was content to sit quiet and carefully pick at Maggie's bones. Two more sips of her Old Fashioned and Maggie would spit out the whole story.

It took only one more sip. "She called me old, fat, and unattractive." She paused. "Well not exactly in so many words but nevertheless old, fat, and unattractive."

Alice looked unimpressed. "Well, two out of three ain't bad, kiddo."

Maggie stared in surprise.

Alice said, "You *are* old and fat; it's the unattractive I don't buy. Though I'd suggest just a bit more attention to the hair and makeup."

"Honestly, Alice," Maggie breathed indignantly, automatically reaching for her handbag.

"Oh, for God's sake, Maggie, stop playing the delicate flower from the Garden State! It doesn't become you. I never realized you've turned yourself into such a naive little dove. First off, we're both the same age, so don't give me this 'young' shit. You're 36—which isn't exactly young. And no, I wouldn't call you fat, but you aren't exactly slim-jenny either. You could well afford to shed a good fifteen pounds, maybe twenty. I'd have to see you stripped. And speaking of stripped, kiddo, where on earth did you get that number you're wearing? You look like something dressed up for the coal miners' dance."

"Stop it!" Maggie shouted. She felt the silence in the room but didn't give a damn. "I'm sick and tired of sitting like some dolt and letting everyone insult me. You and Rita Gant can go to blazes for all I care," she said, fighting back the tears again and at the same time trying to push the chair away from the table as she got to her feet.

She had wanted a dramatic exit, chair flying backward against the wall, the upset cocktail glass, preferably breaking, the audible gasps of the onlookers. But the chair's feet were stubbornly caught in the shag of the carpeting, her purse had slid under the table, the cocktail glass was sitting there looking virginal, the other diners had resumed their own private conversations—and worst of all, Alice was smiling and softly clapping her hands.

"Speaking of jobs," Alice said, "Have you considered the theatre?" She stopped her soft clapping and her expression went very grave. "Sit down, for God's sake, Maggie. If you value my friendship you'll listen to some good advice."

Maggie hesitated. After a moment she felt awkward standing there with the feeling of being naked before strangers. She did not want to hear anything Alice had to say yet she found she could not bring herself to turn and storm out, the way she did back in the office. Inwardly she shook herself, like a shaggy dog coming in out of the rain. She said, "Really, Alice, sometimes you infuriate me."

Unperturbed, Alice said, "I always have, remember? Come on, finish your drink and we'll have another." She sipped at her glass. "Maybe if you repeat that 'irate woman' scene one more time we'll be able to sell it to MGM." She toasted her with her glass. "Twice in one morning! Practice makes perfect."

Maggie rested her hand on the back of the chair, supporting her terrible indecision. Finally she could stand the weight no longer. "Well, I'm certainly not old and fat," she said defiantly as she sat down. She pouted, staring at her unfinished cocktail. Her hand, as if operating independently, reached out and lifted the glass to her lips. She polished off the Old Fashioned in one gulp and punctuated her defiance by banging the glass down on the table.

"Good," Alice said as she motioned to the waiter for another round. "You know, Maggie old friend, yesterday when you confessed how bored you were with your life, I was very quick to suggest that you do something about it, like getting the hell out of that house and enjoying yourself and not sit around moping, waiting for Doug or the kids to need you. But after I left your place I did some serious thinking about you and I came to the conclusion that my advice might not have been good for someone like you."

"What do you mean, 'someone like me'? How am I so different?"

"You belong to a different breed than me. The advice I gave you was advice I'd have given myself, or someone like me."

Maggie started to object but Alice held up her hand. "When we were growing up, at first we were closer than two loving little sisters. But as we matured we grew apart."

"You discovered boys."

Alice shook her head. "I was searching for love. I remember going to your house and seeing how well your father and mother got along; it was obvious that there was a great deal of love among you. I used to get very jealous of all that affection, even the affection they gave to me. I wanted my parents to love me and care for me the way yours did. But we both know what an unstable household I grew up in and then my stepfather died and. . . ." She fanned out her hands. "The minute I found out that boys treated girls lovingly and warmly, I rushed into as many of their arms as I could, hoping to find the love my parents never gave me. By the time I was all grown up I'd faced just about every disappointment a woman can face, so the big bad world wasn't much of a disappointment to me. So, when I started to think about you leaving all that security, all that love, I kicked myself for giving you bad advice. You've been sheltered too long and I doubt very much if you can be house-trained for the bitterness that exists outside your present way of life."

When Maggie started to interject Alice quickly said, "Yeah, I know. You've always been a strong-willed, even-tempered sort who makes good no matter what the odds. I said to myself, 'What the hell. Why should you try to protect Maggie? Everybody's protected her all her life. Let her take her own chances, if that's what she wants.' So, I decided to let my advice stand, but I decided that rather than waste a lot of time finding out whether you have the guts to stand up to harsh realities, I'd give you the fire and water test right off the bat. That's why I had you counseled by Rita. If anybody would show you the scars of making one's own way in this world, it would be good old rotten Rita. She really isn't one of us."

The waiter put their drinks in front of them. Alice continued. "You know, Maggie, after all these years, I think you've remained the same little girl I knew back when we were the same age."

Maggie tasted her fresh cocktail. "We're still the same age, Alice. You just reminded me of that."

"Like hell we are, kiddo. I'm eons older than you now." She fished a cigarette out of the pack and lit it. "You are still that innocent little brown-haired tot who keeps wanting to add more and more toys to her toy box, and at the same time wanting to make sure nobody takes away any of the old toys. You keep filling your box and filling your box, piling more goodies on top of other goodies until you can't see the bottom of the pile any more."

Maggie frowned. "You're talking in riddles again."

Alice said, "You keep putting good stuff on top of good stuff until you don't know what you have. You only see what's on top and you lose sight of what it's all based upon, what it's all about." She took a drag of her cigarette. "Rita Gant is, I bet, the first time you had to look square into the eyes of something unpleasant."

"Oh, Alice, you're making me out to be some dumb little Nell from the farm."

"You are."

"That's ridiculous. Whether or not you believe it, I know all about the hard cruel world you're trying to protect me from."

"I seriously doubt that." She took another drag from her cigarette, made a grimace of distaste, and crushed it out. "Hell, I don't know why I smoke those things, I don't enjoy them." She took a sip of her drink. "You've never worked for a living, Maggie. Things take on an entirely different perspective when you have someone giving you dollars for time and labor. Money makes a big difference. It makes people hard and cruel and insensitive to everything except their own needs and wants. Rita Gant saw an enemy in you today. You're a woman who really doesn't need to earn her own living. You're a woman who could easily be taking food out of the mouths of babies whose mothers need a job. Many of her Spanish-speaking applicants are no more qualified or experienced than you, and on top of that many of them speak little or no English. She, of course, is much more interested in seeing them earning money than a woman like you."

"That stupid Rita Gant is like so many other blind, dumb women who think they're protecting their own minorities by fighting the very people who could help them."

Alice raised one eyebrow.

"Alice, you're bright enough to know that I'm intelligent, efficient, ambitious, hard-working. Put a dozen women such as me to work on any job and you know in your heart that more and more jobs would be created as a result of our hard work. We would make more openings for minorities, people less qualified, because our diligence would create expansion. Given the right opportunity I could be more help at creating jobs for more underprivileged people. Look, what happens when a bunch of people with a drive get together? They produce, right? And the more they produce the more they market, and the more they market the more they sell, and the more they sell the greater the demand, and the more the demand the more help needed to produce. See what I mean?"

Alice looked impressed but said nothing. She occupied herself with her cocktail.

Maggie said, "From what I saw of Rita Gant she seems to be a woman carrying a grudge not only against people of another race but against everyone. She don't give a damn about her people, as you say. She'll place them in the worst possible working conditions just so she can say she found them a livelihood. What in hell does she care what kind of work it is, or how little the pay? She cares only about commissions and statistics, and her poor applicants are so happy with any kind of income that they uncomplainingly go to work and Rita reaps her percentages and everyone is supposed to be happy. Well that's not what going to work means to me, Alice. I may be bored with my life at home, but I know I have all this energy that's bursting to be put to use, and if there is an employer out there who will hire me, he won't be sorry. I'll work as hard for him as I would in my own home and I'd make a success of whatever I do.

She was suddenly all fired up, anxious to show her side of life. "I don't want to sit idly by and have my vitalities go unneeded. I'm going mad in that house." She pointed in the direction of New Jersey. "Some women are satisfied with cleaning and cooking and being content with the chance to tell everyone how hard it is to keep a house. I'm not."

"You're not going to win many friends with remarks like that, kiddo."

"Oh, I didn't say it very well, Alice, but I didn't mean that housework isn't hard—it is; it's damned hard, but it's also fun, or at least it's fun for those who continue doing it. It was fun for me for awhile, but the fun's gone out of it. I need a new challenge."

Alice sat quietly for a moment. She'd been impressed with what Maggie said; in fact, it was the first time she'd ever heard her friend get riled up about something she obviously felt deeply concerned about. "Okay," Alice said finally. "You've convinced me that you want to work and that you'd be good at whatever you get hired to do, which brings us back to Rita Gant."

"How so?"

"You aren't qualified or experienced and . . ." she hesitated. ". . . and you could take a little closer look at yourself. You've let yourself go." She quickly added, "But I must admit you haven't gone beyond redemption. I have a feeling that there might still be something worth saving under all those drapes and flounces of blue silk."

Feeling defensive and self-conscious Maggie snapped, "Damn it, Alice, I came looking for a job—not an entry in a beauty contest!"

"I didn't say you had to look gorgeous, just attractive."

"I'm not looking for a man either."

"Aha!" Alice hooted. "I think I just heard a Freudian slip." She leaned back, looking smug. "Why did you mention a man, Mag? Is that really what's in the back of your pretty head? Sex?"

"Jesus, Alice, you do make me furious at times."

Alice continued to smirk. "It was you who mentioned a man, not me, kiddo. Now let's level. Way back in that brain of yours is the longing for a wild, impossible romantic fling with an unobtainable stranger, right? Something right out of a *Cosmopolitan* romance."

"Stop it," Maggie said sharply. "A new man is the farthest thing from my mind. I'm quite content with the one I have, thank you."

"Ah, but the thought of something new and young and fresh and different wouldn't exactly turn you off now, would it?"

Maggie fidgeted. She twisted her mouth until an unattractive sneer formed. "First of all, as everyone is so quick to remind me, I'm far too old to attract any young bachelors; I'm far too young to be the desire of any elderly widower who might be looking for a replacement for his recently deceased wife of fifty years. As far as divorced men are concerned, those who are of eligible age never divorce their wives until there's a little dish already waiting in the wings." She felt herself calming down. "No, Alice, it is not sex I want; it really is a job, something to make me feel useful again."

Alice winked. "I don't believe a word of it. I've always known you were the dedicated type, Maggie, but never so dedicated that you'd turn your back on the prospect of a little adventurous romance—something to make you appreciate Doug all the more."

"I don't need any kind of stimulus to appreciate Doug."

They sat silent for a moment, each digesting the other's thoughts. After a while Maggie glanced at her watch. "I'm famished and these drinks have made my head swim. We'd better order."

For the next several minutes they immersed themselves in the menu, although it was obvious that neither of them was giving much thought to the selections. Maggie refused the third cocktail; Alice reordered. "Okay, kiddo, I'll see what I can come up with by way of a job, but I really and truly think you should do something about the way you look."

"Stop picking on me, Alice," Maggie pouted.

"I think my picking on you is long overdue." She saw the anger begin to boil up again and held up her hands. "Go ahead and get mad all you want, kiddo, but I'm speaking as a friend—your oldest friend—someone who cares a lot, believe it or not."

Maggie fell back, looking defeated. "I guess I know down deep that you're right, but it isn't right to kick a gal when she's down, and that awful Rita Gant really put me down."

"Sometimes a kick is the only way to make the message stick, Maggie. Look," she said brightly, reaching across and taking her friend's hand. "I know this really great spa in Arizona. I told you about it . . . The Golden Cactus."

"It would cost a fortune by what you've said about it."

"Don't give me that, Maggie. Doug makes enough bucks to foot the cost of you coming with me for a couple of weeks. We'll get ourselves the complete treatment. Neither of us need any lifts or tucks yet so we should come out looking like Tinkerbell in two or three weeks, maybe a month. We'll go for the complete overhaul and then I'll take you on a shopping spree."

Maggie shook her head. "Out of the question. I wouldn't think of wasting Doug's money on something as vain and frivolous as that. A new hairdo, a couple of new dresses maybe, but this complete overhaul, as you call it, would be far too expensive and a complete waste of time and effort. If I have to shed some weight I'll go on a diet at home."

Alice nibbled at her Cobb Salad, shaking her head. "Home diet plans take too long and they generally fail."

"Well, an Arizona health spa is out."

Alice decided she wasn't hitting hard enough, that she needed heavier ammunition. She bit down on her lower lip thinking about the facts she'd uncovered about Doug and Phyllis Bracken, but debated with herself as to whether telling Maggie might be overstepping the boundaries of fair play. Still, what she'd found out was true; she'd substantiated that. She decided to chance it. "Seeing the way you've let yourself go, it's no wonder Doug is rumored to be looking at Phyllis Bracken again."

Maggie's knife clanged down on her plate. Alice could feel Maggie glowering at her but she refused to look up. She continued picking at her salad.

"You'd better explain that, Alice," Maggie said in an even, cold voice.

Alice shrugged and slowly chewed a piece of lettuce. "Just something I heard at the Club."

"That was a long time ago; you know that. It's over and done with."

"Sometimes things like that can start up again." She laid aside her fork and dabbed the corners of her mouth with her napkin. "Have you given Doug any reason to run back to Phyllis?"

"Of course not. And what you heard is all wrong. Doug mentioned that he was seeing Phyllis, but it's strictly business. He isn't the type to lie about a thing like that."

Alice laughed. "Knowing your beautiful husband, I'm sorry to say I'm sure he wouldn't know when he's being seduced. You two are the most naive oldsters I've ever met. Phyllis Bracken has never taken her claws out of him and Doug is such an innocent baby he will find himself all involved again and wonder how in hell it happened. I know, kiddo. I've seen it happen to two of my ex's, and they weren't half as naive as Doug." She thought for a moment. "You know, I believe it's in the nature of man to be promiscuous; whereas women generally aren't unless they're provoked into it."

Maggie sat thinking back over the past several months. It was true that Doug seemed to be obsessed with sex recently, sometimes wanting it too often for Maggie to contend with, but she'd faked it when necessary. But faking it was only occasionally. Upon closer examination she remembered several times in the last several weeks when she'd begged off or, again, pretended to climax. It was more than possible that Doug knew she was faking it and had gone back to Phyllis for the real thing. Oh, damn it to hell, it was so easy to be a mistress to a man and so difficult to be a wife. Mistresses only had to satisfy a man's sexual needs, they didn't have to put in a full day of kids and housework, shopping, social engagements before climbing into bed to satisfy a sexually aroused husband. It wasn't fair. It just wasn't fair.

Maggie said, "I think you're wrong about Doug. He isn't all that naive and innocent about other women. He loves me and he knows he came damned close to losing me the last time, so I don't think he'll chance it again."

"He also knows you love him and you'll take him back no matter what."

Maggie felt her whole body sag and put her hands in

her lap. "Oh, God, Alice, I hope and pray what you say isn't true. I don't think I could bear knowing he's in bed with that woman again."

"You fought and won the last time; you will again."

An encouraging thought hit Maggie. "But you said it's just gossip. I doubt if it's true. Doug told me early this morning that he'd be seeing her on business today."

Alice saw she wasn't making any headway and decided to go for the throat. "Did he tell you she was at that four-day convention he went to in Philadelphia?" She saw Maggie's eyes drop and the hurt creep across her face. "I see he didn't." Alice said. "So I assume he also did not tell you she was in Chicago last month when he was there on that construction meeting."

Maggie felt trapped. She had to fight back but didn't know why she should fight for a man so unfaithful. It was all circumstantial, she kept telling herself. She said so out loud. "Pure coincidence." But there was little conviction in her voice.

"I fudged a little when I told you it was gossip, Maggie. I checked it all out before telling you. It's true enough."

"It's still circumstantial evidence."

"Good, keep thinking that way, but in the meantime give serious thought to my suggestion about coming to Arizona with me." She motioned for the check. "You know how I feel about throwing monkey wrenches into motors before finding out whether they can be fixed."

"Go to Arizona and give Doug a free hand with me out of state? If he is seeing Phyllis. . . ."

"Let him get it out of his system without making a fuss like we did before. And if it were my husband I certainly would not mope around the house, as I know you will, while he's shacked up with another lady. I'd give him every reason to wonder about my fidelity and to have lots of time to miss me. Then when you come back all lovely and ravishing, he'll be quick to see the error of his ways and, *voilà*, Phyllis Bracken will be pushed off the shelf again, more than likely for good and always!"

Chapter 4

On the way back to Saddlebrook Estates, Maggie had a terrible time keeping back the tears. The day had been a total disaster. Her feelings were rubbed raw; even the feel of her skin was like sandpaper—it hurt to touch it. She'd almost forgotten the insults from Rita Gant, the equally harsh criticism from Alice. The thorns she felt now were thorns of disappointment, of anger with Doug for having been so weak as to let Phyllis Bracken get him back into her clutches. And much worse was the fact that Doug had lied to her, hadn't told her about Phyllis being with him at those out-of-town affairs.

She was still in her blue silk dress sitting in the dark when Doug finally came home. "Hey, why are you sitting alone in the dark?" he asked. "Where are the kids?" He clicked on the lamp on the table in front of the windows.

Maggie blinked and put her hands to her eyes. "Oh, they called. They'll be home later."

"Later? Hell, it's almost nine o'clock now."

"Is it?" Maggie said. Her voice was miles away.

"What's wrong? Something's bothering you." He sat down on the footstool near her chair and looked anxiously into her face, taking her hands in his. "Did you have bad news about something? You look terrible."

"I feel terrible," Maggie said, easing herself out of the chair, away from his touch. She didn't want to be near him, to look at him, yet she knew she couldn't keep everything bottled up inside her. "I think I'll fix myself a drink."

Doug frowned as she walked toward the liquor cabinet. "What's wrong?" he asked again.

"How's Phyllis Bracken?" she asked with malice.

She heard him hesitate before saying, "Ah, so that's it." He came over and tried to put his arms around her waist. Maggie stepped out of his embrace. "I told you this morning that seeing Phyllis was strictly on business. You know I wouldn't lie to you, Maggie."

"You have before, I hear."

"Oh, for Christ's sake you know Phyllis and I were finished a long time ago. It's dead history, so let's not start that old rag up again."

"Not from what I hear."

"Who's been gossiping? Alice? You saw her in New York today, didn't you? You went to her employment office, right?"

She didn't want the highball but she sipped it anyway, knowing it always bothered Doug to see her drinking for no reason but to drink. "Yes. I told you I was going so I went."

"Well, well, aren't we getting independent." He watched her for a moment. "What kind of shit has Alice been feeding you?"

"She merely filled me in on the fact that Phyllis Bracken just happened to be at those last several out-of-town business things you attended. And, wasn't it coincidental that she had her rooms at the same hotels as yours, and on the same floors, according to the hotel registers."

Doug scowled and turned his back. To show his anger he turned and said, "For your information, Maggie, it *was* a coincidence; whether you want to believe that or not is immaterial to me." He felt cornered. "I'm telling you the truth. I knew Phyllis was going to be at those affairs but it certainly wasn't at my invitation. For crying out loud, Maggie, Phyllis and I are business associates. It's only natural that we'd find ourselves at the same conferences and conventions."

Maggie continued to sip her highball. "If I remember correctly, Doug, that was how it all started the first time. Business colleagues and all that kind of thing," she said derisively.

Doug knew better than to argue when Maggie was in one of her moods. Besides, Phyllis had talked about renewing their affair and Doug hadn't exactly discouraged it. He also knew that the more he talked about Phyllis the more obvious it would be that the affair had sparked again.

It wasn't that he wanted the affair, or needed it. He felt himself at that stage in life when the attentions of other women represented living proof that he wasn't getting as old and unattractive as he imagined himself. He loved Maggie; there was no doubt about that, but Maggie was his wife. She was his. It was as if the contest was over insofar as they were concerned, and their sex together proved that. He hated to admit it but the plain truth was that Maggie was dull in bed. She was so . . . "normal" was the only word. Much as he wanted to experiment she refused.

Naturally it was wonderful to think that Maggie and he were married forever; he'd never be alone. Yet he yearned for a little more excitement, a little more sexual diversification.

Blame it on second childhood, senility, whatever—he wanted to go back to when he was eighteen and did all sorts of wild things with girls, experimented with the strange and unknown, knowing that anything considered unnatural would be excused because of his youth. It was wrong, he knew, but it was human, which made it not so wrong in his mind.

Naturally, thinking as he did was a danger to his marriage, which was the reason he'd stopped seeing Phyllis when they had their first affair. And he'd stop seeing her again before he became addicted. He didn't want Phyllis Bracken; it was what she did to him sexually that he found so fantastic. She fed his animal inclinations, which was something Maggie wouldn't let herself understand.

He said, "It's senseless to talk to you when you are in one of these moods, Maggie." He started to leave the room. "I'm going into the study. I have paperwork."

"And I'm going to Arizona."

"Huh? Did you say Arizona?"

She took a long sip of her drink. "Yes. Alice and I are going to a desert spa she knows of there."

"A desert spa? What in the world are you going to do at one of those places?"

Maggie caught herself before she bumbled out the

truth. Why tell him she needed to lose weight and get a complete make-over? He'd only argue that she didn't need it, but far back in his mind it would register that she *is* overweight and wears mousey clothes and has a matronly hairdo. She learned a long time ago never to tell anyone your flaws; they'll always be the first to point them out next time they see you.

Casually she said, "I've never been to one. I want to see what it's like. Alice says they do wonders for your outlook."

"I bet they'll do wonders for my pocketbook too."

"We can afford it."

He thought of Phyllis. He decided he owed it to Maggie. "Yes, of course we can."

Maggie interpreted his admission as permission. Was it a guilty conscience that he was trying to assuage by humoring her? More than likely. Of course he didn't come right out and say that she could go, but she didn't like the way he so easily agreed money wasn't a concern, just as he'd easily consented to her going out to look for something to occupy her days. He most likely was thinking that it might not be a bad idea to get her away from home for a while so he could get things settled with Phyllis. He hadn't even asked about what was to be done about the children, which was generally his first excuse for being against anything. Well, if he was so concerned about Phyllis, then Maggie decided she'd give him something else to be concerned about.

She said, "If you intend to see Phyllis Bracken I see no reason why I shouldn't look around for something with which to flatter my ego."

Doug stared at her. After recovering himself he said, "Are you standing there telling me you are going to a health spa with the idea of trying to find yourself a lover?"

"No, that's not my express intention. I said 'something' to flatter my ego, not 'someone.' " She finished her drink. "However, to put your mind at rest, I believe it is a spa exclusively for women. Of course, that doesn't mean that I intend to wear blinders for the rest of my life."

"This is disgusting. From what I gather, you're going away to make yourself glamorous so that you can start picking up on other men? You're a married woman, for God's sake, with grown children, a lovely home, a husband who loves you. . . ."

"And you have the same, including a wife who loves you, but it doesn't seem to stop you from chewing up Phyllis Bracken's backyard!"

"I swear to God, Maggie, there is nothing between Phyllis and me."

Maggie gave him a withering look, then went over to refill her glass. "When you start swearing to God, Douglas, I know there's something to start worrying about."

He ran his fingers through his hair and began pacing. He started to deliberate with himself as to whether or not he should confess his affair with Phyllis, swear that he'd never see her again, and throw himself on Maggie's mercy. It would be the truthful, honorable thing to do, but he just could not bring himself to do it. He would not prostrate himself before his wife; it would make him weak and Maggie would never look up to him, or trust him again. From here on she would always look on him as some spineless jackass who couldn't be trusted with another woman, a pushover for every female who flirted with him. That wasn't the case at all. His attraction to Phyllis was strictly a sexual one. He didn't want other women; he didn't even want Phyllis, but he found himself helplessly trapped by her sexually. She made sex so different, so unusual, so undemanding on his part. She offered him things Maggie had never offered.

Doug said angrily, "Well, if you intend to shop around for a love affair, I'll be goddamned if I'll finance it."

"I didn't say I was going to shop around for a lover, Doug. To repeat myself, I said if you and Phyllis are getting back together again, I have every intention of following your example. What is sauce for the goose, et cetera. . . ."

"I am not starting up with Phyllis," he lied. He felt he had to lie.

Maggie shrugged. It made her sick at heart to listen to his outright lies. He'd never lied to her before, yet there was something pathetically desperate about the way he was defending himself. "Then I have no intention of shopping around for an affair of my own." She leveled her eyes at him. "But just step out of line one more time, Doug, and it will be your last. I was made a fool of once before by that woman and if it happens again you will regret it. I have my pride just as you have yours."

Doug felt himself crumbling under her look. He knew she saw the truth behind him. He turned sharply and left the room.

There wasn't the least doubt in her mind that Doug was courting Phyllis again. There had been fear and embarrassment in his eyes. She was quick to recognize it and she knew he was aware of it. There had been no harm putting the fear of God in him as well. She could never bring herself to leave him, however, despite his growing weaknesses, and for the first time in her life she realized that Doug was getting old.

She had spoken the truth when she talked of her injured pride. It wasn't so much Doug's having sex with another woman that worried Maggie; she knew she could handle that phase of it. She thought she was a formidable opponent to any woman insofar as sex was concerned. But that first time Doug took up with Phyllis it was a smear to her integrity. Before Alice had told her about it she'd suffered the sneers of her friends, their pitying looks, the condescension with which they'd treated her. It all had hurt terribly. Well, if Doug was involved again, Maggie had no intention of sticking around and giving all their friends and acquaintances the opportunity to pity her.

She'd go to Arizona whether Doug approved or not. And Phyllis Bracken had best be out of the scene when she returned.

Behind the door of the den Doug sat slumped in the chair behind his desk. There were papers in front of him, but although he was staring at them he didn't see them. Now that he was alone he could think more clearly about the predicament in which he once again found himself. The quiet solitude of the room granted him the luxury of facing the truth about his situation. He felt completely confused about what he truly wanted or needed. Everything was all muddled again. Every time he tried to focus on his love for Maggie, Phyllis appeared from out of nowhere.

He propped his elbows on the desk and rested his chin

on his fists. He cleared his head of everything except the two women who were important to him. Yes, he had to admit that at this point Phyllis was important. She represented a soothing balm that did wonders for his male ego, but then so did Maggie, but in a different way. Maggie was more fun to be with out of bed, he told himself, feeling suddenly guilty. Well, if he was going to face facts, then damn it, it was true. The only reason he was seeing Phyllis was for sex and flattery. Sexually, Phyllis did things that would horrify and repulse Maggie. Oh, Maggie was all right in bed—but she still clung to that old-fashioned notion that a woman was supposed to be passive. Even when fully aroused, she was careful to stay in her role. Maggie never did anything imaginative or innovative. To her, the husband was supposed to be on top and the wife on the bottom. The man did all the work and it was the wife's duty to respond, even if faking it was necessary. It was this whole Victorian attitude in Maggie that made Phyllis so damned attractive. Phyllis knew when he wanted to play the passive role, and her aggression never made him feel unmanly.

Tonight, for instance. He could still feel the tantalizing sensations he'd gotten from the vibrator she'd used on him. How in God's name could he bring a vibrator home and ask Maggie to use it on him? She'd have him committed, thinking he'd turned queer or something. Or suppose he asked Maggie to straddle him, letting him relax on his back while she did all the work, the way Phyllis did?

He felt a stirring between his legs and tried not to think of the maddening, thrilling sensations Phyllis created in him. He thought with throbbing need of the way she tongued and caressed every part of him, parts of him that Maggie would consider disgusting. To want this from Maggie was unthinkable, and yet he could think of nothing he wanted more.

With a sinking heart he knew deep down that for the present he could only get what he needed from Phyllis Bracken. Was her sex more important than his marriage and his family?

God forgive him, but in his present state he'd almost convinced himself that it was!

Chapter 5

Arizona was hot and dry and after the first day Maggie began having misgivings about coming. But they were registered for four weeks and it was money down the drain if she didn't stay for the full time. No refunds at the elegant and exclusive Golden Cactus. The place itself was unbelievably beautiful. The spa held everything a woman could possibly hope for, excepting, of course, all those marvelous things like chocolate cream pies and banana splits with crushed walnuts and cherries. The Golden Cactus was an emporium for the health-minded. There were saunas and swimming pools, both indoor and out, two gymnasiums—three if you counted the workout room beside the steam room. There were mirrors everywhere. It was the spa's philosophy that the woman who looked at herself loved herself, and loving oneself is the first step toward happiness. Corny but effective.

The rooms were large and sumptuous. Numbers were kept to a minimum so that the visitors felt individually attended, not just another body to be pounded and dieted, exercised and fed, then herded together with the other bodies, sheared like sheep in the spring, and sent back into the world.

There were only ten other women in their group, all pleasant and obviously rich. Surprisingly, there were several young men working in the place. Alice had known of this beforehand but had failed to mention it—on purpose.

"It's the only one that employs men. That's why I like it," Alice said when Maggie gasped at the young fellows in tight shorts and T-shirts who were on hand for the welcoming.

Alice nudged Maggie. "Whoever their personnel director is she certainly has a good eye for handsome hunks. God, look at the shoulders on that one—not to mention the bulge in the crotch of his shorts."

Besides the male attendants, the only other objection Maggie had was to the heat, and the sun in particular. "I'll be a potato chip inside a week," she complained.

"Not to worry," Alice assured her. "They see to it that you get plenty of good stuff in your diet, and three times a day you'll get rubbed down with lotions and creams and oils." She winked suggestively. "And by men if you like."

"I don't like," Maggie said.

Alice shrugged. "There's no extra charge, kiddo, and you can bet your fat fanny I have every intention of availing myself of every one of the place's freebies. That's what I put my money down for."

Everything at the spa was supervised personally by Miss Markum—not Clarissa or Clarissa Markum, just Miss Markum—although, as Alice whispered, Miss Markum definitely looked more like a madam than a miss. She was one of those deeply tanned, thin-as-a-rake ladies who had the body of a teenaged cheerleader, the face of a female athlete and the expression of a woman who has seen far too much of life and been bored by it. Yet she was always jovial and overly anxious to accommodate her "girls," as she called them. The word jangled in Maggie and Alice's ears.

During their orientation, Miss Markum made it emphatically clear that she was there for the express purpose of pleasing her guests.

"Look upon me as your friend, your confidante, your advisor, your paid servant, if you like. I am here to please you in every way, just as long as it's slimming and healthy." She paused and, in an aside, said, "And I believe sex is very healthy for every woman, regardless of age."

The male attendants weren't at the orientation but the "girls" all knew what Miss Markum was referring to, especially when she added, "And there are no extra charges for any of the services at the Golden Cactus. Everything—without exception—is absolutely free."

On her first afternoon Maggie sat alone in her room looking out over the desert that surrounded them. She felt herself in a different world; but somehow she'd taken with her all of the troubles of the world she'd left behind. Already she was lonely for Doug and the children.

She went to the desk and opened the drawer, taking out the picture postcards that the spa provided. Without hesitating she addressed one to Doug. After writing "Darling Doug," she felt her hand tighten around the pen, almost snapping it in two. What in the devil was she doing sending a card to Doug the first day here? It was only an admission of how much she needed him. It was destroying the very reason for her being here—which was to show Doug she could be as independent as he.

And the same applied to David and Julie, she told herself as she angrily threw the postcards back into the drawer and slammed it shut.

She started to pace the room, then glanced at her watch and reminded herself that she should place the phone call she'd promised. When Doug had said, "Call me when you get settled so that I know you've gotten there all right," she'd said, "Why waste money talking long distance? I'll place a person-to-person call to myself. That way you can refuse the call and at the same time know I've arrived safe and sound."

Doug had objected, of course, saying they could certainly afford to exchange hellos, but Maggie had insisted, and rather than risk another argument he had agreed.

Before leaving, Maggie had no doubt in her mind that Doug was seeing Phyllis again. It was Alice who had advised her to play it cool, to come to Arizona and let Doug stew for a while. And she supposed Alice was right in reminding her that throwing the proof in Doug's face would only cause a rift that might never be mended. Alice had come up with a lot more facts to substantiate the story. Doug was seeing Phyllis every single day, usually after work. But what good would it do to prove him a liar? He'd only run to Phyllis for reassurance and consolation, and maybe he'd never come back. Maggie had learned from experience that when people go out of their way to prove their point they usually wind up alone with their argument.

Standing alone on the terrace of her room, Maggie watched the sun dipping deep into the desert sands. Her life felt terribly empty. She twisted the gold band on her left hand and said, "Mrs. Douglas Hampton." It had a beautiful, solid sound; she wondered if she were destroying that sound. She turned and looked toward the telephone. Perhaps she should call Doug and tell him she'd made a mistake, that she was coming home, that she loved him in spite of everything.

She stood deliberating until the sun was almost gone. Then with a positive stiffening of her back she walked toward the telephone.

"Maggie, are you in there?" Alice called as she tapped loudly on the door. A second later the door opened and she came in. She saw Maggie standing there with the receiver in her hand. "Oh, sorry, kiddo, were you on the telephone?"

"It's all right, Alice," Maggie said as she dropped the receiver into the cradle. "I was just going to call home." She explained about the code. "It can wait."

"I was just wondering if you planned on dressing for dinner."

"I thought everything was casual here."

"It is, but there are the young men to think about. I thought I'd try and make a nice impression our first night out. Get the pick of the litter, as they say."

Maggie laughed in spite of herself. "You never stop, do you?"

"When it comes to money and sex you're right, I never stop." Alice seated herself on the edge of Maggie's bed. "Jeff, one of the guys who takes care of the pool and exercise equipment, met me in the hall just now. He specifically mentioned your name," she said, fixing a suggestive curve to her brows.

Maggie gave her a wary eye. "How come?"

Alice tried to sound casual. "Oh, he just asked if there was anything he could do for me, and when I said 'Not at the moment,' he said, 'If your charming friend, Mrs. Hampton, needs anything, tell her my name is Jeff.'"

"Jeff," she said flatly.

Alice examined her fingernails. "Yep, just Jeff." A sly smile crossed her lips. "I think you have an admirer, Mrs. Hampton."

"And I think you're plotting something, Mrs. Maitland."

Alice widened her eyes in mock hurt. "Me? How can you accuse me of such a thing, Mrs. Hampton?" She laughed. "Seriously though, kiddo, he did introduce himself and asked if you'd gotten settled. At least he took the trouble to find out our names."

"I believe that's his job," Maggie said as she started to undo the buttons of her dress. "I think I'll take a quick shower." She stepped out of the dress and started toward the bathroom. "And you can tell Jeff-the-Stud that I am very settled and have every intention of staying that way without any help from him or any of his swaggering young co-workers."

"Speak for yourself, Mrs. Hampton," Alice said. "I have every intention of doing just the opposite—being very unsettled and constantly in need of help. Before I leave here I intend to work my way through each and every one of those lovely males, starting tonight." Maggie had disappeared into the bathroom. "So what's your decision, dress or informal?" Alice called.

"I brought along a couple of long dresses—so I might just as well get some use out of them."

"Good. Long dresses it is. See you in forty-five minutes."

Alone under the shower she let the water sluice over her body. Oddly enough, she found herself humming. Although Alice had more or less exaggerated her meeting with Jeff what's-his-name, it was pleasant to know that the young man had known her name. Maybe she wasn't that far over the hill after all. She reminded herself that the guy was being paid to fawn over her, but her argument to that was that there were many other ladies at the spa, why had he singled her out of the flock of twelve?

Secretly she knew she was indulging in a foolish fantasy but it had been a long time since any man other than Doug had complimented her in a way that reeked with sexual overtones, and there wasn't the slightest doubt in her mind that Jeff's remark had a sexual overtone.

When she stepped from the shower and began drying herself in front of the full length mirror, her mood veered sharply in the opposite direction. She saw the telltale lines around her eyes, the sausage roll of fat around her middle, the thick thighs.

"Good God," she said to her reflection. "He's nothing more than a paid stud. What in heaven's name would he want with a fat, middle-aged woman like you? Rita Gant was right. I'm old and fat and unattractive and I should thank God I have a husband who says he loves me. If you want to buy sex, you can do it back home for far less than what it's costing in this place."

She tucked the towel around her nakedness and hurried away from the mirror. Her jaw was set and her eyes hard. She'd see the month through by concentrating on losing pounds, firming her muscles, getting herself back into shape so that she could be as beautiful as possible for Doug, and not for any one of these peacocks who charged by the inch. She didn't need their lies, their false flatteries. To hell with them. She had Doug and she'd fight to keep him.

She dressed without much attention to careful detail, reminding herself that there was no need to impress anyone here. Even the gown—white with a full skirt and high neckline—she chose was the plainest of the lot. Julie had once said it looked like something left over from a wedding.

She had fifteen minutes before Alice would call for her. Now was as good a time as any to call Doug, and she decided not to use the code. She wanted to talk to him, bare her soul, forgive him anything. She felt her heart beating faster as the telephone on the other end started ringing, and ringing, and ringing.

On the seventh ring Julie said, "Hello."

"Julie? It's me, Mom."

"Oh, hi, Mom," she said, sounding disappointed. "How was the trip?" She also sounded uninterested.

"Fine. Everything's fine. I just wanted to let everyone know I'd arrived."

"I thought you were going to use your code."

"I changed my mind. A woman's prerogative, you know." She hesitated when Julie said nothing. "Darling, I don't want to build up the charges with a lot of unnecessary chit-chat; can I talk to your father?"

"He isn't here."

The words stabbed her so sharply that she actually

winced. "Oh, I see." She put her hand over her heart to still the pain.

Julie was quick to pick up the disappointment in her mother's voice. "What's wrong?"

"Nothing," Maggie said quickly. She purposely brightened her tone. "I'd forgotten the address of someone I wanted to send a card to," she lied. It was the only thing that popped into her head.

"So what do you need to talk to Dad for? What's the name? Your address book is right here next to the phone."

Maggie felt foolish. Her lie had forced her into a corner and now she had to continue the sham. She gave a friend's name, cursing herself for adding to the telephone charge. After Julie gave her the address Maggie couldn't stop herself from asking, "Did your father say what time he'd be home, darling?"

"Nope. Do you want me to ask Aunt Flora if he said anything to her?"

"No, that's all right. Just tell him I called and that I got here all right."

"Right."

"Everything else all right at your end?"

"Super."

"Good. I'll see you in a month then."

"Enjoy," Julie said and hung up.

Maggie stood with the telephone receiver frozen in her hand. It took a moment or two to realize that she wasn't trembling with fear but with anger, better still, with rage. How dare he!

It was your own fault for inventing that stupid code, a voice told her. Doug knew he wouldn't have to sit at home waiting for your call; whoever answered would talk to the operator and he was free to go to Phyllis Bracken.

"You fool!" she said as she slammed down the receiver. "You stupid, old fool!"

Maggie threw herself across the bed and started to cry. Even Alice's knock didn't stop her tears.

"Maggie! Good God, what's the matter? Why are you crying?" Alice asked as she put her arm around Maggie's shoulders.

Maggie felt embarrassed at the sound of Alice's concern, the touch of her hand.

"I'm so mad I could spit," Maggie said, forcing back the tears even though the sobs contracted her throat. She sat up and patted the wet from her eyes.

"What happened?"

"I called Doug." She found her throat tightening again.

"And?"

"He wasn't home."

Alice glanced at her watch. "It's almost ten o'clock back home."

Maggie's eyes glinted like steel. "Exactly."

"Well, maybe he's just working late."

"Don't try to make excuses. We both know damned well where he is. He knew I was going to call tonight, using that ridiculous code I'd devised. No, Alice," she said, getting up from the bed. "My darling husband couldn't wait to fly to the arms of his mistress."

Alice saw the set of the jaw, the anger in Maggie's face. She'd never seen her friend so livid with rage. "So what are you going to do?"

Maggie walked over and stood in front of the full length mirror. She studied herself for a minute then said, "The first thing I'm going to do is get out of this white tent and put on the lowest-cut dress I have. I may have a roll around my middle but my cleavage is still pretty damned terrific, if I do say so myself, and men still stare at my legs." She began unzipping and unbuttoning and threw the dress in a heap on the floor of the closet. "And then, dear friend, we are going to go down to dinner, after which we will check out the availability of manly shoulders on which to rest our weary heads."

"Bravo! If he can do it why in hell can't you?"

The dinner was a collection of attractive dishes that tasted like raw cotton and seaweed. Although everything was seasoned well enough there was no texture to anything. Still, it was filling enough to satisfy Maggie's lack of appetite. She wouldn't have cared if they'd served cooked cactus. For all she knew, perhaps they had.

She made empty conversation with the other women. Everyone was enthused about the forthcoming four weeks, everyone comparing the number of pounds they hoped to lose, everyone playing the health-minded, happy housewife and everyone eyeing and flirting with the young men who were so accommodatingly waiting table.

Maggie was still seething inside, swearing to get even with Doug, so when Jeff bid her good evening and placed a salad in front of her she forced herself to smile and leaned back slightly so that that he'd get a good view down the front of her dress. Then, as soon as she felt his eyes she moved forward again and tugged the neckline higher.

A second later she had regrets. Good God, if Doug had to act like a tomcat that was no reason for her to do the same. As she ate her salad she told herself to act her age, reminding herself that regardless of her good legs and great bust she was still a fat, middle-aged housewife from New Jersey.

She said the same thing aloud to Jeff when he remarked later, walking along the edge of the pool, that she looked lovely.

"I'm old, fat and not particularly attractive, so don't waste your attentions on me, Mr. Cochran."

To her surprise he laughed. "Hardly old, Mrs. Hampton, and certainly not unattractive. As far as the fat is concerned, that will be gone inside a week. I give you my personal guarantee." He smiled with his eyes. "Personally, I never have objected to women with a little excess meat. Skinny women turn me off."

She was still furious with Doug and didn't feel like being pleasant to anyone, especially some hired male prostitute. That's all he was really, she told herself, a hired stud. "Tell me, Mr. Cochran, how does Miss Markum go about assigning you gentlemen? Do you draw lots to see which guy gets which woman, or what?"

His smile never faltered. "You're angry about something, Mrs. Hampton. Was it something I said?"

"No, I was just wondering about how the call system worked here, that's all."

His smile faded just a little. "We get to pick our own . . . uh . . . preferences, if that's what you mean."

"You mean to say, your own 'marks,' right?"

He shrugged indifferently, still smiling but not as

broadly as before. "Why are you being so hard on yourself, Mrs. Hampton? You're really teed-off about something, I can tell, but instead of taking it out on me why don't you tell me about it?"

Maggie's expression stayed as cold and hard as the tiles they were standing on. "Oh, I get it. Now you switch on the broad-shoulder-to-cry-on-bit."

He looked hurt. "Only trying to help, Mrs. Hampton."

As she looked at his bowed head she felt ashamed for her rudeness. He was just doing his job. He was a perfectly available male body put at her disposal to do with whatever she wished. Unfortunately, she didn't want to do anything with him. Jeff was young and handsome, strong and pleasant, but he was also without any trace of morals or character. He was merely a beautiful voice in a beautiful body and nothing more, just a machine Miss Markum had hired to help relieve the tensions and frustrations of her clientele, the same way she bought and paid for the exercise equipment, the food, the utilities. Jeff Cochran was one of the spa's facilities—so why shouldn't she use it?

Maggie tossed a pebble into the pool, then laughed. "I guess I shouldn't have done that. Whose job is it to clean the pool tomorrow?"

"Mine."

"Then I apologize for the pebble." They walked a few steps. Maggie took a deep breath and let it out slowly. "I also apologize for my rudeness, Jeff. It's just that I came here with a splinter under my skin."

"Oh. Shall I have the nurse look at it?"

Maggie laughed accommodatingly. "Not that kind of splinter. I meant a problem, or as they say in westerns, a burr under my saddle."

"Oh, I see." He paused then asked, "Husband problem?"

Maggie nodded gravely. "But then I suppose most of the women who come here have that type of a problem, or claim to have."

Jeff stayed silent.

"Mine isn't a convenient invention, something I dreamed up for the purpose of tossing you into the sack. You're a stunning young man, but I happen to be very much in love with my husband and intend staying that way. I don't want to do anything to complicate my life any more than it is."

"I fail to see how you'd be complicating it," Jeff said. "You said yourself a few seconds ago that you know we are just call boys. So if you know that, then what's the harm in availing yourself of our services?"

She gave him a strange, uncomprehending glance.

"Look," Jeff said sternly. "I know what I am and I don't feel ashamed of it. Maybe you come from a different background, but where I grew up it was perfectly natural for young guys to satisfy themselves with older women and vice versa. I happen to like sex for what it is, and I intend to get all I can of it while I can. If it comes with a salary, so much the better. I haven't any hangups; you obviously do. I only wish you didn't."

"In my day, young man, we didn't call it having *hang-ups,* we called it *morality.*"

"Don't call me *young man,* like that. For Christ's sake, I'm no more than ten years younger than you."

It was the first time she found him capable of anger. She smiled and said, "I've made you break one of the spa's cardinal rules, I'll bet. I've made you angry."

He turned away from her. "Yes, you have."

"Okay, so I'm not all that old, but you're right," she said, putting her hand on his sleeve. "We do have a different set of morals and we're stuck with them. I just can't bring myself to flop into bed with a man I don't know or don't care about. It may be easy for you but it isn't for me. Now take my friend, Alice. She's more your type. Concentrate on her, Jeff. I think you two would hit it off beautifully."

"If I'd wanted Mrs. Maitland," he said, sounding cocky, "I would be out here with her right now instead of you."

Maggie smiled at what she took as a compliment. "You're very sweet, Jeff, but you're wasting your time on me."

"Let me be the judge of that, Maggie." He hesitated and looked anxious. "It *is* all right to call you Maggie, isn't it? You don't mind? I'll call you Mrs. Hampton when there are others around, but when we're alone together, I thought. . . ."

Maggie chuckled. "It's all right, Jeff. I'm flattered."

He took her hand. "All I ask is that you think about it. I'd love to go to bed with you, but I certainly won't force myself on you. I just want you to think about it, okay?"

"Okay, I'll think about it, but I can assure you my answer will be the same on my last night here as it is tonight: No. Thank you, dear boy, but no."

He smiled down into her face. "I'll let the 'dear boy' crack go by. All I have to say is, we'll see about that, dear Mrs. Hampton."

He leaned closer and tilted her mouth up to his. Maggie started to pull back but he held her firmly and kissed her lightly on the lips. It was no more than his lips brushing against hers but there was more excitement in that gentle touch than if he had crushed his mouth over hers in a passionate embrace. She felt the tingling running through her and quickly eased herself out of his arms.

Maggie put her hand against his chest and forced him away, reluctantly. "No, I mustn't, Jeff," she protested when he tried to pull her back against him. "I've got to go to bed." She turned and heard him following. She stopped and smiled at him. "Alone, Jeff."

He shrugged. "I won't stop trying, so you'd better get used to my pestering you."

"It won't do you any good, I'm warning you."

"As I said, let me be the judge of that, Mrs. Hampton."

She bade him goodnight and hurried to her room, quickening her steps as she went, fearful that she might weaken and call him to her. It would serve Doug right if she brought the young man into her bed. After all, Doug was more than likely in Phyllis' bed right this minute.

She lay in bed a long time debating the question of fidelity. She remembered someone telling her one time that most people prefer to be those who are fun rather than those who are loyal. That was obviously Doug's attraction to Phyllis; he found her more entertaining. But then why shouldn't he? Phyllis didn't have kids to yell at, didn't have to wash out Doug's sweat-socks and athletic supporters, scour toilet bowls and scrub the soap-scum rings off the tub, all while Doug was around. Phyllis had only to concentrate on being fresh and pretty with everything in its place, fixing a simple dinner that looked lavish, and being up-to-date with the latest gossip and jokes when Doug showed up for their rendezvous.

Oh hell, why did husbands always see the drudgeries of a wife and never see the same in a mistress?

The more Maggie thought of Doug's affair, the more she began to seethe again. She could picture the intimate little table set for two, so romantic, so charming, so exact in every detail, while at home he had to put up with a table set for two brash, hurrying teenagers who talked at the top of their lungs and shoved food into their mouths like it was going out of style. No candlelight and wine at home; no, there he got simple meat and potato dishes and had to help with the washing up afterwards. She could easily understand his desire for romance.

But damn it, she wanted romance too, and if Doug found it then so would she.

Chapter 6

She awoke feeling less determined, although she was still furious with Doug; and as the days passed she found herself drawing further and further inside herself. The idea of actually having sex with a strange man was frightening. She knew she'd never be able to enjoy it; she'd be too tense, too nervous; so why bother risking it?

As a result, she ignored Jeff Cochran completely. After a while he seemed to get the message and stopped trying to talk to her.

She fell quickly into the daily routine of the spa, which worked wonders in keeping her occupied and her mind too tired to think about Jeff Cochran's charms, although he always seemed to be there whenever she looked up.

Her day started early, seven-thirty, with a substantial breakfast. At least it was substantial by her standards. Normally she had coffee and toast, but here it was required that each of them consume juice, eggs, toast, cereal, fruit, coffee. After breakfast they were ushered into a room where they were massaged and lectured on beauty tips and fashions.

There followed an hour of exercise, light calisthenics usually, nothing too strenuous. At eleven o'clock they had a choice of lessons in swimming, fencing—for poise, they were told—tennis, racquetball; or if they preferred they could study a foreign language of their choice or any academic subject. They could ride horseback, play bridge or any number of games, do anything that was active and participating. Reading was forbidden during the daylight hours, being considered by Miss Markum as too inactive and closeting.

"This is a social club as well as a health spa," she reminded her charges. "We stress involvement and activity."

After a light lunch of salad and iced tea the real work began. Now came the pounding and rolling, the wearing away of the layers of fat, the heavy exercises, some sessions lasting as long as two and three hours. After that there was an hour in the sauna or the steam bath. By five o'clock the women were utterly exhausted, and some of them slept right through the dinner hour.

Before coming to the Golden Cactus the ladies were required to bring with them a recent doctor's report of his medical examination, from which their individual charts were compiled. Each day the charts were updated with the guest's individual progress. If the weight loss was not according to schedule, penalties were imposed, certain "treats" were restricted. By the end of the second week fruit and cheese seemed to Maggie the most sumptuous dessert imaginable; the glass of white wine with Sunday evening's dinner of fish was a delicacy undreamed of.

"You're doing well, Mrs. Hampton," Miss Markum said, glancing at Maggie's chart and noting the twelve-pound weight loss. "We'll ease up on your restricted foods. You'll join Mrs. Maitland's table for dinners hereafter . . . that is, unless your weight starts to climb."

"It won't, I promise," Maggie said. "After all this torture I believe the mere sight of a chocolate square will make me sick."

Miss Markum laughed. "Surely it hasn't been all that painful?"

Maggie had to admit that it hadn't. Despite all of the sweat and work and sore muscles, it had been fun—so far. The competition was very sportsmanlike and everyone seemed really to enjoy herself.

Alice said, "Of course, if you were doing as I and most of the others are doing before going to sleep, you'd have lost a lot more than you have."

Maggie knew to what she was referring. Miss Markum had lectured one morning on the healthful benefits derived from sexual intercourse. "It's wonderful exercise, and depending upon the duration and degree of activity, untold hundreds of calories are burned away."

Jeff was always there, looking only too eager to help

Maggie burn away hundred of calories merely with the nod of her head. She hadn't nodded. Not yet.

"What's wrong with you?" Alice asked at the beginning of their third week. "Jeff Cochran is moping around like a sick cat, according to the other guys."

"For someone moping around like a sick cat, he sure is bright and chipper whenever he's with Patricia Castleman. She seems to have an exclusive on him."

"You're a fool. Jeff is a real hunk."

Maggie munched a celery stick. Having seen him every day, he'd grown out of the realm of "stranger"; yet she couldn't bring herself to be friendly toward him, because she knew he'd only take it as a sign that she wanted him. On the other hand, she resented the fact that Patty Castleman was occupying all of Jeff's time lately—or was he occupying hers? Whatever, it bothered Maggie more than she cared to admit. Of course she could see why Jeff would be attracted to Patricia. Patty was one of those streamlined types, attractive, youngish, easy to like.

Ever since Jeff took up with Patty, Maggie had missed his attention, his always being there. She rather wished she hadn't discouraged him so completely; she missed the flattery he'd expressed that first night and his puppy-dog devotion by following her around while she ignored him.

Now he was acting as though she didn't exist. Of course she could hardly blame him. But why did she care? Even now, if he did proposition her, she'd turn him down flat, of course.

Would she? The thought disturbed her. She hadn't spoken to Doug since her telephone call to Julie. She'd received two letters from him, short, sweet, signed with love, reminding her that he was writing, not calling, according to the promise she'd extracted from him before she left. Back then Maggie had decided to play at being cool, distant and aloof. "Don't call me, I'll call you," sort of thing. She thought she'd make Doug suffer for want for her, but the tables turned; it was she who needed and wanted him, but her pride would never permit her to admit it, especially to Doug.

By the end of the third week Maggie actually found pleasure in admiring herself in the mirror. She was as trim as she had been on her wedding day. She shook her head, reminding herself not to think of her wedding day or Doug; he didn't belong here.

Her skin actually glowed with health and vitality. Her eyes hadn't sparkled like this in years, since she was a girl. She felt pretty—and young—and really looked it.

"You know," Alice said, admiring Maggie as she walked toward her at the swimming pool. "You look like hell in that sagging bathing suit. You really have lost tons haven't you?" She gave her a critical eye. "Beneath all that excess lastex there seems to be a terrific body. I can't get over the change in you, kiddo. You look twenty-one again."

Maggie laughed self-consciously, but felt happier than she had in years. "Hardly twenty-one. I might settle for thirty."

"We'll compromise. Twenty-five."

"You're on."

Maggie settled herself in the chaise next to Alice's. "With all this weight loss I've got to start thinking about a new wardrobe. Nothing fits. My clothes are hanging on me."

"They have a seamstress on hand, I understand. It's expected here so they're prepared."

"Yes, I forgot. I'll pay her a visit later."

"Speaking of wardrobes, kiddo, I think before we head home you and I should go on a shopping spree. I thought maybe Dallas. It's on the way and Neiman-Marcus should have everything we need."

"Hold on, Alice. Doug would have a fit if I spend any more money than I have."

"What do you care what Doug says? We don't have to spend a fortune, just half a fortune." She saw Maggie hesitate. "Look at it this way, kiddo. Dallas is on the way home, a free layover insofar as the airline fare is concerned. We'll be saving his lordship some money. He'll approve of that."

"I suppose," Maggie said.

She saw Jeff coming toward them. As usual he was with Patricia Castleman. Maggie turned sideways toward Alice and began smearing suntan lotion on her legs. Her heart started to thump faster as they went by. She wanted him to stop and speak to her but he didn't; he seemed overly engrossed in a whispered conversation with Patty. Then, when she was sure he was bent upon ignoring her he turned, said something to Patricia, and came back toward Maggie.

Alice said, "Here comes lover-boy, kiddo."

"Hello Mrs. Maitland," Jeff said, then to Maggie, "Mrs. Hampton." He waited for Maggie to look up at him.

"Oh, hello, Jeff," Maggie said, acting surprised to find him standing over her. "How are you?" Damn it, why was her heart pounding like that? she asked herself.

"Fine." He hesitated, glanced at Alice, then leaned closer to Maggie and said, "I was wondering if I might speak with you privately after dinner tonight."

"What about?" She found she could not look at him, knowing that if she did the desire in her eyes would give her away.

"A personal matter." He saw her look doubtful. "It's very important. Please."

"Well, if it's important, of course I'll see you. Eight o'clock say, here at the pool."

"I'll call for you at your room."

"Here at the pool, Jeff," Maggie said emphatically.

"Right. Eight o'clock." He was smiling, or was it a smirk? Maggie wasn't sure, and for a second she was tempted to call him back and tell him she couldn't meet him, but she let him go, hating to see him with Patricia Castleman.

Maggie was ready for the rendezvous at seven-thirty, pretending not to be anxious. Purposely she moved her thoughts away from Jeff to Doug. She had a very strong urge to call him and tell him she was leaving him, that he was free to go to Phyllis forever. The urge disturbed her, making her wonder why she was suddenly so willing to give Doug his freedom now while she hadn't been the last time he'd strayed into Phyllis' bed. She tried to convince herself that Jeff Cochran had nothing to do with it, that he was merely a paid gigolo who'd be out of her life in a week's time. No, it wasn't Jeff, she rationalized; she was merely giving Doug his freedom because she considered it a sacrifice on her part done in a spirit of kindness, not revenge.

She stood up and walked toward the small terrace. She

didn't really want to divorce Doug. She wished some miracle would happen to save her marriage, to make Phyllis go away forever and leave them in peace. But there would be other Phyllis Brackens . . . and other Jeff Cochrans.

"Good God," she breathed, putting her hands to her mouth. She ran her fingers through her hair. "I'm letting things get away too far out of line."

She snatched up her evening bag and started toward Alice's room, intent upon sending her with a message that she wouldn't see Jeff. Alice wasn't in her room and when Maggie started toward the pool area Jeff was already there, although it was only fifteen minutes before eight. The minute she saw him looking so young, so trim in his tight white trousers and open-necked shirt, all her determination melted away into nothing.

"You're early," she said, hoping to hide the nervousness she felt.

He grinned. "So are you."

"I saw you standing here. I was on my way to find Alice for a moment."

"I'll wait."

"It isn't important." She settled herself on a chaise. "Now what's all so important and personal?"

"Us," he said simply.

Maggie pretended to be perturbed. "Really, Jeff. I'd hoped you weren't going to start in on that again."

They looked toward the terrace when they heard a group of ladies chattering and laughing together as they came out of the drawing room. Jeff said, "Please, Maggie, let's go somewhere where we can talk in private. I've so much to say to you."

"If it's . . ."

"Please," he said in an urgent whisper.

He looked so miserable, so desperate that Maggie felt she could not refuse him a kindness. If he insisted on talking her into bed she'd just have to be brutally firm with him. "Oh, very well, Jeff," she said, letting him take her hand as he helped her up.

"This way," he said, keeping her hand in his. Maggie was unnerved as she felt the hot, tight firmness of his touch.

He led her toward the buildings where the horses were

groomed and stabled. It smelled of fresh straw and saddle-soap and leather. "I do all my thinking in the tack room, back here," Jeff said as he coaxed her toward the cubicle near the rear.

"No," Maggie objected. "I'd prefer to walk somewhere," she said, refusing to let herself be tempted into any compromising situation in a private room far from any possible prying eyes.

She started out toward the desert and cactus plants but this time Jeff objected, telling her that the snakes and lizards came out at night, and could be dangerous. They compromised by walking around the tennis court area, which was dimly lighted but deserted.

"So now," Maggie said, trailing her fingers across the tops of the high green hedge. "What's so personal and important?"

"I told Patricia I couldn't see her anymore. I'm afraid she is very angry with me. I'm afraid she might go to Miss Markum with some cock-and-bull story that could get me fired."

"Why would she do anything like that?"

"Because I'm turning her loose. She's not the type of woman who takes rejection well. You meet a lot of her type in places like this, rich, spoiled, always getting their own way."

"So why did you incur her anger by giving her the gate?" It was an old expression which Maggie instantly felt dated her.

"Because I couldn't pretend to myself any longer. Every time I was with her I pretended it was you."

In the moonlight she saw he was looking straight ahead, as if conjuring up the courage to say what he had to say and get it over with.

Jeff lowered his head and said in a soft, pathetic voice, "I can't stop thinking about you, Maggie. I do it all day and all night." He turned to her, pleading, "Please, please don't continue to shut me out."

"Jeff," she said firmly, putting her hand on his arm, stopping their walk. "I am a happily married woman and you are an attendant at a desert spa that caters to older, lonely females. I really can't believe that you are doing anything else but overreacting to my initial turn-down. I hurt your ego. I'm sorry, but it isn't anything more than that—an injured pride."

"It's much, much more than that," he said, taking her hands and hugging them to his chest. "You're driving me crazy, Maggie. I've got to have you or I'll go out of my head."

Maggie pulled herself away. She laughed nervously and said, "I doubt that very much, Jeff. I'll be gone in a week and we'll never see each other again. Nothing can possibly come of our attraction for each other." She knew the moment she heard her words echo inside her head that she'd tripped herself up.

Jeff was quick to catch it. "Then you *are* attracted to me." He took her hands again as he tried to pull her close.

She resisted as best she could. "Yes, of course I'm attracted to you, Jeff," she said, seeing no way out of the trap she had fallen into. "What woman in her right mind wouldn't be? You are young and handsome and charming and bright. You'd make any woman proud."

"Then why do you refuse me? Don't you want to go to bed with me?"

Maggie felt the trap tightening. "To be perfectly honest, I don't know. One part of me says 'yes' while the other says 'no.' If you want the truth, I'm a little frightened. I've never been with any man other than my husband. I don't know how I'd feel afterward. I put a lot of value on my marriage," she said. She felt as though a cock should crow three times, the way it did when Peter denied Jesus. Just a short time ago she sat seriously contemplating divorcing her husband; and here she was spouting off on the sanctity of marriage and all that rot. She was a traitor to herself. If only she didn't have a conscience; if she were more like Alice, freeloving, no hangups, always on the go, never a care for anything but her own happiness and pleasure.

All her life Maggie felt that she was apart from the mainstream of living. Since puberty she'd developed a separateness from everyone, even from Doug. It was as if she lived only to satisfy others by devoting all her attention to them, yet never involving herself with them completely. Maggie knew she wasn't being fair to the world; she jealously coveted her privacy too much.

As though reading her mind Jeff said, "You are too

much inside yourself. You should share more with others."

"Like you, I suppose?"

"Yes, of course. Hell, I know very little can come of our relationship if you set your mind to that. You've put up a smoke screen before we got off the ground. Can't you be a little more considerate of my feelings, as well as your own? I know you want me as much as I want you—so why shouldn't we satisfy our own needs?"

"Don't confuse me, Jeff. I've got to think."

"You've had weeks to think. I haven't bothered you since you told me to get lost. Surely you must know whether you want me or not?"

"Of course I want you, but. . . ."

"But what? I want you. You want me. That's all there is to it," he said as he tried to pull her closer.

Maggie resisted. "Please, Jeff. Don't pressure me."

He pulled her hard against his body and held her tight. She could feel the hardness of him against her thigh. Hard as she tried, she could not stop the shivers that were coursing through her. She felt his breath on her cheek and she knew he was going to kiss her. Every fiber of her being fought against it but she was helpless. His strength overpowered her as his mouth moved over hers. The kiss was deep and passionate and shared. She found herself clinging to his young, broad shoulders, her nails digging into the material of his shirt. He kissed her mouth, her eyes, her throat. She felt the wetness between her legs and her knees started to buckle beneath her. His arms held her as his mouth worked its way back over hers.

"Oh, Maggie, Maggie, please say you will," he breathed.

"Yes, Jeff. Yes," she answered, not recognizing the voice as her own.

He eased her away from him and looked imploringly into her face. "Tonight?" he asked, his voice boyish and humble. "Please."

"Ten o'clock. I'll leave my door unlocked."

"Darling," he breathed, again pulling her into his arms and kissing her passionately. "My dearest, darling Maggie. You've made me very happy."

She could still hear his voice and feel the touch of his lips on hers when she closed the door to her room and leaned back against it. She tried to still the shaking that was convulsing her. She felt weak and lightheaded; most of all she felt terribly frightened. Afraid of what, she did not rightfully know, but whatever it was it was a delicious fear, like kissing a boy for the first time, thinking that that's how girls got pregnant.

She glanced at her watch and pushed herself away from the door. Jeff would be there in an hour. She'd shower again and redo her makeup. She wondered if she should be naked in bed when he came or be waiting for him in a negligee or dress? Doug usually liked seeing her in something transparent, but she hadn't brought anything like that with her, having expected to be among women.

Alice, she thought. Alice surely had something she could borrow. Of course it meant giving the whole thing away, but Alice could certainly be trusted not to gossip. In fact, Alice would be overjoyed about the whole thing.

Maggie pulled on a dressing gown and went to Alice's room. She wasn't there. Miss Markum was coming out of one of the rooms and Maggie asked if she'd seen Alice.

"She was in the game room playing backgammon just a few minutes ago. I suspect she's still there."

Maggie looked down at her dressing gown and hesitated. She wasn't accustomed to roaming about the spa dressed as she was but she had to get Alice's help so decided to chance it. She hurried across the deserted reception area toward the west wing which housed the dining room, a small reading room, then the game room. She paused in the darkened dining room when she heard the sound of men laughing; it was coming from outside the French doors, which were standing open. Trying not to be noticed, she walked on tiptoe, being careful not to bump into anything and betray her presence. She wasn't really listening to the men's conversation but when her name was mentioned she stopped.

"Mrs. Hampton finally said 'yes,'" one of the men said.

"Goddamn it," the other swore. "That is going to cost me a hundred bucks. Shit, I was sure she was the cold-assed type who'd never give in."

"You know old Jeff. He can defrost a refrigerator with one flicker of his boyish smile."

"That prick! How did he do it?"

"I suppose in the usual way. He put on the old 'I'm miserable without you' bit, or 'They're going to fire me but I can't concentrate on my job thinking about you all the time.' You know these frustrated old broads fall for his line every time." Maggie tried to move but couldn't; nothing would cooperate, as if her power switch had been turned off. Finally she pushed herself away from the chair she had been clutching; without its strength she would have fallen to the floor. She started to move back toward her room. She didn't remember how she got there but somehow, her eyes blinded to everything but the humiliation and anger she felt, she staggered down the hallway and found herself sitting on her bed staring at the plain tufted print of the bedspread. Her nails were digging deeply into the palms of her hands.

"You rotten son-of-a-bitch," she swore as she felt reality gradually coming back to her. "Bastard!"

Chapter 7

The next morning Maggie told Alice.

"That little prick!" Alice started for the door. "I'm going to give him a piece of my mind, and then I'm going to cut his friggin' balls off."

Maggie grabbed her arm. Through her tears she said, "No, forget it, Alice. I don't want to make it any more unpleasant than it is. Besides, Jeff has no way of knowing I was lying in bed when he came to my room last night. I'd just as soon prefer he thinks I stood him up. It will hurt more that way."

After Jeff had stopped his anxious tapping and calling her name, Maggie spent the entire night crying and thinking about how humiliated she felt. So now, what good would it do to compound things by making a scene, possibly going to Miss Markum to lodge a complaint about him, get him fired? She'd been humiliated, but at least her humiliation wasn't known to anyone but herself and Alice, and pretending to have stood Jeff up at least saved face. It would be he who lost the hundred-dollar bet. In the eyes of the other men, Maggie felt she'd earned an element of respect, and she made up her mind that she'd see to it personally that the others would know he hadn't gotten her. It was a rather empty victory but it was the only one she had and she must satisfy herself with that.

Alice said, "Well, we're not staying here another day. Get packed. I'll tell Markum we're leaving."

"Not just yet, Alice. I have something I must do before we leave."

"What?"

"Come along. You'll see."

Last night she'd thought she would never want to see Jeff Cochran again but somehow the light of day brought with it a new sort of determination. She blamed it on all the hard work she'd subjected herself to over the past weeks, the sweating, the glamorizing, the dieting, the slimming. She felt she looked beautiful and with her new beauty came a new self-assurance with a firm, imposing bearing and a direct gaze. No insignificant, cheap little hustler was going to destroy all her efforts.

She would play her little scene with Jeff and then leave with her empty victory. But the others wouldn't know it was empty, which was all that mattered. All right, so her pride had taken a beating. She'd just have to swallow that pride and be on her guard against future beatings.

She hurried along ahead of Alice until they came to the dining room where she knew Jeff and the other boys would be setting up the breakfast tables. Her luck was good. He was at a table in the center of the room. When she saw him he looked different somehow. How could she have ever considered giving in to someone who was nothing more than a cheap, conceited call-boy without morals or character; just a plastic mannikin, all surface and shine with nothing underneath?

"Jeff," she called in an unusually loud voice. She forced a little laugh and said, "Sorry about last night." She glanced to make sure all of the others were watching and listening. "Alice and I got into a heavy backgammon game. Oh, don't set a place for either of us this morning. Alice and I are rushing back to New York on the noon flight." She kept her smile sparkling. "Something important has come up."

She saw him start toward her, his eyes staring at her. It sickened her to look at him. She turned quickly and with Alice playing rearguard, blocking any possible interference, they hurried along the corridor toward Miss Markum's office.

"Well played, kiddo," Alice said as they hurried along.

Jeff called her name but as he did, Miss Markum turned the corner and started toward them. Without turning around Maggie could hear Jeff's footsteps stop, hesitate, and turn back toward the dining room.

Miss Markum was distressed to learn of their unexpected departure, but she had to admit that they'd both accomplished just about everything they'd come to accomplish. So she wasn't too reluctant to have them leave, especially when they weren't insisting on any kind of refund, which she reminded them they were not entitled to.

Later, while Maggie was packing, she found small consolation in her scene with Jeff. She packed quickly, haphazardly, hoping Jeff wouldn't come to her room, but then she knew he was kept very busy every morning with his usual duties—which he couldn't possibly neglect if he wanted to keep his job.

She looked at herself in the mirror and again she felt genuinely pleased by what she saw. She looked terrific, trim and lovely and fresh, even though there was a dullness in her eyes, a dullness she knew would disappear with thoughts of Jeff Cochran. She'd actually enjoyed the ordeal, she had to admit, but a month was far too long a time for a wife to be away from a husband if she intended to keep—and contrary to all she'd thought about before this morning, she wanted to keep Doug.

Alice hadn't completed her packing when Maggie came to her room. As she helped Alice finish Maggie said, "You know, when I was with Jeff last night I felt weaker than I ever felt in my whole life. I knew that I was letting myself become involved in a foolish affair that was totally wrong, but in my heart I honestly believed there was something right in all that wrong. I suppose it was thinking of Doug and Phyllis that made me feel that way. Oh, what an utter ass I've made of myself! Just because Doug is blind, how could I have been?"

"Kiddo, we all get taken in at one time or another during our lifetimes. And as far as Doug is concerned, I suggest you not think of him or Jeff Cochran or Phyllis Bracken or anything except our going off to Dallas and spending a bundle."

"I honestly think I should get home, Alice."

"Not on your life. You look absolutely magnificent in your new body and there's nothing in the world like tons of new clothes to help you get over a disappointing experience. Believe me, by the time we finish in Dallas you'll have forgotten all about Jeff Cochran, I guarantee it."

Much as Maggie objected, she found herself agreeing by the time they got to the Phoenix airport. "I'll call Doug and tell him of our change in plans."

It was strange to hear Doug's voice over the telephone. Oddly enough she had expected him to sound like Jeff Cochran.

Doug didn't object as strenuously as she would have liked. He merely said he missed her and wasn't expecting her for another week anyway, so go ahead to Dallas and he wished her a good time, laughingly pleading with her not to bankrupt him.

After hanging up, Maggie felt a new kind of understanding of Doug. Although she hadn't actually had sex with Jeff, the desire was as sinful as the act; so in a way she was just as unfaithful to her marriage vows as was Doug. The thought made her feel less resentful toward him.

To Alice she said, "Well, I have His Highness' blessing."

Alice gave her a wry look and said, "Which I interpret as meaning he's still shacked up with the lovely Miss Bracken."

Doug was still shacked up with Phyllis and hated himself for it. He held the dead receiver, wishing he'd told Maggie how deeply he loved her, how he wanted her more than anything else in the world.

"You stupid jerk," he said to himself. "All you said was that you missed her. What in hell kind of a thing is that to say? Why didn't you beg her to come home, plead with her to try and understand your weaknesses?"

He felt ashamed and guilty as hell, yet in spite of himself he could not break the hold Phyllis had on him. He didn't love her, he was positive of that, but every time he thought about her body and the way she used it, he trembled with need of her. His sexual desires were much stronger than his mental love for his wife. They were on two different planes, one physical, the other almost spiritual.

The phone rang again and Doug, thinking it was Maggie calling back, snatched up the receiver. "Darling, thank God you called back. I have something I must say to you."

Phyllis' smiling voice said, "There's several things I

have to say to you too, lover boy, but I'll wait until I see you. Same time tonight? I'm fixing Cornish game hens."

Doug's heart sank; her voice sounded so rasping after hearing Maggie's. Furthermore, he hated Cornish game hens, those small meatless little things that left an empty space in his stomach.

"Oh, yes, Phyl, I suppose I'll be there as usual."

"You suppose?"

"I'm sorry, yes, I'll be there."

"You sound funny."

Doug tried to think fast. "It's just that I talked to Maggie earlier. She's changed her plans."

"She isn't coming home earlier than expected, is she?"

"No. She left the spa earlier, but she and Alice are going on to Dallas to do some shopping."

"Good. I have so many things planned for us. I'd be very disappointed if anything happened to change them."

"I'll see you this evening, Phyllis."

"You sound as though you're trying to get rid of me. Is anything wrong?"

"No, nothing. I have a lot of work to do, that's all."

"Well, don't tire yourself out, lover boy. I'll do that myself when you get here—so come prepared."

Why in hell couldn't he tell her to get lost, to go fuck herself? As much as he wanted to he couldn't bring himself to do it. Phyllis was like some drug that had gotten into his system and he had to keep feeding it or he'd go crazy. He admitted that her type of sex was perverted by many people's standards, including Maggie's, but to him it was a narcotic. He craved it more than anything. He thought of it all day long. Hard as he tried to satisfy the itch that gnawed at him, he found no satisfaction, no substitute for Phyllis but Phyllis herself. If only Maggie could generate the same sensations all his problems would be over. But he knew if he suggested, merely insinuated such things to Maggie, she'd think him deranged. She'd leave him for sure.

What troubled him most was that he truthfully believed Maggie's position to be the right one. He remembered reading somewhere that what is moral is what one feels good about afterward, and what is immoral is what one feels bad about afterward. He always felt bad after his sessions with Phyllis; he felt dirty and guilty. So therefore his relations with her were immoral. There was no doubt about it.

His argument was immediate. He felt dirty and guilty afterward because the act was performed with Phyllis; it would be different with Maggie, if only Maggie would do to him the things Phyllis did. It wasn't the acts themselves that were immoral, but the person who performed them. Thinking this way, he hated Phyllis all the more for keeping him enslaved to her wiles.

He stared at the papers on his desk without seeing them. He pushed them into a pile and pushed himself out of his chair. Work was impossible. Two different voices kept echoing around inside his head, like the tormentors of a sinner. On one side Maggie, on the other Phyllis. There was a golden ring to Maggie's voice, all clear and bright and singing. Phyllis' was dark and enticing, like the song of the siren, lush with sinful temptations.

He'd break his date with Phyllis, he decided suddenly. But before he finished dialing Phyllis' number, he dropped the receiver heavily into its cradle and fell into his chair, burying his face in his hands. It was no use. He wasn't strong enough to fight the devils that tormented him. Perhaps with Maggie beside him he might find it possible to oppose Phyllis, but without Maggie he was lost; there was no way in hell he could resist Phyllis Bracken.

The scent of Phyllis' perfume lodged in his nostrils, the touch of her against his naked skin was like tiny sparks dancing over a watery surface. Everything about her reeked with sensuality and sin, making him feel deliciously wicked and evil. Doug admitted that his wickedness was nothing more than a temporary weakness, that his strength lay in Maggie. . . . But she wasn't here.

He lifted his head sharply. Why should be bemoan his guilt? Maggie was most likely no better than he. Where he was given to sexual perversities, she more than likely was being rampant in sexual infidelity. As long as they were both engaged in plowing the same pastures, what difference did it make if he spent his time in whatever manner with Phyllis? How could Maggie point an accusing finger?

She was having her flirtations, no doubt, so why shouldn't he?

Yet later, standing at Phyllis' door, he hesitated before ringing the bell. He felt queasy, letting himself believe that Maggie could bring herself to be unfaithful to him. It wasn't in her nature, regardless of how many veiled threats she'd made before leaving with Alice for Arizona. It ripped at his heart, thinking that Maggie would ever find comfort in the arms of any other man than himself. This thing between him and Phyllis was nothing serious, merely an escapade into a different kind of sexual experience. It was new and different and utterly perverse; but it was no different from visiting a prostitute once every so often, like eating lobster on occasion, just for a change of diet.

"Hey, you're late," Phyllis said in answer to his ring. "I keep forgetting to give you a key so you can let yourself in."

"I don't want that; Maggie would be sure to notice it on my keyring."

Phyllis pecked his mouth. "Poor pet, still worrying about upsetting Maggie. Surely you realize by now that she is well aware of what's going on between us."

"I prefer to think that she isn't."

Phyllis smiled. "What an innocent. Honestly, Doug, if I didn't know any better I'd suspect you of being sixteen and a virgin."

"There are times of late that I wish I were."

She saw the dark frown crease his forehead. "I have a feeling it is going to be one of those sin, suffer, and repent nights. Okay, lover boy, come on in. I'll fix you a good stiff drink and you can pour out your guilt. Let's get it over with before dinner—which will be in about forty minutes," she said over her shoulder as she went into her tiny kitchen.

The dinner never did get served. Doug wasn't hungry and after several generously laced scotch-and-sodas he lost his appetite completely. The Cornish game hens got cold. Phyllis nibbled. Doug talked.

She had heard it all before—too many times—but she listened. She sat there asking herself why she so desperately loved this man with all his weakness and his guilt, not to mention his wife and two children. She couldn't answer her question. She supposed it was because of all these weaknesses. She knew she thrilled him by her sexual expertise, the various ways she dreamed up to bring him to climax after climax. It was the whore in her that he loved; she knew that, and she would act the whore as long as he kept coming back to her. She'd crawl through the dirt if he asked her to.

If only she'd known Doug as early in life as Maggie had, things might have been different. There were so many things about Doug that he tried to keep buried. If only he'd realize that bringing all his true, inborn wants and needs out into the open he'd feel less frustrated, less guilt-ridden. She'd given Doug a glimpse of his true nature and she knew he would never be able to deny that part of him again. He'd never be able to shove it all back under cover and go on living with Maggie knowing there was a part of him lying dormant, needing desperately to breathe air and feel the light of day and receive expression.

She propped her chin on her hand and listened to his slightly drunken voice complaining about how the bank was trying to shaft him on the interest rate. She couldn't help but smile. He belonged here with her and she was sure that eventually he would realize that. It would take time, but she'd spent most of that time already. She was in the home stretch now. A few weeks, perhaps a month longer, and Doug would be hers. When Maggie came home he'd be forced to choose; and Phyllis was positive she'd win the toss. And she didn't care how she'd win, just that she would.

"Come on, lover, I think we'd better get you into bed and let you sleep it off."

"No," he said, pulling his arm away. "I've got to get home. The kids will think. . . ."

"To hell with what the kids think, or what your sister, Flora, thinks or says. She knows you're over twenty-one and I'm certain she won't call Maggie and rat on you for staying the night here."

"I can't stay here," he argued, trying to get to his feet. He fell back.

Phyllis laughed. "I don't think you have any choice."

Doug's head was all fuzzy and her voice sounded so far, far away. He felt himself being helped across the room, then everything was dark and quiet.

He didn't know how long he'd been asleep. He awoke with a start and fumbled for the light on the nightstand. Nothing was where it was supposed to be and something crashed to the floor.

The light clicked on and Phyllis said, "What's wrong?"

It took a minute before he connected the voice with the person, the room with the bed. "Oh Christ. What time is it?"

"Not late. About one o'clock."

"I've got to get home." He threw back the coverlet and put his feet over the side of the bed. He noticed that he was naked. Casually he draped the covers across his crotch.

Phyllis saw his gesture and laughed. "You sweet, little prude." She leaned over and kissed his bare shoulder.

"Don't." He shrugged and started to reach for his undershorts.

Phyllis slipped her arms around his waist and began inching her fingers slowly toward his penis. Much as he wanted to leave there was a tingling that started in his toes and was gradually rising higher and higher until he felt his whole body engulfed in one huge, hot wave of sensation. He sat rigid, unable to move.

"Do you really want to go?" she cooed.

Doug let out a sigh. "I should."

"But not immediately, Doug. Please. Lie back." She pressed her hand on his chest and gently eased him back against the crisp cool sheets. The sleek silky fabric of her nightgown pressed suggestively against his muscled, naked body. She snuggled closer, laying her head on his shoulder, coaxing his arms to enfold her.

Doug didn't move; he couldn't. He lay still and quiet, trying to keep his breathing even, refusing to let her know how excited he was getting. His body tensed suddenly when he felt her hand on his waist. Her fingers moved slowly, deftly across his abdomen, tangling momentarily with his thick wiry growth of pubic hair. He gave a sudden jerk as her hand encircled, squeezing urgently, feeling him react.

"Please, Phyllis, I've got to leave," he breathed, shifting slightly to escape her touch. "They'll worry about me."

"Ah," she cooed, snuggling even closer. "This won't take long, darling." She cupped him in her hand and slipped a finger between the crack of his buttocks.

Doug reached down and pulled her hand away. He tried not to tremble with his need for her. He couldn't let her see how much he wanted her kind of love. He mustn't let her know how enslaved he'd become to her. "Sorry, Phyllis, but I really should get the hell out of here."

She didn't answer. Instead, she wrapped her arms around his naked body and moved one leg between his. She tensed her thigh, relaxed it, then tensed it again. She could feel his already hard flesh begin to get even harder as she teased him with her pressure.

Doug sighed and pressed himself hard against the bed. "I see you're not going to take no for an answer." The hardness in his groin had turned into a demand. In spite of his resolution, the urge was suddenly unbearable. Phyllis' body felt hot—as hot as human flesh could feel—as it ignited his need. He encircled her, pulling her on top of his naked body. "I should be going," he said, but his voice held no conviction.

"I know." Her smile went unnoticed as she gazed into his dark, handsome face. "So go," she grinned, beginning to nibble at his ear lobe. Her tongue licked the sides of his neck, then kissed and caressed his broad shoulders.

"You aren't helping," he breathed, fumbling with the soft material of her nightgown.

Phyllis didn't answer. Her mouth busied itself with the sharp points of his chest, biting them softly. Doug's fingers tightened on the filmy material, clutching it into a ball, ripping it from her body as her lips continued their downward course. She reached his navel and paused long enough to free herself from the shreds of her nightdress. Doug sighed, feeling her breasts as they fell free and brushed his groin.

Phyllis shifted position. She raised up, then lowered herself into a sitting position on his lap, sucking him hungrily into her. Their arms wound around each other. Phyllis' breasts were smashed tightly against his hairy chest as their mouths crushed together. Slowly she began to rotate her hips, drawing Doug deeper and deeper into her hot, passionate body. She moved faster and faster, swaying wildly as she felt his hardness pulse and throb deep inside her. Tiny little groans of pleasure escaped her mouth only to be sucked from between her lips as his mouth remained glued over hers.

"God," he gasped, pulling at her breasts, refusing to allow her mouth to move away from his. His gasp made her move more violently, bouncing, churning her body over his exploding desire. He groaned again as if in agony, as he felt the last wall collapse and the flood start to pour out of him.

Phyllis ground out the last throes of her own ecstasy, groaning, moaning, almost screaming out her delight. Then suddenly she froze in an attitude of complete satisfaction. Slowly she allowed her grip on him to loosen and she fell forward on top of Doug's body. After a moment she slid, heavy and exhausted, to his side.

The quietness of the bedroom seemed to wrap around them as they lay, trying to regain their normal breathing. Phyllis stirred finally, propping herself up on one elbow, and looked into Doug's face. His eyes were closed, his lips half-parted.

"Now you can go home if you wish," she said. She kissed his mouth.

"In a little while." There was a calmness inside him that was like the flat sea after a heavy storm. Nothing stirred, no quarrels, no disagreements, no controversies plagued him. He was at peace with everyone and everything. If only all the rest of time would pass with such hushed serenity, such peaceful quiet, almost like the peace of the grave.

His eyes shot open as he remembered that there was no peace for the wicked. He sat up and swung his feet over the side of the bed.

"Oh, Doug, lie back down," Phyllis said. "The kids are in bed by this time and if you think your sister, Flora, is worried about where you are, call her and tell her you're playing poker with the boys or something."

"Calling will wake the kids, and Flora *will* be worried," he said as he hurried into his pants.

"Are you concerned about Flora's worrying or is the guilt starting to build up again? Honestly, why are men so damned anxious for sex and the minute it's over they feel they've committed the most mortal of sins?"

"Don't lecture me, Phyllis." He finished buttoning his shirt but the buttons weren't in the right buttonholes. He didn't notice.

Phyllis gave him an exasperated look. " 'Don't lecture me,' he says. He spends the entire evening talking about himself, his wife, his business, his bank problems—and now after one remark from me he says, 'Don't lecture me, Phyllis.' "

Doug ignored her.

"Doug, why can't you relax?" She went to him and began correcting the shirt-buttoning. "Everybody knows about us. Why are you being a hypocrite to yourself?"

"I guess I can't help it."

"Well, what about me? Don't you ever once think about my side of this whole thing? What am I supposed to do, sit here and wait for you to get around to me?"

"Let's not go into that, Phyllis. You agreed to the arrangement when it started."

"With the object in mind that you were eventually going to talk to Maggie and come to a decision. You promised me that much, Doug. You know I promised to abide by whatever decision you reach. If you say you want Maggie and never want to see me again, then okay. It'll hurt for a while, maybe forever, but I'll honor my promise never to bother you again. But damn it, Doug, you have got to decide! You've got to talk to Maggie and either tell her you want a divorce or tell her you'll never see me again. One or the other. I'm tired of sitting on the fence waiting to see which backyard you want to play in."

"We've been all though this years ago, Phyllis."

Phyllis saw him starting to get angry with her. "I have a feeling that this little absence of hers is having its effect. Absence makes the heart grow fonder and all that jazz." Still quoting, she added, "Just remember that absence also diminishes little passions and increases great ones, just the way the wind blows out candles and fans fires."

"Spare me the maxims. I've got to be going." He started for the front door.

"Not even a kiss goodbye for the mistress?"

He turned to kiss her. She pressed herself tight against his body and slipped her leg in between his. Her tongue darted between his lips and crept into his mouth.

He eased her away—reluctantly.

"Phyl, I'm sorry. This whole thing is getting to me. I'm really sorry. It's late, I had too much to drink, I'm upset about Maggie. I just don't know about anything anymore. I'm all mixed up inside, I can't think straight."

Phyllis looked up into his face. His eyes had a remorseful look, as if trying to hide the anguish that was in his heart. He was a strong and virtuous man, she knew, but she had to remind herself that the virtuous often use virtue as a mask to hide their secret vices and strong men are usually melted by their weaknesses. But Phyllis had never been able to put Doug into any one category; he was virtuous, sinful, weak, and oftimes quite lewd when he let down his puritanical guard. Although he wasn't aware of it, he was indeed a hypocrite to himself, but certainly no one's fool. He was a terribly confused man, being pulled apart by his own indecision, his own innocence. He wanted the beautiful with the plain, the sinful with the virtuous. At heart he was still a boy, filled with illusions and the truthless ideals that were instilled into him, bruising and hurting himself every time he came into contact with reality. The one great danger about Doug was that he had deceived himself by his own sincerity. He honestly mistook his sensuality for romantic emotion. He could no more change Maggie into Phyllis than Phyllis into Maggie, but that was what he hoped would happen one day, and through that metamorphosis his dilemma would be resolved.

In short, Doug was an idealist—and she loved him for it.

Chapter 8

Maggie spent more money than she intended, but she didn't care; she couldn't remember when she had felt and looked so young and attractive. Men actually stared at her when she passed, and more than once the younger, bolder types whistled.

Alice commented, "You always know when you're looking terrific when you begin seeing resentment in younger women's eyes. They're the ones who can spot us 'remakes' right off the bat, and when our remodeling is successful they hate us for it." She nudged Maggie. "Did you see that blonde with the football player type? She grabbed his arm when we glanced over, just to show us that he's hers and we'd better not try to wander into her territory." Alice laughed. "Isn't it wonderful to be competition again? I love it!"

Alice kept firing her resentment of Doug with insidious reminders of his infidelity, reminding Maggie that she'd fought against temptation and had won. The reminders always left her with fewer regrets about the amount of money she'd spent during the day as well as a nagging regret that she didn't go to bed with Jeff Cochran after all. What did it matter to her if he won or lost a bet? She'd have had him, which was all that would have mattered. After all, she wasn't the dumpy, plain little housewife she used to be; perhaps he really did want her sexually for herself and not just because of the stupid bet. The more she saw her reflection in mirrors the more she was convinced that Jeff Cochran really had wanted her for herself, not the money.

After the end of the fifth day of doing the shops, Maggie decided she'd had enough. She telephoned Doug, who promised to meet her plane in Newark. When the plane touched down at the airport Maggie had the oddest sensation of being nineteen years old again and just starting over, anxious to be out in the world and all its excitement.

Doug wasn't in the terminal when they got off the plane. His sister, Flora, waved to Maggie and hugged her as she came through the gate. Flora said, laughing, "Hey, don't let your disappointment show so much. I'm not all that hard to take, am I?"

Maggie was more than disappointed, she was furious, but told herself she mustn't show it to Flora. She had wanted to walk into Doug's arms, have him stare at the new Maggie Hampton with love and admiration. She'd wanted to make an entrance, as they say, but it had all been wasted on Flora. Flora wasn't the noticing type.

Maggie had always liked Flora, an open, cheerful woman who seemed to live her life for the mere pleasure of living it. She had a grown family of her own and a husband who spent all of his time running a farm in Ohio. Flora was Doug's oldest sister, who adored her young brother and never refused him anything. In Flora's estimation, Doug could do no wrong. Maggie reminded herself of that when she asked about him.

"Doug got tied up at the office again. Hi, Alice," Flora added over Maggie's shoulder. She extended her big, meaty hand, and although her smile was genuine enough, she never really approved of Alice Maitland. She disapproved of all she'd heard and seen of her.

Alice shook her hand and returned the smile. Alice had never cared much for Flora either, and the exchange of greetings was about the only contact Flora and Alice ever had. They both liked to keep it that way.

Flora looked back at Maggie. "That rest cure didn't do you much good. You look a little peaked; and look at you, skinny as a rail."

Maggie laughed self-consciously. She ran her hands over her hips. "This is what is called svelte, Flora."

Flora shook her head. "Too skinny to suit me."

Alice chuckled and said, "That's just the idea, it's your brother she wants to suit."

"Take it from me, honey, Doug was satisfied with the way she used to look."

Alice curled her mouth sarcastically. "That's why he sees so much of Phyllis Bracken, I suppose."

Flora gave her a fierce look, but said nothing. When Alice was looking for her luggage, however, Flora whispered conspiratorially, "I don't much care for that Alice Maitland. And who in blazes is Phyllis What's-her-name?"

"Oh, just some woman the gossip mill says Doug is seeing on the side."

"Hell, don't believe a word of that kind of stuff, Maggie. Doug is true blue, let me tell you."

"Then I take it he's been home every night after work, waiting anxiously for his prodigal wife to return?"

"He's been working a lot of overtime."

"I'll bet."

"Look here, I don't know what's going on between you two; but I can tell you, Maggie, it isn't Doug's fault, whatever it is. You should know better than to go traipsing around the country with the likes of Alice Maitland. She was always a troublemaker, as I remember."

"Alice happens to be my oldest friend, who likes to look out for my welfare."

"Doug does that. You don't need any woman friend to give you direction. She's divorced again, I hear."

Maggie ignored the comment. "I went away to straighten out my thinking. Just so it won't come as too great a surprise, Flora, I gave serious thought to divorcing your brother just before I went to Arizona."

"So I hear. Doug and I talked when you were away." She gave Maggie a quizzical look. "I take it you changed your mind about the divorce."

"That, my dear Flora, will all depend upon Doug. So far," she said, noting his absence, "he isn't making too many points."

"Hells bells, Maggie, he's tied up at the office."

"Just like he was tied up at the office every night that I was away, right?"

"He's a family man with the need to earn a living."

Alice rejoined them. To Flora she was an intrusion into a family matter, and family matters were not aired in front of strangers. Flora said, "Doug promised he'd be home by the time we get there."

He wasn't, and by the time they went out of their way to drop Alice at her apartment on the Palisades, a good two hours had passed. "So where is he now?" Maggie asked a rather embarrassed Flora.

"I'll call his office."

"Don't bother, Flora. His secretary will just give you some vague excuse." Maggie threw her purse on the chair. "Honestly, you'd think he would at least think enough of me to meet my plane." Just then she heard his car pull into the driveway. Unfortunately, by this time she was not very pleased to see him. His lack of consideration had tarnished her high spirits, had chipped away at her beauty. She felt plain and petulant. She turned her cheek when he tried to kiss her.

"Mad, hon?" he said, grinning like a naughty boy. "I really did have to work, Maggie. I was out at the Fort Lee construction site again."

"Oh, Doug, you could have at least freed yourself long enough to meet our flight."

"I'm sorry but something came up that needed my personal attention."

Flora tactfully excused herself.

Maggie said, "Honestly, Doug, when I left with Alice it was on such a sour note that I was sure we'd both try to be on our best behavior when I returned. You can't imagine how disappointed I was not to see you when I got off the plane."

He took her in his arms. She let him. "I truly am sorry, darling. I know I should have been there but I just couldn't get away. At least I sent Flora." He grinned, trying to attract a grin from her. "Which is better than your having to take a cab." Seeing her pout he said, "I love you," in a little sing-songy voice.

He kissed her deeply and lovingly and she felt herself melting in his arms. When he released her she stepped away from him and pivoted. "Well, how do you like it?"

"New dress? Very pretty. And I won't even ask how much it cost," he joked.

"Not the dress, silly, my figure. I lost over twenty

pounds. And how do you like my new hair style? The latest Paris fashion, we were told."

He crinkled his nose. "Too glamorous. It isn't you somehow."

She wouldn't let him dampen her mood about her new self. "You are just going to have to get used to a little more glamorous wife. This is the new me," she announced proudly.

"I liked the old you," he said stubbornly. She was acting rather strange, almost brazen; he wasn't sure he liked it. She didn't even look like herself.

Maggie chucked him under the chin and winked. "You're going to like the new me even better."

"Why, what did they teach you out there, adult sex education?" It slipped out without him realizing what he'd said.

She glowered. "What in hell is that supposed to mean?"

"I don't know." He shrugged. "It was just something to say. I was just trying to be funny, I suppose." Hell, she'd given him a perfect opening to tell her about the kind of sex he enjoyed with Phyllis, but his courage suddenly deserted him. He just stood feeling extremely awkward and tongue-tied. How did a husband go about telling his wife he thinks she's ordinary in bed and that he'd like a little variation, a bit of experimentation? Maggie would only construe that to mean that he wanted to have Phyllis—or someone else. The old quarrel would start up and they'd be right back to where they had been before Maggie left. He shrugged again, feeling her scowling at him, and said nothing.

Maggie felt miserable. The dieting, the gruelling regime of the spa had accomplished nothing. Doug wanted her to be the same common little woman she'd been before, overweight, ordinary, middle-aged; and it was obvious that despite everything else, he'd always want her that way. Well, to hell with him, she decided as she scooped up her purse and started toward her room. She'd worked too long and hard to accomplish what she had and she had every intention of enjoying the new Maggie Hampton—even if she had to change back to Maggie Booth.

"I'm tired," she said. "I'm going to lie down. I assume Flora is planning on preparing dinner?"

"I thought we'd all eat out tonight. Sort of to celebrate your coming home."

"Fine," she said coolly. She turned and went up the stairs.

Doug watched the sway of her hips, the trim waist, the fantastic hair, the sleek curve of her legs. Damn it, she looked terrific! Why couldn't he tell her how beautiful she was?

As he thought about it, he supposed he wanted Maggie as she used to look because he never had to worry about other men trying to steal her away from him. He had always had a possessive nature as far as she was concerned, and selfish as it sounded, if he couldn't have her then he didn't want anybody else to have her. It wasn't fair but that was the way he felt. He supposed it was the way he loved.

However, the same did not apply to Phyllis. He didn't care about her that way. She was welcome to any other guy she wanted and it wouldn't bother him, just so long as Phyllis wasn't having other guys at the same time she was having him.

After an hour Doug timidly came into the bedroom carrying her suitcases. "You'd better unpack before everything gets too wrinkled."

She was standing at the window and didn't turn around.

"Besides," he added, "I'd like to see what you spent my bankroll on." There was a smile in his voice.

"Our bankroll," she said crossly. "We're married. Remember? What's mine is yours and what's yours is mine."

"Ah, Maggie, come on, let's not fuss at each other." He tried to put his arms around her. "If you're mad because I didn't notice your new figure and your new hairdo I'm sorry. You know what a klutz I am. When you walked out of the room I had to pinch myself to make me believe I'm married to such a beautiful woman. But hell, you didn't have to turn yourself into a glamor girl just for me. I don't care what you look like. I'll love you forever and ever. Nothing will change that."

She spun around. "I didn't do all this just for you!" She slowly moved her head from side to side. "I never realized it before but you are really a very selfish man, Doug."

"Maggie!"

"Well, you are. All you think about is Doug Hampton and what is good for him, what he wants. How about me, Doug? In case you're interested, I sweated off those pounds for me," she said, emphasizing her point by jabbing herself with her thumb. "Me, Maggie Booth."

She saw him start to get angry.

Maggie hurried on with, "You're always satisfied with everything just so long as it's what you want. Well, things are going to be a little different, Doug. I want a change. We talked about this before I left and we left everything unresolved. I did a lot of thinking in Arizona. I'm not happy and I intend to do something about it. I'm tired of being taken for granted by you and the children."

"Christ! That damned Alice is preaching equal rights again, I see."

"Don't put the blame on Alice. You're as much responsible as anyone. If you'd be a little more considerate of me and what I want, we could be happy together, but you are so damned selfish about having everything your way that you're suffocating me. You have your work and all your conventions and your other on-the-side interests, and what do I have? Nothing."

"You have a house and kids and a husband who loves you."

"And I also have boredom and dirty dishes and hours upon hours of being alone." She felt the tears starting to come, but refused to give in to them. "The house, the kids, and your love just aren't enough anymore." She could see the sudden hurt in his face. "I'm sorry, Doug, but I mean that. I need something more. I need to have an interest in something I can get involved with."

"I suppose you want to be like Alice with her cocktail crowd and her steady stream of boyfriends."

It occurred to her that people always suspect you of wanting what they themselves would want, but she didn't want to open up that can of worms. "Oh, for God's sake, Doug, I'm not referring to that kind of involvement. The only thing I envy Alice for is her work, just as I envy you yours."

"You have your work," he said making a sweeping gesture to indicate the house, their family, their life together.

She shook her head again. "You just don't understand,

do you, Doug?" She sat down on the edge of the bed and folded her hands in her lap. "I suppose I could talk until doomsday and you'd never understand because you won't let yourself understand."

"When I see you wanting to uproot everything we've started together, pull down everything we've built up, everything we've worked for, no, Maggie, I don't understand."

"I'm not trying to destroy everything we have, Doug. I just want to do something with the rest of my life besides sit here at home and wait to be needed by you or the children. I'm like an electric appliance that you plug in and turn on whenever you want to use it."

"Nobody takes you for granted. You just imagine that we do."

She shook her head slowly. "Imagined or not, I feel that I'm having my life gradually squeezed out of me. I just want to be Maggie Booth again."

A heaviness fell over the room. It hung there for a moment before Doug said, "Does that mean you want a divorce?"

Maggie looked up quickly as she got to her feet. "Oh, no, Doug. It doesn't mean that at all. I just meant that I want to feel that I'm alive, just the way I did when you and I first met, when we were first married. I want the happy days back again. I know I can't bring back the ones we've already spent but I can't help feeling that there has got to be more than my sitting around in a dead house waiting for you to grow old enough to retire and join me. As for me, I'm already retired."

She slipped her arms around him and laid her head on his chest. "Admit it, Doug. Regardless of the work and the long hours, you manage to enjoy being with the people who are around you every day. You like being caught up in all the emergencies of your job, all the hassles, the problems. You're doing things with your life. I'm not. I'm just vegetating now, like an orchid in a hot-house, waiting for my petals to wither and fall off."

"Okay, okay," he said with a sigh, hugging her close. "You want to go to work, right?"

"Yes, if I can find a job."

"All right." He eased her away from him. "But promise me one thing."

She hugged him and said, "Anything."

"Just make sure in your mind that you want a job because you're bored and that you won't start running around the way Alice does."

"I promise."

"Okay then," he said, running his hands up and down her back. "Then I suppose from here on in I'll have to get used to the fact that I'm married to a working woman."

He didn't like the idea of her going to work. It somehow made him feel less a man to know his wife would be independent of him. Her arguments were sound enough and reasonable, but at the same time he could not help but feel less in control, less a husband and more just a friend. It was idiotic to feel this way, he told himself, but that's the way it was. Part of him was being taken away and he didn't like it. He was back to admitting his selfishness.

On the other hand, a little voice reminded him—a spiteful little voice that said he should try to get even with her—he was being given the chance to be more independent himself. Now Maggie couldn't much argue about his coming home late, his being away from home more often. She would be at work, a working woman, and would begin to realize how a job and outside interests have a habit of becoming a preoccupation. He would have more free time which he need not explain away. All in all, he decided, there might be some advantages to letting Maggie get a job.

He thought of Phyllis but swore to himself that he was going to put an end of that affair once and for all. Maggie's getting a job didn't mean he had more time for Phyllis. Absolutely not. That was over for good.

Somehow an old saw about good intentions paving the road to hell came to his mind.

Downstairs the front door slammed and they heard David's unmistakable footsteps clomping up the stairs to his room. Maggie went to the door and called, "Hey, sport, the old lady's home!"

"Hey, Mom!" He started into her open arms, eyeing her

appreciatively. "Holy cow, where were you anyhow, at some glamor school? You look positively terrific. A real honest-to-goodness Class Triple A knock-out."

"Thank you, kind sir," she said, giving him a bear hug. "I needed that."

He looked her up and down again. "You are one classy lady. Man, if you weren't my mother I think I'd put the make on you, sweetheart," he said in a bad imitation of W. C. Fields. "Oh, hi, Dad," he said when he noticed his father standing just inside the door. "I saw you this afternoon."

Doug looked curious.

David leaned close to his mother and in another bad imitation—this time of Groucho Marx—flicked an imaginary cigar, fluttered his eyebrows, and said, "Watch it, Madam, your old man was seen with another woman, but one not half as lovely, I might add." He turned and did a little shuffling step. "See you at dinner, kids."

"We're eating out," Maggie called as he went to his room.

"Then I won't see you at dinner. I'll grab something here. I'm catching an early movie."

Maggie went back into her bedroom. When she closed the door she said, "Phyllis Bracken, I suppose." It was a statement not a question.

She saw him try to hide his guilt by looking down at the carpet. "Yes," he admitted, "As a matter of fact it was. She's doing a cost study on that Fort Lee job."

"I'll just bet she is."

"Now stop it, Maggie. I told you that there is nothing between Phyllis and me."

"And you lie through your teeth," she said calmly. She unsnapped one of her suitcases and began hanging things on hangers. "I told you before, Doug, that I know for a fact that you've started up with Phyllis again. I have proof in black and white."

"Christ, what did you do, hire detectives to spy on me while you were away?"

Maggie froze. Then she turned and faced him squarely. "I take it by that remark that you have been seeing Phyllis while I was away."

He felt he couldn't let her browbeat him. "Yes," he said.

"We spent a few evenings together. Strictly business," he insisted.

"I don't believe you. How do you like them apples?" She threw the dress she was holding across the bed. "I know that woman too damned well to trust her. I don't know what kind of a hold she has over you, but whatever it is, I know you can't resist it."

He looked away. "You're talking nonsense."

"No, I am not. She's been in your blood from the very day you met her. I can see it in your face. I've wised up a lot in the few weeks I was away. I think I can look at things a little more rationally than before. I made this threat once before to you, but I'm making it again, Doug. If you persist in seeing Phyllis Bracken, you are going to lose me, this house, the children, everything we have. Just remember that, Doug."

She let her arms drop to her side showing her palms, as though presenting herself to him. "I made myself over for several reasons, Doug, one of which was so that I could fight Phyllis on her own terms. I intend to do just that."

"You don't know how," he muttered.

A car was heard screeching to a halt in front of the house. The shouting of youngsters stopped Maggie from asking her question. She went to the window and looked out. "Julie's home," she said as she patted her hair into place and she left the room and started down the stairs.

"Julie!" she cried as she hurried to take her daughter in her arms.

"Hi, Mom," she said without enthusiasm. "We missed you."

"I bought you the loveliest blouse from Neiman-Marcus. I hope you like it," Maggie said.

"Hey, what have you done to yourself?" She stood back and eyed her mother critically.

Maggie beamed and made a full turn. "How do you like your new mother?"

"You look perfectly ridiculous!"

Maggie's face fell.

From behind her Doug said, "Julie, you're being unkind. It took a lot of work and perseverence on your mother's part to lose all that weight."

"It's not just the weight," Julie said, studying Maggie's

new hair style, the new clothes. "She's just too flashy. She looks funny."

Maggie felt her back stiffen, her hands clench.

David saved the threatened scene by trotting down the stairs past his father. He was carrying books. He said to his sister, "You don't like Mom because she suddenly looks better than you. Don't listen to Julie, Mom, she's just jealous because you're prettier than she is."

Julie stuck her tongue out at him and said, "And you're just being mean because Nancy Hendricks won't go to the rock concert with you."

"Jealous?" Maggie said more to herself than anyone.

And as the weekend passed she began finding out that Julie and Doug were resentful of her new look. Both of them, as if by conspiracy, were constantly offering her slices of pie or cake, tempting her with ice cream sodas and sundaes, anything fattening for which they knew she had a weakness. Julie complained that her hair style was too young for her face. Doug complained that every dress she'd bought in Dallas—oh, never mind the price—had either the wrong hemline, the wrong fit, the wrong color, little things that made it obvious he knew nothing about fashion, only that he wanted her to return to the way she used to dress, the way she never intended to be again.

Rather than being annoyed by their petty jealousy, she found it amusing, actually complimentary, and the more they tempted her the stronger her resistance became.

On Monday morning, Flora went back to Ohio, Doug went to his office, and the kids went to school. Maggie decided to call Alice. As much as she dreaded facing that awful Rita Gant again, she made up her mind to do so. This time she felt a little less insecure and a little more knowledgeable about what to expect. But before she could dial Alice's number in New York, Alice called her.

"How's it going, kiddo?"

"Can't complain."

"How did everyone take the new Maggie Hampton?"

Maggie hesitated. "About sixty–forty. Sixty against, Forty for."

"Who's in the minority?"

"David and I."

"Figures. I always thought that besides you, the boy had class."

Maggie laughed. "How's it with you?"

"The usual. Another fiasco date with Eddie. I wish to hell I'd learn to stop beating a broken drum. Well, at least I got laid in the process, so I suppose it wasn't an entirely wasted weekend."

"I wish I could say the same," Maggie said.

"What? No nooky every night from the great lover?"

"I can't say none, but what there was of it was very half-hearted, like I was something fragile that might break, or that he was somewhere else."

"Like with Phyllis Bracken."

"Oh, I just don't want to think about it, Alice." She felt a mood of dejection setting in.

Alice sensed it. "Listen, I didn't call you to open up sores. What I wanted to know is whether you are still interested in going to work?"

"Sure. What's up?"

"One of my girls quit. God forbid that she'd let me know. Oh no, not this one. She just didn't show up and when I called her home her mother said she left for Louisiana Saturday morning, with no apparent intention of coming back." Alice chuckled. "The dear old thing sounded glad to be rid of the little slut."

"What do you want from me? I don't know anything about the employment placement business."

"What's to know? An applicant comes in, you have them fill out their qualifications, you check the register of job openings, and if there's a fit you have a job placement."

"I'm sure it's a hell of a lot more complicated than that."

"Not at the start. Later it gets complicated, but it's nothing you can't learn. I'll have the kids help you along."

Maggie felt a shiver run through her. "Like Rita Gant?"

Alice laughed. "I'll give my solemn word that Rita will be on her best behavior. Honest injun."

She felt her pulse start to race. "When would you want me to start?"

"How about in an hour?"

She swallowed hard. "This morning! Oh my God!" She wanted so desperately to get out of the house, to find herself a job and now that she was being offered one she was frightened. "Gee, Alice, I don't know."

"Don't give me that 'I don't know' business, kiddo. Just get yourself in gear and get your skinny new ass in here on the double. We're swamped." Alice hung up.

"It isn't skinny," Maggie said into the dead line. For a minute she sat staring into space, then, as if jabbed with a pin, she jumped up and hurried upstairs to her room. She started to hum as she tried to select just the right outfit.

Everything was going to be perfect after all.

Chapter 9

New York seemed different, somehow. She supposed it was because of the sudden change in her outlook. The city didn't appear as ominous or forbidding as it had. The last time she was here she'd been timid under its overpowering force. Her timidity had been due to the vagueness of her reason for being there; she hadn't known where she was going or what was ahead. Now she had an aim and a purpose. She was going to work in an office where she knew people, where she wouldn't be a complete stranger. She even remembered the name of that nice-looking young man who'd treated her so courteously: Andy Carver.

Alice had filled her in on Andy when they were wiling away their time at the Golden Cactus. "Andy is as gay as pink ink and makes no bones about it. He used to be a chorus boy and still thinks he can be one. Gay men never think they age—they think growing old only happens to straight people."

Maggie wasn't at all familiar with gay people; in fact, Andy would be the first gay man she'd ever associated with—as far as she knew. She wondered idly how she'd react to being around a homosexual.

Then there was Rita Gant to consider. Walking toward Fifth Avenue, her steps faltered as she remembered the surly, vindictive woman with the heavy Spanish accent, obviously hating anyone who was of a different nationality. And hadn't Alice mentioned that Rita even disliked her own people? How would she get along with a woman like that? By ignoring her, Maggie decided as she picked up her pace.

The office looked the same, but like the city outside, it too had a different aura. There was the same chairs and desks, the same white walls with the glass partitions, but somehow it had a warmer, more intimate feeling than it had the first time she was here.

She stood at the reception desk waiting for the girl to finish a personal conversation, obviously with her boyfriend or husband. The conversation made Maggie realize that she'd come to work without calling Doug and letting him know she was starting a job this morning. He'd more than likely be furious with her but she didn't feel concerned. She was here and she intended to stay and work for as long as Alice wanted her, provided, of course, that she could do the work. She would be as independent as Doug and the rest of the family, and if dinner wasn't ready on time, well too bad; they'd just have to get used to the fact that she was a working woman now.

"Hi, Mrs. Hampton," the receptionist said. "As usual the boss lady is tied up but I'll call Andy. Hey, I hear you're going to be one of us."

"Yes. And as long as I am I'd like it if you called me Maggie."

"I'm Caroline."

They shook hands.

"If you need anything, just pick up your phone. I'll help all I can, Maggie."

Andy Carver was the same jovial guy she'd remembered. He took her under his wing, seating her at the desk next to his, and before an hour had passed she felt herself relaxing into the work. It wasn't difficult, but Andy warned her that he would feed her only the run-of-the-mill stuff at first; later on he'd show her how to go about testing applicants, handling the employers, and the telephone work involved in finding new customers on both the hiring and the employing ends.

"That's what the business is all about," he told her. "You don't just sit here and wait for someone to come in looking for a job. You have to practically live on the telephone when you aren't interviewing, talking to personnel heads, trying to get their business, trying to sell them on an employee; or on the other side of the scale, you're calling prospective employees we have on file, trying to get them to take a job that's opened. You'd be surprised at the number of people who come in looking for work, fill out all the forms, and then have a million and one excuses why they can't take a job. Remember, it's a hell of a lot easier for some people to stand in an employment line to pick up a government check than it is to get up every morning and go to work. So the first thing to learn is not to take 'no' for an answer, be it from an applicant or an employer. You have to sell yourself and, more importantly, the agency."

"I've never sold a thing in my life," Maggie said, feeling suddenly that she would never qualify for a job like this.

"It isn't difficult. All it takes is personality, and you impress me as having lots of that." He leaned closer. "And incidentally, I absolutely adore your new look. Sensational."

She thought she'd be uptight with Andy, knowing what he was, but there was something very relaxing about the man, something she found very comfortable—almost like being with another woman. Maggie thanked him and said, "What do I say to convince someone who's on unemployment that they should take a job?"

"That is sometimes a pretty hard nut to crack, but the way I do it is to find out, without being obvious about it, just what they don't like about being unemployed and I jump on that. Usually, if you tell a married woman about how great it would be for her to get out of the house and be around new people all day, as well as have an excuse for being late getting home at times, stuff like that, you can often win them over. But it isn't easy. The usual complaints are that the job is too far from home, they have to have a wardrobe, or that it's cheaper to stay on welfare or unemployment rather than go to work."

"How do you get around those arguments?"

"Surprisingly enough, most of the people who are unemployed want to work, in spite of how easy they have it on unemployment or welfare. First, because a salary usually means much more money, even after taxes. Second, they don't have as much idle time on their hands. Third, they meet other people like themselves and generally make a lot of new friends. These things usually outweigh being at home and going out once a week or once a month for a government check. Besides, welfare checks, food stamps, and the like require swallowing a lot of personal pride, and most people are very proud. You'll find it pretty simple to talk them into a job if it is a good one."

"You said something about finding jobs for applicants?"

"You call employers just as you call employees. In the case of employees it's a matter of talking them into going to work; in the case of employers it's a matter of talking them into hiring someone . . . sometimes someone they really don't need. That's where the book-learning comes in. You should know statistics on the percentages of unemployed so you can talk to the employer knowledgeably, convince him that what he's doing is for the good of his president, his country, taking a lost soul off the streets and giving him a purpose in life . . . garbage like that. But don't worry about that end of it, right now just concentrate on fitting prospective employees to the openings we have here on these file cards," he said, touching a large card index.

Rita Gant walked into the office and caught Maggie's eye. Maggie smiled and nodded, but it took a lot of courage. Rita tilted her chin and pretended to ignore her. Andy noticed the exchange. "Ignore that bitch," he whispered.

"Is she always so rude to everyone? That first time I was here . . ."

"Yes, I was sitting here, remember? She's just an evil bitch. I think her real problem is that she needs a good lay."

Maggie felt her face flush but she reminded herself that she wasn't at home in her proper little circle, she was in the middle of Manhattan where people said what they wished and did what they wished.

Andy veered sharply. "God, I just cannot get over the change in you, Maggie, especially the clothes and the hair. I absolutely adore that outfit, but then I told you that already, didn't I? I'm always repeating myself so just ignore me or tell me. You see, I say the same time to so many different people on the telephone and to applicants who come in that it's just a terrible habit I've gotten into of being repetitious. Whenever you find me doing it to you, just tell me. I have a thick skin, believe it or not."

She didn't believe it. There was something very vulnerable about Andy Carver.

"It's as thin as tissue paper," a very overweight girl said as she walked up and put a stack of papers on Andy's desk. To Maggie she added, "Hi. I'm Louise McCartney."

Andy said, "No relation to the Beatles, much as she likes to tell everyone there is. The truth is her mother is the Goodyear Blimp. Actually she was just a twenty-dollar tramp off Madison Avenue, back when she was half her present size. I picked her up one night when I was in one of my straight moods."

"The only thing straight about you is that thing between your legs," Louise joked. "And there's talk going around that even that's about as bent as you are, love."

"Isn't she sweet? That's the way a girl talks when she's swallowed too much joy juice. She doesn't believe me when I tell her there's a million calories in that stuff."

Louise said, "Then you should weigh at least five times what you do for all you gulp down."

Maggie was very uncomfortable under this barrage. "I'm Maggie Hampton," she said. "I'm pleased to meet you, Louise."

"My desk is just around the corner, Maggie. If you want to take a breather from this swishy prima donna, come on over and I'll buy you a cup of coffee."

As she poured herself a cup of coffee Maggie asked, "Do you always talk to each other like that?"

Louise laughed. "It's all fun and games. Bitchiness is part of Andy's makeup; I think all queens have it."

"Queens?"

"Boy, you are from square city! Queen. Queer. Fag. Fruit. They all mean the same thing." She offered Maggie the sugar, which she declined. "You'll get used to it. When I started here I was just about as green as you."

"Then I take it Andy didn't find you on Madison Avenue?"

Louise laughed again. "Good God no, that's just his way of defending against my cracks about his being gay. I was a school-teacher out on Long Island. Long Beach to be exact. Mafia town, they called it once. My boyfriend was killed in Nam and I let myself balloon up to tent size. I've been drowning my sorrow in calories ever since."

Maggie sipped her coffee, not knowing whether she should sympathize or make no comment. Louise obviously wanted to talk about it or she wouldn't have made mention of her being so fat. She was reaching out, looking for someone to help her share her unhappiness, and even a stranger like Maggie seemed a welcome source of understanding. But then again, Louise might be one of those women who merely liked feeling sorry for themselves. Her obesity could certainly be overcome by dieting, so why feel sorry for someone who refused to help herself? If Louise McCartney didn't have any willpower or self-pride, then that was her business and of no concern to outsiders.

"I know how difficult it is to lose weight," Maggie said. "Thank goodness I'll never have to go through it again."

"How much did you lose?"

Maggie told her and Louise sneered. "That's nothing compared to what I'd have to burn off if I ever decide I want to."

"Believe me, you'll feel so much better. I feel as if I've dropped a rock."

"I have no willpower."

"One of these days a good-looking guy is going to give you the eye and you'll have an excuse then to start thinning down. You're very pretty, you know."

Louise sneered again. "All fat girls have pretty faces, didn't you know that? But that's what I'm afraid of, that I'll drop a hundred pounds and wind up looking like some scarecrow, all elbows and knees and sunken cheeks."

Maggie didn't feel comfortable. Louise, like all weak women, laid an exaggerated stress on not wanting to change. Maggie said, "I'd better get back to my desk. I wouldn't want the boss to see me goofing off on my first morning."

"Coffee breaks are allowed by law. Besides, Alice does more goofing off than any of us."

Later when Maggie and Andy were talking, Alice's name came up and Maggie mentioned what Louise had said. Andy objected. "Louise doesn't know what she's talking about. Sure, Alice is out of the office a lot, but it's usually on business. The agency isn't a success because of our dazzling smiles and efficient work force. Alice breaks her butt getting inside various groups that can refer business to us. So what if it costs a dollar or two on entertaining? It's worth it in volume."

Maggie was rather pleased to find that Alice kept more or less to the background and wasn't watching over her like a nervous sponsor. She'd put Maggie in Andy's charge and left her there. Twice during the day Alice came over to see how Maggie was getting along, but there wasn't any evidence of their long friendship and no offers of personal supervision. Alice treated her like the employee that she was. Their only meeting in private was toward the end of the afternoon and that was about salary.

"You'll be on what we call an 'advance.' You will receive a thousand dollars a month. That's money the Fifth Avenue Agency loans to you—and you'd better treat it as a loan and not a salary because you have to pay it back."

"Pay it back?"

Alice nodded. "That's right, you have to pay it back. If you don't, then I'm out the grand and you're out on your can. Here's how we work it. You get a percentage of the first month's salary of every applicant you place. In this office, the employer pays the agency fee. You get X percent of that fee, which goes toward reducing your advance. The more people you place the more percentages you make, the more of the thousand you eat up. Believe me, if you work hard and diligently that thousand will disappear in no time and you'll start building on it. Anything over the thousand is yours free and clear. That's why it's important to hound the personnel offices in town because the more openings you create the more money you can make if you fill them."

Maggie didn't see how she could miss. If she didn't place anybody at all, the agency still gave her a thousand a month. Of course it was a loan that had to be paid back, but at least she didn't feel any pressure because in the long run she could refuse the advance—inasmuch as she didn't need the money—and just work for her percentages.

Maggie had always known that Alice ran a successful business, but she'd never known its actual scope before today. The agency handled everything, Maggie found as she paged through the interoffice telephone directory of names and extensions. Where Maggie worked was just one of fifteen floors occupied by the agency, and each floor was devoted to and specialized in every conceivable area of employment. Maggie's office dealt exclusively with female office help, in particular general secretarial, reception, and filing, and they covered all five boroughs of New York.

At four-thirty Maggie was interviewing a young English girl who had come over with a Gilbert and Sullivan troupe from London and wanted to stay permanently. Maggie was having trouble with the customs regulations regarding work visas, and Andy was helping her out. Alice sauntered by and said she had an appointment uptown and left. In a way Maggie felt relieved that she wouldn't have to spend time with Alice. She was beginning to look upon Alice as her boss and herself as a hired hand—like Andy and Louise and the dozens or so others she'd met.

At five she pushed herself away from her desk and stood up to stretch. She felt exhausted but entirely happy. Her first day had been hectic and wonderful. She was alive and living in a thriving, interesting world of people who breathed and cried and laughed and complained. She was back among the living.

"We usually gather down at The Rail for a couple of drinks," Louise said. "Want to join the rest of us workhorses?"

Maggie shook her head. It dawned on her that she hadn't tried to call Doug again, and heaven only knew what the children thought when they got home from school and found her not there. They must be worried sick, she thought as she reached for the telephone. "I'll pass, thanks, Louise. I'd better call home and let everyone know where I am. I came out this morning without even leaving a note."

David was just going out again, to a basketball practice and Julie was over at her girlfriend's where she planned to have dinner. Maggie was bitterly disappointed that neither David nor Julie—who had come home from school with him—even wondered where she was. All David said when she told him she was working in Alice's office, was "great." And "See you when you get home, Mom."

118

When she called Doug at his office he was in a conference but his secretary put her through.

"You're where?" he asked.

She told him and made it sound as though she was merely helping out for a few days, until Alice could get someone permanently. She felt a stab of conscience but when he said he would most likely be working late on the Fort Lee problem her guilt vanished. Whenever she heard *Fort Lee* she automatically assumed it meant Phyllis Bracken.

She hung up and sat for a moment with her hand on the receiver. Louise was slipping into a jacket. "I think I've changed my mind, Louise. I'll join you after all, if that's okay."

"Great."

Maggie wasn't late getting home, and as Andy pointed out, the nice thing about unwinding at The Rail was that the commuter trains and buses weren't as crowded after six and seven o'clock.

She was glad the house was empty when she got there. It was only a little after seven and she was tempted to fix herself a cocktail, having had only Perrier water at The Rail. But she pushed the temptation out of her head, reminding herself that every cocktail had at least a hundred calories and she was only too well aware of the effort it took to burn off a hundred calories.

Thoughts of the spa brought with them thoughts of Jeff Cochran. Strangely enough they weren't unpleasant thoughts; in fact, they were pleasantly disturbing.

By the time the children came home she was in the final stage of cleaning up the kitchen. Julie disappeared up to her room and her private telephone which, Maggie knew, would be the last anyone would see of her until tomorrow. David vanished into the garage out back, a portion of which he—with Doug's help—had converted into a so-called crash pad, where he could play his rock music as loud as he liked and there was no one he could disturb. It was David's sanctuary and even his sister wouldn't cross its threshold without being invited.

When Doug finally came in about ten o'clock, Maggie was curled up in the den watching some inane program on television. Her mind wasn't on whatever was going on on the screen. She was just watching, letting herself unwind after her chaotic day and looking forward to tomorrow.

"How's the working woman?" Doug asked as he pecked her brow.

She patted his hand, pretending to be engrossed with the television. "A little tiring." She didn't want to show her excitement for fear he'd decide he didn't want her to go back.

He didn't press her. He seemed preoccupied with whatever was on his mind, business or Phyllis, Maggie didn't know which . . . and she didn't feel up to asking. They chatted for a moment or two, then Doug said he had to go over some figures and disappeared into his study.

Half an hour later he came out and kissed her on top of the head. "Coming up? I'm bushed."

She was still staring at the picture tube but not seeing it, feeling deliciously tired and pleased with her day, as well as with herself. "In a minute, Doug."

Doug walked slowly up the stairs, glad that Maggie wasn't coming with him. At last he'd done what he should have done a long time ago. Still, he felt a terrible loss, an emptiness was gnawing at him like those first days and weeks after he gave up cigarettes. He had a craving for Phyllis but he was glad he'd told her they were finished, that he would never see her again except for business.

He wanted to be alone to lick his wounds and pat himself on the back for his courage and strength. It hadn't been an easy choice, but it was the only one he felt he could make if he wanted to preserve his marriage. Now he had to figure some way of adjusting himself to live without the sexual excitement Phyllis gave him. He would never get that kind of excitement from Maggie, so he would just have to live without it. After all, hadn't he been sexually satisfied during all those years *before* Phyllis? So why couldn't he be again? He'd just have to steel himself against the temptation. Just like any bad habit, Phyllis could be broken and forgotten. The hard part would be seeing her almost every day at the office, always acting as a reminder.

"You mustn't give in again this time," he said to the empty room as he slipped out of his clothes. "Maggie is what is most important."

But at that very moment he would have given a million Maggies to have Phyllis walk through the door and relax him and satisfy him sexually without his having to move a muscle. If only he could teach Maggie to take the initiative once in a while. How did a husband go about changing a sex pattern he'd lived with most of his life, the only sex pattern his wife knew? It was impossible, so he might just as well put it out of his mind and forget about it forever.

Downstairs Maggie sat till very late, tired out but too happy to move as she thought about the people who'd occupied her day. It had been loads of fun to be with the jovial little knot of employees at the agency as well as at The Rail. The excitement was still with her and when she slipped in beside Doug she found she was still wide awake. For a moment she lay listening to Doug's even breathing, but after a while the exciting noise of New York came back to her. She felt herself a part of that sound, a sound which would again be a part of her tomorrow.

Chapter 10

As the days passed, Maggie found herself beginning to sort her impressions of the people with whom she'd been thrown in contact. She began taking a more deliberate interest in people; she was more inclined to examine and to criticize and not take anyone at their face value, as she had always done. She supposed this new critical look at people was due to the fact that she'd never worked closely with any group of people for hours on end, day after day.

Of the fifteen or so people who worked in the various sections of her office—full-time, part-time, male-female—she narrowed her preferences down to two, Andy and Louise. She was, of course, very friendly with Alice, but the employer/employee relationship was awkward for them both. At times she walked the tightrope between boss's friend and hired help and did it well. If she went off with Alice too often, the others kidded her about brown-nosing, and if she was too friendly with the employees Alice accused her of slumming.

But it all seemed to work nicely.

At home, things weren't much changed from that first day on the job. The kids were as independent as ever and Doug was always busy with one thing or another. Maggie was generally home on time so no one seemed to care whether she was working or not. All that initial hoop-dee-do about her getting a job was forgotten by them. The thing that surprised her most was that Doug never questioned her very much about her days at the office. But then she continued to make her job seem like a part-time thing, a temporary help for Alice.

Maggie sensed a subtle change in Doug, but she was sure it had nothing whatsoever to do with the fact that she was working during the day. He acted strangely, especially when they were in bed together. It was as if he wasn't sure whether or not he wanted her sexually. It was a kind of indifference on his part. He would lie on his back staring up at the ceiling, waiting for her to make the initial advance. Maggie wasn't particularly shy after so many years of marriage, but when she would coax him on top of her she had to keep teasing him into continued excitement. As a result she got the impression that he was bored with her. This bothered her a great deal but she couldn't bring herself to ask him about it for fear Phyllis Bracken's name would crop up.

On the other hand, perhaps she was imagining it all. Perhaps the excitement the office generated was making the old excitement with Doug seem tame. Sex had always been the highlight of her days. Maybe her work was replacing that excitement. Suddenly she could understand why Doug was often completely wrapped up in his job. The variety of the day seemed to dim her enjoyment of the night.

On Monday of her second week, Andy Carver did not show up for work. Alice was furious and so was Maggie, because his complete work load—and Mondays were always the busiest—fell on her and Louise.

At three o'clock Andy straggled in looking not the least concerned about his absence, his appearance, or the chaos he'd caused. He fell glumly into his chair and put his hands over his ears, drowning out everybody's complaints. When Louise put a stack of work orders in front of him, he shoved them onto the floor with an angry swipe of his arm and stormed into the men's room.

Louise and Maggie exchanged one of those women's looks that meant he'd best be left alone, that something more important than his job was eating him alive. By the time he came out of the men's room the work orders had been gathered up and Andy's desk was as uncluttered as it had been at the beginning of the morning.

Maggie let him sulk but when she ran across something she couldn't handle she went over to him, apologized for disturbing him and asked him to help her with the problem. Then she said, "Do you want to talk, Andy? Or are you like my husband and would rather be left alone?"

"I'm in a rotten mood, Maggie. Just ignore me. Here, give me those Wayland Industry orders. It'll take my mind off things."

She handed him the files. "If you'd rather not . . . maybe you should go back home."

"I didn't come from home," he said. He flipped open the tov file and started to scan the work order. "Have a drink with me later, okay, Mag?"

"Sure, okay."

Louise didn't join them at The Rail, she said she was supposed to meet someone and maybe she'd stop by with him later. Maggie and Andy settled themselves into a corner table and Maggie ordered the usual Perrier water while Andy gulped down a straight bourbon and called for another. "I'm going to get rotten drunk," he announced.

"To celebrate what?" Maggie chanced.

"Being stuck at Fifth Avenue Agency for the rest of my life it seems."

"And is that all that bad? You make a pretty good wage, don't you?"

"It isn't the money, darling. It's just not what I had in mind for myself. I'm a lot like you in that I took the job more or less on a temporary basis until. . . ."

"Until what?"

He took a deep swallow of his bourbon and made tiny circles of wet on the table top. "I'm a chorus boy, did you know that?"

Maggie nodded. "Alice said something about it. But I thought that was all in your past."

Andy's expression went wistful. "Once you get the theater in your blood you never get rid of it," he said.

There was something hollow in the sound of his voice, somewhat plastic and unreal, as if he were reciting lines in a play, and reciting them badly. His voice was dramatically exaggerated, like the expostulation of a Shakespearean actor. Even the pose was artificial and stiff. He held his head tilted back and upward, as though projecting to the topmost balcony of the theatre. "I'll always be an artist. It's my life."

Maggie was tempted to laugh but she could tell that he was being serious. She knew he felt he was being sincere but it was so fake, so artificial that she wondered why he couldn't see the artificiality for himself. But then who ever sees themselves as they are? One only sees the image one wants to see.

When she looked at Andy all she saw was the effeminate young man with whom she worked and whom she was growing fond of, an effeminate young man wearing a ridiculous mask that covered nothing. She so wanted him to be Andy Carver of The Fifth Avenue Agency and not Andy Carver, ex-chorus boy. She was tempted to amend the latter to "aging ex-chorus boy" but decided it would be too unkind, even though true. Andy Carver didn't deserve unkindness right now and he certainly didn't want truth. She supposed that for all his life he'd suffered enough of both of those—unkindness and truth—from too many others.

It was the terrible hurt in his eyes that made her want to try to lighten whatever disappointment was bearing him down. "If you believe the theater to be your life, Andy, then you should be working in the theater, not in an employment office."

"Employment offices pay salaries."

"But wouldn't you be happier scrubbing the floor of a stage or painting scenery or whatever they do rather than placing mundane people in mundane jobs all day long?"

His answer surprised her. "No. I don't scrub floors or paint scenery. I dance."

"But until you dance, you would be in the environment you love most."

He answered her with a long harangue, a tirade about the injustices of the world, employing all the usual cliches, the cop-outs, as Doug called them. Andy didn't really want to be a chorus boy, he wanted to be a star, he wanted to start at the top without any of the drudgery it took to get there. Oh, sure, he'd dance in the chorus but it had to be an On-Broadway chorus line of a hit show. "I've already paid my dues to those two-bit off-Broadway productions. I could be dancing in those right now, but I walked out on my last job of that kind. If you don't show your independence you're in the friggin' chorus forever."

"But being in the chorus at least gives you the chance of being recognized. They won't come looking for a headliner in The Fifth Avenue Agency."

Andy shook his head. "It's obvious that you know nothing about the theater."

Another cop-out, Maggie told herself. That was the answer everybody gave when they had no argument against reason and common sense.

"Maybe not about the theatre, but I certainly know that if I wanted to be an actress I'd live, eat, and breathe acting, not treat it as some happenstance that I pay attention to when a chance looks promising, when it might not take much work to get a brass ring."

Andy scowled at her and drained his glass. He banged it on the table and called for another. "I suppose you think I don't work at my dancing."

"I'm sure you do, honey, but I'm talking about complete dedication. From all I understand, that's what it takes to make a success; complete and total commitment to one's art, not a part-time sort of thing." She found herself talking to him as she would have talked to Julie or David, but then there was something immature about Andy, as though he were hiding from reality, living his own private dream in his own private world.

Andy found Maggie was annoying him. She sounded so much like his father, always lecturing, always the voice of experience, even experienced in fields he knew nothing about. Why did older people always have to lecture?

He was surprised and disappointed that Maggie was acting the same way. What in hell did she know about professional dancing? How dare she sit there and give advice about something as alien to her as her stupid, dull life was to him?

When his drink was set before him he took a gulp, trying not to listen to the sensible advice Maggie was mouthing off. He cut her off angrily with, "Oh, what in hell do you know about theater and theater people?" He didn't mean to be insulting but he heard her gasp and sit back, staring at him.

Just then Louise and a young man pushed their way toward the table. "Oh, oh," Louise said as she heard Andy snap at Maggie. To Maggie she said, "I didn't think you'd see this side of our beloved Andrew quite so soon. He must have flunked another one of those auditions he keeps going out on." She put her hand on Andy's shoulder. He knocked it off. "Don't mind Nijinsky here, Maggie. Andy always gets impossible when these moods hit him. And he always piles booze on top of disappointment, neither of which he can handle very well."

"Shut the fuck up, Lousey," Andy growled.

The young man with Louise said, "Hey, old buddy, that isn't any way to talk in front of pretty ladies."

"You can go fuck yourself too, Mike." Andy picked up his glass and drank almost all of it. He sat trying to focus on the blur in front of his eyes when suddenly he felt his stomach lurch. He got unsteadily to his feet. "I think I'm going to be sick," he managed as he started to push himself away from the table. The young man named Mike grabbed him as he started to totter and rushed him into the men's room.

Louise chuckled and sat down in the chair Andy had vacated. "Poor Andy. He can sure be one helluva mess when he sets his mind to it. I don't understand why he persists on thinking himself nineteen and a boy. A lot of the gays I know are like that; it's like they're afraid to grow up and become men. Gay women are just the opposite; they think they're thirty-five when they start into puberty."

Maggie sat trying to pull herself together after the shock of Andy's temper. Initially she decided she didn't really like Andy Carver at all, but as the impact started to wear off she tried to understand him. "I feel so foolish having tried to advise him. I was only trying to help."

"Don't sweat it, Maggie. I've seen Andy go through this a dozen or more times. Tomorrow he won't remember any of it, not even flunking the audition. He's queer in more ways than one," she said. "He refuses to remember anything unpleasant. Tomorrow will be like today never happened. If you ask him about it he won't know what you're talking about. That's the way he's always been since I've known him and—I've know him ever since I was a size seven." She laughed and added, "Which is more years than I care to remember."

"I just can't get over the way he seemed to change right before my eyes."

"Andy likes to think of himself as a temperamental artist, so he acts like one. Deep down is a latent ballerina fighting to get out. Fags," she said derisively, "Who can figure them? I have enough trouble with the straight guys." She brightened. "Speaking of which, how do you like the hunk I brought with me. Ain't he a piece though?"

"I didn't pay much attention, but he seemed nice."

"His name's Mike Ballantine. I was waiting for my date, who didn't show—per usual—when Mike happens along and invites me for a drink. He used to work for Fifth Avenue for a short while. He's from over in your neck of the woods."

"Saddlebrook?"

Louise shrugged. "Somewhere on the other side of Fort Lee. Hackensack, I think."

Mike Ballantine came back to the table. Andy wasn't with him. To Louise he said, "I left him in the stall throwing up. I'll see that he gets home when he's emptied out his stomach." He smiled at Maggie and said, "We haven't met. My name's Mike Ballantine."

He had shaggy black hair, startling blue eyes, and hard tanned skin, the result of too many hours at the beach. In a number of years his face would take on that rugged, weathered look of a dedicated outdoorsman. He was unmistakably good-looking, but it wasn't the prettiness of someone out of the pages of a magazine. Mike Ballantine looked more like a professional athlete than a model.

"Maggie Hampton," she said, putting her hand in his. She looked into his electric blue eyes and felt herself hypnotized.

Mike threw one leg over the back of the chair and lowered himself into the seat next to Maggie. She found his masculinity too powerful to ignore. He said, "Do you work at the agency with Andy and Louise?"

Maggie nodded and told him she'd started last week. As they chatted idly about work, Maggie couldn't help but feel herself staring at him. He was almost beautiful, but in a very masculine way.

Louise said to Mike, "This is the one I told you had the run-in with Rita."

"Poor thing," Mike said, grinning. "Now there's one bitchy lady. She's one of the reasons I'm glad I'm not working at Fifth Avenue anymore."

Louise sipped the drink she'd ordered. "Like everyone else, old Rita has had her share of problems. Maybe if we had her troubles we'd all be bitches too."

Maggie said, "Yes, Alice mentioned something about Rita having had a hard time of it. What's her story?"

"She had a tragedy a couple of years back," Louise said. "Her husband was burned alive when their house caught fire. From what I heard, Rita was suspected of having set the fire, but it was never proved."

"How dreadful."

Mike said, "Don't let your heart bleed for that one, Maggie. Knowing Rita, she'd drown you in your own blood." He shook his head. "I've never met so cold and vicious a woman. I wouldn't put it past her to burn up her old man."

"Mike," Louise admonished. "You shouldn't say such things!"

"Well, I wouldn't." He turned to Maggie and said, "Take my advice and stay clear of Rita Gant. She spells trouble in solid caps."

"Maybe that's why she's so cold and miserable, because nobody befriends her," Maggie said.

"Everybody's tried," Louise said. "Rita just doesn't want friends, at least not our kind. Our skin is too light to suit her." She looked at Mike and added, "A couple more weekends in the sun and you might pass."

Before Mike could reply, Andy staggered back. He was white-faced with tinges of green around the eyes and in the hollows of his cheeks. It was easy to see he felt as bad as he looked.

"Here," Mike said, pulling up another chair. "Sit down before you fall down."

Andy tumbled into it and put his head down on the table. "I want to go home."

Mike said, "Let me finish my drink and I'll take you."

Louise got up. "If you intend to play nursemaid to the Queen for the Day, I'm going to see what happened to my date." She waved to Maggie. "See you in the grist mill tomorrow, Mag."

Maggie started to collect herself. "I ought to be going too," she said. She glanced at her watch. "Oh damn, I just missed a bus."

Mike asked her where she lived.

"Jersey. Saddlebrook Estates."

He frowned slightly, which was flattering to his looks. "What did you say your last name is?"

"Hampton."

"You wouldn't by any chance know David Hampton?"

"I have a son by that name."

"Well, it couldn't be the David I know. He's almost eighteen."

"That's David." She blushed under his flattery.

He stared at her. "You have an eighteen-year-old son?"

"He's only seventeen, really." She found she couldn't look at him. "However, if David were here he'd be quick to correct me by saying 'seventeen and a half.'" She found the courage to look at him. "How do you know David?"

"Actually I know him only casually. He's a good buddy of my kid brother's."

"Ballantine," Maggie said, recalling his name. "Of course, Timmy Ballantine. He and David are classmates and they're on the basketball team."

"I saw a lot of David when I was living at home."

"Then I take it you don't live in New Jersey now."

"No. I have my own place on 24th and Third."

Andy was forgotten as they started their questions and answers, each finding himself becoming more and more comfortable with their conversation.

Suddenly Maggie glanced at Andy and laughed. "Good heavens. I think he's fallen asleep."

"Passed out, you mean," Mike said, shaking Andy's shoulder. He was dead to the world. "I'd better get him home."

"Do you know where he lives?"

"Yep, about three floors below me." He started to struggle with Andy's uncooperative weight.

"Here, let me help," Maggie offered.

She never once thought of how late it was getting as she helped Mike manage Andy. It seemed to her more important to get Andy home rather than get herself home. Doug would understand. This was a kind of emergency.

131

Mike's company was extremely comfortable, his conversation easy and interesting, and there was something "her age" about him although it was easy to see he was no more than twenty-three or twenty-four years old. He didn't speak as a man his age would. He had too much maturity, too much sophistication for one so young. She reminded him so much of the young men one found in Victorian novels, all chivalry and charm and steeped in polish and good manners, yet with a rough undertow of manly crudity that left no doubt in any feminine mind that this was a man who scoffed at danger, a man capable of the most strenuous tasks, a man capable of captivating any woman with his sexual prowess.

She felt herself slightly unnerved by these and other assorted flattering thoughts that passed through her head, as she waited in the living room while Mike undressed Andy and put him to bed.

She thought of Jeff Cochran; compared to Mike Ballantine, Jeff was a child. Her interest in Mike made her forget her manners and when he came out of the bedroom she asked, "How old are you, Mike?"

He laughed and said, "If I were a woman I'd pretend to be indignant." He fanned out his hands, showing himself, "But as you can see I definitely am not a woman. I'm twenty-three. Why?"

"No reason. I was just thinking about someone I met recently in Arizona." She didn't want to think of Jeff. He was spoiling her delicious mood. "Are you and Timmy the only two in your family?" The question brought her back where she belonged and left Jeff Cochran in Arizona.

"The only two, which according to my father is two too many. He believes me to be a good-for-nothing bum and Timmy is girl-crazy."

Without thinking she said, "Better girl-crazy than like Andy." She reddened. "Oh dear, that wasn't very kind of me."

"Andy would be the first to understand. He wears his homosexuality like a cop wears a badge. Believe it or not there are thousands and thousands of men and women like Andy who are downright proud they're gay. Surely you've read the papers and see how they're coming out of the woodwork."

Maggie didn't like the topic; homosexuality was out of place in a conversation with Mike Ballantine. "I seldom read anything in the papers except the comics and the fashion pages. Current events depress me."

"A woman after my own heart," he said. "Two ostriches with our heads in the sand." After a beat he said, "Come on, I'll buy you a cocktail and some dinner."

Maggie's hand flew to her throat. "Dinner! Oh dear, I should have been home hours ago. Doug—my husband—will be worried sick."

Mike nodded toward the phone. "Call him and tell him you'll take a later bus, that you're eating in town."

"I appreciate the invitation, Mike, but I really must get home." She found the words difficult. She wanted to stay. Just looking at Mike was a pleasure.

"Come on, Maggie. I hate eating alone. At least call your husband and see what he says. We'll leave it up to him. If he's upset, tell him you're on your way. If not, we'll go down to the Village to a little place I know." With a sly expression he said, "Very Bohemian."

Doug wasn't home. Julie said she was just going over to her girlfriend's and David was at some school meeting. "Dad called and said not to hold dinner, so don't hurry home on our accounts, mother."

Maggie found that Mike Ballantine had mastered the difficult feat of talking just enough to suggest conversation without tempting monologue. She was captivated. Although he said little that was new or clever, his personality in conversation had a curious power. He had an intoxicating voice and an irresistible way of turning a phrase.

"You should write," Maggie commented after Mike finished a particularly amusing little story about an elderly woman who thought her female cabbie was a man.

"I should do a lot of things, according to my father." He pushed aside his plate. "Unfortunately I have, and so far nothing particularly suits me."

Jeff Cochran popped back into her head and her heart sank. Surely Mike wasn't another one of those? The reminder cautioned her against getting too comfortable with Mike.

"As I sometimes ask my two children . . ." she glanced

at him to make sure he got the reminder that she was a married woman with a family, "pretend your fairy godmother comes down and grants you guaranteed success in any career you want. What would it be?"

Mike thought for a moment. "Gee, I don't know. I really don't think there's anything I want to do yet. Maybe play professional baseball or be an Olympic athlete, but as for a career, that's a tough one. I'm not ready to settle into anything."

"Not even work *toward* settling into something?"

"No."

As he talked about himself she realized that he was just another young man without any purpose, without any aim in life. He was beginning to look more and more like Jeff every minute. She suddenly wanted to hurt him by reminding him that he wasn't getting any younger.

But then he said something that turned everything around for her. "Hell, I know I'm not a teenager any longer and I'm certainly no cover boy. One thing I can't stand is a guy who depends on his looks and his sex appeal to get ahead. This place is crawling with them. I'm not like that at all. I've worked at a lot of different jobs . . . hard jobs. I make my own way, despite what my father thinks. I'm really not a drifter. I'm only searching for the right niche, and when I find it I'll know it and then I'll settle in."

Maggie smiled broadly. Mike wasn't anything like Jeff Cochran, whom she shoved into the past, hopefully once and for all. It seemed right somehow that Mike should be without a definite purpose, a precise goal which, upon reaching it, would mean his end. She felt he should be allowed to remain the free spirit he was, unencumbered, unattached to the rest of the mortals. There was something almost godlike about him; he had an unusual aura that commanded respect, needed separate space, and demanded a free rein. He wasn't the type who'd even consider pouring himself into tight shorts and a T-shirt and demean himself by fawning over sagging women who sweated their lives away in one exclusive health spa after another. Mike had too much character, too much class for that sordid type thing.

"You should travel," she suggested.

"I've done a little, but I get tired of living out of suitcases and I'm not the type who could live out of a backpack. I like my creature comforts too much. I have a couple of buddies who grew beards and long hair, wear scruffy clothes and bum around Europe in sandals and a beat up old VW with a stash of grass." He shook his head sadly. "That's not for me. I gotta change my clothes several times a day, scrub my teeth as often as possible, bathe before crawling in and out of bed. . . ." He winked. "Regardless of how many times a day and whether alone or otherwise."

Maggie laughed. She hated to say what she did. "Speaking of crawling into bed, I've got to be heading for the other side of the river."

"So early?"

She glanced at her watch. "Early for you, perhaps, but we happily married women have our obligations."

"Are you happily married?" He looked quite serious.

"Very." She found her voice shaky and her eyes drifted away from his.

"That's too bad." Then he laughed. "Come on, I'll ride with you up to Port Authority."

Just before Maggie boarded her bus they shook hands and said goodbye, but as she took her seat she found her heart thumping louder and louder and hoped it would not be a real goodbye. She wanted to see Mike Ballantine again, and deep down inside she knew that she would. She didn't know where or when, but it seemed as definite as her getting out of bed tomorrow morning.

Chapter 11

"God only knows where in hell she is," Doug fumed as he paced back and forth across the living room. He kept slapping his hands on his thighs and cursing the night, the empty house, his son—who was God only knows where—and Maggie, out there someplace, maybe run over by a car, maybe raped and lying in an alley. At least Julie had had the sense to call and tell him she was at her girlfriend's.

He needed another drink to calm himself, he decided as he went into the den. He didn't feel like wrestling with the ice-cube trays in the refrigerator so he drank the scotch neat. It was warm and burned his mouth and throat but he didn't care. He didn't give a damn about anything but the fact that he was alone and there was no one he could take his anger out on.

"Where in hell is everyone?" he shouted to the empty house. As if in answer, the front door opened and slammed shut. "Maggie!"

"No, it's me, Dad." David stood on the threshold. "What's up? Mom not home yet?"

"Where have you been?"

David saw his father's furious expression and shrugged innocently. "We had a meeting of the Graduating Committee. What's the big deal?"

"The big deal is, young man, that you should tell somebody about your Graduating Committee meetings and all the rest of the damned rot that occupies your time. This is your home, where people are concerned about you."

David stared at him. "For cripe's sake, Dad, why are

you making a federal case out of my being a little late getting home?"

Doug waved his hand in disgust. "Go to your room. I don't want to hear another word out of you tonight."

"Jeez!" David breathed. "Can a guy at least get a sandwich or something or would you blow your stack about my eating too?"

"Go!" Doug shouted.

David disappeared.

The minute he was alone again he started to chastise himself. Why had he blown up at David? The answer was right there: Because he was the first one to come in. No matter who had come through that front door they would have felt the lash of his anger.

He sipped his scotch and tried to calm down. Why in hell was he angry at anybody when all the time it was himself he was pissed off about? After all his fine intentions, why had he gone to bed with Phyllis again? Why was he so damned weak when everyone else was so strong? He'd never before been a weak man, but something was happening to him lately which he couldn't understand. He refused to listen when his older friends joked about male menopause. He was too young for that, and besides, that was all a crock of shit. Men didn't go through menopause.

But why in hell was he turning into some kind of perverted lecher? Why couldn't he leave Phyllis alone? She wasn't all that gorgeous or even young. Maggie had her beat on all counts, but damn it all to hell, he couldn't say no wherever that damned she-devil licked her lips and offered to rub him down.

"At last," he said as he caught sight of Maggie starting up the walk.

She had her key in the latch when Doug yanked it open and demanded to know where in hell she'd been. "It's after eleven o'clock, for God's sake!"

Taken slightly aback she said, "Well, I had dinner and then the buses were running only every forty-five minutes and I'd just missed one."

"Good God, Maggie, you know it isn't safe for a mature woman to be wandering around New York in the middle of the night."

The "mature woman" stung her. "Really, Doug, it is hardly the middle of the night and I wasn't wandering around New York. I went to dinner and came home. What in heaven's name are you all steamed up about?"

He ignored her question. "I suppose you had dinner with Alice and a couple of her business associates." The way he sneered "business associates" he implied unmistakably two men.

"As a matter of fact, no. Andy Carver. . . . You remember my mentioning Andy?"

"Yeah, the fag."

She got annoyed. "Honestly, Doug, what is wrong with you? What are you all wrought up about? Andy Carver is a very nice young man." And he *was* nice, she thought. She'd only known him a short time and here she was defending a homosexual against Doug's attack. But damn it, the way she felt right now she preferred Andy's company to her husband's, even if Andy had lashed out at her in the bar.

He sneered. "A *homosexual* young man, kindly clarify."

"You are being particularly obnoxious. What happened? You certainly can't be all this upset just because I'm a little late getting home?"

His anger at himself refused to leave him. "Why would you want to have dinner with some fairy?"

Maggie straightened her spine. "If you persist upon being crass and ungracious toward someone you've never met, I will not stand here and listen to you." She started up the stairs to their room.

Doug followed close behind. "Ever since you came back from Arizona and started going into New York every day, you're an entirely different person. Good Christ, you never would permit yourself to look at a queer before, and now you're all palsy-walsy with one."

"Andy got sick. Someone had to look after him."

"What do you mean *got* sick? He is sick."

She decided that whatever it was that was bothering him, it wasn't going to surface. He was upset with himself about something, but knowing him so well, he never talked things out once he started taking his anger out on her. In cases like this, Maggie's usual course was to ignore him. He'd try his damnedest to drag out her temper and then blame the whole mess on her. Not this time, she told herself as she started to slip out of her dress. The echo of Mike Ballantine's voice seemed to mollify her agitation.

"So little Andy got sick," Doug persisted. "What did you do, tuck him in?"

If he insisted upon being spiteful, then she could give as good as she got. "No," she said flatly, "Mike Ballantine did that."

That shut him up for a second or two. She could almost feel his mind clicking away a mile a minute. "Who in hell is Mike Ballantine?"

"The man I had dinner with," Maggie said boldly.

"Oh." He paused. "I suppose one of Andy What's-his-name's fag friends."

"Really, Doug, you're are being impossible. What's eating you?" Her plan to ignore his ill-humor fell apart. She sat down at her dressing table and began removing her makeup.

"Hell, I don't know, Maggie," Doug said in a quieter voice. "I don't like the idea of coming home to an empty house."

"And I don't like being in one all day and sometimes all evening, so I can commiserate with you."

Doug paced, screwing up his nerve, then said in a firm voice, "I don't want you working any more. I want you to quit that damned agency."

Maggie swirled around. "No. And I will not hear another word on the subject."

Doug shook his finger at her. "I'm not asking you, Maggie, I'm telling you. You are not going back to that office tomorrow. You're turning into another Alice, just as I warned you you would."

"And you're being ridiculous."

He was being ridiculous and he knew it, but damn it anyway, if he'd known Maggie was home waiting for him it would have been easier to not give in to Phyllis. That excuse hadn't worked in the past, he reminded himself, but he refused to think about the past. His misery was now and now was all that mattered to him.

He said, "Ridiculous or not, it's that damned job or me. Make your choice."

Maggie felt equally defiant. She knew she was in the

right and he was acting like a spoiled little brat who was threatening to hold his breath if he didn't get his way. Well, she had no intention of giving in to him. She knew exactly what he'd do, grab a blanket and a pillow and storm off to the couch in the study.

That's exactly what he did and she let him go.

She lay alone feeling her determination grow weaker and weaker. If she gave in to Doug now she'd be finished forever. The thought kept her steadfast. She heard Julie come in, and although it was long past her curfew Maggie didn't feel like a confrontation with her. It surprised her when she didn't hear Doug yelling at Julie, but then Julie was his favorite; he hardly ever found much fault with her.

She heard Julie go to her room, then she heard the door to Doug's study bang open and the liquor bottles on the bar in the den rattled louder than necessary. He was pouting and he'd have a hangover in the morning, but maybe that was what he needed.

She got up, took a valium and went back to bed. Everything would be all right in a day or two.

Strangely enough, it wasn't Doug she thought about as she drifted off to sleep, it was Mike Ballantine. But a metamorphosis set in and Mike's face turned to that of Jeff Cochran. Maggie felt a cold hand grip her heart. She tried to conjure up her husband's face but it refused to come. With an uneasiness settling throughout her body she rolled over on her side, cradled her pillow, and waited anxiously for sleep. It took a while for the valium to work and between her tossing and turning she was tempted to go down and coax Doug back to bed.

She wanted sex.

But she knew she wasn't going to have Doug tonight so she forced herself to think of the work she had waiting for her at the office. She had several good applicants coming in, and lunch with the personnel manager of a chain of hotels. Alice promised to take her to her meeting with the ERA people at three o'clock.

Andy and Louise were such great fun to work with, always laughing at something or someone, always so full of interesting stories and hilarious happenings. Her life was so different from what it had been so short a time ago.

She knew she was a different woman, and perhaps Doug had a right to be annoyed with her. Perhaps she should go down stairs and try to make up with him.

However, while she was deliberating, she fell asleep.

Doug stayed in his snit for the better part of the week and Mike Ballantine seemed to disappear back to wherever he came from. Once when Timmy Ballantine came in with David, Maggie had asked about Mike but Timmy had shrugged and said they never hear from Mike, that their father didn't exactly welcome him at home.

Although Doug and Maggie slept together, Doug ignored Maggie's sexual overtures, and Maggie's pride would not permit her to pressure him.

By Saturday night she was becoming edgy for the need of sexual release. "Aren't you ever going to be my husband?" she asked when he slipped between the sheets. The smell of his naked body made her go hot all over.

Doug stretched out on his back and put his hands behind his head. "If you want me, I'm right here," he said stubbornly.

Maggie curled up next to him, slipping her leg over his. She began toying with the hairs on his chest. "Does my having a job really upset you so much, Doug?"

"I don't care one way or the other."

She rested her cheek on his bare shoulder then moved downward slightly and started to kiss his naked skin. She felt his hand at the back of her head, urging her toward his nipples. At the same time, she felt him hardening beneath the pressure of her leg between his. She kissed the nipple and played with it with the tip of her tongue, surprised to find it hardening and pouting much the way her own did when she was sexually stimulated.

She was content to arouse him like this, but suddenly the pressure at the back of her head increased. Doug was forcing her mouth lower, down toward his navel, down toward his crotch. The pressure of his hand grew more demanding.

Maggie forced herself away from his hand. Her eyes widened as she realized what he had wanted her to do. "Good God," she groaned. "What whore taught you to like that?"

Doug threw aside the covers and jumped out of bed.

He jammed himself into a robe and stormed off into the bathroom. Minutes later she heard him rummaging around for a blanket and pillow and going off downstairs.

They didn't speak unless when absolutely necessary all day Sunday and by Monday morning Maggie was anxiously looking forward to going to the office.

With the passing of each day, the silence between her and Doug lengthened while the hectic pace of the office grew. Andy was back to being his old flighty self and Louise always had something to eat either in her mouth or in her hand and was constantly promising to start her diet the next day. Alice had started introducing Maggie to the various employer contacts and this necessitated some social obligations such as dinner and cocktails, so Maggie was often very late getting home. Doug said little, but the kids—David or Julie, depending on which was being inconvenienced the most—were always griping. Maggie shrugged off their selfishness and replaced it with a selfishness of her own. She felt entitled. She was getting a magnificent taste of independence and loved every minute of it. She knew the rift between her and Doug was widening but she was too pleased with her days to see the danger brewing in her nights.

School was finally out and David was being particularly peevish because Doug had refused permission for him to bum his way to California with Timmy Ballantine (the name always gave Maggie a start) and a few other of his grubby friends, as Doug called them.

The change in her husband was astonishing. Doug, in the short span of weeks, was cold and indifferent to all his family, including his favorite, Julie. Where once he deprived Julie of nothing, he now resented any show of individuality or independence, accusing her of being as rebellious as her mother.

Maggie bore Doug's disdain and her children's blame with a jutting chin and a stiff determination. Doug's behavior was her fault—according to David and Julie—and the more they reproached her, the more she was determined to wring every drop of happiness out of her job at the agency and all her new friends.

She hadn't seen anything of Mike Ballantine; neither had Louise or Andy. But why should she expect to, she asked herself. Hadn't she made it perfectly clear to him that she was a happily married woman?

As much as Maggie tried to befriend Rita Gant, she failed miserably. Yet Maggie, compassionate to any unhappy creature, be it human or otherwise, was convinced that the others were wrong by snubbing Rita. The woman simply needed understanding, a warm smile, a few polite words. Maggie persisted with the tenacity of a bulldog, and with each failure she felt more secure that her next try would be a successful one.

"Don't forget my Fourth of July party next Saturday," Andy said as Maggie finished screening her last applicant of the day. "Are you going to bring Doug, or don't you trust me enough yet?"

Andy's annual Fourth of July blast had been the talk of the office for several weeks. Every year, it seemed, he gathered all his friends together someplace out of doors, where he'd provide the food and everyone would bring whatever they wanted to drink. Each year he held the party at a different place—in the park, at the Jersey shore, at Jones' beach—and this year Andy's latest lover was a man with a house on Fire Island. Andy had the use of the place; the guy was in Europe on business. The entire office, excluding Rita Gant, was looking forward to the bash, which was to last the whole holiday weekend.

Maggie said, "I asked him but he may have to work."

"On a weekend, and a holiday to boot? Ridiculous. You tell that hunk that I personally will come to Saddlebrook and make a scandalous scene on your front lawn if he doesn't come."

It took a lot of persuading, and when Maggie repeated Andy's threat Doug actually went white believing it. The mere thought of a group of queers camping it up on his front lawn scared him to death, and having heard the stories of how zany the guy was, Doug wouldn't put it past him to carry out the threat.

So Doug agreed to go with Maggie to Fire Island, but only for the day. The idea of going to a party hosted by a queer was bad enough, but having it on Fire Island made it worse. He knew he'd have a rotten time, but better go to the queers rather than have the queers come to him.

The party was all Doug feared it would be. To him,

even the straight people acted queer. Alice and some of the other women wore ridiculous bathing suits that left very little covered and Doug absolutely refused to look at any of the men, some of whom wore less than the women. There was a pool at the rear of the huge, weather-beaten house—just this side of the ocean—but Doug refused to go near it, for fear he'd find the partyers wearing nothing at all.

"This is nothing but a goddamn orgy," he complained, herding Maggie away from a particularly masculine woman who was trying to occupy all of Maggie's time. "Let's get the hell out of here."

"It isn't all that terrible, Doug. Relax. Most of these people are perfectly ordinary."

"Ordinary? I heard someone say they were swimming naked in the pool."

Maggie shrugged. "So steer clear of the pool if that bothers you."

"For Christ's sake, the next thing I know they'll be screwing in the middle of the room and you'll be wanting to join them."

She didn't think the slur deserved an answer. She turned and went over to talk to Louise and her new boyfriend. Maggie had to admit, however, that the party was just a bit more raucous than she'd expected; but she'd be damned if she'd let Doug know that. Although the people she met and talked to seemed perfectly nice and amusing, the drunker Andy got the louder and freer everyone else seemed to get. By the time the sun started to go down things really were a little out of hand.

Much as she didn't want to admit to Doug that they'd made a mistake by staying too long, she swallowed her pride and went looking for him. She found him in the kitchen pretending to be polite to a bunch of guys who were talking football.

Maggie glanced at her watch and said, "Doug, I have a feeling we've missed the boat and the next one doesn't leave for another hour. I'm afraid we'll have to make the best of it, but it is getting a little out of hand in there."

She could see the terrible distaste, the hatred in his eyes, and for the first time in her entire life she felt separate from him.

At that moment he did hate her for having brought him here. For God's sake, didn't she see that these people were ten, twenty years younger than they? Okay, so she looked young and lovely in her new outfit and with her perfect figure, but surely she wasn't deluding herself into forgetting how old she truly was and that she was a married woman with morals.

He took her arm and started to lead her through the house toward the front door. The party had definitely gone past the risqué point. In Doug's eyes it was depraved debauchery with naked men and women cavorting around, all too drunk to know exactly what they were doing. And as he watched Maggie's eyes move over the crowd of people he imagined that she was approving all this. She was lost to everything that was once real in their life. The newness of her life had obviously taught her to hate all that was sensible and reasonable. He could almost see the battle that was raging inside her. She wanted so desperately to be a part of this young, unethical crowd but another force was saying, "No, you can never belong here. You are from a different time, a different set of values and ethics."

He opened the front door and pulled her after him. But he caught a glimpse of her looking back at all the carefree people, the wanton lust that glimmered in their eyes, like Lot's wife turning to catch her last glimpse of Sodom and Gomorrah.

"Come on, Maggie. We'll wait for the next boat at the hotel."

On the front porch they bumped into Louise who was shooing a cluster of half-naked boys into the house, the oldest of which Maggie guessed to be nineteen or twenty at the most. "Look what I found strolling around the beach. Poor babies were looking for something to do." Louise was obviously drunk. "I told them that I had enough for everyone."

Doug pulled her past the group and as they started along the boardwalk Maggie spied Mike Ballantine coming toward them.

"Hello," he said as he removed the wide-brimmed hat that shaded his face. "I was wondering if you had the guts to come to this shindig."

"Well, hello," Maggie beamed. She found herself feeling self-conscious as she stared up into his handsome young face. "Oh, Mike, I'd like you to meet my husband. Doug, Mike Ballantine. He's Timmy's brother. You know, David's little friend."

Mike shook Doug's hand and said, "Don't let Tim hear you call him 'little friend.' He'd skin you alive."

Doug said, "Maggie can't get used to the fact that the kids are practically adults." He meant it as a dig and saw that he hit the mark he'd aimed at.

Maggie's expression went sour. "We were just splitting." Doug grimaced.

"There's no place to go that isn't more crowded than right here. The hotel is a madhouse, the beach is turning into an orgy and the next boat to the mainland isn't for an hour. There's a little guest house toward the back; it'll provide us with an empty corner where we can have a drink and talk. I've been out in the sun all day and I'm beginning to feel like a potato chip."

Doug didn't like the guy, and he liked him less and less as the hour grew later and still they talked—but then what husband likes any guy who comes on strong with one's wife, and this guy was really turning on the charm. Doug found him superficial and phony, but obviously Maggie was intrigued, judging by the way she seemed to hang on his every word, laughing at everything he meant to be amusing. Of course Doug had to admit that he had several redeeming qualities that any woman would find attractive: he was young and good-looking. Personally, Doug distrusted good-looking men.

When Doug finally managed to get Maggie to leave for the boat he said, "Is that Mike a fag too?"

She had obviously been wallowing in her lovely, lingering thoughts of Mike because her face grew dark and her eyes narrowed in anger. "Damn you, Doug, do you have to throw muck on everybody who doesn't fall all over you?"

"You sure star-gazed enough at him."

"If he's queer, as you suspect, then why would you give a damn?" she spat.

They didn't speak to each other until they got to the mainland and started the drive back to Jersey. Doug was jealous of the young guy's attention to Maggie and he was mad at Maggie for having acted like a stupid teenager, completely taken up with thoughts of herself and be hanged with everyone else, including him. Okay, Doug told himself, so she looked twenty years younger than he did: she was still pushing forty and she was still his wife.

He glanced at her sitting sulking in the corner of the front seat. She was so beautiful, more beautiful than he ever remembered. Watching her mingling so freely with all those people at the party was like watching a stranger. She was the same Maggie, of course, but there was a change in her that wasn't merely physical. She was acting as young as she looked.

Doug let his shoulders slump. He felt very old. Maggie was making him feel old, which was something Phyllis Bracken never did. Phyllis never tried to hide the fact that she was aging.

He felt his hands tighten on the steering wheel as the car picked up speed. As they moved faster he saw Maggie glance anxiously at him out of the corner of her eye but she didn't say anything.

He'd had enough of her friends and her young admirers and her new freedom. If that's what made her so happy then she could have all of it. He'd have what he wanted.

David and Julie had gone to a fireworks display and rock concert. They were always out somewhere, Maggie thought as they let themselves into the empty house. Several weeks ago the thought would have upset her; now she didn't seem to mind. It was right that youth should spend their time without cares and worries and responsibilities; there would be time enough for all that later on. Let them enjoy themselves while they can, she told herself as she went up to her room and started to change out of her sundress. Doug had gone into the den without a word, and she'd heard him click on the television.

The television, she thought despairingly. All those people at Andy's friend's house and here she sat with nothing to look forward to except another boring evening of television with a husband who was pouting because Mike had flattered her. How she wished she was back where they were having fun, laughing and talking and making the time pass so quickly, so happily.

She hated being where she was. She looked around at the room she'd decorated, the room she loved. It was smaller than she remembered, and seemed to be getting smaller every minute.

She didn't want to be alone, yet she didn't want to be with Doug. This latter thought frightened her. What was happening? Perhaps Doug was right, perhaps she should give up her job; she was becoming a stranger both to Doug and to herself.

My God, she was a middle-aged woman passing for a youngster! She knew it was wrong, but the thought pleased her.

Chapter 12

Mike Ballantine felt the cold night air chill his skin but he didn't want to go in to that mass of people trying so hard to enjoy themselves. He sat on the veranda listening to their laughter and gaiety and wondered where Maggie was at that exact moment, resenting the obvious fact that she was with her husband.

He'd never felt like this about any of the women he'd been with, and for the first time in his life he actually ached with the need to be with Maggie Hampton. He yearned for her. He thought of taking her in his arms, kissing her full luscious mouth. He wanted desperately to slide his hands down over her smooth, silken cheeks, press her hard against his chest, feel the softness of her body against his own.

All his life he had thought of falling in love with a woman . . . not a girl but a woman. Girls had never held much attraction for him; they were silly, empty things that always needed to be taught and encouraged. Their giddiness annoyed him.

Maggie Hampton was everything he'd ever wanted, ever hoped to find. That first evening when he saw her in that crowded, smoky bar, he knew he loved her.

Why did she have to be married? In his dreams, the woman he eventually fell in love with and married was divorced, childless, moneyed, sophisticated, and terrifically experienced in bed. He had always supposed that being in love meant being consumed by a kind of rapture that filled him with ecstatic joy; but this love for Maggie made him miserable. It was a hungering, painful ache such as he'd never known before.

He sat there alone, trying to pinpoint the exact moment when he'd first known for certain that he loved her. He supposed it was when he left her at the bus terminal; he had felt an emptiness consume him and even after picking up that girl on 45th Street the sex hadn't come close to satisfying his emptiness.

He hadn't wanted to come to Andy's party, but Louise had mentioned that Maggie was planning on being here. He had to see her again. Yet he hadn't had the nerve to come to her office for fear one look into his eyes would expose his love and she'd run away from the temptation.

"What are you brooding about, handsome?" Louise asked as she carried her drink out onto the darkened porch.

Mike sighed. "I think I'm in love for the first time in my life," he said, rubbing his hands together as the coldness nipped at him.

"Maggie, right?" She lay back on a chaise.

Ever since he'd met Louise he'd found her easy to talk to. They were close to the same age and right from the start they'd hit it off together. There was no sexual attraction on either of their parts, especially not on his, and he found Louise always sympathetic to whatever bothered him. Louise was a terrific listener, wise for her age, and there was something about her bulk that made her motherly and protective.

Mike nodded. "Yeah. Now ain't that one hell of a mess. Me in love with a happily married woman."

"Who says she's *happily* married?" She sipped her drink. "Something tells me her marriage isn't all that great."

Mike's face lit up with encouragement. "What do you mean?"

"I can't put a finger on it," she said, sitting forward, "But every time I'm with Maggie she seems like she never wants to go home. She's always still plugging away like a fire engine when five o'clock rolls around. Everybody else has their desks cleaned up, their files put away, everything closed and waiting to get the hell out of the office. Not Maggie. She'd work all night if someone didn't tell her to quit."

"But you told me she wasn't a regular with you, Andy, and the bunch who go to The Rail for drinks."

Louise shrugged. "She doesn't drink. She's watching her figure—and who wouldn't with a figure like hers?—but I can tell she wants to go with us instead of on that bus bound for Jersey." She tapped the side of her head. "Woman's intuition, Michael."

Mike continued to warm his hands by rubbing them together. "I can't stop thinking about her. She's everything I've ever wanted in a woman. I'm really in love, Louise. I feel terrible."

Louise laughed. "Then I guess you *are* in love." She looked into his face. "You don't look too hot either. Come on, let's go inside and get another drink. Andy's going to do a drag number."

"Spare me. I've seen all of Andy's numbers. I think I'll walk over to the hotel and get something to eat if they're still serving."

"Oh my, you do have it bad," Louise said as she got up, patted him on the cheek and walked into the house.

As Mike started off for the hotel he tried to figure out how it all could have happened so quickly. He'd spent only one short evening with her alone, and an hour or two in company with her and her husband, but there was something in the way she looked at him that completely unhinged him. He inhaled, remembering the lingering scent of her perfume, seeing the shine of her hair, the fullness of her hips and breasts. She was his fantasy come true, the dream he'd always dreamed, but in his dream he walked into a room and saw her standing in a group of admirers, her hair studded in pearls, her gown the softest of whites. The moment their eyes met he stood quite still as they stared at one another, forgetting everything and everyone around them. And then they danced an oldfashioned waltz, swirling around a polished marble ballroom lined with mirrors and crowned with dazzling crystal chandeliers. He told her she was the woman he had been looking for all his life and she whispered that at last she'd found her only true love. And on they danced while people stared and men tried to sweep her away from him. At last the night grew late and they fled the hall at the stroke of twelve and hurried into a carriage that sped them off through the silent, starlit evening, off into the distant, romantic unknown where they would live happily for ever afterward.

"Watch where in hell you're going, buddy," a man grumbled as Mike bumped headlong into him. The man was staggering drunk.

Mike mumbled an apology and walked on.

He ordered a drink at the hotel bar and as he waited for it his eyes fell on the public telephone just outside the door. If only he could hear her voice. If only he could tell her of his revelation.

She'd only laugh at him, he told himself as the bartender put his drink in front of him. And besides, what good would it do? But then he remembered what Louise had said and it gave him hope. The first day back after the holiday he'd call her at the agency. If she accepted his lunch invitation it would give him the courage he needed to tell her how he felt.

Although Maggie accepted his luncheon invitation, Mike's courage deserted him. He kept glancing at the wedding band on her finger and asking himself what right he had to jeopardize a woman's marriage. And as he sat listening to her quiet voice, all the brashness of his youth paled before her quiet dignity. She was so much a woman, so different from the brainless girls he knew. He told himself that if he babbled out his love like some high-school sophomore, she'd more than likely laugh at him, whether his declaration pleased her or not. He'd make a fool of himself and would lose her forever by his impetuosity. She'd never think he was serious.

He decided to change the tactics he'd spent so much time mapping out. He'd show her he was just as reserved and as adult as she, that there was nothing frivolous or flippant about him, that he wasn't some cow-eyed boy mooning over an impossible love, wanting that love simply because it was impossible. He was twenty-three years old and a full-blooded man in every sense of the word. He'd prove it to her.

Little did he suspect that Maggie's impression of him was completely different from his own. She saw nothing boyish or inane in anything he said or did. Maggie found herself leaning on his every word, loving the masculine tilt of his head, the deep male timbre of his voice. He was as nervous as she, she noticed. They both knew why they were here; this was much more than a casual lunch between friends. Those unsaid words, those knowing glances usually reserved for a romantic rendezvous were all there. She saw the desire in his eyes and knew he saw the same reflected in hers.

The rules of the game had to be observed, and this game they were playing had more complicated rules inasmuch as one of the players was married and the other almost fifteen years her junior. However, the increased complication seemed to make the stakes more exciting.

They asked more questions of each other, not really wanting answers, just an excuse to prolong being together.

"Will you have a drink with me after work?" Mike asked as he sipped his coffee and waited for the check. He saw the hesitation and quickly added, "I know you have to get home to Doug but just one short drink. Please."

She knew she should not but she said, "All right, one Perrier water and then my bus home."

They didn't go to The Rail, which was Mike's idea. Maggie didn't object too strenuously, agreeing with Mike that she saw too much of Andy and Louise and the rest at the office all day. They both knew why they didn't want to join the gang at The Rail; they wanted to be alone together.

Afterward, on the bus home, Maggie told herself that what she was doing was wrong. She was encouraging a man almost her son's age. Oh, so he was several years older; however, that didn't alter the fact that he was still very young . . . too young. But when she closed her eyes and found his handsome face smiling at her, it didn't matter somehow.

It was late when she got home but, as usual, the house was empty and she kicked herself for not having stayed longer and caught a later bus. The vacant rooms vibrated with her loneliness. If only Doug had been here to reassure her that her attraction to Mike Ballantine was just a caprice. At least Doug could serve as a reminder that she was a mature woman with a mature husband and mature children, living in a middle-aged world, a world that frowned on non-directional youth, aimless innocence, purposeless fledglings.

Her annoyance with herself turned to anger by the time David and Julie got home. David said, "What's going on around here lately? You and Dad are always on our case. Yesterday you were complaining about me being home and tonight you're yelling because I was out. Make up your mind," he groaned as he headed for his retreat in the garage.

"Just one minute," Maggie said sternly. "Yesterday you were blasting the whole neighborhood apart with all that racket you and your friends call music."

"It was just Pink Floyd and it was the holiday weekend."

"I don't care if it were Green Gerald. When you disturb people it's called a nuisance."

"Hell, a guy can't win around here," David said as he changed course and went up the stairs.

Julie had disappeared into the kitchen as soon as she'd come in, now she emerged with a peanut butter sandwich and a glass of milk. Maggie said, "I thought you were dieting?"

"Don't start on me, mother. Just because you're fighting with Dad doesn't mean you should jump all over us kids."

"Who's fighting with your father?" Maggie asked indignantly.

"Oh, Mother. We do have ears, you know. You and Dad don't exactly argue quietly, you know."

"We aren't arguing."

"Excuse me all to pieces, Mother, but you two have been jabbing at each other all weekend—when you talk at all." She bit into her sandwich. "I take it the party on Fire Island was too far out for Dad's tastes?" She went into the den and flopped in front of the television.

Maggie felt confused. Stupid as it seemed, she never counted on the children overhearing their arguing, and it had never occurred to her before that Julie nor David were very intuitive about the disturbances that riffled their parents' relationship. She'd always looked on them as children, and like all children they sat quietly and neither saw nor heard anything you didn't want them to.

156

She looked at Julie and although she knew her daughter's bra size, her size pantyhose, it never dawned on her that Julie was a young woman, not an adolescent with stringy hair and splotchy skin. And David was eighteen now, old enough to vote. And drink, she tacked on.

While she waited for Doug to come home she spent her time filling it with a firm resolution to try to forget about Mike Ballantine and concentrate on trying to make things better between Doug and herself. True, Mike was a fantastic shot to her ego, but reality had to be faced: he was much too young.

She sat in front of her dressing-table mirror and began making a mental list of what was fact and what was fancy. First she loved Doug; that was a definite fact. Mike was a wonderful temptation but he was purely physical; he didn't have the depth or quality about him that Doug had. Fact two, she had two bright, wonderful children whom she cared deeply about.

And by the time she finished her mental calculations, the fact column far outnumbered the fancy, although the fancy column was by far the more attractive—but just not sensible.

Her resolution to make peace with Doug was still firm when she heard Doug come in. It vanished the moment she smelled a woman's perfume when he pecked her cheek.

"You've been with Phyllis," she charged.

He didn't deny it this time. "Yes."

She forced back her anger. "We have got to talk, Doug. Things are getting too far out of hand."

"There isn't much we can talk about these days, Maggie. You're a stranger to me lately and you obviously refuse to turn back into the woman I married."

"I'm still me," she insisted.

"No you are not. Look at yourself," he said pointing to the mirror. "You don't even look the same."

"No, that's true, Doug, but I think I've changed for the better in that regard."

He nodded. "I was watching you at that party the other afternoon and I admit that I was very proud that you were my wife. You are very beautiful, more beautiful than I ever remember seeing you. And I admit I was very jealous that the men all flirted with you but the thing that worries me was that I saw you were really enjoying yourself. You were acting so differently than I've ever seen you act at parties; you were so much freer, so much bolder."

"What's wrong with my enjoying myself?"

"I don't resent that. It was the way you were enjoying yourself. I thought we left off enjoying kids' parties years ago."

"So that's it. You're annoyed because I was accepted as one of the young crowd and you weren't."

It astonished her to see him agree. "Truthfully, yes. And the thing that hurts the most is that you *think* you belong to that crowd. You don't, Maggie. You never did and you never will."

"I disagree with you. I may be older than all those people at that party, but that isn't any reason to accept middle-age as some kind of germ that you're afraid to pass on, so you stay home alone. They could care less about how old I am; that's only in your head. You resent my looking so young because it makes you look older by contrast." She saw him flinch. "You are a very selfish, vain man, Doug."

"Then there is no reason for us to discuss this any further. I've decided that the best thing perhaps is for me to move out for a while so that we both can have some time to think without the other being underfoot."

She began to shake with fear but to hide it she said, "You've decided to move in with Phyllis Bracken." It was a statement.

"No," he said calmly. "I'll take a room at the Holiday Inn for the time being. If things don't work out between us I'll find myself an apartment somewhere."

Their marriage was falling apart and she knew it, but there was something about the look of him that made her suspect he wanted it this way. Despite what he said, he was going to Phyllis. She hadn't any doubt about that.

"Perhaps it is for the best," she said, thinking suddenly that the hiatus would give her a chance to find out her true feelings about Mike. "Maybe some time away from each other will clear things up for both of us."

"I sincerely hope so, Maggie. I love you very much, whether you care to believe that or not."

"And I love you, Doug. I really do."

She wanted to go into his arms, take him to bed, make mad passionate love to him, but that would only put them back on square one. She had to move forward into an unknown that was capable of either destruction or preservation. She had to find out which.

She'd never thought about separating from Doug, and if it had ever crossed her mind to do so she would have imagined it to be a terrible ordeal. Strangely enough it happened quietly, simply, and Doug was moved out before the full impact of the whole thing hit her. Even then, though an empty fear gnawed at her, she didn't believe anything fatal could come of it. After all, he was just at the hotel in town and could easily be at her side within minutes if she needed him, so it wasn't that she was completely alone and abandoned.

Surprisingly, the children were very adult in their reactions to their parents' separation. David said, "Is Dad going to marry that Phyllis Bracken? Everybody sees them around together almost every day."

"I don't think so," Maggie told him, trying not to show her hurt. "I doubt if it will come to that. We both just have to have some time to get our heads together, as you kids put it."

Julie said, "Well, it's not like he's moving to Alaska or someplace. He'll still pay our allowances won't he?"

The Lord be praised for the selfishness of youth, Maggie thought; it heals a lot of pain.

The most difficult thing about Doug's separation from her was the seemingly endless evenings Maggie spent alone. It did not seem right to run directly to Mike and tell him she was free—for a while. That would be tantamount to an open admission that she wanted him, and much as she was taken by him she could not throw herself at his feet. They saw a lot of each other after work but she never once told him she had to go home to a house with no husband.

However, as the weeks passed she discovered that she was spending more and more time with Mike after work. One evening the time grew so late that she almost missed the last bus for the night. Mike laughed and said, "I keep hoping you miss that last bus so you'll have to stay with me all night."

It was the first time he'd openly propositioned her, but it had been more or less established that they wanted to go to bed together. Doug was all that was standing in their way and even though he wasn't living at home, he was still her husband and sleeping with Mike would definitely be an act of adultery, grounds for divorce.

The word frightened her too much to take the risk.

As the summer wore on Mike got into the habit of stopping by the office every noontime, pretending he just came to lunch with Louise, Maggie, Andy and the rest of the gang. To both himself and Maggie it was an innocent enough occurrence, being as blind as they were to everything except themselves. Louise and Andy were hardly taken in by Mike's sudden interest in his old friends. Even Alice was surprised when she saw Mike there several lunch-hours in a row.

"Is it my great cafeteria food or are you out of a job again and freeloading on my staff?"

He took it good-naturedly. "I am among the employed, Miss Alice," he said sweetly. "But I find I cannot tear myself away from my old co-workers at The Fifth Avenue Agency."

"Any one particular co-worker?" Alice asked in an aside.

Mike grinned. "You never can tell."

It never occurred to Maggie that people were gossiping about her and Mike. She wasn't conscious of the time and attention she and Mike paid to one another, or that she was acting like a school-girl. She never thought the others noticed their lingering soft glances, their smug little smiles of happiness, the way they always found themselves next to each other. So when Alice brought up the subject Maggie pretended indifference.

Alice said, "He's nuts about you, you know."

"Who?"

"Come off that Little Miss Innocent, kiddo. You know damned well who I'm talking about. Why haven't you told him Doug moved out?"

Coolly she said, "How do you know I haven't?"

"Because he's still looking at you like he wants to undress you. There is a certain look that comes into a young man's eyes after he knows what a woman feels like and looks like naked."

"Alice, really."

Alice persisted with, "Why don't you put the poor boy out of his misery and shack up with him? I know you want to."

Maggie looked up sharply. "Because you just put your finger on it. . . . He's a boy, and fifteen years younger than me. I still remember Jeff Cochran."

"There's no comparison and you know it. Mike's a very sensible guy, not some street hustler."

"I'm still a married lady." She hesitated before adding, "And far too old for him."

"So go ahead and keep frustrating yourself, kiddo. You're the one who's suffering . . . and Mike, of course."

She couldn't imagine that Mike was suffering, and it seemed right somehow that she should suffer. She'd turned her husband against her, she was threatening their marriage, her home, her whole past life for the sake of a young man who didn't have a steady job and didn't seem to have any desire to get one, a young man who—for all she knew—was no better than Jeff Cochran.

But then she mustn't take all the blame on herself. After all it was Doug who'd started the whole mess—so why should she feel guilty just because she was enjoying the company of a younger man, regardless of his intentions? The fact was that she enjoyed Mike's company more than anything else.

Almost every evening she found herself with Mike. David, with minor supervision by her and Doug, was doing a good job of taking care of himself, and Julie had gone away for the rest of the summer to her girlfriend's cabin at Java Lake near the Canadian border. Night after night Mike introduced her to something entirely new and always fun. They never went any place overly expensive and their dinners were generally eaten at some nondescript little place that didn't charge an arm and a leg. Mike even accepted her treats every once in a while, but not often enough for it to offend either of them. On one occasion she tried to slip him extra money but he became angry, which pleased her no end.

Mike made her feel so young and alive. To her, they

were just like any other ordinary young couple sharing fun and experiencing things together. She never thought she'd like rock music, having had it forced on her by David, but with Mike it took on an entirely new dimension; it wasn't all that loud grating and noisy stuff she'd heard blasting out of David's garage. Mike taught her to concentrate on what the music was all about, to listen to the lyrics and fit the music and rhythm to the meaning of the words. After a lot of exposure to Fleetwood Mack, Pink Floyd, Blondie, and the rest of many of her son's idols, every time Maggie found herself mentioning David's name, she started to think of him as a kindred spirit, a fellow music-lover and not her teenaged son.

She got to love the nights he took her dancing. Disco seemed to have been invented exclusively for her. It made her feel alive and free and so uninhibited. She was self-conscious at first, but later she noticed that nobody was paying any more attention to her than she was to them. The music and lights stole reality from everybody and left them with the emotions.

"Just relax with the music," Mike said as he moved sensuously in front of her. "Let yourself go, Maggie. Just let yourself do whatever you feel."

She wondered now why she had thought the movements of disco dancers so suggestive; they weren't suggestive really, just wonderfully unwinding.

She worried a lot about the complete change in her, especially when she was alone. She saw little of Doug, feeling he'd only dampen her new happiness and she felt guilty letting him see how truly happy she was. But with Mike she talked openly of how she'd changed, anxiously listening to his reassurances.

She didn't see much of Mike on weekends, feeling that the least she could do was to spend as much time as possible at home with David, although he was seldom there and when he was he spent his time with a pack of buddies or holed up in his garage sanctuary. She never worried too much about how Mike occupied his weekends; he said he usually called her three or four times every day and moped about until he saw her at lunch Monday.

One Saturday afternoon, however, she went to the stock car races with David just for want of something to do to occupy her time. She'd called Doug at his hotel to see if he wanted to join them but he wasn't in. The clerk had mistaken her voice and said, "He hasn't come in yet, Miss Bracken, but I'll see that he calls you as soon as he does."

Until then she'd almost forgotten Phyllis but proof that she was still on the scene only intensified Maggie's joy at seeing Mike at the car races. He'd come with his brother Timmy and admitted later that Timmy had told him they were going to be there.

She never thought she'd enjoy stock car races, but that afternoon was one of the most exciting she'd ever spent. Even David, on the way home, said, "Gee, Mom, I never knew you were such a barrel of laughs. You really had a time for yourself." A little while later he said, "Mike's sure a terrific guy, isn't he? He knows just about everything there is to know about race cars. He used to drive one once."

"Oh?"

"Timmy said he used to be a member of one of the driving teams but lost interest. Still, he's sure smart about everything. I should ask him over some time, okay? Maybe he'd be able to tell me what's wrong with that motorbike I broke down and can't get back together."

"God forbid," Maggie breathed. "I hope you never get that thing working."

She was pleased at the idea of David liking Mike. And perhaps she would let him invite Mike over. After all, Doug obviously was spending his weekends with Phyllis, so why shouldn't she have some adult male companionship? It didn't mean she'd entertain him in bed.

The idea made her radiate and when she told Mike that he'd made such a big hit with David, Mike said, "Good. One down, now only one more to go." He leaned forward and tried to kiss her.

She let him.

Chapter 13

Since sleeping alone, Maggie had developed the habit of getting up at the ungodly hour of five A.M. Although the world outside her window was still dark, inside herself the day ahead was bright as polished silver. David was working for his father during the summer and Doug called for him about seven. Lately, though, Doug began staying for coffee and then wound up staying for breakfast.

It was nice seeing Doug every morning; but there was something different about him, which she supposed was expected in view of their complete change in lifestyles. Doug was quieter, more withdrawn than his usual self. She appreciated the fact that he never questioned her too closely about her work, how she occupied her time at night. Sometimes she got the impression that he was merely feeding her enough rope with which to hang herself, because she talked openly about Alice, Louise, and Andy, but she was careful never to mention Mike and Doug never asked about him. She often told him things she'd done which ordinarily would start an argument, or at least a discussion, like telling him about a see-through blouse she was admiring. But whatever she said was all right with him and if he did disapprove his only comment would be, "I don't like that," or "I'm surprised you found that enjoyable." He never censured or criticized. Underneath, however, Maggie felt he was smoldering, biting his tongue to keep from telling her exactly what he thought of her new tastes.

And she did indeed acquire many new tastes and interests, and oddly enough she found that Doug had also discovered some new interests which they both shared. Their taste in music, for example, had altered drastically; Doug even mentioned how much he liked the discos and recommended one particularly popular place in Fort Lee.

Phyllis didn't seem like the disco type and Maggie was tempted to ask him who'd introduced him to rock music and disco dancing. Was Doug seeing a younger woman? The idea bothered her, though she didn't see why it should.

Major changes always came from unfamiliar sources, she supposed, because in their life together Doug and Maggie had always found themselves interested in the same basic things but had never gone out of their way to add to or augment the things they shared. It had taken strangers coming into their lives and introducing them to new interests. Before, when she and Doug were completely happy together, change was something she feared; now they both welcomed it.

It hurt a little to see Doug leave, knowing that he would not be back until the next day. His deliciously masculine body would not be lying naked and warm beside her, welcoming her touch, her kisses. She'd been without his sex for weeks and the strain was beginning to bother her, yet hard as she tried she could not bring herself to go to bed with anyone except Doug, simple as it would be to have Mike Ballantine.

The hurt at seeing Doug leave was quickly replaced by the thought of seeing Mike in a couple of hours. She loved being with him; he was more fun than anyone she'd ever met, including Doug—which she found difficult to admit but it was, nevertheless, the truth. While Doug was fun in a quiet, friendly way, Mike was zany, reckless, carefree, uninhibited, and he was bringing out the same in her. She'd found a part of her that had never been allowed expression before, something wild and frivolous and daring. She'd never realized before that she had a sense of adventure inside her; generally she was timid about anything different or novel.

She occupied herself with the usual routine of cleaning up the kitchen and getting ready for work, asking herself if it wasn't time for her and Doug to sit down and discuss their future before more time pulled them farther apart.

An arguing voice asked her if she really wanted to go back to her old ways, to Doug's way? She wasn't ready for that, but neither was she ready to be totally free of Doug. The word divorce still frightened her. Was that because she'd no longer have an excuse to refrain from having sex with other men?

"Good Lord! Other men? I don't want other men." She felt that if she couldn't have Doug then it would be Mike Ballantine and she was adult enough to admit that the idea of having sex with Mike was very exciting.

But afterward? Ah, that was what she was most afraid of. Afterward.

Maggie walked out to a comfortable sky and the promise of another busy, pleasant day of people and activity, then a quiet dinner with Mike. Tonight he was taking her to a baseball game. She'd never been to a baseball game, never even watched one on television, even though it was one of Doug's favorite sports.

As she got on the bus she hoped Andy wasn't still in his bitchy mood. All day yesterday he'd been snarling because the lover with the house on Fire Island had taken up with some teenaged singing star, grumbling about the disgusting way "kids" run after older, richer guys.

"Goddamn hustlers, that's all they are," he'd said. "The lousy punk just wanted to see if he could break us up." Never once did he mention the fact that he had taken the older gentleman away from his earlier lover, a man several years older than Andy—according to Mike.

That was the one single thing about Mike that she didn't much care for—he was very involved with Andy and his gay friends. She kidded him a few times about having a gay streak in him and he laughed about it but never admitted or denied it. The one way to find out, by Maggie's way of thinking, was to go to bed with him.

Now that she thought of it, there was one other thing she didn't like about Mike. He smoked marijuana on occasion . . . "pot" as he called it. No way would she participate when the "joint" was passed around; although she didn't object to their using the stuff, she didn't approve of it.

As she walked from the Port Authority terminal toward Fifth Avenue her spirits lagged, realizing that today was

Friday and another weekend alone lay ahead. Doug was picking David up early tomorrow and they were going to some lake with Doug's business partner. "Just us guys," David had told her when he mentioned his father's invitation. It struck her as peculiar that Doug and David seemed so much closer all of a sudden; lately they were always doing something together, while they had never seemed all that interested in each other in the past. Of course David would be going off to college in a month or so, so she supposed it was natural that his father wanted to spend as much time as he could with his only son. After all, everybody who went away to college always returned an adult.

"T.G.I.F.," Andy hailed, and it was easy to see that his foul mood was gone.

"Who did you meet last night?" Maggie asked as she hung up her suit jacket.

"How did you know I met anyone?"

Maggie grinned and shrugged and Andy launched into the beauty and virtues of some body builder he'd met at the Hollywood Disco. "Of course he doesn't have a dime," Andy added. "But this time I am really in love."

Louise put in, "For the umpteenth time this year, lover."

Andy wasn't phased. "No, I really mean it. I'm truly in love for the first time in my life. This one's different. He's a Virgo."

Louise winked at Maggie and said, "In other words, they didn't make the scene yet."

Andy scowled. "All you think about is sex, Louise. This is something loftier, more sacred, something you'd never understand."

Louise and Maggie rolled their eyes and went back to work.

Maggie's phone rang and Caroline, their receptionist, asked her if she could come out to the reception room. When Maggie got there she found Caroline trying to talk pidgin English to a dark-haired girl of about eighteen who apparently spoke no English.

"Rita's not in yet," Caroline explained. "Andy told me you speak a little Spanish. I can't get her to understand that she has to talk to a counselor in order to get a job."

Maggie's Spanish was rusty now that she wasn't home during the day to keep it fresh by talking to the cleaning woman who came three afternoons a week. "I'll try," Maggie said and launched into faulty Spanish, only to be rudely cut off by Rita who came in behind her and took charge of the girl. Maggie's Spanish was good enough to translate, "Don't listen to the stupid white woman," which came from Rita.

Maggie was tempted to tell her to go to hell, but stopped herself.

When she got back to her desk she was still shaking with anger and more than once she had to keep herself from getting out of her chair and going over and giving Rita a piece of her mind. All her earlier ideas about trying to be the Good Samaritan had vanished as Maggie saw up close just how terrible Rita Gant could be. Understanding Spanish made Rita more of an ogre than the others in the office realized, especially Alice, because Maggie heard Rita constantly cursing at her girls, belittling them, degrading them if they came up with any excuse not to accept a particular job. Rita actually browbeat her applicants into going to work—so it was no wonder her commissions were the highest in the office.

The girl was still sitting at Rita's desk when a workorder turned up on Maggie's desk which belonged to Rita, an order for a Spanish-speaking receptionist in a car agency uptown. She picked up the file and walked over to Rita.

In Spanish Rita was saying, "Look, dummy, you either sign this contract or you don't go to work—at least not from this agency and believe me I have a lot of friends at all the other agencies in New York so if you don't get placed through me here you won't get placed at all, understand?"

The young girl looked confused. She said in faltering Spanish, "But the newspaper says that this agency does not charge any money, that the jobs are free."

Rita glowered. "Look, I'll say it just one more time, either you sign this agreement to pay us your first salary as the employment fee or you don't get any salary at all, from nobody, at least not here in New York."

The girl reluctantly took the paper, handling it as if it

were contaminated. She mumbled something and hurried off.

"What are you doing?" Maggie asked as she dropped the file on Rita's desk. She pointed to the retreating girl. "You were asking that girl to pay you her first month's salary."

"So?"

"This is an 'employer paid' agency; you know that. You can't collect double commissions."

"You mind your business and I will mind mine," Rita said.

"The business in this office is all of our business, Rita. Anything shady will only bring trouble and we could all be out of work if the State revokes Alice's license for such dealing as you are obviously trying to pull. How many other poor kids have you collected double from?"

"Look, white woman," Rita spat. "You are so stupid you do not deserve an explanation, but I will give you one anyway. In the first place, that job I was sending that Mexican slut out on was an 'employ*ee* pays.'"

"But . . ."

"Employ*ee* pays," Rita emphasized. "Second, for your information, whatever goes over this desk of mine has nothing to do with this lousy agency. I rent desk space from Alice. I am not a part of her organization, so I lay down the rules with my own people, nobody else. Alice does not tell me what to do and I do not interfere with her. Got that straight, white woman? Now do me a big favor and take your friggin' white ass away from my space. And in the future keep your nose out of my business and as far away from me as you can."

Maggie stood unable to move a muscle. What Rita had said came as a surprise, but of course it was possible that what she said could be true, that she merely rented desk space here. It had to be true, she decided, thinking back, Hadn't Alice once said that Rita wasn't "one of us." Yes, that was Alice's exact words right after Maggie's initial interview. She'd said then she hadn't wanted her working there. So Rita must be an independent, not a part of Fifth Avenue Agency.

Which explained a lot of things, Maggie decided. She felt suddenly foolish for having butted into Rita's territory.

170

Rita was right, in the employment agency business one counselor never barges into another's applicants or job placements unless asked to do so. Jobs were their bread and butter and the counselors' personal property as well as their stock in trade.

Well, Maggie thought, it would be just another reason to stay completely out of Rita's hair. She'd never have to try and be nice to that awful woman again.

Maggie was too embarrassed about having broken the unwritten rule about meddling with another counselor's applicant to mention to anyone, even when Alice stormed through muttering, "That damned Rita. One of these days I'm going to kick her ass out of here."

Maggie said, "I just had a little run in with her too."

Alice raised a questioning eyebrow but Maggie didn't elaborate.

Alice put a stack of job cards on Maggie's desk. "What are you planning for the weekend, kiddo?"

"Nothing much. Why?"

"All alone, or could David do without his chaperone for one weekend?"

"All alone. David's going to the lake with Doug."

"How about Mike Ballantine? Not planning on sneaking him over while everybody's away?"

Maggie gave her a disgusted look. "You know me better than that, Alice. If I had any intention at all of going to bed with Mike, it certainly wouldn't be in my husband's bed."

"So do it out in the garage in David's pad."

"Be serious."

Alice did go serious. "Tell me something, Maggie, just between us girls. How do you really feel about Mike? I hear from the water-cooler-set that you two are seeing a lot of each other. True?"

Maggie nodded. "He's great company and you know I hate empty houses."

"And empty beds."

"Not that far."

"Yet."

"Ever," Maggie insisted. "I'm still married to Doug and I hope to stay that way."

"And you wouldn't give a moment's thought to anything so awful as sleeping with another man, right?"

"That would be reason for divorce."

"Not if no one knew but a select group of closed-mouthed friends."

Maggie looked up, eyeing Alice suspiciously. "What are you driving at? You certainly don't have to match-make as far as Mike anl I are concerned. We're both adult and Mike is very well aware of how I feel on the subject of sex with a man to whom I am not married."

"I wasn't exactly referring to Mike Ballantine."

"Who, then?"

"What makes you think it's a 'who?' "

"I know you too well."

"Okay then, here's the deal." She propped herself on the corner of Maggie's desk and leaned close. "Remember that big shot we had lunch with at the Four Seasons, the one from Consolidated Industries?"

"Yes. Stanley Stanmaster."

"Right. Well, he took a liking to you and. . . ."

Maggie shook her head. "Forget it, Alice. As much as I love my job and am loyal to your agency, I will not prostitute myself for either."

"Who's asking? Here's the plan. Eddie has the use of his boss' private jet this weekend and we're flying to Vegas. I was going to invite Stanmaster with the promise that you'd be with the party. Once in Vegas all you have to do is be civil to old Stanley without being too encouraging. Eddie's promised he'd see that the guy doesn't get too over-anxious with you, and when old Stan's blood gets too hot, Eddie knows a couple of girls who will gladly take over from there."

"No."

"How's this as an incentive. Consolidated Industries is opening up three branches throughout the area, one in Jersey City, one out on the Island, the other in Brooklyn. They're going to need scads of office help and Fifth Avenue Agency is getting the exclusive. Now if you play your cards right with me, kiddo. I'll give you first crack at filling all those lovely jobs."

"No." But this time she wasn't as definite. Her mind started to click along. It would mean hundreds of dollars in commissions. Not that she needed the money but after working in the office for so long she'd automatically fallen into the competition regarding commissions earned. Everybody boasted about how much they made every month. It wasn't that she wanted to earn more money than Andy and Louise, it was just that they might stop treating her as someone temporary, someone green and new and someone who wouldn't last. As hard as she'd worked at it, she'd never been able to convince any of them that she was someone other than a close personal friend of the owner's who'd been called in to help out.

Alice said, "No one here will know where all your job openings came from. You'll have brought them in through your own efforts, which won't be a lie if you decide to come with Eddie and me to Vegas."

"Louise and the rest of the kids will easily put two and two together and come up with prostitution."

"How will they find out? Come on, kiddo, if not for yourself do it for me and my business."

"No. As much as I would like to start showing everybody around here that I can keep up my end, I don't want to do it this way."

"You're concentrating too much on the sex angle, which isn't right because there won't be any sex as far as you're concerned. It's no more devious than taking Stanmaster out for dinner or lunch. Now no one thinks there's anything wrong with that."

"It's just wrong, because it's devious."

"Devious is just a dirty word for clever."

"I'll pass, Alice, if you don't mind."

"But I do mind," she said, getting up from the desk. "Tell you what, kiddo. Why not come with Eddie and me anyway, just the three of us. It'll do you good. I promise I won't invite Stanmaster. Just bring a couple of hundred for the Blackjack tables and we'll forget our cares and woes." She raised two fingers. "Just the three of us; scouts' honor."

Maggie relented. "Okay, let me check with Doug."

"Dear God, Maggie, the guy walked out on you and you have to check with him if you want to go away for a weekend. I just do not believe you."

Maggie reached for the phone. "It's called being honest

and open. I do not want Doug to be in any way suspicious of me."

"But's it's okay, I suppose, if he makes you suspicious of him?"

"What's to be suspicious of? I know he's sleeping with Phyllis, but just because he has a troubled conscience doesn't mean I should have one."

"You're crazy, do you know that? If he were my husband I'd have him in a divorce court so fast he'd come in naked and unshaven."

"That's why you have three divorces to your credit while I will never have any."

She knew the remark hurt but it was good to speak her mind for a change. Her new life taught her to do that, and she felt better for it. No more holding everything in, letting people step all over her while she just smiled back when they did, excusing them for their lack of manners. Those who stepped on her now did it only with her permission. Maggie was learning to retaliate when the hurts were uninvited.

Alice said, "What about Mike? Are you going to string along both him and Doug?"

"Nobody is stringing anybody along, Alice. Doug is free to do whatever he wishes until he gets it out of his system and comes back to me."

"And Mike?"

"The same applies to Mike. He doesn't exactly pine away for lack of a sex partner. We have a very friendly relationship. He knows Doug comes first with me."

"Does he?"

"We've never spelled it out in so many words but we both know how things stand."

"How do they stand?"

"I'm very fond of Mike. In fact, I think I could fall in love with him if Doug weren't in the picture."

"Then you intend to sit around and wait for Doug to make up his mind—thereby making up your mind for you."

"I suppose you could put it that way."

"It sounds like a cop-out to me." Alice looked perplexed. "I don't understand you at all, Maggie. You can be in love with one man and keep yourself from falling in love with another until you find out if the first one returns your love."

"What's so confusing about that?"

"It just doesn't seem natural. It's kinda callous."

"I won't let myself fall in love with Mike. I call it will-power."

"But people don't let themselves fall in or out of love, kiddo. Things like that happen, they aren't planned."

"That's child's talk. Love, like any other emotion, can be controlled."

"Crap! You're afraid if you lose Doug, Mike might not be as perfect a replacement as you might have hoped, so you keep him at arm's length until you have no other choice. Personally, I think that's petty and selfish." She walked back to her office.

Maggie sat back. She never realized that she'd been using Mike, but it was true and the realization made her feel ashamed. She could understand how she felt about Doug: he was actually like a child who could go away from her, but like a mother she could not go away from her child. Mike was entirely different. He wasn't like a child at all; she didn't love him and care for him in the motherly way she did Doug. Doug was both a lover and a son; Mike was just a lover, and technically, not even that.

By her way of thinking it was right that she should suffer for Doug's sake, for his right to what made him happy, because she was a woman and women suffered more easily, more willingly than did men. Her life could be bearable when it was only she who suffered. It was easy to put up with one's own suffering but not someone else's, like Doug's for instance, or David's. She could not bear to see either of them unhappy for any reason. She wouldn't like to see Mike suffer either, but his suffering wouldn't be as important.

It wasn't that she considered herself a masochist, or that she was self-sacrificing. She had what she wanted, for the time being. She had a wonderful sense of freedom. Knowing that Doug was being unfaithful put him in a position where he could not dictate to her, could not complain about anything she did. She could do anything and not feel guilty, anything, that is, that did not disturb her conscience.

Doug certainly knew she was seeing Mike Ballantine. She'd told him that she was not sleeping with Mike so that he would feel doubly guilty about his adulterous affair with Phyllis. If anything, Maggie was ashamed of the secret pleasure she got from making Doug ache with remorse for his weakness.

When she spoke to Doug on the phone she could tell by his tone that he wasn't particularly pleased that she was planning on going to Las Vegas with Alice and her ex-husband, of whom Doug never did approve. But he said, "Don't lose too much at the tables and don't let any of those slick card sharks turn your head. I love you."

"I love you too."

Only someone who's gone through a relationship such as theirs could understand, Maggie told herself as she thought of Alice's failure to understand. Theirs was a quiet kind of love that had ripened with age into a deeply profound sense of respect and need. The physical passion of their love was still there, only imbedded deeper under the layers of their years together. No man would ever excite her sexually the way Doug did; that part of their love affair would never change, even though he was sleeping with another woman and the day might come when she was sleeping with another man. Even divorce could never take away from her the pleasure and sexual excitement they'd produced together.

There would be no divorce, she told herself as she took her hand off the receiver. Phyllis was only a temporary diversion; how could a woman like that endanger a life that had been built from scratch? Doug had been as inexperienced a lover as she when they met and married. They'd taught each other everything. She was his sexual roots as he was hers; and like any living thing, if the roots are pulled the thing will die.

Maggie frowned. Perhaps, though, Alice had a point. Perhaps Maggie was afraid to compare another man's lovemaking to Doug's for fear Doug might lose—or win!

She started into Alice's office to tell her she'd join them for the weekend. She began mapping out her timing as she and Alice talked about the trip.

Alice had her car. They'd drive to Maggie's where she could change and pack; then to Alice's where she'd do the same. "Eddie said there will be food aboard—nothing heavy, just enough to keep us from starving until we get to Vegas. And he was guaranteed reservations at the Sands. We can have ourselves a sumptuous dinner when we get in."

Maggie had promised Mike earlier that she'd join him for their usual Friday night dinner, but she'd have to cancel that, much as she didn't want to. But Mike would understand. Besides, they never spent weekends together anyway so it didn't matter very much about a single Friday night dinner.

The thought also crossed her mind that with Doug and David away together, going to Vegas with Alice would remove any temptation she might develop of inviting Mike over to the house, or of her staying at Mike's.

To her surprise Mike didn't seem all that disappointed when she cancelled their date. That bothered her. After she hung up she wondered if Mike had made plans for the weekend with someone else and was just as pleased to be able to move them up to include Friday night as well. He'd sounded so pleasant, almost relieved when she told him she was going to Las Vegas.

Alice said, "You look funny," as she pulled into a string of cars queuing up for the ramp to the George Washington Bridge.

"I feel funny," Maggie admitted. "I talked to Mike a while ago and he sounded almost happy that I was leaving town."

Alice shook her head. "There you go again, kiddo, confusing the hell out of me. Why should you care if Mike has another girl on the string? You told me yourself that he understands he's second in line."

"I know, I know. I don't understand it myself all of a sudden."

"You wouldn't be jealous, would you?"

"Jealous? Me? Don't be ridiculous." She turned her face away.

"It's known to happen to the best of people, kiddo."

"Mike and I are just very close friends with everything else on the back burner by mutual agreement. I could learn to love him, but after all, Alice, even if Doug didn't. . . . Oh, hell, Alice, Mike is years and years younger than me, which is a very important consideration."

"Aha, I think I'm finally beginning to see what's going on. Why are you letting the difference in your age be such a big issue? Personally I think you two make a divine couple."

"I told you," Maggie said adamantly, "I like Mike very much; I do not love him."

"You *think* you don't love him. Damn it, Maggie, if I were in your shoes I'd at least give the poor guy a chance. I have a feeling that every time you find yourself thinking seriously about him you start seeing the difference in your ages."

Maggie didn't say anything.

"To hell with the age difference. Go to bed with him, kiddo, if you have the desire. That way you'll be able to find out how much you really like him. Believe it or not, having sex can make or break the most ideal love affairs. You know yourself that plenty of romances fall apart after the couple have had sex. Either the girl finds out she doesn't like the feel of the guy or that he's too big or too small; or he finds out she's too tight, too dry, she doesn't move her ass to suit him. Sex is an equalizer and a deciding factor. It bares everything—excuse the pun. Everything is brought right out in the open and we can't hide anything. So if you want my advice, take Mike to bed."

"I couldn't, Alice. Don't ask me why, but I couldn't. I know I'm procrastinating when I talk about adultery and fear of losing Doug. It's just that I can't bring myself to have sex with another man, Alice, something inside me makes me afraid. I honestly would love to go to bed with Mike, Alice, but I just can't."

"You almost gave in to Jeff Cochran at the spa. What did he do to lower your resistance?"

Maggie thought. "I truly don't know. I suppose it was that helpless, love-sick con job he gave me. I'm a sucker for someone who's miserable and needs me."

"Then maybe I can help, kiddo."

"What do you mean?"

"I might be able to give you the needed boost over the hurdle."

Maggie didn't grasp Alice's meaning until later when

they ran across the tarmac to where the private jet was waiting, its engines beginning to churn. The pilot was waiting for clearance from the tower while Eddie helped Alice and Maggie aboard.

The plane taxied to the designated runway. The pilot, through the open door said, "You'd better all take your seats and buckle up."

The plane began to pick up speed as the door to the lavatory opened and Mike Ballantine slipped into the empty seat next to Maggie.

Chapter 14

"Surprise!" Mike said as he reached for her hand. Maggie snatched it away.

She had been set up and it made her furious with both Alice and Mike, even with herself. She wanted to reach out and hit someone but sat gripping the arms of the seat tightly to keep her anchored from attack.

Alice turned in her seat and said, "We knew you'd never go along with the idea so that's the reason for the surprise."

"You're damned right I wouldn't have gone alone with the idea," Maggie snapped. "How could you do this? You all conspired against me."

"Come off it, kiddo. You know damned well that you're secretly pleased."

"I am not pleased," Maggie said through clenched teeth. "What am I supposed to be pleased about? Being set up like some yokel? I'll never forgive you for this, Alice."

Mike tried to take her hand but she pulled away so violently she cracked her elbow against the bulkhead. "Don't touch me, Michael," she said. "Don't ever touch me again."

Eddie said, "Come off it, Maggie. For Christ's sake, you aren't some teenie-bopper who's being kidnapped, you know. You are reading a lot more into this than there is."

"I detest sneaks." She leveled her remark at Mike.

"I'm sorry," he said. "I just thought it was about time. . . ."

"About time for what?" Maggie demanded. "Sex?" She spit the word out of her mouth.

"Not if you don't want it," Mike said, feeling hurt.

"Then I don't want it."

"Okay, so we'll just have a fun weekend." Again he reached for her hand.

"I told you I do not want you to touch me, Michael!"

He backed off, huddling himself in the furthest corner of his seat. "Okay, okay, so I won't touch you."

Maggie sulked for the entire trip, making it twice as long as it was. By the time they landed at the Las Vegas airport everyone was in ill humor. Maggie went off to her room the minute she checked in and said she'd have her dinner alone in her room while she checked for a return flight to New York.

Mike tried to talk to her but she cold-shouldered him and stormed off to pout.

Mike, Alice, and Eddie agreed to dress for dinner, all three of them knowing it was going to be a frosty weekend. As Alice slipped into her dinner gown Eddie said, "It looks like another of your bright ideas backfired."

"Don't start in on me, Eddie. How in hell was I supposed to know Maggie would pull her Puritan Priscilla act?" She slammed shut the closet door and started out of the room. "Well, I'm not going to let her spoil our weekend. She's going to get a piece of my mind if I have to shove it down her throat."

Alice didn't bother to knock; she barged into Maggie's room, finding her sitting at the window watching the myriad of colored lights blinking and flashing, beckoning for attention and fun. Maggie turned and jumped up when Alice slammed the door.

"Leave me alone, Alice."

"No." Alice grabbed her arm when Maggie started to retreat into the bathroom. "You're going to listen to what I have to say so sit down before I knock you down."

"You have nothing to say that I want to hear."

"You are a stupid little fool, Maggie."

Maggie glared at her. "Fine. I'm a stupid little fool, so now leave me alone. I'm waiting for the airlines to call about a seat back to New York."

"Honest to God, Maggie, I should shake you for acting like this. You really hurt Mike and you are spoiling a perfectly marvelous weekend for Eddie and me."

"That's why I'm flying back to New York."

"That won't make things any better. Why don't you stop acting like some prudish old maid and relax. Nobody is throwing you into bed with Mike. Isn't that the conclusion *you* jumped to? All we intended was for the four of us to have a good time."

"Like hell," Maggie said accusingly.

"It wasn't Mike's idea, if that's what you think."

"I'm pleased to hear that, but it still doesn't excuse him from going along with it."

"Wouldn't you have if you were he?"

"I don't have my mind in the sewer all the time, like you do, Alice."

"Well goddamn it, maybe it's about time you put it there because it's where you've wanted it whether you like admitting that or not. I'm really sick and tired of this holier-than-thou attitude you've adopted. Just because Doug is shacked-up with some wild broad is no reason for you to run to the far side of the pasture whinnying and neighing about how righteous and good you are by comparison. My God, Maggie, it isn't natural for you to deprive yourself the way you are! The next thing we know you'll be taking the veil."

"I am a married woman who happens to be in love with her husband. I have no intention of flopping into bed with someone young enough to be my son."

"You find more goddamn excuses. First it's because you refuse to commit adultery, then it's because the guy is too young. What will the next prerequisite be, that he be three feet six and have crossed eyes?"

Maggie wouldn't be angered. "Doug is the only man I've ever had and he is the only man I ever want. It's as simple as that."

"Nothing about you is simple, kiddo. You must have everything your own way no matter how it affects others. You're heartless and selfish. You think only of what's good for you and be damned about whether anybody else is happy." The telephone rang and Alice snatched it up before Maggie reached it. "Yes," she said into the mouthpiece. "Good. Now cancel it." She slammed down the receiver.

"How dare you!"

"Because you aren't leaving," Alice said defiantly. "We all came here to have fun and by God we are going to have fun. You are *not* going to spoil this weekend with your pettiness and your pouting. Nobody gives a shit whether you get laid or not, so stop putting all your emphasis on that. And start acting like what you are, a grown-up sensible woman." Her voice softened. "You can enjoy yourself if you let yourself, kiddo, so why not give it a try?" She smiled. "For my sake, Maggie." She touched Maggie's arm. "All you'll go back to is an empty house and loneliness. If you intend to be miserable at least do it here where you'll be with us." She let her fingers tighten on Maggie's wrist. "I'm sorry if I overstepped my bounds, kiddo, I was just thinking of you. We all were. You know I've always been pretty good at butting in where I don't belong. Forgive me, Maggie? Please?"

Maggie stood very stiff but felt her insides beginning to collapse. She let her shoulders droop. After letting out a long, deep sigh she said, "Yes, all right, Alice. I suppose you're right. I over-reacted. But I was just so mortified. I felt as if I were being sold on an auction block."

"I never thought you'd take it that way, kiddo. I really didn't. I wanted you to be tickled pink, but as usual I botched things. Even Eddie just got done reminding me I pulled another one of my boners. But let's not toss away the weekend because of my goof-up. Mike wants to be with you whether it's in bed or out. He's crazy about you, Maggie."

Maggie lowered her chin and looked at the floor. "That's just the trouble, Alice," she said softly.

"How's that?"

"I'm afraid. Mike's too perfect. There've got to be flaws in him somewhere. It's all so pat and perfect. It isn't right somehow that a young, good-looking guy like Mike would fall for an old gal like me."

"Why not? You're not exactly hard to take, looks wise. In fact, watching you at the office, you stand out like a swan on a lake. You're an extremely lovely lady, Maggie

Booth Hampton. Don't you know that?" She gave a little laugh and said, "The only one lovelier than you in our office is Andy Carver."

Maggie laughed in spite of herself.

Alice patted her hand. "Come on. Change into something ravishing and let's go down to dinner."

"I've already ordered dinner. They're sending it up."

"Leave it. Eddie's company is picking up the tab so to hell with the expenses."

An uncomfortable notion passed through Maggie's head. "Did you tell Mike that when you invited him along?"

Without thinking Alice said, "Sure." She saw the cloud pass across Maggie's face. "Hold on, kiddo. Mike isn't any Jeff Cochran. He's Eddie's and my guest. Eddie may have slipped him a couple of bucks for the tables and slot machines; I suspect that he did. But that doesn't mean anything. The guy isn't exactly rolling in jack—so what's the harm in Eddie wanting to share his wealth?"

Maggie shook her head. "It's mercenary, like you hired a gigolo for me for the weekend."

"There you go again, hinting at sex when sex doesn't have to be in the cards."

"I can't help feeling dirty."

"Maggie, my love," Alice said as she tipped up Maggie's chin, "there is absolutely nothing to feel dirty or guilty about. I made a mistake in inviting Mike, so beat me, but please don't drag this martyrdom of yours into the ground. What went on between Mike and Eddie isn't any of our business. If Eddie wanted to give him some money, fine and good; that has nothing to do with you. If you want to sleep with Mike, that's fine and good too, but it is for you to decide—and Mike, of course."

Maggie flinched. It was possible that he liked her simply because of her maturity, her good company, her motherly ways. It was she who was putting all the emphasis on sex. Alice was right, Mike might only want to cuddle with her, like a child.

Alice saw Maggie's pained expression and asked, "What did I say?"

Maggie shrugged. "I just started to think that you might be right. I am selfish. It's possible that Mike doesn't want to have sex with me."

"Oh, I wouldn't go that far." Her laugh was almost indecent.

"But it is a possibility," Maggie insisted. It was a relaxing idea. It took all the emphasis from herself, like finding out the real killer in the murder novel and closing the cover: you're glad someone you didn't like was the bad guy.

"Get dressed, Maggie. Wear that black slinky job I saw you pack." She winked and said, "Now don't tell me you packed that for Eddie's benefit." She winked again and fired a finger-gun. "Whether you like to admit it or not, kiddo, you were hoping for a little excitement this weekend, otherwise you'd have left that black number at home. So you can't be too angry with me for trying to fulfill a fantasy."

Maggie smiled. "Get out of here. I'll meet you in the dining room in twenty minutes."

She'd never seen Mike in a dinner jacket. He looked so handsome she felt herself begin to tremble as she made her entrance into the handsomely appointed dining room. Eddie was smiling as she approached the table but all Maggie saw was Mike and his deep blue sparkling eyes, dancing with desire under the candlelight, and the seductive, sensuous curve of his mouth, the square solid jaw, the broad muscular torso that strained against the white linen of his jacket. He looked very humble and almost sad.

"I'm sorry, Mike," Maggie said, putting out her hand. "I behaved very badly. Please forgive me."

His eyes grew moist as he smiled. "God, I'm so sorry I've upset you. It's the last thing I'd ever want to do, Maggie, hurt you."

Eddie held a chair for her. "You look ravishing, kiddo."

Maggie laughed and said, "You've been hanging around Alice too long, Eddie. She's the only one who ever calls me *kiddo*."

"Sorry," Eddie muttered.

"No," Maggie said putting her hand over his as he took the chair next to hers. "I've spoiled enough of everyone's weekend as it is. Let's all start over again and I want to make one unbreakable law: no more sorrys and no more apologies." Her eyes sparkled. "Everyone is hereby forgiven of everything and I decree that we will all have a wonderful time."

If the dinner was a portent of the following days, it was to be a magnificent holiday. The only touchy moment was when Eddie announced that he was paying for everything, which brought a dagger-look from Alice. Maggie didn't rightfully know how to handle it when Eddie pressed two one-hundred-dollar bills into her palms and said, "Just so you don't think I'm playing favorites." He laughed.

Maggie knew what he was referring to and tried to give the money back. Eddie shook his head and unheard by anyone but her said, "It'll put everyone on the same footing, so to speak, Maggie. Alice took hers," he added with a shrug.

It didn't make her feel any better but she pocketed the two hundred dollars. She'd give it to a charity as she intended to gamble away her own money.

After dinner Mike and Maggie cut out on their own. "To explore," Mike said.

Las Vegas was a wonderland, they found. Neither one of them had ever been there before and everything they saw they marvelled at, relishing each other more than anything else. She felt like a senior on her first date, all dressed up and caught up in the magic of a fairyland.

Maggie said, "I wonder why they called it 'The Meadows' when it's out here in the middle of a desert."

"The Meadows?"

"That's what 'Las Vegas' means in Spanish."

The city was breathtaking with its bustling pace and modern architectural beauty, its brilliant lights and balmy nights. There seemed to be just as many people at three o'clock in the morning as at mid-afternoon; nothing ever closed and no one ever slept, it seemed. Maggie had always thought of Las Vegas as a gawdy, plastic-covered movie set where people caroused and debauched themselves indecently, but it was not like that—unless, like everywhere else, you reached deep below the surface. The lights and activity were intoxicating, and Mike made it all so new and fresh and scrubbed. How unfair she'd been by thinking sex was the only thing on his young mind! He was so decent, so innocent.

There was nothing innocent about his goodnight kiss. He held her tightly in his arms, pressing his firm body hard against hers, forcing his tongue between her lips, kissing her deeply, passionately. She felt his need for her and also felt herself weakening to that need with an answering one from within herself. Somehow she managed to ease herself out of his embrace before it was too late.

"No," she said softly as he reluctantly let her go. "I'm sorry, Mike. I can't. Not yet."

"I love you, Maggie," he whispered.

She smiled a tolerant, motherly smile. "You don't know what love is, Michael."

"Please don't say that, Maggie. I'm not a child. I know what I'm doing and how I feel."

"Then behave yourself," she chided as she patted his cheek. "I've grown exceedingly fond of you, you know that; but let's keep it there for the time being."

He smiled and said, "I'll unlock my connecting door if you'll unlock yours."

"Alice thought of everything, didn't she, even connecting rooms." She wagged a finger at him. "My side stays locked, young man."

He shrugged, pretending indifference. "Mine doesn't, so in case you get cold or lonesome all you have to is turn the latch."

"Stop tempting a vulnerable woman."

"Are you vulnerable, Maggie?"

"Very," she admitted.

"Then sleep with me. Please." He started to take her into his arms again but Maggie resisted.

"I've got to get to bed," she said as she slipped away. "I'm very tired and it's very late. Goodnight, Mike. Call me when you get up. We'll have breakfast at the pool."

"If you change your mind about that connecting door, don't hesitate."

"I won't change my mind, so get some sleep."

Maggie did have a change of heart while she lay tossing and trying desperately to satisfy the itching, the burning in her loins. She needed Doug very badly; it had been too long and it wasn't fair that Alice had conspired to put this terrible temptation in the adjoining room. It took every ounce of determination to keep from throwing back the covers and unbolting the door. She tried not to think of Doug and Phyllis but found herself wondering how Phyllis reacted to Doug's lovemaking. Did she bolt and thrash about when he pushed in and out of her so forcefully, so deeply? Maggie could almost feel the heat of Doug's body, the strength of his muscles, the smell of his sweat as they clung together in the throes of sexual excitement. She wanted to feel his hairy chest brushing against her soft breasts, tickling her nipples, making them harden and pout just as they were doing now as she stroked them.

In the next room Mike lay nude, the sheets thrown back, his mind fired by the closeness of Maggie. He tried to force the need for sex out of his mind but the harder he tried the greater the need became.

"Maggie," he breathed, running his hands over his smooth, hot body.

The torture was too intense. He had to at least try, he decided, as he flung himself off the bed and went to the connecting doors. He stood trembling with anticipation, fortified by the confidence of youth. He tapped lightly on the door, whispering her name with an urgency that surprised him. He pressed his ear tight against the panel and listened for the slightest trace of movement.

He tapped again, this time slightly heavier.

Nothing.

"Maggie," he said harshly, almost demanding.

He leaned his whole naked body flat against the door, feeling the coolness of the air-conditioning against his bare skin, the thick pile of the carpeting under his bare feet. He heard nothing from the other side of the door and his whole being sagged under the weight of his disappointment. He heaved a heavy sigh and started to turn back toward the bed when suddenly the bolt on the other side opened and the door slowly opened.

Maggie was standing in a shaft of light, her eyes alive with wanton desire. She couldn't bring herself to look directly at his nakedness but she knew he was naked. She kept her eyes carefully fixed on his, praying her courage would not fail her.

"Maggie," he breathed, staring at her loveliness. Her hair hung loose, the outline of her nudity was silhouetted through the transparent nightdress.

She teetered slightly from the strain of her emotions. Mike saw her falter and rushed toward her just as she collapsed into his arms. He swept her up and carried her toward the bed.

Their mouths clung together; they kissed deeply, passionately, as Mike fumbled with the gauzy material of her dress. Their bodies shook with desire mingled with the excitement of fear, fear that this one single act might be the culmination or possibly the ruination of a beautiful relationship.

Maggie opened her eyes and looked into Mike's handsome, young face. She found herself staring, trying to understand why Mike's face was over her—where Doug's face was supposed to be.

"Mike," she said in a dazed, far-away voice.

"It's all right."

It didn't seem right, somehow, but she could not do anything to prevent what she knew to be inevitable. Further, she could not help thinking how young, how handsome, how beautiful Mike was. He was something from her youth, a carry-over from her single years. He was her past coming back to be with her for a short while. He was Doug when they first met; he was their honeymoon, all those wonderful carefree times before David was born. She found herself beginning to respond to his inexperienced caresses, the way she once reacted to Doug's.

"Darling," Mike breathed as he covered her breasts with his kisses. He suckled her nipples, one at a time, then licked between the creamy mound of flesh as if searching for her heart. Maggie felt the fires begin to build inside her as Mike's tongue busied itself over her raging flesh, moving down, down to regions she knew were forbidden.

"No," she whispered as he reached the tangle of pubic hair that grew at her groin. "No," she said again, this time more urgently as Mike tried to part her thighs.

"What's wrong?" he asked, softly touching his lips to hers.

"It's wrong," she said, trying not to emphasize his inexperience.

He smiled endearingly and encouraged her with his smile. "I love you, Maggie. I love every part of you.

There's nothing wrong in what I was doing." He began to move down over her again.

She stopped him by cupping her hand under his chin and bringing his face back to hers. "I guess I'm just old-fashioned."

He smiled again and said, "Then I'll have to teach you the way it's done these days."

He started to kiss her mouth again. After a while Maggie found herself staring at him, engraving his features on her mind; she also found herself needing him desperately as her legs seemed involuntarily to wrap themselves around his waist as Mike fitted himself into her.

He was quick and anxious, not patiently tender as she was accustomed to with Doug, but the excitement of his penetration stirred her as she began to move under his forceful thrusts.

Maggie clung to him, her hands rubbing through the slick sheet of perspiration on his back, and the smell of his male odor made her all the more ardent. Mike moved like a young, fleet animal, light as air, yet there was a power that made her head swim under his assault.

When they came together every bone and muscle of her body jarred, her throat felt parched, her head throbbed with delicious ecstasy as her nails raked his naked back. She was delirious with her need to climax and urged Mike on to fulfill that need.

"Oh, Mike," she moaned as she felt her climax building and building.

"Darling," he breathed, covering her mouth with his.

His onslaught grew more intense as he pounded into her vulnerable body. Maggie squeezed shut her eyes and gave herself up to the tantalizing sensations that coursed through her.

And then it was over and she found herself drifting down from some lofty peak, floating on currents of air that soothed and cooled her burning flesh.

They slept very little that night, dozing, making love, dozing again. The sun was far up over the desert horizon before she untangled herself from Mike's young, sinewy limbs and said, "You'd better get back to your own room."

"Why?"

"Because I'm still a married woman and I have a reputation to think about."

Mike laughed and said, "It's a little late to be thinking about that now, isn't it?" He pulled her into his arms and kissed her again.

"Go!" she said as she pushed him playfully away.

Mike kissed her again and got out of bed. He started for the door and as Maggie stretched out on the bed he stopped and turned back. With a flying leap he threw himself on top of her, forcing her legs apart, wedging himself between. Holding her flat on the bed, he moved himself down at an impossible angle and plastered his mouth against her vagina.

Maggie gave a yelp and tried to push him away.

Mike looked up at her and said, "I love that too . . . almost as much as I love you." He got quickly off the bed and went into his room, closing the connecting doors.

She lay for a long time trying to decide whether she had done the right thing by giving in to her lust for Mike's body. The sex had been wonderfully exciting, but different from anything she'd ever known with Doug. Mike had been so inexperienced in certain ways and too experienced in others. His oral fetish she attributed to his youthful enthusiasm and she wondered idly where he'd learned to enjoy such a thing.

Mike had managed to make her metamorphosis complete by returning her to her sexual beginning. The night had seemed like her first time with Doug, a flight back to earlier days when everything was pure and good and clean.

"Doug," she whispered as she closed her eyes and snuggled into her pillow. Her eyes suddenly opened, and she whispered instead, "Mike!"

Chapter 15

She blamed her newfound interest in sex on the novelty of the affair. Mike was so zealous, so full of youthful enthusiasm, constantly and easily aroused and always hungry for the delights of her body. She found his exuberance gratifying and flattering, convincing her that her middle-aged body was still capable of intriguing, exciting, and captivating a man years younger than herself.

Maggie didn't try to hide her affair from anyone, with the exception of Doug and the children. However, as time passed Mike became so demanding of her that she found it difficult to deprive him and keep up a front with her family. As a result, whenever Maggie put her husband or children first, Mike grew peevish and sulked, which caused Maggie pain as well as pleasure. He was like David in many ways in that he pouted when deprived, punished her in little ways whenever he didn't get his own way.

Her motherly approach didn't work with Mike as it did with Doug and David. Mike wanted her to be as frivolous and playful as himself, chiding her for her prudishness, laughing at her strict sense of morality. She usually gave in to whatever he wanted, except when it came to certain "modern innovations" which Mike tried to introduce her to while having sex.

"You really are Victorian, Maggie," he complained one evening after having had sex in his apartment.

She was just finishing slipping into her clothes. Mike was waiting to walk her to the bus terminal. She knew what he was referring to and, as usual, disliked talking about sex, especially with the lights on and both of them fully dressed. "You're just too loose for my rigid sense of morality, Mike. Remember," she said, trying to sound flippant, "I am an older woman, brought up in a stricter society than exists today."

"For crying out loud, Maggie, why can't you relax with me and do whatever you feel like? You always go strictly by the book."

She pecked his cheek. "You know I hate these discussions, Michael."

Whenever she called him Michael he knew it was time to back off or else it meant going without seeing her for several days. It was *her* way of punishing *him* for doing something *she* didn't like. Or was she punishing herself? he wondered.

David was still up when she got home, sitting in the kitchen drinking milk and eating a ham sandwich while he pored over several brochures spread out on the table. He said, "You're late again." It wasn't a complaint, just a comment.

"Yes." She refused to lie and didn't want to explain. "What are you reading?"

"College pamphlets."

"I thought you decided you wanted to work for your father for a year before going to college?"

David ignored the question and out of a clear blue sky asked, "Mom, do you know that Dad is seeing Phyllis pretty regularly?"

Maggie's hand froze on the milk carton as she was putting it back in the refrigerator. "Yes," she said in a feeble, hesitant voice.

"Are you and Dad going to get a divorce so he can marry Phyllis?"

"You've met Phyllis?"

"Yeah. Dad introduced us. I didn't like her much."

"If your father likes her then there must be something there to like," she said trying to skirt around the main issue.

"I guess I just don't want to like her. I know I'm old enough to know about divorce and all but I don't like the idea of you and Dad living apart. Isn't there any chance of you two making up?" There was a pleading in his voice.

"I don't know." She thought of Mike. "Right now it doesn't seem very likely."

"Are you seeing someone else?"

She put the milk carton in the refrigerator and shut the door, then picked up his empty glass and rinsed it out in the sink, giving her time to think about her answer. David was eighteen now and certainly had the right to know what was going on in his own house. Besides, she was getting tired of sneaking around, of feeling sordid and dirty whenever she had to pretend. She steeled herself and said, "As a matter of fact, I am seeing someone."

"Oh?"

"Mike Ballantine, to be precise."

"Mike? Timmy's brother? You've got to be kidding!"

She saw the laughter in his eyes, heard it in his words. She grew angry but didn't want him to see it. "What's so humorous about my seeing Mike Ballantine?"

"He's my age, for cripe's sake."

"He's a lot older than you, David," she said, trying to keep her voice even.

David shrugged. He was still grinning when he said, "Don't they call that cradle snatching?"

"That's enough, David!"

David got up and kissed her cheek. "Only kiddin', Mom. If Mike's what you want then good luck to you. In my book he's a great guy, and I gotta admit you don't look anything like the mother I grew up with." He shuffled the pamphlets into a stack and tucked them under his arm. "I'm going to hit the sack. See you at breakfast."

"David," she said as he was leaving. He turned. "Do me a favor and don't say anything to your father about Mike . . . not just yet, okay?"

"Sure. My lips are sealed." Although he was smiling she thought she saw a pained expression in his eyes, as if he were dreadfully disappointed with her.

After an uncomfortable night of deliberating with herself, Maggie made up her mind that she should stop seeing Mike, that David was right, she wasn't acting her age and should face facts. She was robbing the cradle. There wasn't any decent future for a woman her age to be married to a man so much younger. Then, of course, Mike hadn't even suggested marrying, hadn't even considered it as far as she knew.

She'd tell him they'd have to cool it for a while, until she could think more clearly, but the following night when she saw him her resolve, as usual, petered out and she found herself in bed with him before the evening was over.

"I told David about us," she said. "He thinks I'm robbing the cradle." Admitting the fear, she found, made it less frightening.

"That's only because he doesn't want to admit that his mother is an extremely sensual, desirable, wonderful, beautiful woman." He kissed her breasts, her stomach. He even ventured to kiss the inside of her thighs and was surprised that she didn't stop him, as she usually did. "Getting used to my vulgar perversions already?"

She shook her head. "Just too tired and contented to stop you." She tousled his hair. "Precocious youth must have its way."

He laughed and said, "I'll make an indecent slut out of you yet."

"Seriously, Mike, I'm worried about what David might think about me. He knows Doug is seeing Phyllis Bracken and might even be considering marrying her."

"Good, then that leaves you available to marry me."

"Marry you?" she asked, surprised.

"Sure. Why not? You don't think I want a harlot in my bed every night? I have every intention of making an honest woman of you, Maggie. I've just been waiting to see which side of the fence you're going to land on, mine or Doug's. I'll be happy to volunteer my services at Doug's wedding by giving away his bride."

Maggie stiffened. The thought of Doug marrying someone else made her feel queasy. "Let's not get too hasty," she managed.

He took her into his arms and placed her head on his bare shoulder. "You really should start thinking about whether you want to divorce Doug, Maggie. If you want my advice, I'd invite Doug over and sit down and have a serious talk about it. I don't care if you marry me or not, just so long as you continue seeing me like this for the rest of our lives, but I really would like to hear people call you Mrs. Ballantine."

Mrs. Margaret Booth Ballantine, she thought. Somehow the alliteration bothered her, or was she just too accustomed to Margaret Booth Hampton?

"Maybe you're right, Mike. All last night I tossed about swearing you and I had no future, but when I'm with you I have no doubts at all. Truthfully, I'm sick to death of our having to sneak around like naughty children. Doug makes no pretenses about his affair with Phyllis—so why should I try to hide you under a rug?"

"That's my girl," he said, kissing her. "Now that we have that settled how about inviting me over for the weekend."

"Hold it, Cowboy Bill, let's not jump the gun. I still have a reputation I'd like to keep. Come to Saddlebrook on Saturday for dinner and a movie, but certainly not for the entire weekend."

"Will you never stop being a product of the Victorian age?"

"Never."

"Okay then, I guess I'm stuck with just dinner and a show."

"I'll see that David is at home. I want him to get to know you better."

"We like each other pretty well already."

"As his best friend's older brother," Maggie pointed out. "I want him to start thinking of you as a possible stepfather."

"Hey, you really are starting to think of me seriously." She nodded. "Wow! I'll put on my best stepfather attitude."

That Saturday was far more successful than Maggie had ever hoped it could be. Mike and David got along splendidly and never once did Maggie get the impression that she was out with two youngsters. Mike was serious and responsible, politely reprimanding David whenever he got too giddy or brash in ogling the girls at the movies. They went to see a Jane Fonda film, which insured that there wouldn't be a lot of rock-talk or punk slang which David and Mike were fond of.

The closeness of Mike and David pleased her immeasurably; but as the weeks passed she started to feel that David was monopolizing Mike's time and she grew a little anxious about it. One Saturday when Mike arrived at the house David grabbed his arm and said, "Hey, I thought you'd never get here. I got tickets for the drag races over at the fairgrounds."

"No, no drag races," Maggie said firmly. "I hope I needn't remind you that Mike came to see me, not you, young man."

"Holy cow, Mom, you see Mike every day, practically."

"David," she warned.

Mike said, "What's the harm, Maggie? We'll all be together. Come on. Let's take in the races. You'll like them even better than the stock cars."

She gave in, but she didn't enjoy the races at all.

And when Julie came home from her vacation Maggie found she had still another rival for Mike's attention. Julie found Mike captivating and was constantly flirting with him until David wised her up on the score.

"Mother and Mike? You're putting me on, Dave."

"Nope. And that's right from the horse's mouth."

"Mother told you she was having an affair with Mike?"

"She didn't say it that way; she said she was 'seeing him,' which is her way of saying she's sleeping with him." In a lower tone he said, "She was always very late getting home when you were away at the lake, and one look at her when she came home, anyone could see sex written all over her face."

"That's disgusting."

"What's so disgusting about it? Believe it or not, Julie, people Mom and Dad's age still have sex."

"It's still disgusting." She made a horrid face. "And with poor Mike! She must have something on him, don't you think? Why else would he want to go to bed with an older woman like Mother?"

David grinned and said, "You'd much rather it to be you, right?"

Julie turned beet red. "Don't be an ass."

"I see the way you're always playing up to him. There was a time or two when I thought Mom was going to haul off and belt you. Every time you see Mike you practically throw yourself at him."

"I'm closer to Mike's age than Mother is."

"Just don't make such a fool out of yourself when he's around."

"Why?" Julie whined. "Are you afraid I'll cut into your time with him? If I didn't know both of you better I'd think you two had the hots—always with your heads together and talking and whispering."

"You have a sick mind."

Maggie complained to Mike about their lack of privacy when the children were around, which seemed to be constantly now that Mike was a regular visitor.

He said, "I thought that was the original idea of my coming over here, to get the kids to like me."

"I hadn't planned on Julie trying to seduce you and David occupying all your time."

Mike laughed and said, "Yeah, Julie has been coming on a bit strong. I'll have to let her down easy or she'll hate me for life. Girls are very impressionable at her age."

Maggie felt a sting. "And I suppose you are an expert on girls Julie's age?"

It was thoughts such as this that she found creeping all too often into her head. When alone she sat for hours trying to figure out the answer to the simple question: Am I really in love and truly happy with a man young enough to be my son?

She couldn't come up with any concrete answer, not one that satisfied her conscience.

To face the truth would be to admit that she still loved Doug and no one would ever take his place. But Doug was lost to her and she had to plan for what lay ahead. She didn't want a solitary life without a man beside her in bed. She was the kind of woman who needed a husband, not particularly for protection or manly strength, but a husband who would make her feel like the woman she was, feminine and soft and comforting. She enjoyed being a woman, and preferably a married woman.

She came to the conclusion after a long period of contemplation, that Mike was the only man she wanted to take Doug's place, if Doug was to be replaced. Mike wasn't exactly an alternate; she really loved him, but she loved him in an entirely different way. Doug and she had been a perfect match being that they were the same age, the same temperament—the same vintage, so to speak. As far as she and Mike were concerned, they were complete opposites in just about everything, but paradoxically they were matching opposites, well suited to be together.

Her only reservation about Mike was that their romance might be short-lived, like a picnic at the beach—different, fun and stimulating, but over too soon, too soon a memory, leaving the pain of a dreadful sunburn. Mike was so active and she feared that her mature temperament would one day stop appreciating his noisy activity. There was a lot of the child in Mike; it bothered her at times, though at other times she found it delightful. When he acted like a child she got a nagging feeling that perhaps she was only attracted to him because of her similar attraction to David and Julie. True, she mothered Doug, but that was all right because she and Doug were the same age and it seemed harmless; in Mike's case he was still young enough to misinterpret her desire to mother him, or conversely she might misinterpret her desire to mother him.

She knew she hurt Mike whenever she jabbed him with one of her barbs about younger girls, but there was something in her nature that forced her into these sensitive areas of Mike's life, like a demolition expert working to defuse a cache of primed explosives. Perhaps one gigantic explosion would be an end to her quandary, yet she feared that the explosion would destroy her as well.

There was no doubt that despite Mike's youthful appearance and occasional actions, he was very mature and thought deeply. He was always quick to reassure her that if he was tempted by young girls he would not be with her, always hurt and sullen when she treated him flippantly or wouldn't take him seriously.

He said, "I'm a very serious guy, Maggie; you should know that about me. I never kid around when I'm serious about something the way I'm serious about you. I am in love with you, Maggie. There will never be another woman in my life who I'll ever love as much as I love you. I want to marry you and I'd very much appreciate it if you'd have your talk with Doug and not keep me hanging any longer."

"Soon," she promised. "Soon, my dearest." She laid her hand on his cheek. "I just haven't found the right time."

To her complete surprise he slapped her hand away so violently that he actually hurt her. She winced and grabbed her wrist. He wasn't even aware that he'd hurt her, she noticed.

"Damn it, I'm tired of waiting for you to find the right time." He stood up and began pacing the room, running his hands through his hair. "Talk to him, damn it! You have me on a friggin' tight-wire and if I'm going to fall off, for Christ's sake let me fall and get it over with but don't keep me dangling like a stupid puppet."

His outburst was so unexpected she found herself staring at him as though he were a complete stranger. She hadn't planned on talking to Doug that Saturday evening but when he showed up at the house unexpectedly when Maggie was waiting for Mike, she remembered Mike's outburst and decided this would be as good a time as any. Mike had called and said he'd be a little late but that he'd be there, never fear, so when the doorbell rang and she saw Doug she decided on the spur of the moment that their heart-to-heart talk was long overdue.

"Hello, Maggie," Doug said. "I hope I haven't come at an inconvenient time?" Before she could answer he said, "I see you're dressed to go out. I won't keep you."

"No. Come in, please, Doug. I was planning on having dinner with a friend but he's going to be late. I thought perhaps you and I should talk."

Doug came in carrying a large cardboard box. "I found that staying at the hotel proved to be a little too expensive so I rented a furnished single over on the Palisades."

Near Phyllis, Maggie thought but she didn't say it. "I see."

"I wanted to get a few of my personal things, if that's okay." He made a self-conscious gesture. "You know, something to make the place feel a little more homey."

"Of course. Take whatever you like."

The stiffness between them was tremendously intense and Maggie could not find any way of bringing the conversation around to what she wanted to say. She thought perhaps she'd better lead into it by putting him on the defensive. "How's Phyllis?" she asked. She hoped she hadn't sounded bitchy; she wanted their conversation to be as friendly as possible.

"Fine. She's fine."

"Doug, I think. . . ." Just then the doorbell rang again. Maggie hesitated, knowing it must be Mike. "We have to talk," she said, then turned and went to the door. Doug went into his study leaving the door open.

When Maggie opened the door Mike stepped inside and immediately pulled her into his arms and kissed her hard on the mouth. She struggled slightly but he held her firmly, turning the kiss passionate and lingering.

She managed to ease herself away and whispered, "Doug's in the study."

Both of them turned and saw Doug watching them from the doorway.

For Doug his life ended at that exact moment. He'd never before seen Maggie in the arms of another man and now that he had he felt as though he'd been dropped into a box and the lid nailed shut over his head, leaving him in empty blackness. This was the terrible price he'd been made to pay for his innocent transgression with Phyllis, his selfish need for physical diversions. The idea that he would ruin his marriage and lose Maggie forever had been nothing more than a nagging threat, a possibility, but now he saw for himself that the threat had become an actual consequence, the possible disaster had become material destruction. He'd flirted with his own ruination and had lost.

There was no escaping it, he thought; he would have no other choice now but to make the best of his difficult lot.

"Oh, Doug," Maggie said, patting her hair nervously. "You remember Mike Ballantine?"

The two men shook hands, Mike smug and smiling, Doug serious. What could Maggie possibly see in this young jerk? Doug wondered. Good God, he was practically a boy. Had Maggie lost her mind? His heart sank. He felt very old, very tired, and could think of nothing to say. He picked up his empty carton again and giving Mike and Maggie a little nod he went back into the study, tactfully closing the door.

Maggie looked anxiously at Mike. "We've hurt him terribly."

"Yes, I guess we have," Mike admitted, feeling concerned. "I didn't want to do that."

"I know you didn't, darling. You had no way of knowing he was here."

"Still . . ."

"Make yourself a drink, Mike. I think I'd better go in and speak with my husband."

As she started toward the study Mike grabbed her hand. "I wish you'd start referring to him as *Doug* and not your *husband*. It would make me feel so much better."

Maggie smiled but she gave no promise and went into Doug's study.

As she closed the door she saw him putting a few books into the box and said, "I've tried not to disturb any of your things."

"It wouldn't have mattered." He sounded so hurt.

"Doug . . ."

"Don't say anything, Maggie. You have nothing to apologize for, if that's what you are intending to do."

The accusation in his tone rankled her. "I was not going to apologize. I have every right to entertain if I so choose."

"Maggie, I don't want to argue. You, as you said, have every right." He put another book in the box. "How old is he?"

She fumed. "Old enough to be in love with me."

"What does he do, park cars at the ball park?"

"You're being deliberately insulting, Doug. Mike Ballantine is an extremely nice young man. At least he doesn't run after every woman who smiles at him."

"Neither do I."

He was right in that, she told herself. He didn't run after women, from what she'd learned from Alice; and in Phyllis's case it had been Phyllis who did the chasing.

Maggie sighed. "Why are we always snapping at one another?" She took a step toward him. "It was never like this before."

"We never lived apart before."

"And whose fault is that?"

Doug shrugged as he put the last of his things into the box. "Mine, I suppose."

Maggie said nothing; she waited expectantly for him to say how sorry he was for having caused this rupture in their lives. He just admitted that he was in the wrong; so why didn't he ask her to forgive him and they could get back to where they once were?

It broke her heart to hear him say, "I guess it's all for the best, the way things have worked out. You deserve better than me. You always have. You're a young, vibrant, beautiful woman, Maggie. I admit that I'm envious of that young guy out there," he said, motioning with his head toward the other room. "But I really don't resent him because he's young; I'll always be jealous of any man you fall in love with."

She wanted to stop him by screaming, *But I don't love anyone as much as I love you.* Unfortunately the words would not come.

"I'll never permit my personal feelings to interfere with your happiness ever again, Maggie. You want a different world from the one I can give you. You want to be around those odd-ball friend of yours, and I have no right to insist you live the kind of life I want you to live." He paused, knowing his next remark would cut her deeply. But it had to be said for the sake of both their happinesses. "And you have to let me have the kind of life I want to live."

He saw her flinch and averted his eyes to avoid her pained expression.

"I'm sorry, Maggie. I hope you and what's-his-name will be very happy together. When you want to get together about the divorce settlement here's my new address and telephone number." He scribbled it on a pad and handed it to her.

She couldn't take the slip of paper.

He laid it on the desk and went to the door. Before opening it he turned and said, "I wish it could have worked out differently, Maggie, but I suppose we both need our different tomorrows."

He went quickly, hiding the tears that were stinging the backs of his eyes. He ignored Mike who was standing in the doorway of the den and as Doug cradled his box under his arm he kept his head down and went out the front door.

Mike stood watching the closed door of the study, waiting for Maggie to come out. He waited several minutes before going over and tapping on it. When Maggie opened it he saw that she'd been crying. He took her into his arms and said, "I love you, Maggie, if that will help any."

She nodded against his chest. "Oh, Mike, I've made a terrible mess of everything."

"Marry me."

She moved away from him, fumbling for a handkerchief. She blew her nose and said, "You'd better watch what you say, Mike, because it looks as if I'm going to be a free woman very shortly."

"Darling." He took her in his arms again. "Please say you'll marry me. I'll do anything in the world to make you happy."

She caught herself before she made the mistake of giving in to her self-pity and accepted his proposal. Things had happened much too fast. Although Doug's cutting remark about Mike's occupation had been meant to hurt her, there was something to be said for the question. What did Mike do? Up until now she'd been having too much fun to care and loved him too much for it to matter. However, if she were to marry him, that was an entirely different matter.

He had a job, that much she knew, but doing what? He never spoke about his work except to say he hated it—whatever it was. She'd pressed him once but he'd avoided her question by saying he didn't like doing his job and certainly didn't like talking about it. He didn't make much of a salary so it could hardly be anything illegal, she decided.

"I've got to think, Mike. I wish with all my heart that I could honestly say 'Yes, I'll marry you.' But I can't. There are too many things to consider."

"Such as what?"

She didn't want to bring up his livelihood, fearing to upset him. "There's the children, the house, my work, our ages."

"Always back to the age bit? The kids like me; we can sell the house or live in it as you wish; you can keep your job if it makes you happy; and forget about the difference in our ages—which isn't all that much and certainly not important. I can never understand why it's considered all right for a man to marry a woman fifteen or twenty years younger than himself but if a woman marries a guy one, two years younger, the tongues start wagging. The big thing for you to decide, darling Maggie, is whether you are still in love with Doug. I honestly believe that you are. So, what I suggest is that you and he get together—just the two of you—and talk it all out without me being in the next room or Phyllis Bracken waiting for Doug around the corner."

"You're so wonderful," she said, hugging him. "And so very wise for. . . ."

"Yeah, I know, for a kid." He grinned then grew serious. "A long talk with Doug will clear the air if you both decide to be totally honest with each other. Lay it all out and don't, for God's sake, get into an argument, just talk to each other calmly and rationally and come right out and ask each other what are your chances of getting back together, if that's what you want." He looked deep into her eyes. "I don't want to see you go back to Doug, but I'm not a selfish guy, Maggie, and if that's what you want, then okay. I'll just have to accept it, I guess."

As usual his maturity and sensibility surprised her. However, when she looked into his face she could see the fear, the difficulty he was having with being so mature. She saw the boy there inside trying to keep from crying out for her love, wanting her to be reckless and run away with him and forget everything except love and all the nice things that went with it.

"You're a very wise young man, Mike," she said.

"You're always telling me that. Why is it so surprising for someone my age to be sensible?"

"Sense usually comes from experience."

"That, dear heart," he said, tweaking her nose, "Depends upon the type of experience."

All that evening Maggie was tempted to bring up one of the major drawbacks to her marrying Mike. His livelihood. It wasn't until after dinner, while they sipped coffee, that she summoned up the courage to ask. "I know you hate talking about it, Mike, but as long as we might be getting in over our heads in our relationship, I think we should talk about your future."

"My future will be with you, I hope."

"No, I mean, what do you want to do? Your ambitions? Your work?"

He shrugged. "Is that important?"

"I think it is."

"There's your old Victorian background coming out again." He put down his cup and said, "Right now I know I don't make enough to support you the way Doug does, but I intend to change all that. Something will come along that pays more than I'm making now."

"A bigger salary isn't necessarily the answer. It isn't the money I'm concerned about, it's you and what you want to do with your life. Marrying me is one thing, but we—God willing—will be married for the rest of our lives and we can't live on love. I don't want you to wake up one morning and feel yourself stuck in a life with which you aren't happy. You have got to like your work as much as you like your wife and family. They all go hand in hand." She shook her head at the waiter with the pastry tray. Mike selected a Napoleon. "You should think about going to college or settle into a career that pleases you."

His indulgent smile returned. "You're confusing me with Doug, Maggie. I'm not that kind of guy. Whatever I work at I'm happy doing—at least for the time being. When I become unhappy I change it."

"But you can't go through your whole life like that."

"Why not?"

"Because. . . . Well, because that's just not the way it's done."

"You mean, that's the way it wasn't done when you married Doug. Everyone's values are different nowadays, Maggie. It's live for today and tomorrow will take care of itself . . . if we're even here tomorrow. That's the one thing about you that I'll have to do some serious work on changing. You've been taught always to make definite plans for whatever lays ahead, for whatever pitfall or emergency. Now I'm of the school that believes you take one step at a time until you get to where you want to be. Believe me, my way is best because it's more adventurous. There are no guarantees in this life so why try to manufacture some? You thought your life with Doug was everything you'd ever dreamed of until you found out for yourself that it wasn't." He tasted the Napoleon. "Making plans is fine but sometimes it takes all the fun out of things. Personally I hate to know exactly what I'll be doing tomorrow because tonight something might happen to prevent me from doing it. It's like the tourists who land in a new city and the first thing they do is rush out to all the old historical landmarks, the places that will always be there. Not me, Maggie. I want to see all those places that are brand new and might be torn down tomorrow."

Maggie laughed and said, "You amaze me."

"Don't laugh, Maggie. I'm being perfectly serious. And after you've had your talk with Doug I want you to sit quietly alone and think about the way I look at life, then ask yourself, 'Is that the kind of husband I can be happy with?' I'm not Doug, Maggie. I'll never be anything remotely similar to him. You've got to understand that."

Mike was right, of course; he wasn't Doug and when she lay in bed alone that night she understood what Mike was saying but wondered if she could adapt to his way of life, a life that seemed to be without any definite future.

She shook her head on the pillow then sat up. She wasn't going to be able to fall asleep if she continued tossing the questions about inside her head. There was only one question she need answer and the rest would take care of themselves. Did she love Mike enough to marry him—a man with different ideas, different outlooks, a man from a new generation? She went into the bathroom and took a valium, and got back into bed to let her mind concentrate.

The answer came smoothly enough. Yes, if she couldn't have Doug.

After that restless night, she didn't wrestle with the question, promising herself that the first chance she got she'd take Mike's advice and pay a visit to Doug and just talk and clear the air without any interference from anybody.

When she called Doug at his office he said, "I'll be home all evening. How about having dinner?"

"No, I think not, Doug." She didn't want anything to act as a distraction. She made up her mind to speak bluntly to Doug, settling once and for all exactly where they both stood. Tonight would decide everything, she thought as she went back to her work and hoped the afternoon would end quickly.

As five o'clock neared, however, she found herself anxious to catch her bus home. She didn't linger over her usual after-work Perrier water with Mike, giving David as an excuse and saying nothing to Mike about her planned meeting with Doug—she didn't want to have him press her for details tomorrow in case it turned out that she and Doug stayed married. In the event she'd have to think of how to let Mike down easily. Even as brave as he professed to be about accepting whatever answer she arrived at, he'd be terribly hurt if she decided against him.

Too often she'd heard him insist that he'd "understand" if she decided to stay married to Doug. She found it hard to believe in his "understanding," because of his age; she had the feeling that it was all surface, not really a part of his true self, just a show at being a man of the world . . . like Humphrey Bogart sacrificing himself for Ingrid Bergman's happiness. That stuff happened in the movies.

On the other hand, perhaps it was envy that someone so young could be so wise and practical—because Maggie had to admit that she certainly wasn't wise and practical, and it seemed unnatural to her that Mike should be.

With a tiny shake of annoyance she wondered why she was always looking for faults in Mike. Why couldn't she accept him as he claimed to be and not be suspicious over every little thing?

At home, she fixed herself and David a quick dinner— steaks on the grill—and took a long time deciding what to wear. She didn't want to wear anything too sexy and revealing, yet she didn't want to be too conservative either. She tried to see herself the way Doug would want her. The only thing that came to mind was her frumpy house dresses and they were definitely *out!* Whether Doug approved or not, that part of her life was over forever.

"Are you going out?" David asked, looking up from the TV.

"Just going over to see your father. I don't think I'll be late."

He winked and said, "With any kind of luck I hope you will be."

David planted a notion in her head which was still there when she turned onto Doug's street and began searching out the number of his building. It was more fashionable than she'd imagined, but then why not? Doug wasn't a struggling construction worker anymore; he now had his own business and a rather successful one at that, so he deserved to live as well as he liked. Yet, something didn't ring true; it wasn't the type of building she pictured Doug living in. It was very luxurious—the kind of an apartment building that would appeal more to a woman.

His apartment was on the top floor. A penthouse, no less, Maggie said to herself as she stepped from the elevator. Why had Doug given her the impression that he'd rented a modest one-bedroom furnished place, a substitute hotel room?

Phyllis Bracken answered the door. Maggie stood there staring at her with one part of her brain asking Why? and the other answering Why not? After all, she hadn't told Doug what she wanted to talk to him about—so perhaps Doug saw no harm in having his mistress present.

Maggie felt utterly humiliated and embarrassed, both of which changed to downright rage.

Phyllis said, "Let's not pretend we don't know each other, Maggie. Doug stepped out for a moment, I guess. He wasn't here when I got here. He should be back any second."

"I . . ." Maggie couldn't think of a single excuse to get her out of there.

"Come on in."

Maggie didn't move; she couldn't. How dare Doug do this to her? It was obvious now that he and Phyllis were far beyond the "mistress" stage. He was living with her.

"No, thank you," she managed. "I've changed my mind. What I came to see Doug about isn't important. Tell him I'll phone him in a day or two." She turned quickly, anxious to get out of there.

She drove home at a reckless speed, not caring if she crashed into a tree or drove over the Palisades. Doug was obviously comfortably settled in with that whore. Thank God he hadn't been at home. Maggie felt that she would only have made a complete ass of herself by trying to see if they could patch things up.

"To hell with him," she swore as she pressed down the accelerator and sped toward home.

Chapter 16

She heard the loud music before she pulled into the driveway, the sound of it only increased her anger. It was after ten and David knew damned well that the house rule was no loud rock music after ten o'clock except on weekends.

She slammed the front door and tore through the house toward the back door and David's garage-retreat. The door was standing ajar, the music blasting, his strobe lights flashing, the colored neons spinning and twirling in every mad direction and design imaginable. She heard laughter and voices and hesitated, trying to identify the one that wasn't David's. She also smelled something sweet and thick, not unlike incense.

"Dear God," she cursed as she identified the odor of marijuana. "David!" she yelled as she pounded on the door, flinging it back.

Mike Ballantine was lying on the floor propped up on pillows with David sitting cross-legged beside him.

"Mike!"

He was grinning lopsidedly. She saw the ashtray on the floor between them and the clip holding what was left of the marijuana cigarette.

David scrambled to his feet and turned down the music.

"Turn it *off*," she ordered, then glowered at Mike. "What in hell do you think you're doing? How dare you, Michael?"

The three of them looked at each other, the varicolored lights moving over their faces, changing their fiendishly colored masks from red to green to yellow and back to red.

"Hold it, Maggie," Mike said as he got shakily to his feet. "We were just listening to some music."

"Damn it, don't take me for a jackass. Who does that belong to?" She pointed to the roach in the ashtray. "Did you bring that into my house, Michael?"

"No, Mom," David admitted. "It's mine." His face was flushed under the changing colors of the lights. He couldn't look into his mother's eyes. "I just thought. . . ."

"Yours? God in heaven," she gasped putting her knuckle to her mouth to keep herself from crying. "Yours?" she repeated.

David kicked at an imaginary object on the floor and nodded. "I thought. . . ." he began again and again he stopped.

This wasn't possible, Maggie told herself. David was lying for Mike's sake. David wasn't the kind of boy who smoked dope. They'd talked too openly about this when David was in high school and admitted then that there was a lot of peer pressure on him about his not smoking grass and said then that he wasn't interested in it. He wouldn't have lied. It had to be Mike's marijuana.

"You're lying," she said to David and turned on Mike. "You brought it here, didn't you?" She drew down her brows in an ugly scowl.

"Is that what you want to think, Maggie?" He made an indifferent gesture. "If it is, then it's okay with me."

David said, "No, really, Mom, it's mine. Some of the guys stopped by just after you drove off, then Mike showed up and the guys split. One of them left a joint." David still couldn't look at her. "When Mike and I got to talking I thought there wouldn't be any harm in our lighting up."

"Is that the truth, David? Look at me!"

He slowly raised his eyes. "Yes, Mom, that's the honest to God truth," he said evenly.

"Very well," Maggie said after a moment. With an imperious toss of her head she said, "I apologize, Michael, but you should not have encouraged my son."

"Maggie," Mike said, still wearing his lopsided grin. "What's the harm in a little grass? It's not addictive."

"Who says it isn't?"

"Everybody knows it." Mike argued.

"I do not approve of drugs of any kind, Michael. You know that because I've always made it perfectly clear when you and the others . . . indulged. I don't approve and I never will."

Mike thought he would tease her and said, "Valium is a hell of a lot stronger drug than marijuana and you're always taking Valiums."

It only infuriated her. "I think you'd better leave, Michael."

"Ah, Maggie, come on, don't be so sore. We weren't hurting anybody. It was just David and me listening to some good hot rock."

He was acting as though he'd been drinking but she knew it was the grass. "Why did you come here anyway, Michael? What did you want?"

"I was concerned about you. You acted so strangely earlier, almost anxious to get rid of me. I just thought I'd check."

"Like everyone else, Michael, I do not appreciate being checked up on. Now if you will kindly go."

He glanced at his watch. "The next bus back isn't for forty-five minutes."

David started to say something but Maggie stopped him with a wave of her hand. Maggie said, "Then you can wait on the corner." She pointed toward the door.

Mike's grin faded. The fact that she was seriously angry with him finally soaked into his drugged brain. "Maggie, I'm sorry. I know I shouldn't have. . . ."

"I shouldn't have either, Michael," she said. She needed say no more. Mike knew what she was implying.

"I'll call a cab," he said after a moment's hesitation.

Maggie felt her shoulders sag. It wasn't entirely Mike's fault, she told herself. As usual she was over-reacting, yet she would never forgive him for encouraging David, which is what it all amounted to.

She said to Mike, "I'll drive you to the bus. We have to talk."

She turned to David who was standing waiting for her wrath to settle over him. "As for you, I'll have your father deal with you in the morning. Now turn off these lights and go to your room this instant."

David said, "I still can't see the big deal. And what's Dad going to say. Phyllis is always trying to get me to smoke with her." He turned off the swirling lights.

Maggie's jaw dropped. "Phyllis. . . ." She cut herself off and said to David, "Go to bed."

Mike tried to take her hand as they walked around the house toward her car. She didn't want to chance taking Mike through the house; it might tempt them both to have coffee and linger. She did not want that. She wanted Mike out of here and out of her life. At least at the moment that's how she felt.

They drove in silence along the parkway toward the Park and Ride lot. Mike said, "I can only apologize again, Maggie, which I now do, but I will not crawl. David is no child. Whether you want to believe it or not, he knows what's going on in the world. You can't continue to shelter him by treating him like a little boy."

"He is my son, Michael, and while he is living under my roof he will abide by my rules. He knows only too well that drugs are not allowed. He broke that rule."

"All right so he broke your rule. You'll only make him sneak around the next time."

Maggie slowed down as they approached the cut off to the lot. "I didn't drive you to this bus stop to talk about David, I want to talk about you and me." She pulled into a parking space, turned off the ignition and turned to face him, knowing that the darkness outside would hide the hurt, the fear, the anger she felt.

"You're upset, Maggie. I suggest neither of us say anything about our relationship because right now we're both in no position to speak or think clearly. You're obviously angry and I'm obviously high." He gazed at her a moment, feeling a temptation to laugh. He suppressed it.

"How did your meeting with Doug go over?" Mike asked.

Maggie frowned at him. "How did you know I went to see Doug tonight?"

"David told me, of course."

She didn't say anything.

"Now I understand why you were so anxious to get home from work. You had a date with your husband." The urge to laugh got the better of him. There wasn't anything particularly funny to laugh at; he just felt like laughing. He knew it was the grass, which made it all the funnier.

His silliness only infuriated her all the more, and the more angry she got the more she needed to hurt him.

She said, "I'm sorely disappointed in you, Michael. I know now that I made a serious mistake in thinking that you could ever set anything but a poor, childish example for my children, being a child yourself. I don't think we should see one another any more."

She achieved her desired result. His head snapped around and he stared at her with bewilderment and disbelief.

"Hold on. Smoking one lousy joint with a guy who's legally of age isn't any reason for that kind of talk, Maggie. You are talking about you and me, not David and marijuana."

"I see them as one and the same, under the circumstances." She turned away from him and looked out at the blackness on the other side of the glass.

Mike grabbed her shoulders and turned her toward him. "Don't trifle with me, Maggie. Damn it, I love you. So I made a rotten mistake about the grass, but hell, I never thought you'd get so upset about such a little, insignificant thing. You can't call it quits between us just because David and I smoked a joint together."

"I think that's reason enough. I don't want my son associating with that sort of thing."

"Jesus Christ, you're unreal," he swore, throwing himself back against the seat. "I thought you were so 'with it,' so relaxed! Why did you lead me on to believe you were something you aren't and can never be?"

"I never led you to believe anything you didn't want to believe, Michael."

"For Christ's sake stop calling me *Michael*. It makes you sound like a nun I had in eighth grade." His head was getting clearer. "I don't believe this is happening," he said. "You aren't serious about not seeing me anymore? Please, Maggie, tell me you aren't serious."

She sighed again and thought for a moment. "Let me put it this way," she said calmly. "Right now I am dead serious about not seeing you again. I didn't like what I found when I came home tonight. However, to be perfectly candid I did not exactly leave my husband's apartment in a very congenial mood."

"Aha," Mike broke in, "So you were pissed off *before* you found David and me. You couldn't blow up at Doug so you blew up at his son and your lover."

"If you wish to put it so crassly, yes, I suppose I did." When he reached for her she pushed him back and said, "But I have not changed my mind about finding you and David smoking marijuana—grass, if you prefer."

Mike laughed in spite of himself. "The way you say 'grass' is like my maiden aunt saying 'shit.'"

"Stop being so damned vulgar. I've never seen this side of you before."

"And I've never seen you act like a snooty old maid. All this primness doesn't suit you, Maggie." He threw himself back again, puffed out his cheeks and fluttered the air out through his lips. "It's the grass," he admitted. "It'll wear off in a few minutes. I'm coming down now."

"I hate to be cruel, Michael, but I have no intention of waiting around to see you 'come down.' There's the bus pulling in now. I've got to get home to David."

"To tuck him in, I suppose."

She ignored his sarcasm. "Good night, Michael."

"I'll call you tomorrow," he said as he got out of the car.

"Don't. I won't be answering my phone."

"I'll call anyway."

He leaned back across the seat to kiss her but she repulsed him. "Don't call, Michael," she said, feeling frightened. "Give me a couple of days to think things out."

"Only if you promise me one thing, Maggie."

She nodded weakly.

"Just remember that we have been together quite a while now and I assume you liked everything you saw about me until tonight. Tonight is just one flaw; don't judge the whole package by that one thing you didn't like. I'm still the same honest guy you got to know and love—or should I say 'know and like'?"

She shook her head sadly. "No, you can still say *love*."

"Thank you for that, Maggie. I'll call you toward the end of the week."

"All right."

Mike didn't keep his promise. He called late the next afternoon, apologized and asked her if she'd please join him for a drink and dinner.

The scar was too new; it would take a while to heal. She was firm in declining his invitation and made him again promise not to call her for the rest of the week. He sounded hurt and depleted. She almost changed her mind, but didn't.

Doug called her when she got home Tuesday night. "You were supposed to come over last night."

"I was there," she said through her teeth. "Didn't Phyllis tell you?"

"Oh, I see."

"So do I," Maggie answered coldly.

"No, you don't. Phyllis just happened to stop by when I was out getting a bottle of champagne."

"Champagne! My, my, since when have you acquired such high-class tastes? Oh, but then I forgot, Phyllis was there, wasn't she?"

"Stop it, Maggie. You know I was getting it for you and me."

"And Phyllis. Let's not forget Phyllis, Doug. Your roomie. Is that what they call girls like her these days?"

"Sarcasm never did become you, Maggie."

"And lying was never a part of you, Doug, and I hate it. As far as I'm concerned we have nothing more to say to one another. I have every intention of going ahead with a divorce."

"Maggie, I really think we ought to talk first."

"I tried that. No, thank you, Doug. I sincerely think the three of us would have little in common to discuss, unless, of course, Phyllis wants to sit in to see what kind of property settlement I intend asking for." Before he could answer she slammed down the receiver.

Maggie spent the rest of the evening wretchedly reproaching Doug, resproaching Mike, reproaching herself. The phone rang several times but she refused to answer it and when David and Julie came in she gave orders that if anyone called—*anyone*—she was not at home. So that they wouldn't have to lie for her, she got in her car and went for a drive.

She tried to think rationally but she was in such a turmoil of emotions that she could not clear her thoughts. She considered doing reckless things, like flinging away all sense of pride and vanity and throwing herself at her husband's feet, professing her love, promising him any arrangement he wished if he would only take her and make wild, passionate love to her; or drive across the bridge and rush into Mike's apartment, insisting they drink themselves into a stupor, wallow in drugs and sex without leaving the apartment for weeks.

Of course she would do none of these and was surprised with herself for such ideas even occurring to her.

Alice, she decided as she turned onto the turnpike and headed east. Maggie felt she needed to talk rather than be alone with her irrational ideas and Alice had a way of making light of everything, even the most serious. It was part of Alice's charm, her ability to treat everything as flippantly as streamers at a parade, always aware that one had but one life and it was wrong to waste any part of it on being unhappy.

"You look either angry or in love, I can't tell which," Alice said as she let Maggie in.

"A little of both. How about a drink?"

"Oh, oh, you really are upset." She fixed her a Scotch on the rocks. "Mixes increase the calorie count." She handed Maggie the glass.

Maggie took a sip and dropped heavily into a chair feeling that in another second the weight she'd been supporting would crush her flat. "I've really made an awful mess of everything, Alice."

"Everything takes in a lot of territory. How about being a bit more specific. Is it Doug or Mike?"

"Both." She leaned her head back against the chair. "I think I'm finished with both of them."

"What happened?"

"I'm just not ready for Mike and I'm past being what Doug wants."

"How do you know what Doug wants? Have you asked him?"

Maggie cocked her head. "Strange that you should mention Doug first and not Mike."

Alice shrugged. "Because you're still in love with Doug. He's the more important. Any fool can see that." She decided to fix herself a drink. "And in view of the fact that you are still carrying the torch for your husband, you haven't let yourself fall madly in love with young Lochinvar . . . yet."

"I think I do love Mike, but in a different way, Alice. As I said, I'm not ready for him. I've got a lot of things to get used to. He's so much younger and he thinks so differently about things."

"And don't forget his whole new set of friends that you'll have to accept if you decide you love him enough to marry. Marriage doesn't mean just a commitment to one person; it includes all their friends and relations, a whole new circle of people whom you'll have to accept, like it or not." She sat across from her friend. "And don't forget that there is one thing Doug and Mike have in common: They're both men, and men's hearts, unlike women's, are chock-full of dark, strange places."

"But not having either of them makes me even more afraid, Alice."

"Afraid of what?"

"Being alone. I've got to change more than I have or else I have to go back to being the way I used to be. And I don't really want to do either."

Alice leaned forward, her elbows on her knees, the glass cupped in her hands. "I think you'd better tell me what brought on this visit. I feel as though I've walked in at the end of a four-reeler."

Maggie told her about going to Doug's and finding Phyllis, about coming home in a rage and finding David and Mike smoking marijuana. "Nothing is the way I want it to be," she concluded.

"Why should it be? Who says the world has to do what you want it to?" She sipped her drink. "Months ago, before you and I went to Arizona, I told you then that you'd lived a sheltered life since the day you were born, that you weren't ready for what goes on in the big, cruel world. Now see how you carry on every time you come up against something you find uncomfortable. Like everybody else, Maggie, you'd like things to be the way you want them, but that just isn't the way it is. You've got to learn to adjust, accept what you don't particularly like."

Maggie shook her head. "That would mean making myself into something I'm not."

"So what other alternative do you have? You just said you were afraid of your winding up alone. You will if you don't start accepting what are facts. For instance, why did you get all riled up because Mike and David were smoking grass?"

"Because it's wrong! And it's illegal!"

"It may be wrong to you, but a lot of other people don't agree, obviously including Mike."

"You surprise me, Alice. I know you are a free-wheeler and all that, but you've always known right from wrong. You don't mean to sit there and tell me that Mike was right in encouraging my son to use dope?"

"No, I admit that was stupid on Mike's part, but you gotta remember, kiddo, that Mike isn't much more than a kid himself. He's got to be taught values too; he's not too old to learn, just as you aren't too old to adapt."

Maggie put aside her drink. "I just don't understand any of it."

"Because you don't want to. That's one of the reasons Doug strayed in the first place."

Maggie's head snapped up. "Don't put the blame for that on me, Alice."

"Who else? You never like talking about your sex life, but I know that's where all the trouble started. Doug obviously wasn't getting something he wanted from you so he found it in someone else. It's always the reason husbands stray. And as you know, I'm quite a little busybody; I did a little checking up on Phyllis besides all that stuff I found out about her weekends with Doug. She's quite a gal. She used to teach school. Did you know that? Bookkeeping and accounting at Montclair High. They kicked her out for going down on the basketball team."

"Going down?"

"Oral/genital contact, Mrs. Hampton."

Maggie made a face.

"Oh for God's sake, kiddo, will you come out of the

Dark Ages and get with it. Do you mean to sit there and tell me you and Doug never . . . experimented?"

"Alice, you're being particularly disgusting." Maggie felt herself flush.

"I happen to know men and I can tell you one thing for sure, Maggie; no man likes to have the same meal every day of his life. He likes variety, just as you do and I do." She eyed her friend critically. "I bet you never once in your life took the initiative with Doug."

"Of course I have," Maggie said defensively, feeling embarrassed.

"No you haven't. I can tell by looking at you that you expected Doug to do all the work while you lay on your lovely backside and let him satisfy you."

"I did not come here to talk about my sex life."

"I had a feeling all along that that's where your trouble started. Maggie, you've got to start recognizing the fact that you want to be a liberated female and that means changing your old ways. Rape Doug—rape Mike, for God's sake, do something you've never done before just for the fun of it! Have sex any way that pleases you. Nothing is disgusting when you love someone."

"You sound like Mike." She knew her face was crimson; her hands were trembling.

"Then good for Mike! Someone's got to get you out of your sexual rut. Sex is pleasure, Maggie, not work. Enjoy it any way you can get it but remember only do it with someone you love and never let it become an obsession or a chore. Don't ever get like me where it starts ruling your life. That happens to a lot of people; they live their whole lives purely for sex; they have a running contest with themselves to see just how many bodies they can perform the act with."

Maggie had her own thoughts. "I just can't bring myself to, as you say, experiment."

"Then let *him* do the experimenting."

"Which *him*? That's my big problem. I don't have a him anymore."

"What's wrong with Mike? Are you certain you want to toss him aside? If you want my advice, I'd have a long talk with myself about which I wanted, Doug or Mike."

It was all sounding like a broken record. "I can't have

Doug—not now, knowing he's lied to me all this time. I'd never be able to trust him again."

"You'd be surprised what you can do when you love someone."

"Then let me put it this way," Maggie said. "I don't think I want him anymore."

"I don't believe that, but if that's how you feel then I would suggest you hightail it into New York and make up with Mike."

Maggie wasn't ready for Mike just yet. She did have some serious thinking to do; and for the first time she stared sex straight in the face and admitted to herself that that was what was wrong with her lately: she wasn't having Doug, the man she loved. And although sex with Mike was very exciting, he was, after all, still a boy and as such she tolerated his strange little foibles, those unnatural things he seemed to enjoy. She couldn't bring herself to experiment, as Alice put it, especially with Mike. If she were going to do anything like that with anyone it would be with her husband, the man she wanted to spend the rest of her life with.

The old question suddenly raised its head. Who would the husband be? Doug or Mike?

"I've got to be going, Alice. Thanks for the talk and the drink," she said as she got up. "You've helped, as usual."

Once she was outside on her way home, she thought about her parting remark. Had Alice helped? Maggie wasn't any farther ahead in her decision than when she started for Alice's. But then, Alice had brought a few things to light. Doug was obviously getting something from Phyllis that Maggie hadn't been providing.

She was mulling that over in her head when she turned the corner to her street. She gave a little start when she saw Doug's car parked in front of the house. A part of her was suddenly tempted to follow Alice's advice and run to Mike in New York, but the other part of her made her face the truth—she wanted to see Doug, even if it meant another argument.

David was sitting in the den watching Merv Griffin. Maggie stood in the doorway and asked, "Where's your sister?"

"Up in her room," he answered without looking up.

"Isn't that your father's car outside?"

"Yeah," David said as he turned and grinned up at her. "He's out back."

Maggie knitted her brows.

"In my pad. He's a little smashed. He and I were out there listening to records. I came in to watch Charo on Merv Griffin so if Dad's car is still out front then he's still out back getting madder and tying one on."

"Don't be so disrespectful toward your father."

"I'm not being disrespectful," he said, still grinning. "Dad said himself that he wanted to get bombed out of his head. He's a real *cat* when he's had a few too many."

Maggie started for the garage.

David called, "But watch out, Mom, he's really tee'd off about something."

How dare he, Maggie thought, and she demanded an answer when she barged in on Doug.

"How dare you show yourself drunk in front of your children?"

"Child," Doug corrected, a little sloppily. He was sitting on the floor leaning against the studio couch, his ankles crossed in front of him, the colored lights flashing and swirling over him. He saluted her with his glass.

Now that he saw her looking so young, so beautiful, so sensual he could understand why he'd never stood up to her, never stopped her from doing exactly what she wanted. She'd accused him of being selfish when all along she was the selfish one.

His love for her had sealed his eyes from everything but the pleasure he received from being her lover and from her being his wife. When he was a boy he'd seen Maggie Booth walking out of her homeroom for first class and made up his mind then that she was all life could ever hold for him. He'd dreamed of her, masturbated to thoughts of her body. He knew his lust was wrong but for all the impure thoughts and acts she provoked in him, she always gave him a sense of purity and goodness of which he felt she was the personification, and as a result he'd never dared show her the kind of man he really was, sinful and sexually corrupt.

All that was in the past now, finished, he decided as he watched the stormy look on her lovely face. She was more than annoyed with him, she was disgusted. Well, goddamn it! Good! Let her be. Maybe it was about time he made it known that he was equally annoyed and pissed off at her. Enough is enough—and by Christ, he was going to show her how much he needed her and how much she needed him!

As Doug watched her he knew she had instincts she never allowed to surface. Instincts, unfortunately, could never be trusted, especially a woman's. He asked himself why she'd always acted as she did, refusing to acknowledge those darker passions that seethed down deep and only surfaced on rare occasions. Why did she act only according to those emotions she determined as being good and righteous? He supposed it was her basic fear of disaster. Life was a confusion of things and people, everyone urged on by forces they didn't know and by purposes that escaped them. Maggie, like so many others, hurried on just for the sake of hurrying.

Well, he decided in his semi-drunken state, it was about time he slowed her down and showed her the real emotions that were inside her before she ruined them both with her Victorian piety.

"Good God, Doug, you certainly are not setting a very good example." She tried to turn down the music but he reached up and stopped her.

"To hell with the example-setting, Maggie. I've left that up to you and your little friend." He touched the glass to his lips and found it empty. He picked up the bottle of bourbon beside him and took a swig directly from the bottle. He knew he was being disgusting; that's what he wanted to be. "Mike. Isn't that the kid's name?" He laid his head back and stared up at the rafters. "David says he's a really nice guy." He straightened up and winked. "But he says he isn't as great as his old man."

"Dear God," Maggie breathed. "I just can't picture you having a drunken conversation with your son about anything."

"Especially about his mother's . . . my wife's young lover. You know, Maggie," he said, feeling his own temper rising, "You think I'm being disgusting by showing myself a little drunk to my kid, well I think you're twice as disgusting for showing him your lover."

Maggie felt her face flame. "I could make the same accusation about your mistress."

"At least she's an adult woman and I do not bring her into my home." He leaned on one elbow. "Did you have each other in our bed too?"

"Doug, for goodness sake, keep your voice down. The children. . . ."

"The children will what? You're behaving like a slutty little schoolgirl, Maggie. How dare you drag that boy here? This is still my house as well as it is yours. You think that I'm the reprobate, the reviler of women, the destroyer of homes and marriages, but what I do is at least discreet! You've always pictured yourself as some paragon of virtue. Let me tell you something, Maggie, in all the years we've known each other I thought you were a decent woman— the most decent woman in the world—but then after being married to you for twenty years I started hoping you'd stop being so damned decent and start becoming a little more earthy, a little more common—like me." He struggled to his feet, staggered over to her, putting his hands on her shoulders. "You're a beautiful brick, Maggie, but you're also a slut deep down."

She slapped his face so hard her hand stung.

His grip tightened. He pulled her hard against him and crushed his mouth over hers. Maggie tried to fight him off but his arms felt like steel bands as they squeezed her harder and harder.

"I love you, damn it," he groaned over her mouth. "I've never loved anyone else."

"Let me go, Doug," she mumbled under his mouth. "Get your filthy hands off me." She struggled, but in vain.

"No." With a sudden shove he knocked her backward onto the studio couch that stood against the back wall. Immediately he fell on top of her.

"Doug! No!" she yelled as he started to tear away her clothes.

"Yes!"

"You can't do this!"

"To hell I can't," he cursed as he continued to undress her.

He struggled with the buttons of her filmy blouse but

grew too impatient and ripped it from her body. Maggie gave a little scream and started to try to get up.

Doug raised his hand. "Just stay there or so help me I'll slap you silly," he threatened.

She cowered back, covering her naked breasts with her hands. "Get the hell out of those clothes if you don't want them ripped off too," he growled as he stood up and started to undress himself.

As he was stepping out of his pants Maggie saw her chance and jumped up, shoving him backward, knocking him to the floor. She bolted for the door but Doug rolled sideways and grabbed her ankle. He pulled her down beside him.

Doug tore apart the zipper at the side of her skirt. He tore at her half slip and ripped away her panties, leaving her completely naked. His erection felt harder, heavier, longer than ever as he fell on her, sucking her nipples into his mouth, nipping them with his teeth as Maggie gave little gasps of pleasure and pain. He didn't care how she begged, how she'd hate him afterward; he intended having her here and now and he didn't give a damn about the children, Phyllis, the world. This was the one woman who meant more to him than life and he would not be deprived. He was going to use her the way he'd always wanted to use her and if she never saw or spoke to him again at least he'd have this one wonderful memory.

"You're insane," Maggie groaned as he tried to separate her thighs.

"Shut up!" He sucked at her nipples as he dug his fingers into her vagina, searching out and tickling her clitoris. He felt her respond in spite of her struggling to be rid of him.

He grinned drunkenly into her face and said, "Your seeping like mad."

She spat at him. He grabbed her head between his hands and plastered his mouth over hers as he tried to kick himself free of his undershorts.

He thought suddenly of the door with its window. He got up, straddling her naked body. "You move, Maggie, and I'll knock you unconscious."

She stared up at his towering strength, his pulsing erection, his magnificently sculptured body with its rippling muscles and black tangles of hair. She felt herself powerless to move.

Doug stepped out of his shredded clothing, staggered over and locked the door, pulling down the shade to insure their privacy.

As he came back to her his eyes glinted with lust. Maggie felt her flesh grow white hot as Doug's eyes wandered over the sensuous mounds and valleys of her body.

His voice was thick as he said, "I intend to have you any way I want, Maggie, so if you want to scream your head off go right ahead and scream. I've already told Dave I was going to pound some sense into you." He grinned his lopsided grin and added, "I think good old Dave knew I wasn't referring to pounding you with my fists. Our little boy is quite a man, Maggie."

"Doug, for God's sake, don't do this to me. You're being disgusting."

"I'm going to be even more disgusting as things progress, so get used to it now because I have every intention of raping you if necessary."

Something blinked inside her head as she realized that this was the second time within the hour that the word *rape* cropped up.

Despite all her willpower and her fear she could not keep herself from looking at his fantastic physique. His body was more magnificent than she remembered, his shoulders broad and muscled, his chest wide and hairy, tapering to a trim waist and well-defined thighs and legs. She couldn't stop staring at the way he'd allowed himself to become aroused. He seemed longer, harder than she had ever noticed.

Her entire body was flushed and sweating under the heat of the lights, the sound of the rock music beating, pulsing, grinding into every pore of her body. The music throbbed and pulsed like the insane beating of her temples. The sight of Doug's nudity was kindling flames hotter than she'd ever felt. This is what she'd so desperately wanted and now that she had it in her grasp she knew it might easily destroy the both of them. She could never bring herself to admit to the pure physical lust that was consuming her. She could never bring herself to show

Doug how much she ached for him to take her, hard and brutally, but she told herself she had to be unyielding, go cold and unresponsive into his arms. If he intended to take her it would be he who did the taking and not she who gave.

Doug's hands pulled away her arms she'd crossed over her breasts. "You want it as much as I do," he snarled, "So why in hell are you pretending you don't?"

"You'll be taking me against my will, Doug. I want you to know that."

He scooped her up and carried her to the coach, marvelling at the various colors that played over her naked skin as the lights spun and danced and the music crashed around them like cymbals on waves. "I don't give a fuck," he slurred as he grabbed her by her shoulders, hurting her, leaving bruises Maggie knew would show, and then he kissed her with such demanding passion and fervor that she could not help but respond, much as she tried not to.

She began fighting back the fires that were building higher and higher in her loins, but struggle as she did she found herself weakening and the seeping warmth of her desire began flowing.

Doug's mouth moved down over the hollow at her throat, down over the luscious mounds of breast and stomach and the slight rise of her belly.

"Don't do this," she pleaded.

He was too forceful, too insistent, there was no way she could be free of him. "Shut up," he growled again as he buried his face into the very core of her body.

Maggie clutched the pillow, digging her nails into the downy softness, pulling it over her mouth to try to stifle the agonizing scream of pleasure that was consuming her. Although Mike had done things like this to her it wasn't the same somehow. Doug was so loving, so hot and powerful, so exacting, so excrutiatingly delicious. She pressed herself against his manipulations without realizing it and felt herself tip over the edge of oblivion and up to the peak of the summit knowing she would again be pitched out into the unending world of lust and sin and whirling sensations. There was nothing she could do to prevent her ruin, and resigned herself to her own destruction.

Doug's body lay on top of hers and the heat of it sent

her head whirling off into another world of different lights and different colors. She knew he was kissing her and that she was returning his kisses but she was scarcely aware of any of it. The secret recesses of her body were yearning for his strength, his hardness. She felt a hunger she'd never felt before as she grew aware of his hard, muscled legs separating her thighs.

His hands explored every inch of her, bruising everything they touched. The painful pleasure of his touch burned her flesh until she could contain herself no longer. Her needy passions burst out of her like huge rockets of fires. She wrapped herself tightly against him and clutched at his naked, sweating body.

"Doug." It was all she could say as she felt herself collapsing into his arms.

He easily parted her thighs and penetrated her with a quick, fast, brutal lunge. She screamed, then lay back and gave herself up to his wanton lust. She tried to rouse herself to fight off his onslaught and began beating weakly against his chest with her fists, but she had spent all the fight that was in her and knew she would spend the rest of her strength before Doug finished with her.

As he increased his need, she moaned and arched and struggled, feeling the last vestiges of her power ebbing away forever. She climaxed again and yet he did not stop.

Sweat covered their bodies, the music blasted out, the lights flashed and blinked and waved over them like sensual wafting veils of desire and heated passions.

Suddenly Doug arched forward, grunting, lunging as he drove into her with such maddened intensity Maggie thought her mind would be torn from her. Another electrifying explosion went off deep inside her, which was the last thing she remembered before the total blackness took over and she found herself drifting into it.

When she gained consciousness she found herself clinging to him. She went limp and fell back, then curled herself into a ball and began to cry.

"Don't, Maggie," Doug said softly as he tried to put his arms around her.

She sprang at him like a ferocious beast. "Don't you ever touch me again, Doug Hampton. I hate the very sight of you."

"Maggie," he implored.

"You're nothing but a filthy, rotten pig and I hate you, I hate you, I hate you."

"Don't talk nonsense. Why can't you admit that you enjoyed it as much as I did? I admit it was a little unorthodox, that I got a little carried away, but. . . ."

She slapped his face again, harder than before. "I hated it! I hate you! Get out of here, Doug. Get out of my sight." She started to try and piece her clothes back together, which she found almost impossible. They were in ribbons.

Doug couldn't help smiling at the look of her, all disheveled, bruised, her makeup smudged and blotchy, her clothes hanging on her like rags. "You'd better let me go inside and make sure the coast is clear. I'll send Dave upstairs if he's still watching TV."

"Don't bother. Perhaps it's just as well for your son to know what a filthy animal you are." She started toward the door and struggled with the knob, forgetting that Doug had locked it.

"Wait here, Maggie," Doug said as he unlocked the door. "You will only embarrass yourself if David is still up."

"This is one hell of a time to worry about embarrassing me."

"Stop being so damned melodramatic. Personally, I thought it was the greatest."

"I meant what I said, Doug. I never want to see you again. You disgust and revolt and appall me."

"You loved it."

She raised her hand to slap him again; he grabbed it. "I hated it! I hate you!"

He frowned at her, seeing that she was being completely serious. "Do you actually mean that? Seriously?"

Her humiliation had been too complete now that she was back to realtiy. "Yes. Yes, I do."

Doug's head bowed. "I'm sorry, Maggie. I thought. . . ."

"Well, you obviously thought wrong. Get out of here, Doug."

He left. His insides suddenly felt like dried, dead leaves.

Chapter 17

It took several days before Maggie could look at herself in a mirror and not be disgusted with herself. The days were torture; the nights were an agony. She called in sick on Wednesday, but on Thursday when she called Alice to say she wasn't coming in, Alice gave her an argument.

"Hell, those people from Consolidated are coming in. I need you here, Maggie. Now if you're really sick, okay, but if you're just feeling sorry for yourself about Mike and Doug, get your ass in here." She softened her tone and added, "Besides, working will help you take your mind off things."

When Maggie showed up Alice ushered her into her office and said, "Do me a favor, kiddo, and call Mike. Go out to dinner with him or go to bed with him. You two are driving me nuts, what with him calling me and pining over you and you pining for God only knows what."

"Mike's been talking to you?"

Alice told her Mike called three times yesterday worrying because he couldn't get an answer at Maggie's house.

"I wasn't answering the telephone."

"And he's called twice already this morning, so call him."

She did.

Seeing him sitting at the corner table of the restaurant made her aware how young and innocent he really was. Her rape by Doug—and that's the only way she could think of it—had left a terrible scar on her mind. She blocked out all remembrances of the pleasure she'd received, reducing the whole episode into one massive, sordid, drunken experience she wanted to forget.

She'd cried enough over her loss of Doug and the respect she had once had for him. She must pick herself up and start fresh. Mike, she decided, was as good a place to start as any she could think of. She knew she had to keep body and soul on speaking terms or she was done for.

"Hello," she said simply as she held out her hand.

Mike took it and kissed it unashamedly. "Hello," he answered. "You look wonderful."

"I feel all grubby and mussed up after working all day," she said.

"Then let's eat fast and go back to my place."

She felt an unpleasant shiver course through her. She felt it was too soon for her to relax into the pleasures of sex . . . or was it the idea that she'd be having sex with Mike and not with Doug that was causing the unpleasant shiver? The memory of Doug toyed with her mind, like a small persistent pain.

"Not tonight, Mike. Let's just have dinner and talk. I might even have a cocktail and let myself get fat again."

"No, you don't. One cocktail, maybe, but you spoil that gorgeous figure and I'll sue you."

"Speaking of suing," Maggie said, "I'm going ahead with my divorce. That's definite."

He took her hands in his. "Please marry me."

Maggie tilted her head and let her eyes play with his. "I am still upset about that incident with David."

"I know, Maggie. I was wrong. I realize that now. I just was being irresponsible. You've got to believe me when I say it will never happen again. It was stupid and childish and I was totally out of line. Please forgive me, Maggie."

It was amusing to see his boyish, cute face try to be so mature and grown up. "All right," she said after a moment. "Let's forget it."

"It's forgotten," he said happily.

The waiter came over and Maggie ordered a martini.

"Just one," Mike reminded her.

The dinner was wonderful, but afterward, much as Mike tried to persuade her to come to his place, Maggie refused.

"Just say you'll marry me then and put me out of my misery." His earlier maturity had disappeared. To Maggie he was a boy again.

Maggie let go of his hand and put her arm around his waist, snuggling close as they walked toward the Port Authority terminal. "I've had a terrible scene with Doug, Mike. I'm extremely fond of you, you know that. You make me feel sixteen again. I really think I'm in love with you, but I honestly don't know. Doug has been too much in my way lately for me to look at you unobstructed. I do know one thing though."

"What's that?"

"I don't love anyone else."

"Oh, Maggie, I adore you."

Much to her surprise and embarrassment he pulled her into his arms and kissed her square on the mouth at the corner of Broadway and Forty-Second. A group of teenagers started to applaud as they walked by.

She was happy, she thought. When she started to undress for bed she was sure Mike's kiss had finally dislodged Doug, but the minute she closed her eyes the flashing lights, the rock music started up again and she felt a thin film of need coat her body.

"Damn you, Doug Hampton," she cursed as she punched her pillow and pinched shut her eyes. The more his image tortured her the more she was determined to accept Mike's marriage proposal.

First thing the following morning she told Alice that she'd decided she was going to marry Mike as soon as her divorce from Doug was final. "I haven't told Mike yet. I think I'll spend the weekend making absolutely sure I'm not doing this to spite Doug.

"Why do you feel you want to spite Doug all of a sudden? Has anything happened you aren't telling me about?"

Maggie immediately found herself engulfed in the swirling lights, the loud music, the hard muscled feel of Doug's body. "No, nothing happened. It's just that I want to be sure I'm doing the right thing, that I'm not marrying on the rebound."

"You're doing the right thing, kiddo, if you feel really happy about it."

That was the trouble, Maggie thought. She did love Mike in her way; sex was wonderful with him—youthful and almost innocent. Mike didn't have the technique of Doug but he did have a way of arousing her with his boyish exuberance, which Doug did not have—but then Doug wasn't a boy.

She was so confused and like so many others who found themselves undecided, she was ashamed of her indecisiveness, knowing it was nothing more than a sign of weakness. So, she made up her mind that she would marry Mike Ballantine. It was the beginning step in solving her problem with Doug. Committing herself to Mike would force her to decommit herself from Doug. Besides, it would serve Doug right for his treating her like some trollop off the streets.

To Alice she said, "I'm always happy when I'm with Mike." She was going to elaborate, more for her own sake than for Alice's, but the telephone rang, cutting her off.

Alice picked up the receiver. She listened to the voice on the other end, who was obviously saying something that deeply disturbed her.

"What's the employee's name?" Alice asked. She wrote the name down on a note pad. "I don't recognize it, but then I'm not familiar with every applicant we send out."

The caller was talking again and Maggie, sensing it might be a long conversation, stood up to leave. Alice motioned her back into her chair.

"Very well," Alice said. "You may be sure, Mr. Elkins, that I'll look into it immediately. Thank you for calling and letting me know. This sort of thing can't be tolerated, at least not by my agency." She thanked him again and hung up.

Alice sat staring at the name on the pad. "Do you know one of our applicants by the name of Mary Andress?"

Maggie repeated the name, searching her memory. "No, I don't think so. It isn't one of my girls."

Alice chewed on her bottom lip. "Something strange is going on here."

"How do you mean?"

"That was Sy Elkins, you know, Elkins Wholesalers, the dress-manufacturers over on Eighth Avenue."

"Yes. I know the firm."

"One of their employees, this Mary Andress, whom they hired from us, was offered a raise in salary and she turned it down."

"How odd—but I suppose she had her reasons."

Alice said, "She really didn't turn it down exactly, she asked them to postpone it."

"What do you mean?"

Alice picked up the pad and studied the name again. "She asked her supervisor if it would be possible for the company to withhold the increase in pay for a month—until her 'trial' period was over, so that she wouldn't have to pay a higher employment fee."

"And she came from us?"

Alice nodded. "Funny, isn't it? Especially in view of the fact that we don't charge employment fees. Sy Elkins wasn't exactly angry but there was that insinuation in his voice that was accusing me of double-charging the applicants." She put the pad down again. "He said that he'd appreciate it if I would personally check the file on the girl and if by chance a mix-up has been made where we've been paid his company's commission as well as the girl paying a commission, he wants his commission back." She frowned. "I have a feeling that we won't be getting any more business from Elkins Wholesalers."

"But we don't charge the employee a fee." Maggie suddenly stopped as something occurred to her. "What was the girl's name, again?"

"Mary Andress. Why?"

"I just thought of something. But no, the name doesn't sound Spanish." She slumped back in her chair. "Besides, you said yourself that Rita wasn't a part of this agency."

"What are you talking about?"

"Don't you remember when we had lunch that day Rita raked me over the coals, you said Rita wasn't really a part of us?"

"So?"

"A while back I overheard Rita sending a Spanish speaking girl out on a job—I didn't know the girl and I don't know the job—but they were speaking in Spanish and Rita was asking the girl to sign a contract to pay her first month's salary as a fee for getting the job. I went up and reminded Rita that we never charge the applicant a fee, that the employers always pay. She told me to mind my own business, that I didn't know what I was talking about and reminded me that she wasn't a part of this agency, that she only rented desk space here."

"I see," Alice said. She was wearing an expression Maggie could not interpret. After studying it Maggie decided it was an expression of no consequence. Alice said, "I'll check it out," not committing herself one way or the other.

Alice stood up and put out her hand, smiling. "And congratulations on deciding on Mike. I know you two kids will be ecstatically happy. Remember, I'm going to be your Maid of Honor. Change that to *Matron* of Honor."

"We'll leave it *Maid*, and don't let yourself get carried away by calling us *two kids*. There's only one kid in this arrangement and that's Mike."

"Just keep thinking like that and you're finished before you start. There's no harm in making yourself young again, kiddo. As long as you've been given that chance, grab on to it and hang on for as long as you can."

"I really do think I'm doing the right thing in marrying Mike. I admit that I'm still a little hung up on Doug, but that just may be habit. I know I could never live with Doug after . . . after his moving Phyllis into his apartment."

"If you're positive Doug is a lost cause then start treating him like one and put him out of your mind."

That was impossible, she found as the afternoon wore on. The more she was determined to tell Mike she'd marry him, the more thoughts of Doug bothered that decision. Could Mike put up with the petty annoyances she knew she caused Doug? Mike had never been married before; he didn't know what it meant to tolerate a woman's ways around the house. He didn't realize that some people were only bearable under the sheets.

The house? she thought. Would they live in Saddlebrook or would Mike insist that she move in with him? Impossible. Julie had to finish school. David would either go off to college or settle into working with his father. She'd want David to keep on living at home—but with Mike there?

Then there was a livelihood to think about. Mike didn't make all that much money, she was certain, and if she married him immediately after the divorce it meant Doug had no responsibilities except to Julie's support, and even that wouldn't go on for very long.

She made up her mind that, before making her decision

absolute, she would have to have a serious talk with Mike about how they were going to earn a living.

Louise broke into her thoughts saying, "You look very serious, Maggie. Love, illness, or did somebody die?"

Maggie managed a smile.

"Haven't you ever noticed that everybody looks the same whether they're miserably in love, have an incurable disease, or just lost someone to the grim reaper?" Louise said.

Maggie made a face. "You're morbid, do you know that?"

"In my case," Louise said, "It's the latter. Somebody just died."

"Oh, no," Maggie said with sincere concern.

"Yeah, my last boyfriend. He just took off for L.A.—so he might just as well be dead as far as I'm concerned. Now if he'd have asked me to go along that would encourage me to look the same but feel differently." She studied Maggie then asked, "So which is it with you?"

"Love, I think."

"If you have to think then it ain't love."

"Okay, it's love."

"Mike?"

"Is it that obvious?"

"Kinda. You're really serious about the guy, huh?" She screwed up her face.

"I think I am."

"There you go again, thinking. You either know or you don't. Come on, you've been married, you know how it feels to be in love."

"That's the confusing part," Maggie said. "I knew once; I'm wondering if it might feel differently the second time."

"You may have a point. I wouldn't know. It's happened so often I've lost both count and memory." She sighed. "That's what's wrong with me, I guess. I don't bring out the material instincts in men."

Maggie flinched. She could see that Louise wasn't aware of the fact that her remark had hurt. Maggie was equally tempted to make a crack about Louise being too fat to run after a man, but trading insults wasn't something she was very good at. Besides, it was beneath her.

239

Louise asked, "How serious is it, Mag, you and Mike?"

Maggie saw a chance to get in her own dig; tactfully, of course. "I'm not even divorced from one man and I have another one waiting at the stage door."

"Mike proposed?" She looked both hurt and surprised.

"Yes."

"Does Andy know that you two might get married?"

"Not 'might'; it's a definite probability. And no, Andy does not know. At least I didn't tell him."

"Oh."

"Why?" Maggie saw an odd look cross Louise's face.

"Nothing. It's just that Mike and Andy were so . . . close." She turned, leaving her last word to linger like an unexploded bomb.

Maggie could understand Louise being a little resentful of the fact that Mike and she were fond of each other, but she could not see why it would be important to Andy Carver. She had to admit that ever since she and Mike were seeing one another regularly, Andy had more or less moved into the background. He wasn't as friendly as he had been, although he was still there occasionally with the flippant wisecrack and the campy expression.

She liked Andy but he was such a surface person, a man with very little depth and absolutely no thought of anything except what was good for him.

On Friday she made Mike promise not to see her until Monday, and after work Maggie had the chance to talk to Andy about herself and Mike. Originally she'd planned on going directly home but Louise and Andy insisted they buy her a drink.

Andy said, "Louise tells me big things are happening between you and Mike. You've got to dish me the dirt, girl. I want to hear it straight from the old nag's mouth." He put his fingers over his pursed lips and said, "Oops, only kidding."

"There's not much to tell yet," Maggie said as they settled themselves around a table at The Rail. "I told Mike I'd spend the weekend giving his proposal serious thought and I'd give him my final answer Monday morning."

"Your affirmative answer," Louise cued.

Maggie gestured vaguely. "Yes, I think it will be affirmative. No, I take that back . . . I *know* it will be affirmative."

Andy hooted. "Hooray!" He calmed immediately. "I just admit, though, I can't see Mike as a married heterosexual."

Maggie felt her mouth tighten. "What do you mean?"

He patted her hand. "Oh, don't look so crestfallen, Maggie. Have no fears, Mike will make a wonderful husband. I should know." He and Louise exchanged looks.

Maggie drew back. "Is there something that I should know?" she asked guardedly.

Louise said, "No, nothing. Andy's just having his sport. He can't stand it when he loses out to a woman."

Maggie stared at her then at Andy. "You and Mike?" she gasped.

"God no," Andy insisted. "At least it never got to that stage. We were just roommates. And let me tell you, Maggie, he is a marvel to live with. Oh, if only he were gay. He's everything I've ever dreamed of in a man."

"I thought you felt the same way about your body builder?"

"What body builder?"

Louise shook her head. "If you did get Mike you'd be bored with him in a week."

"Never," Andy insisted. He grew serious. "Actually, Maggie, if the truth were known, I really tore my heart out over that man."

Louise made a face. "Come off it, Andy, you were never serious about any man in your whole life. You just pretend to be because you think it's dramatic. There hasn't been one man in your life in the past five years you haven't claimed to be madly in love with." She looked at Maggie. "Andy's latest is always the really big one, the one he's waited for all his life—until the next one comes along. I've never seen anyone fall in love as easily as he does. He meets them at two o'clock and moves them in at three—lovers for life."

"You're being a bitch," Andy snarled.

"I'm also being truthful." In an aside to Maggie, loud enough to be heard, she said, "Andy wouldn't know what love is if he had it for breakfast ten days in a row."

Andy fumed. "Why are you being so mean, Louise? Because Maggie took Mike away from *you?*"

"I didn't," Maggie breathed. "If I thought for one minute. . . ."

"Oh, don't let him get to you, Maggie. There was never anything between me and Mike. We were just friends—at least that's the way it was on his part. I had a thing for him once but I never stood a chance of getting within a foot of him."

"Of course not," Andy sneered; "Not with that fat belly."

Maggie had heard them bantering before but tonight it had a malicious bite to it. They weren't being campy; they were being cruel.

Louise fought back with, "At least I'm a woman, which Mike obviously prefers."

Andy wouldn't be outdone. "He may have a preference for women but it doesn't stop him from letting me suck his cock."

Maggie knocked over her glass of Perrier water. An instant hush fell over them. Maggie fought to recover herself from the shock.

Andy looked contrite. "Now don't jump to conclusions, Maggie, it wasn't any big thing."

Maggie felt herself beginning to feel queasy.

Andy said, "Mike was 'trade,' that's all." He hurried on with, "Trade is when one guy does all the work and the other one just lies back and enjoys it. Mike didn't participate; he didn't reciprocate, if that's what you're afraid of."

Maggie was horrified that Mike had permitted the filthy act in the first place. She felt revolted and began gathering up her things. She had to get out of there, out of the sight of Andy's gloating smile.

Louise saw Maggie's anger and Andy's smugness. She tried to come to the rescue. "Maggie," she said, putting her hand on Maggie's arm. "You mustn't get the wrong idea. Mike's as straight as a board. I wouldn't pay any attention to what this big-mouth says. Chances are he's made it all up just to be bitchy."

Like so many people who have to protect their pride regardless of how serious the consequences and how much damage it might cause, Andy said, "It only happened once, but I still had him."

Louise said, "Shut the hell up, Andy. You're a real bastard for telling Maggie such a thing."

Andy truthfully could not understand what everyone was so upset about and said as much. "I don't know what the big deal is. Just because I blew the guy doesn't mean anything. I've had hundreds of straight guys." But he couldn't resist adding, "Of course, as they say, 'Today's trade is tomorrow's competition.'"

"Andy!"

Maggie fumbled with her purse, making sure she had everything; and then, without even saying goodnight, she turned and walked hurriedly out of the place. Her insides were in knots and her mind felt as though it had been dragged through garbage. How could she ever have considered getting involved with someone as decadent as Andy Carver? she asked herself. Of course she and Mike were finished. She doubted if she could ever let him put his arms around her without knowing that he had had sex with another man.

"Maggie," she heard Louise call but Maggie didn't stop. "Maggie!" Louise called again, catching up to her and grabbing her arm. "Hey, you've got to listen a second." She slowed her down. "Don't go off half-cocked just because that stupid faggot shot off his mouth to protect his own vanity."

Maggie didn't feel she wanted to be placated. She didn't know why, but part of her wanted to believe Andy while another part of her did not.

"I'm sure Andy made the whole thing up just because Mike wants to marry you. Andy's the type who has to win and if he can't, he's got to destroy. Surely you know that queen by now."

Maggie felt her pace slowing. "But what a horrible thing to say, Louise, especially about Mike."

"Hell, it isn't all that terrible. You're just not used to what goes on with these younger single guys." She saw that Maggie was beginning to cool down. "Mike is as straight as they come; surely you know that, Maggie. Haven't you had sex with him?"

Maggie didn't answer; she couldn't.

"Haven't you?" Louise persisted.

Against her will, Maggie nodded.

"Then you know he couldn't possibly have a gay streak in him. He was all man I bet, wasn't he?"

Maggie thought about their sex together and had to admit that there hadn't been the slightest trace of Mike being anything but totally heterosexual. No man could fake the desire he'd shown. There wasn't a part of her he hadn't wanted to devour, she thought with a sudden delicious blush.

Louise had to be right, she decided. Andy was just trying to start trouble. She said, "Why would Andy tell me a thing like that, Louise? Even if it were true, it isn't something a man's fiancée wants to hear."

"I told you. Andy's more of a cunt than we are." They strolled along, not saying anything. "I suppose I shouldn't bring this up, Maggie, but I'm going to tell you anyway." They stopped and waited for the traffic to clear. "This happened long before you and Mike started going together, but I knew a couple of girls Mike used to date. Believe me, from their gossip, what Andy said is absolutely untrue, and this was when Andy and Mike shared an apartment."

"How long did they share?"

"I don't know. Not long. Maybe a month. Maybe less. I know Mike didn't like it much because he used to complain to me about Andy's parade of tricks every night." The traffic stopped and they walked on. "You should know better than to let Andy needle you that way. You should have laughed in his face and told him that at least you won, that Mike's marrying you and not him."

Louise linked her arm in Maggie's. "I know I'm the last one to give advice, but what I want you to do is go home, closet yourself for the weekend and think nothing but glorious, wonderful thoughts about becoming Mrs. Michael Ballantine. Oh, my, doesn't that have a fantastic ring to it?"

She and David went out for dinner—David's treat, since it was payday on the job. Then he went off with a crew of his buddies to the inevitable Friday night party somewhere.

Maggie was glad she hadn't given in to the urge to call Mike and tell him what Andy had bragged about. "Andy was just being cruel," she decided as she yawned and started to get ready for bed. Louise was right. She mustn't let Andy spoil things between her and Mike.

She sat on the edge of the bed and purposely went over each and every time she could remember that she'd had sex with Mike, and hard as she tried, she could not find a single hint of stain on his masculinity.

"Mrs. Michael Ballantine," she repeated. "Then Mrs. Margaret Booth Ballantine." She still didn't like the alliteration but it didn't matter much, she supposed.

She lay back and stared up at the dark ceiling. Something her mother once said crossed her mind. It had been when they were talking about the change in her initials after she married Doug; they were discussing the monograms on her linens. Her mother had said, "A change in the name and not in the letter is a change for the worse and not for the better."

Going from Booth to Hampton was good; going from Booth to Ballantine was a change for the worse.

"Stop it," she said as she rolled over on her side and shut her eyes. "Why was she digging so deep to find reasons not to marry Mike?" she asked herself.

She knew the answer to that—but refused to admit it.

It hadn't been the physical rape she resented so much now; it was the affront to her dignity as a woman and mother.

Dignity be damned, she scoffed, twisting her mouth. She thought back to Doug's and her early years and realized that dignity and love didn't go together. Like oil and water, they didn't mix. She had never considered herself truly dignified and wondered now where she'd acquired it; nobody was ever born with dignity.

"What does any of that have do with anything?" she asked aloud as she pounded her pillow again and wondered if she should take a Valium.

Chapter 13

Saturday was quiet. David was visiting a buddy and they were going to check out some college town up-state that they thought they might want to go to next semester. Julie was spending the day at the shore with a girlfriend and her family. She'd be home for dinner, she promised.

Maggie spent the morning cleaning up around the house, but by noon time the house was spotless and she found the empty weekend yawning before her. She puttered in the garden for a while. She was tempted to straighten up David's garage crash-pad but she found herself unable even to approach the door without shaking with anticipation. She thought of calling Alice but decided against it. This might well be the last weekend she'd have alone if she decided to follow Mike's suggestion that if she agreed to marry him they could get Doug to agree to a quick divorce in Reno and marry right away.

As she walked through the house the same question kept recurring: Why had she been putting Mike off? Why hadn't she come right out and told him she'd be his wife? Why did she need still more time to think about it? Was it stubbornness that kept her from committing herself to him?

As she looked around at the room she realized that she was afraid that marrying Mike would mean the end of everything she'd ever had. It meant uprooting her whole life, changing everything about it.

Her children wouldn't change, she reminded herself. And as she walked into the cozy den with its warm browns and soft contrasts, she felt that she could never lose this room. With a sinking feeling she supposed she would have to.

She ran her hand over the back of Doug's chair. Everything here was hers and Doug's. Mike didn't belong in this room and she would never be comfortable having him here.

She'd sell the house, she decided as she went toward the bookcase and took down one of the small silver trophies that sat on a shelf. It was one she and Doug had won one year, when they had come in first at the tennis doubles contest the local Chamber of Commerce sponsored. It seemed so long ago.

She put back the trophy and wandered toward the fireplace, looking at the framed pictures of David holding up a trout he'd just caught, and Julie in her first formal. The house had seen so much, heard so much, was so much a part of her that she had no choice but to give it up if she intended to start over with Mike. It wasn't fair to him that she should force her wonderful memories on him.

The doorbell caught her by surprise. She looked at her watch and frowned, wondering who it could possibly be. She peeked through the curtains that framed the doorway and her breath caught in her throat.

It was Rita Gant.

"Rita," she said, being unsure whether she should smile or not.

"This is not a social call," Rita assured her with a thick Spanish accent. "I have words to say to you, Mrs. Hampton."

A little hesitantly Maggie opened the door farther. "Come in, won't you?" she said uncertainly.

"This will not take long," Rita snarled as she stepped inside and looked around. She leveled her angry eyes at Maggie and said, "All I have to say is that I will get even with you if it takes my lifetime."

Maggie took a step back away from the woman's raised fist. "What . . . ?"

"Don't play the innocent with me. You know very well what you have done. Alice has fired me on account of you."

"Fired you? On account of me?" She was flabbergasted.

How could Alice fire someone who didn't work for her? "I don't know what you're talking about."

"The hell you don't. Let me tell you something. You are nothing but a rich, spoiled bitch who takes jobs away from poor innocent minorities. You will not get away with it, that I promise you."

Maggie was actually frightened by the rage in her face and voice. "But believe me, Rita," she stammered. "I don't know what you're talking about. I said nothing to Alice about you. And if I did mention you, how could . . . ?"

"You told her about the girl who I asked to sign the fee agreement."

Maggie was completely confused. "I mentioned it, yes. But you aren't part of. . . ."

"But you told her, that is all that is important." She raised her fist and shook it in Maggie's face again. "You will regret that." She turned and left Maggie standing there with her mouth agape, her eyes wide.

It took several seconds before Maggie recovered from her shock. When she did she went to the telephone and dialed Alice's number.

Alice said, "I thought you were being incommunicado for the weekend."

Maggie didn't stop for the niceties. "Rita Gant just left here. She is furious, threatening me with God only knows what."

She heard a little intake of breath. "I was afraid she'd go gunning for you."

"Why me? I assume that it was one of her girls who Elkins called to report?"

"Yes, it was. I found that Rita's been doing it with every one of her applicants—taking double fees."

"I don't understand. You told me Rita was just hiring desk space from you."

"I never said that, did I?"

"Not in so many words. No, now that I think of it, Rita told me that."

"It isn't true. Rita was an employee just like you and Louise and the rest."

"Why did you tell me she was different?"

"Did I say she was different? If I did, I must have been

referring to her outlook toward things, certainly not her employment status."

"Oh, Alice," Maggie moaned. "You've put me in a very awkward position. Lord only knows what that crazy woman will do. She was simply livid."

"She won't do a thing, kiddo. Just let off a lot of steam, that's all. Forget Rita Gant. I'm glad I finally got a good excuse to get rid of her. Which reminds me, as long as you can stumble along in Spanish I was thinking about giving you Rita's accounts."

"I couldn't, especially under the circumstances. Rita will be convinced I sabotaged her job. She'll come after me with an ax."

"Forget Rita. She's gone for good. Think about what I said." Alice paused. "So how's the decision-making coming along? Have you decided to become Mrs. Mike Ballantine?"

"I was all decided yesterday until I talked with Louise and Andy after work."

"And?"

Maggie told her everything Andy had said and what Louise had said in the way of argument.

"So what's the big deal?" Alice asked. "Even if what Andy claims is true—which I very much doubt—it happened when they shared an apartment, I assume, and that was years ago . . . three at least. Mike was practically a child. I'm sure there are isolated incidents in your life that happened during a weak moment that you're not too happy about. Forget it, Maggie. If you love Mike, marry him despite any possible fault you may find in him. And if you insist on dwelling on the matter, deplore the deed, not the doer."

"Always there with the *mot juste*," Maggie laughed.

The rest of the afternoon she spent sitting alone staring out at the all-too-familiar lawn. It was difficult to imagine that in a very short space of time she could well be transplanted into an altogether different existence. She wasn't totally convinced that she could manage it.

What choice did she have? Doug was lost, one way or the other; there was no possibility of her going back to a man she thought she once knew, a man who had turned into some kind of "thing" overnight. *All right*, she said to herself as she got up and began pacing, *I admit there was an element of excitement in the way he treated me in the garage, but it was a barbaric act and certainly not one to look back on with pleasure. If that's what Doug found in Phyllis, then fine, he was welcome to her. I am a normal, properly oriented woman who believes in the normal, the sane, the usual—and I will not be tempted into perversions which I find abhorrent.*

No, Doug had shown his true nature. It had taken years for it to emerge but now that it had there was no denying it. Maggie folded her hands and put back her head. He had behaved like a beast—and in his own son's room. To her it bordered on incest, which made it all the more abhorrent in her eyes.

Was Mike any different? she wondered. In time would he, like Doug, find animal lust lurking inside which he needed to expose? Were all men like that? She tried to picture Andy and Mike in bed together and shuddered. Did men have such black hearts that they'd go to any extreme to satisfy their lechery?

Comparing the two: Mike's supposed sexual episode with Andy and her violent rape by Doug, she had to admit that Doug's behavior at least had been heterosexual, which she understood.

Then there was that uncomfortable incident of David and Mike smoking marijuana and from out of nowhere she drew an alliance between the marijuana and Mike's tolerating a homosexual act.

Mike and David?

"Oh God, surely not." She put her forehead against the cool mantle of the fireplace. "I'm being depraved to even entertain such an idea." She felt a sudden attack of nausea which she fought down.

Thinking about the marijuana and the rape, she decided she'd have to do something about cleaning up that garage, the place where both incidents happened. Of course David would be going off to college, she presumed, and perhaps Julie would like to redo the place as her own private sanctuary. No, best not, she told herself. Clean it out and put the car where it belonged.

By the time Julie came home from the shore Maggie was still where she'd been, sitting in the den gazing out the window, more or less resigned to accepting Mike's proposal and unsure whether it was the right thing to do. A hundred times she told herself that if she was undecided, she shouldn't do anything. But her fear of being left alone took precedence and as much as she tried to deny it, she felt a horrible need to spite Doug. It was proof that her new life, her new look had reaped its proper reward. Doug had been wrong. She could be a young bride again with a young husband; and if they moved into New York and started a new circle of friends there was no reason why she couldn't continue being as young as Mike.

Julie said, "Is that all you've been doing all day, sitting here moping like a sick cat? You look exactly like David when he's mooning over some girl."

Maggie got up. "I wasn't moping, I was trying to sort things out."

"Like whether you want to split with Dad and marry Mike?" Before her mother could answer Julie wrapped her arms around herself and said, "I think Mike is positively the most dreamy man in the whole wide world."

"I thought your father was that?"

"He is, but in an older way. Mike isn't my father, so I can think about him in a different way."

Maggie felt a pang. "What kind of way? If Mike and I marry he *will* be a father to you."

"Oh, yeah, a stepfather, but that doesn't really count like a real father. Besides, Mike is far too young for anyone to mistake him for my father."

Maggie didn't like the way she found herself interpreting Julie's remarks. The question was there, sticking on her tongue—but she knew she had to ask it. "Do you mean you think about Mike in a . . . physical way?"

Julie was nonplussed. "Really mother, must you always be so provincial? The word is 'sexual.'"

"A little provincialism wouldn't hurt you, young lady. You are becoming a little too brazen to suit me."

Julie fell on the couch and said, "When do you think you'll divorce Dad?"

"You're so casual about it." Maggie shook her head. "Does it matter so little that your father and I might divorce?"

"Might? I thought it was all set, at least that's what

David told me." She sat up. "And you yourself have been hinting around to see what we thought of Mike. You're as transparent as cellophane, mother."

"What did David tell you?"

"Huh? Oh, David said that Dad told him that you asked him for a divorce." She tugged up her sagging socks. "David said he thought it had something to do with Phyllis and Mike. You know, Dad gets Phyllis and you get Mike."

"As cold as all that?"

"Really, Mother, you must realize that David and I are all grown up. We aren't exactly children who think babies are brought by the stork."

Maggie felt miserable. "I'm only too well aware of that fact, Julie. I just thought it might matter that your father and I remarried."

"What's to matter? David and I will be getting married ourselves one of these days and believe it or not, mother, kids today are a lot more sophisticated about divorce and stuff like that than they were when you were a girl."

"Obviously," she said.

Julie said, "I suppose it would be a different matter if David and I were still tots. We've talked about this kind of thing in our Social Studies and we agreed that a couple should stay together, if at all possible, where there are small children to be considered. However, when the children are grown, then the parents should think of their own happiness, their own future."

"How very mature of you all." Her sarcasm went unnoticed.

Julie stood and clicked on the TV. "There's an old Greta Garbo movie on. Want to watch it?"

"Being Greta Garbo it could hardly be a new movie." She let a sigh escape her. "Sure, why not?" Then after a pause she asked, "Are you in for dinner tonight?"

"If you want the company."

"Good. Rather than eat in why don't we get ourselves all dolled up and go into town for dinner? Just the two of us."

Julie eyed her suspiciously. "You want to continue to feel me out about Mike, right?"

"Of course not," Maggie said, then laughed and added, "All right, so I want to make sure you agree that I'm doing the right thing by marrying Mike. But I'm really up in the air about it, to tell you the truth."

The movie was just starting. "Okay, but on one condition, Julie said. "You let me wear my hair up, put on makeup that makes me look older, and have a Barcardi cocktail."

"That's blackmail."

"Yep."

"We'll see."

Unfortunately the expensive dinner didn't settle anything; on the contrary, it upset her all the more, especially when Julie bluntly reminded her that although Maggie looked young on the outside, she was still middle-aged inside, while Mike was young through and through.

For all Julie's professing to be adult and sensible, she was as brainless as a child and twice as selfish and stuck-up. She was turning into an insufferable snob, as far as Maggie could see; putting on airs with the waiters, flirting like a little tramp with the other men in the room, slipping in words she thought made her sound sophisticated but were in fact nothing more than vulgarities. Maggie had to warn her about them several times—to no avail.

It was a long time after Julie was asleep that Maggie came to the decision that even if she and Mike did marry—which seemed inevitable—Doug would have to do something about setting to the task of straightening out their daughter. Left unattended Julie could easily turn into a real problem, and Maggie doubted if Mike were experienced enough to know how to deal with her. Mike might even encourage her to do 'her own thing'—which left Maggie more awake than before.

Maggie got up and took a Valium. As she waited for the pill to take effect she supposed Alice and the others were right that she was pretty out of step with what was going on today. She didn't mean the drug scene—that was totally wrong and she'd never go along with that stuff—she thought of the new sexual morality that people had adopted.

Maybe it wouldn't be such a bad idea to buy a couple of books and read about what was going on. She admitted to herself that she'd been very lax about educating herself with regard to the ERA also; and she really should try to find out more about the new sexual mores and ethics, including sexual perferences like Andy's and the oral thing Alice talked about. If she were going to have a young, modern husband, she'd better make up her mind to become a young, modern wife, and know how to handle it.

She started to make a list in her head of the subjects she would like to know more about, but fell asleep while wondering what constituted rape between a husband and wife.

Something tickled her nose, then made her cough. Maggie opened her eyes and tried to identify the odor. The valium made her eyesight fuzzy and her mind muddled. She glanced at the clock on the nightstand and it took a couple of seconds before she read three-fifteen. The moon was shining large and full through the window and the house was dead still.

She sniffed again and coughed. Then it occurred to her what was happening. "Good God!" she said as she sat straight up in bed. "Smoke." She sniffed again, hoping she was mistaken, but there wasn't any mistake. It was smoke, all right, but where was it coming from?

An instant terror gripped her as she switched on the lamp and noticed that tiny wisps of smoke were seeping in around the bottom of the door leading to the hall.

"Julie!" she screamed as she leapt out of bed and threw herself into her robe and slippers. "Julie!" She raced to the door and stopped. It might have been her imagination but the knob actually felt warm in her hand. She tried to think clearly but her terror was mounting.

"Julie!" she screamed as she tried desperately to remember all the sensible things one was supposed to do in such an emergency. Feel the door for signs of heat, she remembered as she ran her hand across the panels. The smoke was coming in stronger puffs from under the door.

The door felt comparatively cool—at least normal, she decided as she turned the knob and pulled open the door. The hallway was filled with smoke, throwing her into a spasm of coughing.

Julie!" she yelled at the top of her lungs. "Wake up, for God's sake."

She worked her way along the corridor, unable to see clearly, and when she reached the door to the bathroom separating David's room from Julie's, she found her eyes stinging so badly she couldn't see at all and her mouth was clogged. She stumbled into the bathroom and soaked a towel with water until it was dripping wet. She slung it over her head, curling one end of the wet towel close to her nose and mouth, feeling that the wet towel would act as a kind of mask to protect her from the deadly poison of the smoke.

As she went back into the hallway the smoke enveloped her like a glove, cutting the air to nothing, choking her until she couldn't breathe, tearing at her eyes until they were burning torture.

"Julie!" she called, listening to the dreadful crackling that was coming from somewhere below her.

She pounded open Julie's door. The room was a mass of smoke and fumes. There were no signs of flames but they'd be on them soon, she knew. The fire was obviously in the den and study directly under Julie's room because the heat seemed more intense through the soles of her slippers. Maggie groped her way through the smoke and found Julie lying unconscious on the bed.

"Dear God," Maggie breathed as she started to shake her. She saw Julie's eyes flicker open then fall shut. The smoke had already overcome her, and it was quickly squeezing the life out of her young body as Julie struggled for breath.

At the far side of the room facing the side garden, French doors opened onto a small balcony that ran over the portico, a balcony that served no other purpose but decoration. Maggie was dubious if it would support their weight even if she did manage to get Julie out onto it.

She had to try. She rushed across the room and tried to open the double glass doors. Too many years of disuse and painting had glued them shut. She snatched up the slipper chair in front of Julie's dressing table and aimed it at the French doors. Something stopped her for a moment as she wondered if this was the correct thing to do. Due to the absence of flames in the room she decided a current of fresh air would give a chimney to the smoke. She sent the chair smashing noisily through the fragile panes and a current of night air began pulling the smoke out. But in the back of Maggie's mind she knew that that same current of night air would eventually begin to attract any flames that were creeping closer. She had to get Julie out of there and fast.

She dropped the chair and went back to the bed. She wrapped Julie in a blanket and eased her off the bed onto the floor. She positioned her on her back, forcing open her mouth by grasping chin and forehead. Maggie tightly clamped her mouth over her daughter's and forced her breath into Julie's lungs. She worked frantically, feverishly, trying to ignore the sound of the crackling fire that was growing hotter and more ravenous by the moment. She felt the tears pouring down her cheeks and the wet towel draped over her head was already beginning to dry. She continued mouth-to-mouth resuscitation, her body wracked with sobs, praying to a God she'd almost forgotten.

After many long, terrifying minutes Julie stirred. Maggie worked faster, breathing harder, forcing the oxygen from her body into Julie's. The telltale signs of life came slowly but more and more definitely. Julie's stomach contracted and she began vomiting, clutching herself as the spasms hit again and again.

"Julie, you must try to help yourself a little. I don't think I could carry you. Come, dear, try to stand up. Please, darling, hurry. Stand up. Please, darling, please."

She half walked, half dragged the poor girl toward the French doors. Just as they were almost to the threshold Julie collapsed again. Maggie dragged her out onto the balcony as the night air wrapped its cool, freshness around them.

Maggie checked and made sure Julie was at least breathing, then propped her up against the siding, wiping her face with the damp towel, encouraging her to breathe deeply.

"That's it, darling, breathe. Breathe deeply. Breathe as deeply as you can. We've got to climb down, sweetheart, so please try to help yourself a little."

Julie started to cough violently.

"That's it, Julie, spit it all out. That's right, sweetheart. Breathe. Breathe," she kept saying as she applied a slight pressure to Julie's stomach, helping her diaphragm to expand and contract.

Maggie knew they couldn't afford to linger on the flimsy balcony; either the fire would devour it or the structure would collapse under their weight—and there was a concrete driveway directly below. She wiped Julie's face again and searched around for some way to escape. There didn't seem to be any. It was a sheer drop from where they were. The outer walls of the house on this side had no trellises or vines; there were no niches or cornices on which to climb to safety. In horror Maggie realized that their only avenue of escape seemed to be back through the house and down the stairs to the front door.

She left Julie leaning against the siding, gasping for breath, and fled back into the bedroom and out into the hall. The smoke was thicker, the air hotter, almost scalding. She went into the bathroom and soaked another handtowel in cold water. She draped it over her head and went toward the stairs leading down to the ground floor. Just as she stepped onto the landing and looked down a piercing scream tore from her throat. The entire lower level was a sea of flickering, roaring flames which were just beginning to eat their way up the staircase.

She fled in terror back toward Julie and the fresh air of the night outside. She stood at the railing petrified and trying to fight back her hysteria. She started to scream at the top of her lungs. Below them a neighbor's dog started racing madly back and forth, furious with its own futility, barking and leaping up on its hind legs trying to get to their rescue.

There was an explosion, like the bursting of a glass bottle, and Maggie screamed again as she looked toward the side of the house and saw the flames had broken through the study window and were licking at the clapboard siding.

Far in the distance she heard the sirens and breathed another prayer. Below her people were beginning to gather. She screamed again and again, and finally several neighbors came around the side of the house and saw her standing yelling and waving.

Her next-door neighbor (the man who always drove away from the house exactly at ten after eight, dressed in a dark blue suit and carrying a briefcase) leaped his hedge and in a moment came back carrying a ladder.

With the help of the others they leaned the ladder against the shaky balcony and started to climb up.

Maggie made them take Julie down first, cautioning them to be careful. She was surprised to see that the man who left the house at ten after eight every morning easily draped Julie across his shoulder and carried her to safety with the expertise of a veteran fireman.

Moments later Maggie and Julie huddled together on the lawn as they watched the brigade of men and hoses fight desperately to save what they could of the house.

Julie clung to her mother as she watched the fire shoot up into the sky. "Oh, Mother," Julie cried. "Our home! Our beautiful home!"

Chapter 19

Catastrophes are supposed to bring people together, but here she was alone, sifting through the ashes of a lifetime. A light autumn wind had come up, definite but not strong, whispering through things, touching the tree branches and flirting with the tired leaves which clung to their stems like old ways refusing to give way to the new.

She hadn't called anyone because her telephones weren't working and there was something distasteful, she felt, about using a neighbor's phone while they stood by and watched her misery, listened to her tears. She would not humble herself, not even to go into their house for food or drink. She'd never befriended any of them at the beginning and it seemed hypocritical that she should use them now, even knowing that their kindness was genuine.

Julie, being young and extroverted, had been glad to go with any neighbor who'd drive her to her girlfriend's house, where she could be fussed over and could brag about the catastrophe in her life. *How easily children laughed at death*, Maggie thought as Julie was driven away.

As Maggie gazed at the house it reminded her oddly enough of an abstract idea that had been scuttled halfway toward completion. From one particular angle it was impossible to tell that what one saw was only half a house. From the opposite angle you stood looking at smoldering wood joists, the collapsed eaves scattered in front of wall-less rooms stacked neatly on two levels with a charred stairway connecting the two. The lawn was mushy from the gallons of water that had finally drowned the flames.

Maggie stood shaking her head, looking at the debris at her feet. If only the fire had eaten away the left side of the house, rather than the side that served as a museum for all her memories. Not a single reminder of her past had been spared. Even the children's school papers, which she'd carefully stored in her upstairs sitting room, were gone. Well, she'd wanted a completely new future; now she'd been given the opportunity to have one.

She stooped and picked up the charred trophy they'd won in the tennis doubles. She rubbed it with her hand and thought of Doug. She knew he'd miss it as much as she.

"We had ourselves a real good time the afternoon we won that baby," Doug said, reaching around her and taking the trophy out of her hand.

Her surprise turned her sharply around. Out of habit she threw herself into his arms and started to cry. He tossed the trophy into the ashes where it now belonged and hugged her tight.

Doug said, "I didn't know, of course," letting his hands smooth her back. "Julie called me. I'm afraid I balled her out for waiting so long to call."

Only after satisfying herself of his strength did Maggie let herself become aware that she was in Doug's arms, feeling his familiar protection, knowing she never wanted to be free of his embrace.

She hesitated, as if pulling the last ounce of comfort out of Doug's body, then carefully eased herself away from him. "I'm sorry," she stammered, fumbling for her handkerchief, dabbing at her eyes.

"For what?"

Maggie merely shrugged and walked a few steps away. Doug followed.

As they stood looking at the burned remnants of their lives a strange sensation came over Maggie. A calm had suddenly descended over her, a calm that emanated from Doug's presence. There was no other possible reason for feeling the way she did now. Doug stepped closer and took her hand in his.

Maggie squeezed and held on, fighting back her tears. A million memories were darting and flashing about inside her head, mingling together to form so vast a mass that everything separate was fused into one entity, the way she and Doug had been fused all these years.

Maggie let out a long, tired sigh. "Funny thing about memories," she said. "Even the dark, unhappy ones have a brightness about them." She found she could not hold back the tears any longer. She let them run freely down her cheeks. "I'll miss all those memories, Doug."

Doug slipped his arm around her waist. "I'll always be your memories, Margaret, just as you will always be mine." He turned and tipped her face up to his. "We are tomorrow's past if we stay together."

Maggie frowned and studied his handsome features. "Do you really want that, Doug . . . to stay together?"

His eyes took on a pleased little gleam and without a moment's hesitation he said, "More than anything in the world, Margaret. I know there are no guarantees that things will be better, but at least we will have what we started out with—each other; and who knows us better than we know ourselves?"

Maggie leaned against him, again reveling in the familiar warmth of his strong body. "I thought we got bored with one another."

"Not bored, Maggie. Never bored. We just grew too contented." He took her hands in his and looked into her lovely face. "I think we got side-tracked for awhile. Instead of banking our fires we threw on some more wood. We kept building up our desires, adding to them, wanting more and more rather than relaxing and enjoying what we already had."

"But I was bored, Doug, completely and utterly bored."

"Because you let yourself get bored, just as I did. The kids haven't stopped needing us, and certainly the house needs us now more than ever," he said, rolling his eyes and letting a tiny smile play around his mouth. "We just stopped needing them." He let his smile broaden. "There is absolutely nothing wrong with your going to work, if that's what you want; but we both have to keep reminding ourselves that our family comes before anything else. You and I are a family, Maggie, even without the kids. The only thing that will destroy us as a family is if we permit either of us to become isolated from the rest."

"But . . ." Maggie's voice was frayed and tired. She

felt as though someone had opened a faucet and was slowly draining away her resolve; or was it the poison of an infection that was being drawn off?

Doug said, "You're thinking of Mike Ballantine, aren't you?"

She nodded, hardly aware that she had.

"This is hardly the place to ask this, but I must, Maggie. Tell me truthfully, just what does Mike Ballantine have to give you?"

"Time," she said simply, without hesitating to think.

Doug found he could say nothing.

After a moment he said, "I guess you'll think it sour grapes, Maggie, but that young guy would be as big a mistake for you as Phyllis would be for me. You and I, we love each other. Oh, maybe not the hot, torrid kind of love we once had, but at least we did have that kind of a love and now we are ready for another kind, a deeper, truer kind of love where we can trust each other and enjoy each other. We still don't know everything there is to be known about one another. Haven't these past weeks proven that?"

His arm tightened around her waist. "We just stopped looking for surprises because we felt too familiar—and getting too familiar takes the edge off admiration. Let's never stop admiring each other, Maggie, not for a single minute."

"It's too late, Doug." She laid her forehead against his chest.

"No, it isn't. Not for us." He paused and again tilted her face up to his. "I don't want you to think I'm butting into something that isn't my affair, but are you really and truly in love with this Ballantine boy? Don't you love me anymore?"

"That isn't fair, Doug."

"I don't give a damn about being fair. I want you to be my wife for as long as I live. Whatever I have to do, fair or otherwise, I'll do if I can get you to stay married to me."

"I've changed," Maggie argued. "You've changed."

"Of course we have, but I think we've both changed for the better."

Maggie frowned when she thought of the night in the garage. "What happened the other night was. . . ."

He gently put his hand over her mouth, smothering her words. "Look deep into my eyes, Maggie and tell me you hated it."

"I. . . ." He took his hand away. "It wasn't right."

"You aren't answering my question." He put his hands on her shoulders, squeezing tightly. "I have always known when you were acting and when you were being honest about your excitement. You weren't acting the other night. You were as excited by it as I. There wasn't any harm in it. It was pure animal sex, sure, but we both liked it."

"Stop it, Doug. You're being obscene." She tried to turn away but he held her fast.

"For the first time in our lives, Maggie, I'm going to say what should have been said years ago. I know this is hardly the place, but at last I have the courage to say it. I suppose it's because our security is half gone and you're too vulnerable not to listen to me."

"Please, Doug. I don't want to hear anything you have to say about. . . ." She choked off her words.

"About sex. Sex!" he rasped, shaking her shoulders. "It's just a lousy word, not something that can only be enjoyed in the dark with the shades down and the door locked. You enjoy it, Maggie, so why treat it like it's some kind of weakness that you are ashamed of?"

"I'm not ashamed of it," Maggie argued, surprising herself that she wanted to argue. "It's just that you seem to be obsessed with it lately."

"Not obsessed by it, I just want variety. I grew tired of the same old thing, the same old ways."

"And Phyllis showed you new ones?"

"Yes. She did. But God, Maggie, you haven't been afraid that I preferred Phyllis to you, have you?" He looked unbelieving. "I can't explain it other than tell you quite frankly that I don't like Phyllis at all in the morning and only moderately in the afternoon, but at night she does things to me that positively send me through the roof with excitement. Things which are twice as exciting when I close my eyes and imagine you're doing them."

She tried to turn away again, putting her hands to her mouth.

Doug wouldn't let her go. "It's all sexual with Phyllis and me, nothing more. If only. . . ."

"Stop it, Doug." She put her hands over her ears.

He forced her hands away. "If only it were you, Maggie. That's what I dream about. It's no good if it isn't you. I know that now."

His strength only served to weaken hers. As always, Doug stood like a steel frame, graceful but stiff as an oak and incomplete without her there beside him. It shouldn't have surprised her to learn that he knew her so well; he'd always been able to see right through her pretense of purity.

It was as if he read her mind. "I've always done my part and I would just like for you to do the same now. It's all a game, Maggie. Can't you see that? I'm not asking much, just that you try something different. We have the perfect opportunity now," he said, looking at the shell of the house. "We can start fresh; we can experiment, just the way we did on our honeymoon."

Maggie's face was apprehensive, but gradually the mask began to chip away as her eyes softened, her mouth lost its stiffness. Doug had mentioned her being vulnerable; he was the vulnerable one, standing there so tall, seemingly strong—but his eyes betrayed him. He was terrified. He was giving one last desperate pitch, taking the chance of losing everything.

She couldn't help but admire his courage, his honesty, the things she'd always admired in him. It was only fair that she match that honesty with honesty of her own. She knew how difficult it must be for him to face his deepseated truths; it was only fair that she do the same about herself.

"I love you, Doug," she said as with her last breath. She breathed in, expanding her lungs. "I want that understood right up front." She could not look at him. "I've never been a particularly cold person."

"No, you never have."

"I honestly don't know what goes on inside your head, Doug, and I'm not too sure I know what goes on inside mine. You seem to hate everything new and different when it involves me, but then you turn around and tell me you're titillated out of your head by things Phyllis does because they're new and different. You have me all confused."

He stood on an opposite scale with his own thoughts still fresh. "You changed so much and so fast. I'm not as able to adapt as you are, Maggie. I've had to start a little at a time." He paused, looking at the ground, not knowing exactly how to proceed on this dangerous ground. "Our trouble, I think, is that we started at opposite sides of a circle and instead of working toward one another we worked outward, away from each other. If we could only turn ourselves around to face each other squarely, honestly, I believe it would all work out the way we want it to." He took her in his arms. "The big important thing is that I *need* you, Maggie. I'll die without your love. It's my whole life."

"But you've lied to me, Doug. How can I ever believe you again? How can I accept what you say? You've humiliated me in the eyes of my friends with your affairs with Phyllis. . . ."

He cut her off. "Just as you used to make me feel like two cents in front of your friends by ignoring me. As I said, we're playing a game, Maggie. I'm sorry if I embarrassed you by my cheating and my lies, but I was only trying to get you to pay more attention to me. Phyllis was too clever for me. You know I was never very bright when it came to feminine wiles."

She smiled in spite of herself.

"I'm not blaming anybody but myself for the way I've behaved toward you. And as far as you are concerned, I'm jealous as hell about you're being attracted to that Ballantine kid. He won't make you happy, Maggie, because I know I'm the only one who can do that and you know it too."

It was true, she had to admit. When all was reduced down to one single element, that element was her love for Doug. Mike was sweet and loving and good; but he was only a salve that soothed her vanity. She could never love him as deeply as she loved Doug. She would never be able to forgive Mike his faults the way she could forgive Doug. It all came down to the fact that she understood Doug and she doubted if she'd have the patience to devote to understanding someone as complex and irresponsible as Mike.

She felt as though a white light had suddenly been

flashed on her heart. She leaned against Doug and said, "I guess I've known all along that Mike wasn't for me, nor I for him. All right, Doug. I'll try. I know you're all I've ever wanted and I don't want to lose you any more than you want to lose me."

She smiled up into his face and said, "I suppose nothing has changed since that first time we went out on a date. We knew we were stuck with each other right from the very beginning and we will always be stuck with each other."

"Because we want to be," he clarified.

She shook her head. "Because we can't help it. There isn't anyone else for either of us. There never will be. Much as we want to fight that fact, it's true."

He kissed her deeply, lovingly, passionately. She pushed him away and said, "The neighbors."

"To hell with the neighbors," he said, pulling her back into his arms and kissing her again.

As their lips parted she smiled with her eyes. "You're right, darling, to hell with the neighbors," and flung her arms more tightly around his neck, pulling his face down to hers.

After several delicious minutes Doug eased her away and said, "You must be starving. And look at you, you look like a washer-woman in that get-up."

"It's the only thing I could find in a box in the garage."

A police car pulled up at the curb and two uniformed officers got out. "Mrs. Hampton?" the one asked.

"Yes."

"We've been asked to show you a photograph and ask if you can identify this woman." He took a photo out of an envelope.

It was a picture of Rita Gant.

"Yes, I know her," Maggie said, slightly shocked. "She works in my office in New York—that is she used to work there."

The officer put the photograph back in the little envelope. He said, "One of your neighbors . . ." he glanced across the street, ". . . noticed a woman scurrying around your hedges last night about eight o'clock."

Maggie frowned. "I was out to dinner with my daughter."

"Yes, he said he'd seen you drive off and that was why he wondered what the woman was doing with nobody at home. He was sensible enough to make a note of the license plate number when the woman drove away. When the Fire Department reported your house fire, the computer came up with the connection, especially when the fire chief said they found two gasoline cans at the rear of your house. We have the woman in custody but we'll need a statement from you as to possible cause, if any."

"Unfortunately," Maggie said hesitantly, "I hate to cause Rita any trouble, but there were certain threats she made yesterday."

"I see."

Doug saw how upset Maggie was and said to the officer, "Can this wait, Officer? My wife is badly shaken and hasn't had any sleep."

"Of course," the patrolman said. "Tomorrow will be time enough. The woman is being held for psychiatric examination. She attacked the officer who went to her home to question her."

"How dreadful," Maggie breathed.

The officer handed Maggie a card. "Just ask for Lieutenant Daniels; he's with the arson squad." He touched his fingers to his cap.

"Thank you," Maggie said, taking the card and glancing at it. "I'll be there tomorrow."

When they were alone Doug said, "I don't understand. You mean some woman deliberately burned down the house?"

Maggie hurriedly explained about Rita's past, about her visit yesterday and about her threats. "The poor deranged creature," she said, almost in a prayer.

"You'll be one too if you don't get away from here. Come on, let's go back to my apartment and I'll start getting you looking gorgeous."

"Your apartment?" she said, pulling back as they started toward Doug's car.

"It's all right. Contrary to what you thought, Phyllis never did live with me. She just got in the annoying habit of dropping in uninvited. I should never have told her where I kept the extra key, especially when she found the apartment for me—three floors above her own."

Maggie laughed, then remembered a pile of things she'd managed to salvage from the house. "Wait, Doug, I have my purse and some cosmetics and stuff in David's garage."

"I'll get them. Go and wait for me in the car. You look all in."

As she sat in the front seat she watched Doug move away from her, swaggering slightly with his new cockiness, his butt moving in graceful defiance. She found herself grinning and feeling devilish. She'd always been fascinated by Doug's butt. Then she suddenly thought of the studio couch in David's garage, the swirling lights, the loud music and somehow the grotesqueness of the burned-out house kindled some sort of obscene need. She pushed down the door handle and hurried after her husband.

Chapter 20

When she awoke in Doug's bedroom on Monday morning, it took a while for her to identify where she was. When she did she sat up and stretched, luxuriating in how wonderful it felt to be a happily married woman again.

Julie was happy at her girlfriend's house; David had slept on the couch in the living room and was presently over at the house with his father, sifting through the debris, she supposed. Doug had said something about the insurance investigators being there first thing.

The only thing that marred the day that lay ahead was that she would have to talk to Mike. She knew how hurt he was going to be, but she'd made the mess so it was her responsibility to clean it up, regardless of how unpleasant, how painful.

It was still early enough to call Mike at his place before he left for work, but she hadn't the courage yet to speak with him directly. She had to formulate in her mind exactly what she intended to say.

Instead she dialed Alice's number and caught her just as she was leaving for the office.

"What?" Alice half shouted when Maggie told her about the fire. "Rita Gant?"

"Yes, the police have her in custody. Oh, it's all right with me, Alice. I'm staying at Doug's place until we can pull everything back together."

"Doug's place, huh?" She chuckled softly. "Well who says trouble doesn't solve problems? Are you there for keeps?"

"Yes, I'm here to stay, at least I'm staying married to Doug."

"Does Mike know?"

"No. I have to find the courage somewhere to break the news to him."

Alice said, "Of course the big question of the day is, are you sure you're doing the right thing?"

"Positive. Not even a glimmer of doubt."

"Good." She paused then said, "What can I do to help out? Whatever you need I'll get for you. And are you still working for me or not?"

"I'm still working if you want me, but of course it will be a few days until I get things organized, and even then it may only be part-time for a while. If I need anything I'll yell."

"Whatever. Take your time, kiddo. You'll always have a job whenever you want one." Before she hung up she said, "Hey, how about you, Doug, and the kids coming over here to my place for dinner one night? I want to keep on the good side of Doug now that he's back being permanent."

"Okay. I'll check with the family and call you."

A little after nine o'clock Maggie called the office. "Caroline. Maggie." She didn't explain about the fire, she just said, "Look, honey, I won't be in today, maybe not tomorrow either. Alice knows, I've already talked to her, but I want you to do me a favor if you will."

"Sure, Maggie, anything."

"Mike hasn't called, has he?"

"Not yet. Knowing him, it'll be any minute now."

"Well, when he does will you tell him I'm not coming in but that I'll meet him at The Rail at about seven o'clock? No, make that at the Chez Nous on Twenty-fourth Street," she corrected, knowing the likelihood of Louise and Andy being at The Rail after work.

"Seven o'clock, Chez Nous on Twenty-fourth," Caroline repeated. "Got it."

When she told Doug he asked if she wanted him to come with her. She said, "You have a downright cruel streak in you, Doug Hampton. You just want to gloat over winning out over a younger man."

He kissed her warmly and said, "What's wrong with my enjoying being cock-of-the-walk?"

She kissed him back. "This is going to be something I have to do alone."

"Don't worry, darling, he's a very young guy; he'll bounce back after a couple of hangovers."

She took her car into New York so that she'd be able to make a quick get-away afterward. Short and fast. Wasn't that supposed to be the least painful way?

Nervously she walked into the little restaurant. Mike was seated at a table in front of the windows. Maggie had hoped they'd sit at a dark, secluded table where the world wouldn't be able to watch her betrayal of a friend. And that was the only way she looked upon it, as a betrayal. She had purposely led him on, knowing deep in her heart that she was being selfish, that she would never be able to be happy marrying him.

What had she told Doug when he asked what Mike offered her? "Time," she'd said. Time wasn't love or beauty or security or even happiness. It was an empty commodity that slipped away regardless of its length, a continuing entity that had an unavoidable end when measured in human life. And she never felt more human than when she walked up to the table and tried to smile at him.

She'd never been able to hide her feelings from Doug, but Mike didn't see the anguish in her heart, the pain in her smile.

"Darling," he said, jumping up and kissing her lightly on the mouth. "You didn't work today and your home phone is out of order. I checked."

"Yes," she said, fumbling with her gloves and purse.

The waiter started toward them. "Perrier Water or a cocktail?"

"Just coffee, I think." She found she couldn't look at him. She saw his frown and lowered her eyes even farther.

Mike ordered the coffee and a Scotch Sour for himself. "Is there something wrong?"

She screwed up her courage and said, "Yes, I'm afraid there is."

He started to drum the tabletop with his fingers. "I see. Despite all of your flowery encouragement, you've found yourself back on the fence again . . . or have you decided this time you're going to stay with Doug?"

She knew he was purposely being distasteful, trying to hurt her. She said, "I've decided to stay married to Doug."

He didn't speak. Only the drumming of his fingers could be heard among the quiet clatter of the restaurant. The drumming got louder and louder, the silence deeper and deeper. Suddenly he slammed his fist down on the table, jarring the water glasses and the silverware, making them jump and clink.

"I will not give you up, Maggie!" To her surprise, his voice held no reproach. "I don't care what you've decided, I will not let you go so easily as this." His voice then turned to pleading. "Whatever made you reach this decision, I'll wait it out. I can change any way you want me to. You know how adaptable I am. Tell me what you don't like about me, why you prefer Doug, and I'll change any way you want me to change."

"There is one thing you can never change, Mike, even if I wanted you to, which I don't. You're very young. I'm too old for you."

"That isn't important," he said, trying to keep back his temper.

"I know it isn't and that isn't the reason I'm staying with my husband. I've discovered that I'm lost without Doug. He's all my youth, all my memories, which he built up into an indestructible wall that will protect me for the rest of my life."

She reached out and touched his hand. He pulled it away as though she'd laid a flame on it. He seemed to curl up inside himself and his features grew darker and uglier.

Maggie said, "I've been very unkind to you, Mike. I thought I loved you, and I do love you in a way, but it isn't the right way, the important way. I'm too selfish, too settled—too vain, perhaps; I have a feeling our passion would soon grow weaker as we grew closer in time and in place. We don't have the foundation that successful marriages are built on."

She tried to encourage him with a smile. "You're very young, Mike. You'd grow restless and empty when the days got to be routine, which they eventually would. Vicarious living isn't for me. I need to know where my roots are, where my children are, where I can go to be needed. I lost sight of that need. Julie is a terror who needs more attention than I figured. My home. . . ." She stopped. There was no reason to go into that. "Doug and the children really need me, Mike. Even if I wanted to desert them, I couldn't. Besides, I don't want to. I know that now. Much as it hurts you now, it would hurt them more, it would hurt *me* more. So if you truly love me as much as you say, then prove it to me by letting me go without bad feelings between us."

The hurt was suddenly gone from his face, she noticed, as he watched her with an amused smile, as though enjoying her discomfort. He said, "Talk all you want to, Maggie, but I know that in the end you'll come back. Go to Doug, go to the devil for all I care! Because wherever you go you won't stay. You love me, I know that, and loving me as you do you'll be back."

She touched his cheek and said, "There are all kinds of love, Mike. You and I knew one kind. It will live inside us for as long as we want it to. It's something no one in the world can share; it's ours and ours alone. So don't be angry with me, and don't be hurt or sad. Everything is determined by necessity, remember that. It's necessary that I stay with Doug where I belong. Think only about the good times we had, the fun we had. We shared a lovely dream and I'll always cherish my part in that dream; even when I'm with Doug I'll remember you and what you did for me."

He kept staring at her with hard, even eyes. "You really think it's that easy to chuck it all over with a pretty speech and a friendly handshake goodbye." He shook his head slowly from side to side. "I don't believe you when you say you're finished with me, because you've had your mind back and forth over the net so often you've worn the fuzz off the ball."

She heard a meanness come into his voice. "I won't take this as final, Maggie. You're too important to me. You are the only really solid person I've ever met and you've been a great stabilizer for me. I need that stability and I have no intention of losing it. You may not feel that you love me now as much as you did last week, but you'll change your mind back again one day. Maybe not tomorrow or next month, but one day," he predicted.

Maggie said, "Don't make things any more difficult than they are. It's over for us, Mike. It has to be, so please accept it—and let's part friends." She put out her hand.

He laughed as he took it and touched it to his lips. He held it tight when Maggie tried to pull it back. He started to say something but the waiter came with their order and Mike waited until they were alone again.

He said, "I really am hopelessly in love with you, Maggie."

"Don't, Mike. You're only torturing yourself."

"If you are serious in what you say, I should hate you. But I honestly believe you're just going through another one of your mental ping-pong matches. You're being stupid, like the time in Vegas, all flurry and fuss and in the end you calmed down and gave in to what you wanted."

"Let's not dwell on what's past."

"No, let's dwell on it, Maggie. Maybe it's about time somebody made you sit down and face facts. You think you can walk into a guy's life and give him all kinds of hope, change his whole head around, then decide he isn't what you wanted after all and just walk away free as air leaving him sitting there like some poor jerk." He leaned forward with a menacing glare. "You can't fool around with other people's lives, Maggie, especially with mine."

"Don't turn this into something distasteful, Mike. We'll only wind up hating each other. Thank you for the coffee, but I think I'd better go."

She started to get up but he grabbed her arm and pulled her back into the chair. "You said all your pretty words, now at least let me say just one simple thing." She waited. "You loved me, I know. You still love me."

He was talking louder, drawing attention to them. "Mike, please," she said looking around. "You're wrong," she said in a quiet, urgent voice.

"Look me straight in the eye and tell me you don't love me," he challenged.

She knew she had no choice but to play out the scene. She squared her shoulders and stared directly into his eyes. "I don't love you."

"You're a liar!"

"Mike, please," she said trying to calm him. She looked around again nervously and inched her chair back from the table. "I must be going."

She expected him to reach for her but he did not. He leaned back, teetering the chair on its back legs and laced his fingers under his chin.

He said, "Do you know what day this is, Maggie?"

Slightly baffled she said, "Yes, it's Monday."

"Monday. September 2nd. Remember that. I promise I won't bother you any more, and you should know that I am good at keeping my promises. I won't call you or stop at the office, but one year from today I'll be sitting here in this same restaurant, at this same table, at this same time. You'll be here, Maggie. I know you will."

"No, Mike. I won't."

"*I* will be," he said. "Just remember that."

She turned and started for the door. Somewhere behind her she heard the sound of a glass being knocked over, a chair falling backward as Mike called, "September 2nd next year, Maggie!"

She hurried out the door and was gone.

As she crossed the George Washington Bridge she could not help thinking of him as nothing more than a romantically arrogant young boy. She knew she'd hurt him deeply—but as Doug had said, he'd bounce back. The resilience of youth could always be depended on, she thought as she turned onto the road that skirted the Palisades.

The air was cooler and fresher here than on the other side of the river; she pressed her foot down hard on the accelerator and pushed Mike into a memory. She thought of home and of Doug and of tomorrow. All her life she'd wanted a tomorrow of her own. She never realized until now that she'd always had it.

A Novel Without Scruples

a novel by
Barney Leason

☐ 41-596-6   448 pages $3.50

With consummate insight and shameless candor, Barney Leason, author of *The New York Times* bestseller, *Rodeo Drive*, weaves yet another shocking, sensuous tale of money, power, greed and lust in a glamorous milieu rife with

From the seductive shores of the Isle of Capri to the hopscotch bedrooms of Beverly Hills, London and New York, Leason lays bare the lives and loves of the rich and depraved, their sins and shame, their secrets and

Buy them at your local bookstore or use this handy coupon
Clip and mail this page with your order

PINNACLE BOOKS, INC. — Reader Service Dept.
1430 Broadway, New York, N.Y. 10018

Please send me the book(s) I have checked above. I am enclosing $_____
(please add 75¢ to cover postage and handling). Send check or money order only—no cash or C.O.D.'s.

Mr./Mrs./Miss_____

Address_____

City_____ State/Zip_____

Please allow six weeks for delivery. Prices subject to change without notice.

Over 1.5 million copies in print!

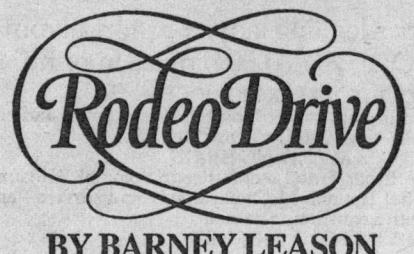

BY BARNEY LEASON

☐ 41-031-X   416 pages $2.95

Welcome to the land of silk and money, where the world's most glamorous—and amorous—come to spend their endless nights dancing chic-to-chic under dazzling lights.

Here, against the outrageously decadent background of Beverly Hills—its hopscotch bedrooms and grand estates, posh restaurants and luxurious hotels—is the shocking story of society dame Belle Cooper and her passionate struggle to become a woman of integrity and independent means.

Not since *Scruples* has a novel laid bare the lives—and loves—of people who have everything...and will pay any price for *more*!

Buy them at your local bookstore or use this handy coupon
Clip and mail this page with your order

PINNACLE BOOKS, INC. — Reader Service Dept.
1430 Broadway, New York, NY 10018

Please send me the book(s) I have checked above. I am enclosing $_____ (please add 75¢ to cover postage and handling). Send check or money order only—no cash or C.O.D.'s.

Mr./Mrs./Miss_____
Address_____
City_____ State/Zip_____

Please allow six weeks for delivery. Prices subject to change without notice.
Canadian orders must be paid with U.S. Bank check or U.S. Postal money order only.

Patricia Matthews

America's leading lady of historical romance.
Over 20,000,000 copies in print!

☐ **41-203-7 LOVE, FOREVER MORE** $2.75
   The tumultuous story of spirited Serena Foster and her determination to survive the raw, untamed West.

☐ **41-513-3 LOVE'S AVENGING HEART** $2.95
   Life with her brutal stepfather in colonial Williamsburg was cruel, but Hannah McCambridge would survive—and learn to love with a consuming passion.

☐ **40-661-4 LOVE'S BOLD JOURNEY** $2.95
   Beautiful Rachel Bonner forged a new life for herself in the savage West—but can she surrender to the man who won her heart?

☐ **41-517-6 LOVE'S DARING DREAM** $2.95
   The turbulent story of indomitable Maggie Donnevan, who fled the poverty of Ireland to begin a new life in the American Northwest.

☐ **41-519-2 LOVE'S GOLDEN DESTINY** $2.95
   It was a lust for gold that brought Belinda Lee together with three men in the Klondike, only to be trapped by the wildest of passions.

☐ **41-518-4 LOVE'S MAGIC MOMENT** $2.95
   Evil and ecstasy are entwined in the steaming jungles of Mexico, where Meredith Longley searches for a lost city but finds greed, lust, and seduction.

☐ **41-516-8 LOVE'S PAGAN HEART** $2.95
   An exquisite Hawaiian princess is torn between love for her homeland and the only man who can tame her pagan heart.

☐ **41-064-6 LOVE'S RAGING TIDE** $2.75
   Melissa Huntoon seethed with humiliation as her ancestral plantation home was auctioned away—then learned to survive the lust and greed of a man's world.

☐ **40-660-6 LOVE'S SWEET AGONY** $2.75
   Amid the colorful world of thoroughbred farms that gave birth to the first Kentucky Derby, Rebecca Hawkins learns that horses are more easily handled than men.

☐ **41-514-1 LOVE'S WILDEST PROMISE** $2.95
   Abducted aboard a ship bound for the Colonies, innocent Sarah Moody faces a dark voyage of violence and unbridled lust.

PINNACLE BOOKS, INC. — Reader Service Dept.
1430 Broadway, New York, NY 10018

Please send me the book(s) I have checked above. I am enclosing $_____ (please add 75¢ to cover postage and handling). Send check or money order only—no cash or C.O.D.'s.

Mr./Mrs./Miss_____

Address_____

City_____ State/Zip_____

Please allow six weeks for delivery. Prices subject to change without notice.
Canadian orders must be paid with U.S. Bank check or U.S. Postal money order only.